The Captain, the Avaeste and the King is a tale of high adventure, undertaken by a boy captain and his irregular crew, in search of a rare treasure. At first reluctant, the hijacked crew grow ever more eager as their captain steers them across the Aethermarinus, and as they learn more of just what it is they are searching for, and why the captain is so determined to find it.

They journey to islands far and wide, to fair beaches, deserts, marshes and winters. Encounters with pirates, goblins, wolves, kings and queens, and raging tyrants are some of the adventures that befall them, they also find themselves caught up in a battle on Meridian.

It is a tale of redemption and self-sacrifice, courage, love, loyalty, and the battle between good and evil.

The Captain, the Avaeste and the King began as an experiment by the author in curiously styled prose, but the characters called for more, and so it grew into this marvellous epic which is sure to delight readers young and old.

the Captain
the Avaeste
& the King

J.M.BARDSLEY

ORATANTO

Chapters:

Chapter 1:
THE SURPRISING USE
OF BLACKCURRANT JUICE

'A Marsh Walump!' two slightly tipsy men exclaimed and slapped their broad thighs, above the sound of the rain outside.

'You can't bring him in 'ere!' They were laughing together at the captain and his crewman, the swamp coloured creature that stood beside him, not much taller than the captain's own knee-boots, but much taller inside despite his hesitant looks.

'Hahaha,' they laughed on in their merry mockery and stirring, and more joined in with them from the bar and the tables surrounding.

The young captain's lip was curling up, like it always did when he was faced with something particularly unpleasant, and his eyes glowered in a way the swamp monster knew did not bode well for this other crew. He was a very proud captain and very loyal friend, and he would stand against all these men for his friend at such an insult. But just as the swamp monster was about to intervene he saw the captain's glower turn into a gleam. He did not say a thing but went to a stool and sat at the counter, completely ignoring that other crew. The swamp monster followed him and sat by his side, over the bar you could just see his eyes.

'Bartender,' called the captain, and the man came grudgingly over. He did not seem to like the presence of this boy and his swamp monster, though he did try to treat them just like any other street urchin that was unknown to him and his counter.

'What do you want, Cap'n?' he enquired, wiped his hands on his apron then itched his moustache which pointed up funnily, like it was held up with wires. You could see he did not like to address a mere boy with a title such as this, but the boy wore his stripes so there was nothing for it.

'I would like a drink, my good man, and you Morris?' the captain turned to his side, the swamp monster nodded and so he replied, 'and one for my crewman here, if you don't mind,' and he gave the bartender his most natural smile.

'You got the blunt to pay for it Cap'n?'

'Aye, I do sir, if you've got what I want.'

'What'll it be then Cap'n, for you an' your 'mate? We serve everything here, beers, wines and sweet ales, from the cheap drop to the vintage first rate.'

'I should like …' thought the captain, with a broadening grin.

'Cider?' helped the bartender.

'No,'

'Lemonade? Tonic and gin?'

'No. I should like, if your establishment has it, the juice of the fruit of the mid-season blackcurrant.'

'Blackcurrant?' said the bartender with a look of surprise.

'Aye,' said the captain with a spark in his eyes.

The bartender looked round him and scratched what was left of the hair on his head. 'Mid-season?' he said.

'Aye,' replied the captain and nodded again.

'Ah, give me a minute,' and with that the bartender left.

'Sent him to fetch some cordial boy have ya!' the laughter went up again; it rose in chorus like the deluge of rain. They were thinking, no doubt, that this captain looked far too young to be out fending for himself, away from his mother.

The captain said nothing but watched all these men and noted to himself their character and aspect, he listened for their names as they called to each other and pretty soon he knew them, the names of their dogs, wives and mothers, the strength of their arm and their intellectual powers, without ever moving away from the counter.

The bartender returned after a while with a bottle in his hands and a half-hearted smile. 'Here,' he said, putting it carefully up on the counter, 'I know it's not quite what you're after, but it's the closest I got, see if it'll do ye.'

The Captain's got good eyes, as he has to have to guide his ship through the drafts and the clouds, and he used them to scrutinize the make of the bottle, the colour of liquid and the words writ on the label.

Then with that, 'I'll take it,' he said.

'Two glasses coming up, soon as I see your blunt,' the bartender said and folded his arms on the spot, for he had had trouble with urchins before, you see, that would order a drink and then couldn't pay.

'I would like quite a few bottles,' the captain pronounced, 'that is, if you have more of the stuff. I'll take all you have in your cellar, if you'll tell me a fair figure.'

The bartender was struck, no vocabulary could he find, for that moment was so unexpected he seemed suspended in time, but his wife, that handsome woman, came to his aid and from behind him she whispered, 'Why, it'll cost you four times your age, in pounds lad, not shillings, and if you don't like it you can be on your way.'

'I'm inclined to accept your offer,' the young captain said, 'after I've seen how much you have.'

'Very well then Cap'n, if you will, follow me,' said the woman and showed him the way. But the captain just sat there, where he was on his seat, and told the bartender's wife to get her regular crew to help her up with the crates. And such was his address that although she hesitated she never once thought to do any other than what he commanded, and so she scolded the loungers until she needled and coerced them into doing her will. 'Up you get, you lazy scoundrels, get this done for your Bette and there'll be a free round for you all when you're back.'

One by one the crates were brought up, there were bottles and bottles and more of the stuff. It had sat in the cellar for many a year, for it seems very few people drank blackcurrant here. The Bartender's face lit up as he heard the young captain's voice, as he heard the words, 'I'll take the lot,' and saw the boy pull out of his pocket the sum of coins his wife had bespoke. 'Just get these men to take it on board,' the captain said, 'and I'll meet them there soon to tell them where it's to be stored.'

So the swamp monster Morris and his fair-haired young captain watched as the crates went by in the arms of the men. The very same ones that had harassed and mocked them were now, round about, working for them. They wanted to finish and quickly have it over so they could return to their free mug of liquor, but after they'd gone out the captain looked at Morris and the little swamp monster wondered just what he was up to, for in his eyes was a sparkle and in the corner of his mouth a wriggling giggle he was trying desperately not to let out.

'Come on Morris,' he said getting up off the chair, 'I think we're done here, time to make ourselves rare.'

Morris hopped down and headed for the door as the captain retrieved his cap, put on his jacket and buttoned it all. It had been raining outside, but the sky seemed to wait just for them before it let go the heaviest downpour.

This odd pair made their way down the street, step by step coating their feet with the mud and the spatter from walking in it. The captain just wanted to be gone from this place, he had only stopped for one purpose and it was well on its way to being fulfilled if he held his nerve and didn't stop now. No matter how his heart faltered, he had to keep the brave face, he had to, he must, and must keep going quickly, so much depended on it. So he picked up the pace and told Morris they must hurry. He lengthened his stride so much that just to keep up poor Morris was running.

They reached the little ship, which had been made secure by long ropes and wooden blocks in a dry dock at the pier, the men from the bar were all under her hull taking shelter, waiting for the directions to come from the boy captain.

Morris ran up and lowered the stairs and proceeded to go about getting ready to leave, and the captain motioned with his hand for the crew to follow after the swamp monster too. Then after the last had disappeared on board the captain ran around, loosened every block and cut every cord, then jumped on the stairs and mounted his spot at the helm, laughing to himself as he thought: that for the price of a few crates of new-season blackcurrant he had acquired a new crew for himself and Swamp Morris.

Chapter 2:
THE TAMING OF THE CREW

Morris hauled in the ropes and the captain steered so by the time the men were finished stacking the crates in the cargo hold they had long left the town and the ground below.

To their utmost surprise and fearful astonishment, this was not any regular ship, nor like any boat of any make they had ever seen. Despite its appearance, of a vessel most usual, oh no this was not common at all, in fact none of these men had ever seen it done before, nor thought it possible, that a ship could fly through the air! The drinkers cursed with swears and with moans and shouted to Morris to take them all home, while holding their stomachs and shivering in their bones.

The swamp monster said nothing but let them ferment, thinking maybe the captain hadn't been wise in letting so many burly gang-types alight. The fellows all jostled trying to get close to him, muttering and calling for death to be upon him. They were looking quite angry, Morris worried, as he ran to the upper deck to get away. Then the captain appeared, he was calm as always, he folded his arms and leaned on the rail looking down on the men, remembering the names of the new crew he'd stolen away.

'Take us back down!' they yelled, still holding their stomachs, 'let us go home! Who are you boy, can't you see with our fingers we could snap your bones.'

But the captain just stood there till the hubbub quietened, he jumped from the high deck to a barrel lower down, as Morris watched on, much apprehensive. He and the captain had come through so much, but did he have what it took to handle this bunch?

The men drew closer and closer around him, their eyes and their faces red from their drinking, their hands were tightly clenching in fury and indignation.

'So, boy, will you take us back then?' said the foremost among them, looking up at the captain, 'or will we have to take it into our own hands, you and this flying contraption?'

'Morris,' said the captain in his calm and soft voice, 'I give you leave to deal with these men; how you do it, is your choice.'

Morris stared down from where he sat on the railing in surprise, now it was his turn to show a gleam in his eyes. He nodded to his captain and jumped down beside him and bellowed out to the men, 'If you lot want an answer to any of your questions you'll have to start addressing him rightly, as Captain!'

For a moment their annoyance seemed to increase, then one of them laughed which brokered the peace, 'Right then, Cap'n, why don't you just take us back down, we were just about to finish our drinks and head home.'

The captain nodded and then he said, 'A legitimate request, but I'm afraid I can't do it. You see I am on voyage of the utmost importance, I seek a treasure of sorts, a very rare thing, but it's a long way off so I need a crew, and I find you're fit for it.'

'Why then, we'll kidnap you, and take over the ship,' they said and made a mad rush for him, but the captain just grinned, stepping up on the banister. 'I'll let you,' he laughed, 'if you can get past Swamp Morris.'

Morris looked at the captain and the captain nodded, a sign that the monster could do what he wanted. Morris rubbed his little claws together as the crew from the bar came closer and closer.

They started the taunts and the mocking again, one said, 'Let me take the Walump!' and so it began. A few of them tried to take Morris down but each one he dealt with as he well knew how. He could dodge like a dragonfly, leap like a frog and fool them easier than the best of them could. Then when the bunch realised they were in for some trouble they went at him all together, but that was the end of the rabble.

Swamp Morris wiped his hands of them and turned to his captain. 'Well done Morris,' he grinned.

'Thankyou Captain,' Morris said, then sat at the wheel as the captain went down to inspect his new crew who lay on the deck all sprawling around.

He looked at them all and stepped over their bodies, in their momentary agony as they moaned and bemoaned their unexpected difficulty, in being held hostage on a flying ship with a boy as their captain and a swamp monster as whip.

'Jennings,' called the captain, then, 'Carter, Banks and Phillips. I'll see you in my cabin soon as you're fit. The rest of you, go down below, find yourself a bunk, and if I were you, I'd make use of it.'

So in a short while the four named men came, hesitantly, wonderingly, into the captain's small cabin.

'Gentleman,' he greeted them, 'please be seated. You must need a drink?' he offered and poured them three quarts of blackcurrant each, before taking for himself one little sip. 'You must be wondering just why you're here, I am about to tell you, so have a good ear. You four men I have chosen, should you accept, to be the lieutenants on board the fair Avaeste. The rewards are high, but in return you must keep a good hold on the hearts of your men.'

'Rewards Cap'n?' Banks asked, with a hopeful eye.

'Aye, rewards Banks, there will be many if we achieve our end.'

'Lieutenant sounds good to me Cap'n,' Carter replied, only ever having been a simple crewman all of his life.

'What's the catch? Cap'n,' Jennings enquired, as he thought to himself that this was sounding better than his current life.

'I'll look after your interests if you look after mine, no overindulging, no slacking, always be on time. Do as I say, when I say, how I want it, but most of all, respect Swamp Morris.'

'But he's a Marsh Walump!?'

Phillips bit his lip as he saw the captain's face, the smouldering ire, the eyes set on fire. He thought in a hurry about the lieutenancy, did he want it? He did. If he stayed in his current job it would take years to attain. So he said hastily, 'Sorry, Cap'n, it won't happen again. And, ah, if there are no hidden clauses and the lieutenancy is a real situation, you can count me in as well.'

'Very well,' said the captain, then for a moment as he glanced at the clock he elapsed into silence over a map. None of them could quite understand the markings upon it, the scribbling type, or where it was, this scattering of islands with space between them. 'Morris,' he called and the creature appeared, peering round the door with his ears plucked up. 'Take these men down,' he said, his eyes still on the canvas, 'show them their quarters and their new responsibilities. You know what to do. Gentlemen, take notice of Morris, choose for yourself the men you want under you. You may tell them they shall be supported if they choose to continue, and if any refuse, then, well, I suppose I shall have to return you to your homes, but take tonight to think it through.'

'Cap'n,' they all said as they nodded and left, but the captain still measured the map with his compass, and scribbled more and more markings upon it. Now that the captain had got what he wanted he just wanted to be off and hear no more of it.

The first mate Morris took the four downstairs, to where the rest of the crew were finding things out. 'This way,' Morris waved with the hand that wasn't holding the lantern and they came to some rooms, small but much nicer than sleeping in bunks with about twenty others. The rooms must have been not quite underneath the place where the captain had his, but definitely towards the back of the ship.

'Lieutenant Phillips and Lieutenant Banks, here are your berths. Lieutenant Jennings and Lieutenant Carter, here's yours just across from them.'

'How do we address you?' Carter asked nicely, 'if he's got to be Captain, then you?'

'Morris is adequate.'

'Alright, Morris, are we to be Lieutenants in clothes such as these? If I'd known I was going away, and going to be elevated to a role like this, I could have packed some things, and dressed more appropriate, not that I'd have the blunt to buy anything much more decent, but maybe I'd have acquired some shoe-shine at least.'

'Don't worry about that,' was all Morris said.

'What do we do now?' Jennings enquired.

'Pick out your men, then get some sleep I suggest. Tomorrow I'll start filling you in on the rest. If anyone's hungry send them down to the galley, they won't be disappointed, the captain's stores are of the best.'

Morris lit the lamps in each of their rooms then disappeared up the hatch into the evening which grew close about with a foreboding gloom.

'Blimey,' Carter sat down on the bunk, 'what an extraordinary turn of events.'

'I'll say,' Jennings said and sat down beside him, Phillips and Banks were also close by them.

'So how many men do we have to split up between us?' Banks asked, but then changed the subject, 'he's just a boy! I can't believe it.'

'I know. What could he do if we all decided to take over the ship?'

'We already tried that, don't you remember, he's got the protection of that little swamp imp.'

'Guys,' Carter said, 'what are you saying? I don't want to be part of any rebellion.'

'But it's not a rebellion Carter, don't you see, it's just taking back our freedom, going back to our families.'

'I suppose.'

'It's true. I wonder what our old Cap'n is doing, in but a day our leave was ending, and we'd be off, sailing the seven seas again.'

'But didn't he say something about a reward? Said he'd support us while we was aboard. Now I never liked old Cap'n Fowler, he'd cuss and abuse and demoralise you. And I don't know what but I think I like this Cap'n; I know he's a young'un but there's that something about him.'

'I know what you mean,' said Jennings and Phillips, and Banks said, 'Well, let's see how it reads, if things look up, then we'll keep playing along, but if things don't work out, we'll pull out the stops. Agreed?'

'Agreed.'

'Agreed.'

But Carter just nodded half-heartedly, he'd desperately wanted his lieutenancy, it was something, if he did right, no-one could take from him. He dreamed of his poor father's wide eyes at his boy turning up in a neat uniform, and cocked-hat by his side, and thought of the pride in his own children's eyes.

The lieutenants sat around a table and wrote down the names of all the men in the stolen crew, and soon they were splitting the group into four till they were left with only two. Including themselves there were twenty-six men, take out themselves that left five men each with two spare, men not one of them wanted as they required too much care, well, a constant eye, that is. One was a ship's boy not much taller than Morris, the other was a man so old he'd nearly no teeth and only a few strands of hair. They must have brought a half empty crate of blackcurrant between them, how else is it that they would have managed to be here?

'So then,' said Carter, 'what'll we do?'

'Oh,' said Banks, 'it shouldn't be too hard to convince this crew to stay on this fine little ship, especially when we explain the benefits.'

'We don't even know what that will be,' said Jennings.

'What could it be?' said Banks, 'he said rewards, and treasure and rare, you were there, you heard him. What else could he mean but some hidden cache or bounty?'

The others mused, inclined to agree.

'And those two, the boy and old Gragan?' said Jennings

'Say to the Cap'n, we've split our men sir, these are for you.'

'Now?'

'No, in the morning.'

'Aye, in the morning, that'll do.'

The empty decks were lit up by a clear starry night and the giant moon shone down with its familiar light. Morris came up just as the captain took to the wheel with a spyglass and put away in his pocket his trusty compass. The swamp monster hopped up to the railing beside him and let his knobbly face feel the cold blast of the wind. He did not say anything but waited to see if his captain would care to explain anything to him. There was always an understanding between them, but something of late had confused him. The captain was planning and plotting and scheming, some things Morris understood, others he knew he needn't, but still he wondered what his captain was dreaming. Never before had he needed a crew of so many men, he'd only ever had a few, and most of the time just Morris would do, was this quest going to take them through circumstances so difficult they would need this many crew?

'Thankyou for your service today,' the young captain said, not looking away from the heavens ahead.

'Oh,' Morris grinned, 'I'm sure you'd have managed without me Captain.'

'You over-estimate me.'

'Oh do I?'

'Indeed.'

Clouds came into view and passed them by, some he drifted past, with others he collided, letting the ship be engulfed in the stuff that Morris liked to think dreams were made of, but really he knew, as the captain had explained, it was just little droplets of gathering rain.

'Morris,' said the captain, in a way Morris knew, he would soon be broaching some serious issue, 'if something were to happen, for better or worse, something that took me away from this berth, I want you to have her, the Avaeste, she's yours.'

'What's going to happen. What do you fear?'

'Nothing I hope, and nothing I know, but there are so many dangers, so many things that could happen out here.'

'But I'm just a Walump, just like they say, you can't leave it to me!'

'Say that again and I won't. Don't listen to them.'

'It's late, Captain, here, let me take the helm.'

'No, get yourself some rest first, I'll be fine,' the captain said. Morris didn't see him lift his hand to rub the sleep from his eyes.

Morris hopped down and went to his bed, which he'd made in a chest in the young captain's cabin. He'd lined it with moss and seaweed and dirt and as a pillow he used the captain's old shirt. There were worms roaming in it and three kinds of slugs and even, if you looked hard, all sorts of other bugs, but Morris was happy and this is where he dreamed because it reminded him of home and all that he missed. So when he was in and comfortably positioned, he pulled down the lid, no one would even know he was in it.

When the bell tolled, at the hour of five in the ante-meridiem, the new crew awakened to find new clothes at the ends of their beds and a wonderful smell coming up from the kitchen. Those with any doubt about being part of this unexpected expedition soon rethought their position and were content, if not happy to stay and see how it turned out. The Lieutenants too, arose and they found neat blue uniforms for themselves, much like the captain's, so neatly laid out.

Carter, naturally, was over the moon, his mind did not ask how, why or where did they come from, he couldn't get them on quickly enough, the breeches, the shirt, the tailcoat and cocked hat, with the neat gilt-brass buttons and trims and all that. 'Lieutenant Carter,' he said proudly to himself, as he went to shave his face for the first time in weeks. 'Lieutenant Carter,' he repeated it over, and promised himself a new self, a start over, no more irresponsible jaunts, no more teasing or taunts, no more neglecting himself and his family.

Jennings was more staid and pragmatic about it. He wondered why any captain would do what this one had done, stolen a crew he didn't know anything of to help fly his ship, into what? Well, it would be interesting, no doubt, to find out just what this boy was about.

Banks buttoned his new waistcoat and sniggered, wondering just how much money was in it. If he could prove to the captain his worth, maybe he could be elevated and order the others about and earn more blunt for himself. Or maybe, just maybe, he could find it – a way to out manoeuvre this boy and take his ship and everything in it.

Phillips just whistled and went about the business as if it were something no other than usual. He resigned himself to the current predicament and was going to do it well till he could get out of it. But what if they were seen by some other crew, serving this boy, it would never do. They'd be the laughing stock, they'd be the butt of so many tales for years to come. And what of taking orders from a Marsh Walump? Oh, what would they say if they were to know that!

By the time the crew were out on the deck in disarray wondering what to do, the sun was blinding and the wind howling through. They saw their four friends in surprise, dressed like naval lieutenants, up to the nines, and these four men went about calling their names and lining them up, and up again, until they got them into position, yelled out, 'Lay forward!' and called them stiffly to attention.

Morris, in his bed, heard the muffled call, and peered out of his chest to see if the captain was gone. But the captain had fallen asleep at the table, strewn with his numerous navigational aids. Morris grabbed a little slug with his tongue and chewed it and licked his lips until it was definitely gone. Then he sighed and he went to the boy captain and dragged him over, across the floorboards to his own little bed in the corner.

Morris went out, ran up to the top deck, and squinted down at the crewmen, and he was very surprised at the sight before him. A neat looking crew, all clean and matching, presented itself to him, at attention.

Carter saluted and smiled at the monster, 'Your orders Morris, or do we wait for the Master?'

'Two of you can take the first watch with your men, the other two can go back below deck. I assume you all know your places on a ship, what you and your men can do?'

'Aye sir, we do.'

'Right then, get to it. Wait,' Morris stopped them as the group broke into quarters, 'what about those two, where do they fit?'

'We thought perhaps the Cap'n would have 'em, otherwise,' said Banks, 'we'd be uneven.'

'Right, you two,' Morris pointed to the boy and the elder, 'follow me will you.'

They went under the stairs and under the upper deck, the first of the new crew to go so far back. Morris had them sit on a bench in the small nook, and said 'I'm not sure the captain can see you yet, but I'll take a look.'

Morris was gone then, into the cabin with the wondering looks of the two crew following. Then they looked to each other, that boy and that old man, and without saying a word they asked the same question. The boy shrugged his shoulders and the old man nodded and tried to hit out the folds in his cap.

Swamp Morris entered the cabin with caution, he did not want to make any noise that would waken his tired young captain. Morris looked on the bunk where he had left him and sure enough, he was still there, soundly sleeping.

'You two wait here, and keep quiet,' he told them, 'the captain will see you when he's ready, alright.'

The two nodded, and when Morris was gone the older said to the younger something about how life always, when you least expected it, would throw up random surprises like this. 'You don't know how you got there or how it's going to end, but how you deal when you're in it is what makes you a man,' old Gragan said.

The sun beat down as the crew worked away, scrubbing the deck and lifting the sails, Morris taught the new lieutenants a thing or two about the ship; their new roles, how to act, what to do, as none of them had been lieutenants before there was much for them to learn that they hadn't realised would be in store. They thought that as lieutenant they would have control, to order about, to command and though that is so, there is more; to be a teacher, an example, a leader, to learn language, science, and navigation, for with greater responsibility one must have greater knowledge and education.

So Morris placed books into their hands, urging them to read them, to learn and understand, for the captain would be asking them all to perform the duties for which their new titles informed.

'But, Morris Sir, I can't yet read,' said Carter, sinking to his knees, thinking this would be the end of his lieutenancy.

'Well, I can't teach you that, but perhaps someone can,' then Morris was off, back to the cabin where outside still lingered the boy and the old man.

'Can either of you read good enough to teach it?'

'Aye,' said the old man, 'I went to school, till I was eight, two days a week sir, aye, two days!'

'And you boy?' asked Morris, 'what can you tell us?'

'I can read a word or two Sir,'

'And what would they be?'

'The Mary Lou, Sir. Well, Mary Lou I can read not *The*,' the boy laughed, 'no, or that'd be three.'

'I see,' Morris did, and waved his claw at the old man, 'you, come with me.'

Gragan followed him at a slow rate but eventually they came to where the Lieutenants were, as Carter paced.

'Go with Lieutenant Carter and help him to read,' Morris said.

'Sure sir,' the old man replied, 'I can do that, but what's in it for me?'

'You'll have to ask Carter and arrange it with him, it's not my business to make dealings between men. I'd leave that to the captain if you can't sort it out, so sort it out because I don't think he'd be impressed if you brought such a trivial thing to him and spoiled his rest when he's been so busy.'

'No, I wouldn't want to do that,' Carter said.

'No,' nodded the elder, 'we'll sort it out.'

'If you ask me old man I consider it part of your duty,' said Morris bravely, then left. He really didn't like being on the same ship as all these men.

Many hours later at the change of the watch the captain awoke at the sound of the toll, he rose and strode out into the noon-day shine, and had anyone seen him they might just espy, the trace of smile, or sort of a grin that comes from a man who took a chance and now sees his plans begin.

He looked at the crew from the shade of the stairs, watching them working and cursing each other, fooling then doing what their lieutenants told them, seeing the lieutenants develop a hold on them. He was very surprised that they were working together, him not having to pull and push them to make it happen. He and Morris could sure run the ship together, but not keep her looking like the beauty that was the Avaeste, and not meet any great danger, and never could they handle a great storm alone, nor other foul weather.

So here were the men, he raised his eyebrows, in the uniforms provided, with the breakfast in their stomachs from his storeroom, doing the things he needed them to do. They were his men, his crew.

He ran up the stairs to check their position, when one called out, 'Ahoy Cap'n!' He saw Carter waving and gave him a nod and saw that the others were now looking up. He lifted his hat to them and nodded again, then went back to his spyglass and his invisible horizon.

When he was certain their course was true, he went back down to plot on his chart just how far they had come, for he knew, that now with a crew under his command they would make better time than that which they had, and so he must check at more regular intervals the line they were heading till his lieutenants could do it.

But as the captain entered under the stairs he noticed a boy sitting on a bench in the nook, who hadn't been their last time he had looked.

'What are you doing here?' he asked rather bluntly.

'Waiting for you sir, to see what you'll do with me.'

'And what have you done that I should do anything?'

'I don't know sir, but I've been here waiting since early this morning.'

'Have you,' said the captain, then asked, 'Are you hungry?' hearing his own stomach.

'Sir, oh yes sir, mightily.'

'Right then, follow me.'

And so the captain went round his table, clearing the charts of the earth and the sky, putting the astronomical and navigational instruments by and sitting the boy down on the other side to the side where he sat where he could see the door, who came and went, and so on and so forth.

'Luncheon will be here soon, do you have a name boy? What should I call you?'

'Tom, Sir.'

'Tom? Is that all, nothing more?'

'Well Sir,' the boy thought then he brightened, 'sometimes they call me Needle, I like that.'

'Needle?'

'Aye Sir, 'cause I'm thin as a stick.'

'A strange kind of logic, but you are, that's for sure.'

'Do you have a name sir?'

'Oh, I suppose, yes.'

'What is it?'

'Ah, well, I very rarely use it.'

'How do you mean sir? It's your moniker ain't it?'

'Aye,' said the captain his frown just beginning, 'but, there are several so it's not really-'

Then the door opened and Morris's entrance interrupted. The young captain's aspect lightened and Needle's eyes nearly popped as they widened as the tray was set down on the table, laden with the captain's luncheon.

On the tray was naught but a cheese and apricot sandwich. The boy stared at it and then at the captain, and said with a start, 'What! Is that it? But you're Captain!'

'Aye, and this is what I like to eat for my lunch,' said the captain, surprised by this outburst, then to Morris, 'Morris, explain him?'

'Lieutenant Banks says you might have him, as if they did they would be unbalanced.'

'I see.'

'Aye,' Morris nodded in understanding. This boy would be trouble if he were mishandled, but with the right direction, maybe they could contain him.

'What will it be Needle, will you have a sandwich, or is it not good enough for you to manage?'

'Too good sir, I'd love one, thank you.'

So Morris withdrew without being asked to acquire another, while the captain sat and watched as out the window flew his quiet repast.

Chapter 3:
A BIRTHDAY WISH LEADS TO…

The days went on, as did the nights, as they flew and coursed at a very great height, with clouds above them and clouds underneath, the little ship, the Avaeste, sighed and creaked. The wind picked up and the wind died down, the men learnt their roles, and the more they did they found that their captain was a fair man, a strong man, a wise man, but he was also distant and mostly unspoken.

If his new Lieutenants had a problem, he knew how to solve it, if they gave the wrong punishment he was quick to resolve it. If the crew were becoming rowdy with boredom, he knew of tasks that could happily employ them. If they were lethargic or becoming nonchalant, he knew the words that would spur or cheer them up. And if they went against orders he gave, he knew how to make the proudest head hang in shame. For he was the captain, and this was his crew, so he made it his business to know them well through.

They learnt how to run a ship thoroughly, from keeping it neat to flying it properly, how to make her go as fast as she could, how to slow her down softly or as quick as she would, how to stand at arms and how to defend in case of attack, many things they knew from before, but they all agreed that no prior commander had the method or skills of this boy captain for certain.

Had they known it the captain was pleased, the Avaeste was transformed with this new company; he knew she was a good ship when he had acquired her, when she was rotting at an old and deserted pier, but if he took her back now to his harbour at home they would not recognise her for her grandeur and glow. Her sails were full and white, her deck shimmering, her rigging was neat; her whole being was singing.

And, thought the captain, the crew had been transformed from a rowdy bunch of drunken sailors into a company, talented and proud. But there was still a long way to go – they hadn't been tested, and not till then would their skill really show, even the captain didn't know how he'd manage, and he worried about the trials before them; could he pull them all through to advantage?

'Captain,' said a gruff voice by his side, as he sat at his desk with the maps one morning.

'Aye Morris, what is it?' he replied.

'Just a little thing,' Morris said gently.

'Aye?'

'In overhearing some of the crew today, I discovered it's Lieutenant Phillips's birthday.'

'I see.'

'What shall we do? Will I double the menu?'

'No, leave it with me,' said the captain, 'actually, no, send him in.'

Not much later there was a knock on the door, and Phillips came in, his bulky frame bending. He was a large sailor, with big bones and muscles that showed even through the shirt, the jacket and waistcoat. He took off his hat and looked down at the boy, saying, 'What can I do for you then, Captain?'

'Sit down Phillips,' the captain said, and waited as the big Lieutenant sat, 'that is the question I was going to ask you.'

'Cap'n?'

'What can I do for you?'

'I don't understand.'

'It's your day of birth is it not?'

'Aye sir,'

'So, is there anything you want?'

'Ah, I don't know Cap'n, no need to trouble y'self, the boys'll help me make a little fun and mischief.'

The Lieutenant made ready to go but the captain stopped him before he could move. Phillips looked worried and the captain could see there was something on his mind that had been there a while.

'What is it Phillips? No need to hesitate, say it.'

'No Cap'n I mustn't, I always say what's inappropriate.'

'Say what you want today Lieutenant, I'll overlook any impropriety in it.'

'Cap'n,' he fumbled with the hat in his hands before looking up and facing the captain again. 'It's just that, some of the lads are getting concerned, this ship ain't run like any other berth. See, like with us Lieutenants, four of us on one ship, just us and the crewmen, no bosun, no cook that we've seen, nor any midshipmen,'

'But everything gets done, does it not, by you four, and the crew, myself, Morris, Santee and Dew?'

'Yes,' Phillips replied, though he did not know who were those last two, 'but that's not everything,' he continued, 'if only you knew; the men are always wondering where we're headed, every day the same scene meets our waking eyes, the same clouds, the same blue skies, the same starry nights. You say it is a voyage of utmost importance, with a reward at the end, but to what end do we fly? And when will we see the land and see our town? When will we be home Cap'n? More'n two weeks we've been away, and though it's not long at all for us sailors, it's hard when we don't know where we're sailing. Banks is getting itchy, and Jennings too, I don't know where I stand, I just want to see land soon, that's all I know.'

'I understand, and you will. You may go.'

Even as Phillips went out the door the captain unrolled his heavily marked map and pulled out another one on top of that, then he slid out a drawer in his desk and he asked for a certain piece. There was a rumble and clatter then it was thrown out at him - an instrument that when looked through, the map could be seen in three dimensions, yes the islands grew up into the air and floated there like you could almost touch them. He found what he wanted and steeled himself for the task, for if he didn't do this right this voyage would be his last. But nevertheless this diversion would be a good test for the men.

The captain ran up to the wheel, and without a word nudged Jennings aside. He changed the course so abruptly that everyone felt it and soon the crew that had been at rest were up on the deck, and Morris who had been dozing in some hidden nook, ran to the wheel thinking something was up.

'Let out the topsails!' the captain bellowed out, 'Needle!' he yelled to his little shadow, 'take this,' he threw him a scope, 'get up to the masthead, keep your eyes peeled just below and this side of the sun.'

'But Harrick is up there already sir.'

'But your eyes are younger and sharper, get up there.'

So Needle ran off, to climb up to the lookout. Though he was scared to go up so high, he wanted to do as his captain commanded, for no one had ever trusted him with much, he being so slight and so prone to running amuck.

More commands the captain gave, all the men followed but wondered what had become of the silent captain that they had known, the boy, so firm but quietly spoken. Phillips hoped that nothing he'd said had made the captain act in a reckless way, hoped that what was happening now had all been his plan before they had spoken.

How they sped, like never before, the clouds passed them by and the wind rushed and roared.

When the captain saw Morris by his side he gave him the wheel and then he stood by, his fair hair and his white shirt rippling, his hands on the belt of his sword which was almost never unsheathed, with his blue eyes he looked left of the sun, and a little below, squinting and peering, was it land yet? It couldn't be far to go.

Then just when the captain was thinking to recheck his course the words echoed down and the crew was suddenly in chorus, 'Land ho!' Needle shouted, 'just above the clouds there're mountains with snow!' he waved his hands, though Harrick still peered Tom Needle was certain and so they all cheered.

'Where are we Captain?' Morris asked in his ear.

'If I have come to where I believe, then this is the Isle, Diamantine.' Then he turned to the crew and called their attention. 'Men,' he said, 'there is land before us, it is not our goal, but I want you to see that you are not sailing with a mad captain through empty heavens. I know I have brought you far from home, and so, in appreciation for all that you've done, for all you've put up with on my behalf, and because it is a special occasion,' he motioned to Phillips and another cheer went up, 'I give you the option of going ashore. But,' he added, with significant emphasis, 'before you decide what you would like let me tell you what I know of this fair Isle.

'Firstly, if we are to go ashore we must get through weather like we've never been through before, and sail into a harbour that's not the easiest of all, and the people there may welcome us, or they may not; they are few, but they are strong. And if you go ashore you may look and appreciate, but nothing from the island can you bring back on this ship, unless, that is, it was purchased or given. What will it be men? This is your decision.'

'Ashore!' one yelled.

'Let's stay on the Avaeste,' some mumbled, uncertain, and others were just silent in thought. Some worried that it sounded risky, but Jennings had run down and into Banks' ear had whispered the words that he overheard; that the Isle to which they were on their way had the word 'Diamond' in its name.

So, soon Banks had begun his stirring, and the crew was whipped up, nearly all yelling 'Ashore! Ashore! Let's go ashore!'

The captain saw Banks milling around, stirring the crew, yelling it out. He was not that dull not to see it, it made him sad, but he decided for now that he'd overlook it.

'Very well,' he said, now back to his quiet self, 'brace yourselves,' he added, nodded to Morris and went below deck to take one more look at the charts before the foul weather hit.

Seeing the clouds gathering before them out of nothing, just as the captain had warned, the lieutenants went about with their orders, getting the unnecessary crew below, hoisting the sails and making sure every man was where he should be to act as fast as they could when the time came to manoeuvre.

The captain went below, past the men, past the lieutenants' rooms, through the kitchen, down the ladder into the cargo hold, then right to the back where he opened a blackened little door, all sooty round the edges from the exhaust of the engine. The noise became louder as he opened it, the churn and the whir and chug-a-chug-chig.

'Mornin' Cap'n!' a jovial voice said, it was shallow and gravelly, with a laughing tilt. 'What can I do fer ye?' the creature said, as the captain bent down and peered in.

The creature was Dew, an undersized goblin, who the captain had found in the engine when he had been completing its tedious reconstruction. Dew was not the prettiest thing that walked the earth, with his pointed nose, his squinty eyes, and his tummy that popped out as though it had a cannon ball in it. He had skin that was darker and swampier than that of Morris, but it did not have quite as many lumps on it, and the darkness was only because of this role, he was really a pale goblin, the only albino; and he had ears like the swamp monster but they were more pointed and further back on his head, and where he had supple claws Morris had webbed hands, but neither knew of the other's existence on the fair Avaeste, a thing the captain wanted to keep, for between the Goblins of Kebatikas and the Monsters of Swamp there existed no greater rivalry, no greater distrust.

'Just thought I better warn you,' the captain replied, 'we're about to hit a rough patch, you might want to hold tight. I'm counting on you not to let the engine die, but if you must, it's alright. You've got to keep yourself safe to keep us alive.'

'You can count on me Cap'n!' the cheery goblin saluted then turned a lever, adjusted a dial and picked some dirt out from under the nail on his toe, then tasted it.

The captain smiled, amused, as he made his way up to the deck, none would stay, he was certain, not even Morris, if they knew their sole engine went on humming only by the cunning of an undersized goblin.

The storm came more suddenly than any had expected, the rain in squalls that came at all angles, down on you hard like needles and vices, it came like it was a storm aimed and made just for them, or any who'd dare to journey closer to see this diadem. The darkness grew and the ship's boards steamed, soon very little at all could be seen, till not a metre in front of you could be discerned through the haze of the rain and the thick foggy cloud.

Voices were silenced, caught by the wind before the words could get out, and bodies were pinned by fear or the force of the tempest to the spot where they clung.

The captain left Morris again at the helm, and went cautiously from mast to mast through the storm. He could hear the sails above him, the ones they had left, they were taking the wind, and carrying them onwards, but would they hold long enough to get them through it? They were being tossed about like a ship on the sea, and the worst was yet to come, just ahead, from the heavens above to the sky below, flashed chain after chain of a furious light show.

He ran into a man coming down on the ratlines, Berens was his name, a man under Jennings.

'How's it look from up there?' the captain shouted.

'Mains'l's chaffing, and the riggin' on the yard is lookin' bad.'

'Will she hold?'

'I don't think so.'

'Anything else?'

'Needle's still up there,' Berens looked to the unseeable masthead, shook his head, 'Harrick left him. The boy tried to follow but he's stuck just below the crow's nest, frightened through, the poor kid.'

'Help me with the rigging, then I'll see to the kid,' the captain yelled and Berens nodded, he didn't want to go back up into the squall, up there where there was so little to hold and so easy to fall, but he followed this boy up into it all, he didn't want to be out done by a child.

They reached the chaffing and loosening ropes as the ship flew further into the storm, Berens had thought it couldn't get worse but everything did, a flash of light seared the cloud just by them, he cursed, and thunder broke, shattering every other sound, the wind pressed, the rain pressed, the air took your breath. Both Berens and the captain at once nearly fell but together they held on and resecured the worn cord so it could hold for another little while yet.

'Get yourself to the deck,' the captain yelled, 'I'm heading up for the kid.'

'Aye Cap'n,' Berens shouted back, no one could call him a coward for wanting to get out of this, his heart wanted to help, but his head knew better, no point staying up here for a near certain death.

The captain disappeared up into the clouds and Berens disappeared as he made his way down. The storm kept churning and writhing about them, the little Avaeste did all she could, as did the crew, the captain, and of course, Dew, who down in the engine room was having the merriest time, humming as he ran about, keeping the ship in the sky.

Then all so suddenly, when it seemed never ending, a break appeared in the sky up ahead, and as the blue overtook the grey blanket a sparkling Isle was before them, shimmering and brilliant.

The isle was floating, like a bird that hovers still in the sky, with mountains of green, of blue and of white standing tall above the horizon, and underneath them were mirrored mountains of gold growing down into the sky below, and where they met lay a great ocean that stretched from the mountains to the edge where it was

24

held in by the hands of the wind that whipped it up and let no water fall into the emptiness.

Then as the crew were mesmerised by the Isle the voice of a boy finally penetrated their minds. 'Help!' Needle yelled, 'quick! It's the captain!'

Morris was first to locate his master, lying on the deck with the boy beside him. He didn't like the look of it, the captain was pale. He was awake and was breathing but his leg, it was bleeding and open where he could see, wide eyed, that the bone was split.

'Can you see Diamantine?' the captain asked, with a pained grin, it was all he could think with so many eyes focused on him while he was in such a position.

'Aye, we can,' Lieutenant Carter said as he knelt to inspect the damage, 'and a beautiful sight she is Captain.' He'd children of his own numbering three, so his heart went out to the captain, kind of fatherly.

'He saved my life!' Needle told the crowd before the captain could say anything to stopper his mouth, 'I were up the masthead, fearing for my breeches, 'cause the wind was acting like it'd have me no matter what I did or how hard I held, then I's just about to give up when Cap'n got a hold on me ankle and we made our way down, and was nearly home, I tell you, we were more'n halfway down when the clouds were clearin' but in the last heave and blast we was shook from the 'lines and tossed aground boys, freak-like, but still he holds on like I'm precious as diamonds and so it is I fell atop o' him, just like that. Maybe I'd 'a died, on this 'ere deck otherwise.'

'Don't be a fool Needle,' the captain said through pain clenched teeth, 'there was nothing in it.' Though many of the crew thought it was the most sensible thing Tom Needle had ever said. 'You lot get to your stations, we've got to get into port yet. Carter, Morris, get me to my cabin.'

'You need a surgeon sir,' said Berens, his eyes worried as were pairs of those behind him, including Phillips and Jennings.

'Aye, I know,' said the captain, looking grimly at his leg, his face further whitening.

A stretcher was brought, the captain taken to his cabin, along with the best physician that could be found on board; a surgeon's apprentice, no less, but no more.

Everyone was sent from the room, bar just a small few, but others waited outside as the apprentice deliberated at the best thing to do for such a terrible wound. Carter forced on the boy a hot tonic that burnt his throat and made his belly and his blood warm up at once. Morris watched the men do what he couldn't do; hold the boy down so they could get done what they needed to.

Carter changed the captain's soaking wet shirt while the surgeon cut away the leg of his trousers and then got to work, pulling out some long ancient pliers he picked out the fragments of splintered bone and debris from the flesh just below the knee. Then gently and firmly the surgeon pushed on the captain's leg, easing the bone back into place. Outside they heard nothing, not one shout, as the captain bit hard on the thick leather glove Carter had found.

'Go,' the captain said to Carter when the worst was over, as Morris washed the sweat from his forehead, 'make ready to heave to, you give the order. Get one of your men to run up the flag, the blue one embroidered with white stars, but first, come back when you're closer, I'll have to guide you down to the water. Oh, and Anthony,' he said to Lieutenant Carter with a face harder and more worn than years could have made it. 'Confine Banks and Jennings to quarters, they will not go ashore on Diamantine island. If they oppose you, send them to me, and before the men go ashore remind them to behave even better than they do on board, and of course, as I said before, nothing comes back on this ship from that shore, not unless it is given or bought.'

'Right Cap'n,' Carter replied, trying not to show the overwhelming feeling he was getting inside, 'I understand, I'll be back shortly, before we come in to land.'

So now only Morris was left to hold down the boy as the surgeon produced a long and curved needle and a length of thread, the captain grabbed the leather in his teeth again as the surgeon worked the string, re-uniting his tortured, torn skin.

The surgeon propped the leg up on a pillow and urged the boy to leave it like that for a while, before saying, 'You're the best patient I've ever had,' and leaving with a smile that was kind and sad.

'Morris,' the captain beckoned, 'go out and see how we progress.'

'But Captain,'

'I'm fine, no protest.'

'Aye sir,' Morris said and jumped down off the bed, and went to do as his captain had bid.

As soon as everyone had left the cabin there was a faint buzzing, like the wings of an insect or a bigger something, then all of a sudden upon the captain's chest a little sprite landed, she was worried and distressed.

'Boy,' she said lovingly, holding his cheeks and peering into his eyes, 'I think you are hurting, are you alright?'

'Nothing time won't heal Santee, don't be upset.'

'Alright,' she said, at once changing her aspect, even down to the colour of her dress, from a dark storm to a bright sunset.

'Tell me,' he asked her, 'I haven't seen you since the men came on board, and tell me, how did you fair in the storm?'

'I hid in your desk.'

'But the men Santee? Are you afraid of them?'

'Aye Cap'n,' she mocked them, then sat down on his shoulder and blew on his neck till he couldn't help laughing. That's when Lieutenant Carter came in, with Morris behind him.

'Good to see you've got your spirits still with you Cap'n,' Carter said, his eyes wide and wondering at why the captain was laughing when he was expecting to be met with a pained grimace. Santee slipped down behind her captain's pillow and found a place behind the fabric where she could peer out but not be seen.

'How's it going out there?' asked the captain.

'Well sir, very well, we're just above sea level now, so I've come as you asked.'

The young captain then explained to his man how to brace the ship, how to come in and land, the rest, he knew the sailors would know, what to do with the sails, how to heave to. 'Go in slowly, and if you're intercepted, or if anyone in authority wishes to speak to the captain, you may tell them how it is, and if they wish it, usher them in, but give me a warning.'

'Aye Cap'n,' Carter rose and went to his station.

'He seems nice,' Santee sighed peering out from the sheets, 'but what would a man do if he saw a sprite?'

'What sprite would want to be seen by a man?' the captain asked.

'I suppose you're right.'

'Have you seen the island Santee?' he asked, his eyes watching her as if in a dream.

'I have, it's more beautiful than anything I've ever seen, I'm so glad you brought me, even though I'm very sorry about what happened to you. Can I go out boy, when we're near the shore?'

'You know I have no hold on you Santee, do what you feel safe to do, I won't leave without you, just don't be away long or I'll miss you.'

'Will you!?' she said, amazed and surprised.

'I will, how will I find anything in my desk without you?' he joked as she crossed her arms and huffed, not impressed at all.

He felt the touch of the hull on the waves, the drag of the water as the Avaeste lowered, then came the sounds and the smells of the shore, before finally the little ship came to a halt.

'Go on,' the captain nudged her, 'just stay out of trouble. But one thing, Santee, before you go.'

'Anything boy, what will it be?'

'Put me to sleep for an hour or so.'

'Is that all? That's easy.'

'Thankyou,' he whispered, sleepy already, as she pulled his eyelids closed.

She looked out the window at the sparkling isle, then looked back at the boy weighed down with worry. She imagined him running on the shimmering beach, like any boy his age might be, then looked again at him here, lying broken and tired. She couldn't leave him, she sat down again, leaning on his shoulder, looking out at the bay and beyond to the mountains.

Santee was as broken inside as shells on the beach. The boy was everything she had, the boy and this ship. She was an outcast, an outsider, a foreigner to her own folk, she did not look like the sprites in her fold, she was taller, brighter, a flyer much faster than any other. There was nothing they could do, but to expel her, as even her brothers and sisters were jealous. Some time in the world would make her think better than to outsmart, outwit and outdo them all in everything. She hadn't meant to, it's just what she did. So she went to hide on this empty ship, it had a name she liked, and better still no one was in it. Or so she had thought, but then one day in her misery she flew straight into a boy, at first both were frightened, the boy thinking that she was some oversized wasp, and she thinking that he was some horrible human, she'd heard nasty things and was scared for her life, but they both stepped back calmly and both were surprised to see a common look in the other's eyes.

Neither had asked the other what was their story, but together they had been since that first day of meeting. And so now she sat, she just couldn't leave him to lie here alone while she went off exploring, she would help him get better enough so that he could go out himself, and then, she decided, then she'd go with him.

After an hour of perfect rest the captain awoke to a tap on his chest.

'Wake up,' the sprite whispered in his ear, 'and get yourself ready, the Governor's here.'

The captain looked at her slightly bemused, 'Wake up boy,' she snapped his eyelid then flew off, 'I'll be hiding in your desk with your toys.'

Before he had a chance to reply he found Needle at the door and Morris by his side.

'Lieutenant Carter sent me to warn you, the Governor of Diamantine is coming to see you.'

'Thankyou, Needle, stay with Carter, he might want you again.'

'Aye sir.'

'Morris?'

'Your coat Captain, your best. I've had the buttons repolished, and I've had it pressed.'

'Thankyou. I didn't ask you Morris, how'd you fair in the storm?'

'Well Captain, no problems.'

'And the rest of the crew?'

'Nothing to bother you.'

'And the ship Morris?' he asked as he did up the buttons, 'the ship Morris, how faired the Avaeste?'

'Nothing a few weeks in port won't fix.'

'Weeks! No. I wanted to be gone by tomorrow. Weeks!?'
'Aye captain, as you'll see when you're fit.'

There were footsteps at the door, the boy sat up, quickly brushing his hair back and clearing the frown from his face.

Lieutenant Carter opened the door and announced, 'The Governor of Diamantine here to see you Captain.'

'Thankyou, show him in.'

Chapter 4:
WELCOME TO DIAMANTINE
& YOU ARE WHO?

Morris quickly hid in the chest where he slept and Santee sunk further into the drawer where she'd hid, as Carter withdrew and the Governor came in.

He was short man, a little rotund, with balding black hair and curled moustache, he carried his top-hat under his arm as he made his way over to greet the young captain.

'Sir Rubra De Silva,' he introduced himself as he held out his hand, 'Governor of the harbour on Diamantine Isle.'

'At your service Sir,' the captain took his hand, 'please take a seat, do excuse my not rising to greet you, but my surgeon has begged me not to move.'

'Ah yes, that they will do,' Sir Rubra said, taking a chair. Behind his smiling, cheery countenance Sir Rubra was studying that of this Capitan with eyes so shrewd there was little he missed. From the shore through his scope he had spied the Avaeste coming through the clouds and the rainbowing mists, and he'd said to his deputy and to his men, 'That, Sirs, is a fine little ship, I think, I think we'll let her come in, even just to see how she is built, and better still, who captain's it.' So now as he sat and looked this boy over he couldn't quite believe he was the one in charge of her, but he'd see in time.

'Capitan, you fly the banner of St Amalric (pronounced *Amery*), you have come far, yes?' he asked.

'Yes Governor, a long way, and we've still further to go. This was an unscheduled stop, I had not meant to burden your fair Isle with my crew, at least, not for long, but I've been informed the ship was damaged in the storm, so we may need to lengthen our stay at your port. If it is a problem sir, you may use your ships to carry us back out beyond the clouds.'

'You have a beautiful ship.'

'Thankyou sir.'

'It will not be a problem, you may stay till you have made the repairs, I will even give you the use of some of my men who are expert in these things.'

'Thankyou sir, you are very generous. To tell you the truth I did not know what to expect.'

The governor laughed as he stood, ready to leave, 'When you are able you must come and dine at my residence.'

'Once more, thankyou,' they shook hands yet again.

'Just remember Capitan, keep an eye on your men.'

'I plan to Sir, I'll do the best I can.'

The meeting went as well as it could have, the captain thought as he looked at the bandage on his broken leg.

'Morris,' he called as he heard the Governor's boat pull away, 'send me the surgeon, I want a splint made.'

Morris climbed out of the chest in the corner, then went to the desk, pulling Santee out of the drawer.

'The captain wants a splint,' he said to her as she shook herself a new colour of dress, 'and I think,' Morris continued, 'what could that mean but that he wants to go out, but should he?'

'Just so, I should,' the captain laughed, 'go on then, fetch my surgeon.'

'Santee, I think you should put him to sleep again.'

'I think you're right Morris,' she said then whispered, 'it's for your own good,' and the captain was asleep before he could say a word.

Lieutenant Carter let the men go ashore in groups of five to ten, but no more. They lowered the row boats and went eagerly to see this new place they had never before heard of let alone seen.

The men were speechless when they reached the shore, the beach alone was far more than they were prepared for. The sand was not sand but innumerable crystals, each one perfect, each one so valuable, and scattered amongst them for as far as they could see where pearls of every shade, so iridescent, and even as they watched more were washed up from the sea.

'Remember,' Phillips warned them, as they stared and they drooled, 'all of this is to enjoy now, not even to think of taking back home.'

They were like men in a dazed dream, everything was so beautiful it almost overwhelmed. They walked into the village by small pebbled paths, marvelling at the people, the animals and everything they passed.

There were houses made entirely of vines, that were silver and gold and bronze intertwined, and they rose into the heavens that shone bright as sapphire. Everything shined and everything shimmered, it blinded them nearly and when they looked to each other they seemed so plain and so simple, even in their best ship's attire. They climbed steps of quartz and walkways of marble, they tried to converse with the people they met, whose laughter tinkled like wind-chimes in a favourable breeze, whose skin even shimmered like the rest of the island around them, and whose eyes were like the gems in the sand, sparkling, glittering, bright and deceiving.

Word of the island got back to Lieutenant Banks who steamed in his quarters that he'd never see it, maybe the captain would come to his senses, or maybe there was a way to get out and back, he and Jennings.

The men took turns in going ashore, the half who were left always worked till they were sore, mending the tears in the sails and the cords, re-scrubbing the deck and making all grand again, but they would have to wait, and this was the hard part, they needed to replace the mast at the mizzen. It hadn't fallen in the storm, but it had come mighty close, and if you took a look at her base she was just as shattered and broke as the captain's bone.

He woke about midday the following day, the ship swaying gently with the heave of the sea, the sun shining warmly down through the window, it would have been perfect if it weren't for the throb that ached his whole body from his head to his toes.

'Morris is summoning the surgeon's apprentice,' Santee said as he brought her slowly into focus.

'You didn't go ashore? Either of you?' he asked surprised as he tried to sit up.

'Don't know about Morris, but I was waiting for you.'

'Afraid Santee, are you?'

'Maybe.'

'You've no need to be, you know, I think you're a brilliant sprite.'

'But you are a nice boy, and you say nice things. I don't understand, how can someone like you exist in a world like this?'

33

The captain just laughed at the whimsical sprite then leaned back on his pillow and closed his eyes. 'What am I to do Santee?'

'About what?' she asked lifting one of his eyelids and peering into his iris.

'Everything.'

'If I could read your books, or your mind, maybe I could tell you. But as is it I have as little idea what to do about anything as you do, in fact, much less.'

'I can't be delayed Santee, I want to leave here in under three days.' He said gently then added, loud and frustrated, 'Where is the surgeon's apprentice?!'

The swamp monster's head appeared timidly round the door, he'd rarely seen this mood in the captain before.

'He's gone,' said Morris, 'he's got leave on the shore, won't be here till supper Captain, they say don't expect him before.'

He was about to shout, to let out a tirade of words against everything that hampered him, but he stopped himself, and breathed calmly out and in.

'I'm sorry, it's my fault,' Santee whispered as she leaned sadly on the golden hair on his head, twisting his long fringe in her little hands.

'Yes, it is,' he replied after a while.

'But I didn't realise,' she sighed, 'I was just trying to do what a good friend would, make you look after yourself.'

'I know,' he said softly as he looked out the window.

'I didn't know time was important, I,'

'Santee, I know. I was the fool for coming in. Don't worry, I'll think of something, and soon, hopefully.'

So while the captain tried not to think of the pain in his leg, but rather the next step he would take, the crew went on discovering magnificent things in this island of unexpected enchantment.

After he had left the fair Avaeste the Governor of the Harbour of Diamantine, Sir Rubra De Silva, made his way to the king.

'What tidings De Silva?' the King asked as his Governor entered the high tower where he studied the harbour with his spyglass.

'The ship is called the Avaeste, her flag bears the St Amalric crest.'

'A friend of old.'

'Yes.'

'And the Captain?'

'Far from what I was expecting, he's a mere child, my King. I'm not convinced it wasn't some form of deception and that one of the others is captain, but he was well spoken, I've asked him to dine with me when he can.'

'When will that be?'

'I do not know, when he is able, for from the flight through our defences he sustained a nasty injury.'

'I see.' The king thought as he tapped his fingers on his chin, fingers that were barely visible for the rings. 'Well, when he does come,' the king carried on, 'also invite me, but do not let him know that I am the ruler of Diamantine. I will question him, I will discover why he's here and who he is.'

'Consider it done.'

It wasn't as long as they thought it would be before the King saw the captain coming to shore from his ship.

'Captain,' had said Phillips, 'let me get you a chair, we can lower you down to the row boat safe in it.'

'Don't be daft,' the captain defied them, 'just give me a loop in a rope and lower me down, I've got two legs, I'll stand on my other one.'

And so he did and they helped him into the boat, picking up the oars and together they rowed with more eagerness, more energy than they had possessed when just rowing together for their own benefit.

The king found it easy to pick out the captain, he wasn't quite as tall as most of the other men, and they all were gathering around to help him up through the diamond sand and onto the glittering pavement. On top of that his way was slow, he walked with a limp, the king focused the glass, he could just make out the splint and the crutches. At once he sent word to Sir Rubra De Silva, the captain was ashore, if his men had not already informed him.

The captain was just as amazed as all the men of his crew had been. He had read in his books tales of this place, but seeing it in person was so much more amazing. He dismissed those of his crew that still hung about, he would explore this place if his time was his own, but he had so much to do, things to get, places to go.

The King saw the boy look about wonderingly but then put down his head and got on with business; that was the first thing that confirmed that this boy was indeed Captain, to this king of Diamantine, but then the boy was lost to his sight, so he sat back and planned what to say if they met tonight.

By noon the captain had located the good harbourmaster, a man under the governor, and requested the necessary supplies for his ship. They would need water and grain, and fruit; if possible, apples and oranges, and anything else they might think of. But of course he would need a figure of cost to make sure he could pay for the things on the list. And lastly, most crucial, a new mizzen mast, he could get the crew to cut it from their forest, but he didn't want to do it without permission from the appropriate powers. Yes, he knew the rules, and he would not take anything without signed permission from Governor or King.

Then after the formalities, and after a subordinate had been sent to get the supplies on the list together as the master didn't think there would be a problem in it, the two men got talking. It was a balmy afternoon and they sat back to enjoy it, the older being interested in this proud young man and the younger finding in him the qualities of a friend.

'It's been such a long time since we've seen ships from so far,' said the kind old harbourmaster, 'tell me lad, how is your father?'

'My father sir?'

'Aye, don't think I don't know who you are, though no one else will. I don't know why you've come so far, I don't think your father would be happy if he knew, but I'll not tell on you if you don't want me to.'

'I would appreciate it if you do keep it to yourself. No one knows who I am, not even any of my crew. I don't want the consequence, nor the image I'd have to live up to.'

'I quite understand you.'

'My father is gravely ill,'

'I'm sorry to hear it, he has my best wishes.'

'Thankyou. That's the reason for my voyage, and I've a long way to go yet, I just hope when I get home my father isn't, isn't dead. But tell me,' said the captain, quickly changing the topic, 'the governor has invited me to tea. Where is his house, could you direct me?'

'Up on the hill lad, not far really, but it will seem so with your leg as it is, I think.'

'Oh, don't worry about me, I'll just take it slowly. Thankyou for your help,' the captain said in goodbye, 'till I see you again.'

'Aye Captain, when you do I'll have those supplies.'

The young captain began the climb up the stone steps to the governor's grand high residence. Flowers studded the corners, little gems in the rough, and vines and shrubs with leaves of every colour flowed over the hillside rocks. There was no one else going this way, they all seemed to be down in the bay, the captain thought as he stopped for a breath and leaned on the crutch the surgeon had insisted he take. He was glad of it now, taking more weight off his leg as he rested his shoulder on it, glad of it too for without it he knew he could not have made this little trip. He turned back now and then to admire the view of the sea, and he felt something like pride well up is his chest as he picked out the shape of his beautiful ship, the Avaeste.

He was not the only one admiring it, many from the village had cast their eyes upon it. There was nothing about the ship that was like this island, Diamantine was sumptuous, the Avaeste rather bare, on Diamantine everything sparkled or shimmered or glowed, on the Avaeste only perhaps her timber rails showed any sign of being glittering and that was only just after a heavy scrub and polish. Other than that perhaps there were a few shoe buckles or buttons that had at one time been something but now only held a faded lustre. And where Diamantine lay-out her best treasures for all to see the Avaeste kept hers hidden humbly. The king wondered just what they were and he could not remove his spyglass, he watched every move of her crew and awaited with pleasure for tonight's interview.

The governor saw the captain coming, slowly with that leg of his, up the long steps to his small palace, and he called his daughter, a beautiful girl who had long dark hair and an affecting smile, to meet the captain halfway down, but Sir Rubra couldn't find her, she'd already gone.

'Hola,' greeted a sweet voice, the captain uplifted his head, and was surprised to see a girl of roughly his age standing there on the next step. 'My name is Yvette, are you one of the sailors from the Avaeste?'

'Ah, yes,' he said, 'I've been admiring the view you have from up here.'

'Tell me,' she said quietly, instantly taking a liking to him, 'have you seen all the world? It must be amazing.'

'I wouldn't say the world, but I have travelled a bit, yes.'

'Is it beautiful out there or is it a world of despair?'

The boy thought hard, then answered, 'It is both.'

'I have often wondered about it. Part of me would like to explore, but the other part just wants to stay home, and that is easier, isn't it, so that's all I've done.'

He just smiled at her as they walked on.

'Tell me about your Capitan,' she began again, 'my father, Sir Rubra, insists I come to dine with them, but I think I'd rather not sit around while old men discuss things of which I have absolutely no interest.'

'You don't like ships?' the captain said, restraining that chuckle of his.

'Oh no, you mistake me, I do – particularly your Avaeste, I think she's beautiful.'

'Why is she so?'

'Her lines are so clean, and she flies so effortlessly, she has no figurehead at her prow just the banner on her mast, of St Amalric, says my father, the white stars of Aeloran, the sign of the wisest king that still lives. Oh, but I shouldn't say that, our king is not so bad,' laughed Yvette, 'and how would I know, I've never been out there, anywhere, I only know the stories I'm told.'

'I'm glad you like the Avaeste, but I don't think you'll like our captain somehow.'

'Oh, really, why not? Is he terrible to look at?'

'Well, I'm no judge of that.'

'Is he old?'

'Not terribly so.'

'Does he swear and curse all day long?'

'Oh no, he might use harsh words but he's far too proud to do that. He has a kind of a limp at the moment, he can't walk very fast.'

'That's not so bad,' she said taking his arm and helping him onto the next step.

'And he doesn't talk much at all really, except when he has to, well, usually. And some of the crew find him irrational, and that might just be so.'

'What else, is he cruel?' she laughed.

'That depends how you look at it. And, he's a little short.'

'Oh no,' she said sarcastically and chuckled as she looked back at this boy as they walked.

'But I hope that's only because he hasn't stopped growing yet,' the captain laughed at her look of enquiring surprise as they reached the last of the steps. Yvette hadn't realised quite how close they were to her own house and so the voice in her throat got caught there as she heard her father call out.

'Ah, here you are, welcome, welcome, do come in Capitan.'

'Capitan!' she choked as she realised she'd been speaking with him the whole time, this boy, nothing like the captains she'd imagined in her mind. 'You *are* cruel,' she whispered with a grin aside, as the governor ushered him in.

'I see you have met my daughter, Yvette?'

'Yes sir, that pleasure I have had.'

'Another thing Capitan, you may laugh at me, but I have forgotten your name it seems, and none of your crew have been able to tell my secretary, so I have to ask you directly, what name shall I provide to my guests this evening?'

'Ashton,' the captain simply replied.

'Ah,' breathed Sir Rubra, 'now, that is easy.'

'Indeed.'

'Capitan Ashton, I thank thee. Will you excuse us for a moment, there are just a few last things to which I must attend, Yvette, come get yourself ready.'

'Boy, I don't trust him,' Santee whispered when the footsteps were gone, she peered out from where she had sat on the fold of his collar around the back, holding onto and hiding in the golden locks of his hair to which she had matched the colour of her dress.

'He's not so bad Santee, every man has a position that binds him to do what he must to get through, the governor is no different. I think he is, in the end, a kind man.'

'Maybe, but look at this place, we thought the island was grand, compared to this it was nothing but sand. Look at it!'

'I have been.'

'Gold, red diamond, turquoise!' she shivered, 'such riches.'

'No Santee, they are not rich.'

'Oh?'

'No, Santee, you and I, we are more wealthy than this whole isle,' the captain said as his face was lit up by a wistful smile.

'Hahaha, how? Or is it a why?'

'Because we know, Santee, that the value of a diamond is only the value men put on it, and there are things out there to be found that have a value far more intrinsic, and that value will always be the same no matter how men flicker and change.'

'But for supplies you still need money.'

'That's true, but don't let it worry you. We'll get through.'

'You always do.'

The Governor ushered his daughter into her room shutting the door and sitting her down, 'Now listen Yvette, the King is coming to dine, but he is not the King, understand me? He will be in disguise.'

'Yes father, but why? Is it because of the captain? Don't you trust him? But he seems nice.'

'Don't ask me, just get yourself ready,' he said and then he left her with a kiss on her head.

He had already sent a message to the palace of the king, which was not far away, telling that they would soon be dining. So now he went to open the door, for the Conte Fra'Antelli, he was no less, but much more, and together they went to the room where the captain was adjourned.

The introductions were made and the room was soon flowing, yes over-flowing with more. More people, more robes, more glittering gowns. It seems the king could even fool his own, without his usual make up, his signets, or his majestic throne.

After the Conte Fra'Antelli, the governor introduced, his hostess, the widow, Mrs Pardue, who made a neat bow and greeted the captain in a volume that echoed across the whole house. She alone was enough to startle him, but still there was more to come. She introduced her son, a tall handsome youth by the name of Armand, and they were as opposites he and the captain, in both looks and demeanour. Then there was a stream of ladies and gentlemen, that the captain found himself quite overwhelmed.

For what the captain had thought was going to be a quiet evening was turning out to be a rather immense, but still casual, function. It seems anybody who was anybody had wanted to come to the impromptu dinner in honour of this unknown captain. After all it was not often they had news of the world so far beyond them. But only disappointment awaited them, for the captain was reluctant with such a crowd before him. They'd have had more luck down in the harbour today where some of the crew were back to their old ways, unwinding their tales at the only bar in the bay.

The governor made excuses, 'He is tired…' and so on, 'maybe another day,' till just the few he had particularly invited remained.

'Do excuse them,' begged De Silva of the captain, 'they mean no harm, they are just the life of the party, but tell them there is none and they'll go away.'

'Thankyou, I am much obliged, I am not one for crowds particularly when I am the mainstay.'

'No trouble, I quite understand, come sit down and relax, we can still enjoy a quiet repast. If you will, Capitan Ashton.'

'Of course. Lead the way.'

The small party entered and were seated along a grand dining table, already laid, with scarlet tapestries, golden cutlery and plate.

At the head sat the governor, adjacent was Yvette, next in line sat the captain, the Conte was placed opposite. Next to the Conte, Mrs Pardue was seated and that made the top end. After that down the table on either side there was Captain De Granya, his wife, Admiral Teodosio, his daughter, and Gualtiero, a pilot, and there were still more.

The Governor's people brought in tray after tray of delicious morsels for all to taste, there were so many things, all so sumptuous Santee even risked a whisper, 'Hey, boy, give me a taste.' Which he managed to do, surreptitiously holding the fork under his ear, just for a moment, while he appeared to have been distracted by something.

'So, Captain Ashton, what brings you here?' asked the admiral as he chewed away.

'The truth Admiral?' the captain laughed.

'Aye,' said the admiral, raising the brow over his left eye.

'Well, it was the birthday of one of my lieutenants.'

At once some were silent, others burst into mirth, 'That's a new one,' said Conte Fra'Antelli, 'tell us, are you always this crazy?'

'How so?' asked the young captain.

'To risk your men, your ship, and everything in it, to show this place to your Lieutenant?'

'And pick up supplies as well,' the captain added, 'not essential yet, but I like to be prepared in advance.'

'And you did do well, that's to be admitted, the last ship that came through was nearly cracked into splinters,' Gualtiero said, 'I'm a pilot myself, who needs sails when you've got wings?'

A sparkle lit up in the young captain's eye, 'I'd like to see your flying machines, if you have the time before I leave.'

'My pleasure Capitan, whenever you're ready,' Gualtiero replied, very eagerly, as he shoved into his mouth another drumstick of chicken without ceremony.

'He loves his machines,' the widow interposed, 'but I think they're such dangerous things.'

'Living is dangerous,' countered Gualtiero, he too had a spark. He was a stocky little man who looked like he'd be the pit-bull if it came to a fight, and he added, 'any of us could die any minute.'

'Here now, I'll have no talk of death at my dinner, another subject my friends, please,' begged the governor.

'I have one,' mused Fra'Antelli as his long fingers grasped the hip of his glass, 'your men, Captain Ashton, come from a little town, is it, called Althorn?'

'Yes sir, you are correct.'

'And yet, you fly the crest of the Isle of Aeloran, St Amalric to be precise.'

'Yes sir, that too is correct,' the captain replied and leaned back, content.

The Conte was irritated that he hadn't fazed the captain yet, so continued, 'Friends, I just can't seem to make sense, where is the town of Althorn, Captain Ashton?'

'Quite a distance, to be sure, it is not on your compass.'

'Every compass has four points my boy,' Fra'Antelli laughed, 'did you not study basic navigation: north, east, south and west; if it is out of our range, it is in no-ones reach, don't you see that?'

'No, you are wrong,' the captain said, and the governor nearly choked as this boy unknowingly challenged the king, 'my compass has six.'

There was a gasp, and then a silence which Gualtiero broke saying with wide eyes, 'I need one of those.'

'Still,' continued the Conte, 'it remains to be seen how –'

The young captain stood, and prepared to go, the Conte looked offended but then was dealt one final blow.

'There are some things that I cannot even tell you, oh King of Diamantine, I do beg your pardon, I was under the assumption I was dining with the governor this evening, if you wish to interrogate me you may come to my ship whenever you wish.'

Then there really was silence as the men summed each other up, but then a smile grew from Fra'Antelli's hard lips, whether he wanted to or not he admired this kid. 'Tell me, how did you know?'

'Your confidence, and your rings.'

'But I only wear three, and none of them denote that I am King.'

'The absence of them. Look at your hands. The love of your jewels Sire, has been your undoing.'

The king did look and he did find the indentations from long wearing the rings he so liked. 'But tell me boy, before you go, truthfully, you are not from this Althorn?'

'You know where I'm from. I have flown the flag since I decided to come.'

'But none have come from that isle for so long, no captain would dare to but a royal one, and you cannot be St Amalric's son.'

'Can I not?'

'But St Amalric only had seven sons? They'd all be older than you, so you see, it cannot be true.'

'I am the eighth one.'

'What proof have you? I'll have you arrested and locked in irons if you can give me none.'

The captain leaned over till they were so close only the king could hear the words that he uttered.

'Then I give you your supplies,' said the king, suddenly altered, 'Governor, see it done.'

'Sire, I cannot accept your generosity,' said Ashton.

'You will accept it boy; let me repay the debt of my father to yours when he gave us his aid all those years ago.'

'For my father, and yours.'

'Yes.'

'I thank you,' the captain bowed, then limped out the door. Yvette followed him with her eyes till he'd gone out of sight, she imagined a life sailing with him, imagined herself so in love and so blithe, but then her wandering eyes were met by Armand. Now he was a far, far staider man, he would not be coming and going doing dangerous things. He smiled at her and in that moment she decided that she would forget the handsome young captain.

*

The captain began to make his way down, wondering how he'd let so much out, he hadn't meant to, he was stronger than that, and far more cunning he knew, but he just let it go. Perhaps he needed to.

'Capitan!' there was a friendly yell behind him.

'Gualtiero?'

'Would now do? To see my machines, come on, I'd love you to, everyone else is scared but I tell you, I think you have the same spirit I do, don't you?'

'I do, but out of necessity Gualtiero, not a recklessness.'

'Hey, I'm not reckless,' laughed the pilot, 'I take calculated risks'

'Oh yes?'

'Yes, there's a chance I might die, there's a chance I might not, I know this, I have calculated it,' he tapped his forehead, which made the captain laugh quite a bit.

'Here, take my arm,' Gualtiero offered, 'my workshop is round the other side of the island, down by the ocean in the rocky part. It's not far really, but there's a bit of climbing down, see, I've got to keep all my work away from the diamonds of the city.'

'You don't like them?'

'Bah, they shine too much, and hurt my eyes when I'm making sparks. I tell you what capitan this is a rare privilege.'

'Yes, thankyou for inviting me to your workshop, I'm very

excited to see this machine.'

'No, not for you, for me. It has been so long since there has been an outside ship come in, it's how I got invited to the governor's dinner, it's a long story I tell you. There has been a long running bet, er, kind of thing, that the first person to see a foreign ship come in gets to dine with the governor or the king on a day of his very own choosing, and I spotted you when I was out testing my machine so, ha, figure that, I get Governor and *you* Capitan, *and* haha, I didn't know it till just now, but lucky man that I am I also dined with the king! Ok, so it isn't so long, but there it is, that's what happened.'

'Is it the storms Gualtiero? That keeps the ships away?'

'Ah, yes Capitan, in some ways. But this isle is unknown to most foreign places, and the truth is the king wants to keep it that way. Who wants trade, he says, when all they do is come to take our diamonds away, but me Capitan, take them! I say, when the rest of what we have we're using up, and rapidly. That's why I build this machine, it doesn't need much to make, and mostly I can use metal in its creation, and here gold is abundant as trees, that's why I made it this way. Are you ready to see it Capitan? My flying machine?'

'Yes, I'm eager to see it.'

So Gualtiero threw open the doors of his workshop, a cave in the rocks beside a place where the water flowed in, and he ran around loosening the covers, then quickly with one movement he pulled off the silk, revealing the most beautiful little machine, a frame where two could sit one in front one in the rear, two wings projected neatly from its sides, and a tail behind.

'The engine is in the front, a two bladed propeller,' the captain observed, 'and what are these Gualtiero, pontoons for it to float on the ocean? A good addition.'

The pilots jaw dropped, 'The Capitan knows so much, how is it possible?'

'We have similar machines at home, but none have come this far, they are still just designing them, I commend you Gualtiero.'

'Thankyou Capitan.'

'Tell me more.'

So they talked and they talked of mechanical things, of specifications, heights, distances and means, till the captain asked, 'One more thing. How much would it be to make one of these flying machines for me?'

'I don't know Capitan, let me think, but where would you fit it on your fine ship?'

'I'll make it fit, it would be easier of course with retractable wings.'

'Yes, yes, but you need a place to take off and land, when you're not at sea but in the air or on the ground.'

'An airstrip.'

'Oh, you are so learned. I barely have room here, look, do you have that much room on your ship?'

'Not yet.'

Gualtiero shook his head, 'But Capitan,' he said, 'it is impossible.'

'Leave it to me, your figure Gualtiero?'

'A six pointed compass,' his eyes gleamed, 'like yours.'

'And the time it will take to duplicate?'

'It's already made, I have two, I just need time to paint. Here, I'll show you.'

The pilot led him to the back of the workshop where pieces of this and that were littered around and he pulled off the covers of the replicate piece, without paint. It nearly took the captain's breath away. For all of the panelling on the entire machine Gualtiero had used a lustrous gold plate.

The pilot took the captain's lack of words the wrong way, 'I know I should not have used gold, it loses its finish, its heavy and so many things, but it was what I had at the time I made it, but like I said-'

'Don't paint it. It's perfect. I'll take it if you can duplicate this, for your payment.' The captain pulled out his six pointed compass; a glass encased contraption shaped like a ball, with one extra point upwards and one pointing down and two brass rings that moved inside, all in all like three separate worlds intertwined. Gualtiero sighed, 'Oh Capitan, no one could do it, where did you get it?'

'I'll tell you that too, when you duplicate it.'

'Oh, Capitan,' the pilot worried, 'what if I break it.'

'You give me your machine.'

'Ah, the choices we make, ah, ok, ok, I'll do it, I can do it, after all, I created the Aeroplane, right?'

'Aeroplane? Yes, Indeed.'

'Capitan, give me until tomorrow night.'

'Very well, where can I stay?'

'I'll bring it to you, don't trouble yourself.'

'I won't let that compass out of my sight.'

'You don't trust me Capitan?' said Gualtiero, clearly hurt.

'Ah Gualtiero, I trust no one. I don't know how you live in this place.'

The pilot nodded and grinned, 'You don't like it Capitan?'

'I feel it would lure me in, and then smother me.'

'My machines will one day take me away. Now, if I make your compass over again, then, ah, then I can go my own way.'

'You'll need maps Gualtiero.'

'I know, I know, I'm working on those. I have seen some in the Governor's house, perhaps I can make copies of those.'

'They are limited Gualtiero. You could come with me.'

The pilot twisted his lips and looked up from the work in his hands, 'You have space for two machines? Yes?'

'Possibly.'

'Ah, let me think, how to do this, how to do it.'

So while the pilot pondered and the captain and Santee watched and waited, as the night crept up and grew around them, back on the ship Carter and Needle and indeed the rest of the crew were quite concerned about their captain's disappearance. Lieutenant Carter continued to pace up and down the deck as the others sat by to wait.

'I shouldn't have let him go out alone, I should have gone with him – wherever he's gone.'

'He's the captain,' said Phillips, 'you couldn't very well stop him.'

'He could be my son! He's young enough.'

'Sure, but he's far too smart.'

'It's no time to jest Phillips, what if something's befallen him, what do we do if he just doesn't return?'

'Have you seen Morris?'

'No, well not since we arrived, have you?'

'Not I.'

'We should ask him how to go about, he's known the captain longer than us, if anyone will, he should know what to do.'

With that the order was given out, find the swamp monster as soon as they could. Failing that, they decided to ask around on shore in the morning, or even this evening if they could ask around quietly without rousing suspicion that the crew were without captain.

With weighted eyes Carter looked at the dawn, the heavy clouds and rainbows on the horizon. Would it be as bad when they left as when they came in? Or would they be able to get a clear run? And where was the captain, and Morris? They hadn't been seen yet.

Then, just as he turned back to face Diamantine two little webbed hands appeared over the side of the ship and Morris's head popped over the railing, holding in his teeth a wriggling fish.

'Morris!' Lieutenant Carter ran over, 'I'm so glad to see you, we've been looking all over.'

The look of surprise on the swamp monster's face had never been equalled by any of his race, for a man, a human, was happy to see him! This would be the first time in the history of their feuding.

'We've a problem, Morris,' Carter admitted, 'we were wondering if you might be able to help us.'

'What is it?'

'Well, we can't find the captain, he's been gone since yesterday morning.'

'So he has.'

'Aren't you worried?'

'When you've known the captain as long as I have,' Morris began to explain but the sound of his voice was drained away.

'Carter, Lieutenant, look,' shouted Needle from the masthead way up high, 'it's the captain, I'm sure it is, coming round the side of the island.'

'Where is that 'scope?' Carter looked to his man, who quickly pulled it from his own eyes giving it to him. 'It is Needle, it is. You were right Morris, no need to worry about him. What is it he's got? Can you make it out?' he handed Morris the telescope.

'No, it's all under covers, though there's another man with him.'

'Is there? So there is.'

'There are more boats coming too,' Needle yelled, 'from the shore Carter, Lieutenant, look!'

'So there are! There's Phillips, I'm sure, and the rest of the crew, and other boats yet with more men on them too.'

Morris just sighed, 'More men! I'm going below.'

The first boat that arrived carried the harbourmaster and his men with a list of everything that was coming. On the second many barrels were balanced up high and as soon as they pulled up the harbourmaster instructed them to be winched topside. The crew saw the barrels all labelled with their contents and marvelled how the captain had acquired all this. Then came a row boat, steadily then avast, carrying nothing less than a new mizzen mast. Which the men got to work with immediately, fitting it into place and strapping it tightly, with the men from the harbour they got it done far more quickly, but were still working at it when the captain returned.

Gualtiero sat in the boat and waited as the captain was winched aloft. He praised Carter for his good job in taking care of the ship and praised Phillips for doing as his instructions had ordered in getting all the men back on the ship as soon as he could, that very morning. Then the pilot clambered up and the captain introduced him saying, 'Gualtiero, my crew, my crew, Gualtiero. Make yourselves known. He'll be one of you for the time being.'

Then the captain left them to their introductions and limped down the ladder to the quarters of Banks and Jennings. Banks was about to make a clamorous protest, about not being able to make a shore visit, when the captain stopped him with just a word from his lips. 'Banks,' he said, so firm and so sure that it made the lieutenant stop suddenly and wonder if maybe he should listen to what this boy had to say.

'My apologies for this enforced detention, but I'm afraid you haven't won my trust yet. The moment you do, you'll know it. But now, as we are about to raise anchor, I need your advice on a particular problem. Come.'

So they followed him down the dark passage to the place where the rest of the crew slept, when they were sleeping, so they weren't there right then.

'I have acquired,' the captain began, 'two small machines, used for flying. Gualtiero calls them aeroplanes. The problem lieutenants, is where to store them and how to get them out, and first of course, get them in.'

'Flying Cap'n? How so?'

'With wings, Jennings, like a bird, but fixed, not moveable. There would need to be a way to get them out at speed, a door or a rather large window, or a ramp perhaps.'

'Could we cut away the rear wall Captain, under your cabin?' Banks suggested.

'My thoughts exactly,' said the captain, 'but what if we're at sea? With a heavy cargo, which we may be, the water would come in the hole and we'd sink.'

'Not up in your cabin.'

'No, that's correct. So what do you suggest?'

'Well, it would mean re-arranging things round a bit,' Banks said, getting excited, 'but it might work if you could live with it. If we put our cabins this way a bit, and if you, Captain, brought yours down here, then if these machines were stored at the front of the ship, they'd have enough room and enough speed perhaps, though I'm no engineer, so that when they reach the rear of the ship, we'd have made a ramp, up and out of where your cabin had been, and we'd have made an opening contraption so the floor and the wall falls away and there you have it – out flies your machine.'

'Cunning Banks, Jennings, what do you think?'

'How wide is this contraption Captain? I think it's rather narrow between the bunks here, how would it get past them, and then past our cabins, even if we cleared the other end?'

'I see what you mean,' the captain said, wondering how long it would take him to make them come up with the plan he already had in his head.

'What about some sort of system, to raise everything so that it lies flat against the walls of the ship, or flat on the floor,' said Jennings.

'Now you're getting somewhere. I don't really like the idea of moving down here, do you think I could get away with just moving my cabin forward a bit, or, of course we could just make it smaller.'

'Indeed sir, that might just work, we could make a ramp that when needed falls outward.'

'Yes, I can see it now. The machines at the prow, a pulley for the bunks, a ramp at the rear. That just leaves your cabins lieutenants. How will the machine get past them?'

'We could put our bunks in here with the men,' Jennings said before thinking.

'Excellent plan,' said the captain, turning his back on them, 'get your men and start building, I'll be rearranging my cabin.'

On deck he yelled, 'Needle, with me. Gualtiero! This way.'

The two followed him immediately. The captain hit Morris's box with his crutch as he entered his cabin and saw the bones of the fish. 'Get up Morris, there's someone I want you to meet.' Morris poked out his head. 'Gualtiero, my new pilot, Morris, the Avaeste's first mate.'

The pilot was stunned as the lid of the chest popped up and a large head appeared with large eyes and large tusks and the scales of the fish still lingering on the creases of his lip.

'Capitan, what is it?' Gualtiero floundered as Needle laughed, the pilot had obviously never before seen a creature like Morris.

'As I said, my first mate, Morris, of Swamp.'

'Don't worry, you're not the first to have a problem with me,' Morris sighed as he stepped out of his hiding place.

'It speaks!' gasped the pilot as Needle went into hysterics.

'He does indeed,' said the captain, 'as he has to being first in command, after me.'

Gualtiero got on his knees and held out his hand to this unknown creature.

'Gualtiero,' he said, 'from Diamantine, pleased to meet you Morris.'

The swamp monster thought, then took his hand, ok, so maybe this one wasn't so bad.

While they talked the captain pulled out charts and maps of every sort, then pulled Gualtiero away and sat him down hurriedly. 'Here,' he gave him a pen and paper, 'start making copies, as payment for your machine.'

'But I don't need payment Capitan, I coming with you, that is the bargain. I don't need these.'

'You will need them, you won't be able to stay I'm afraid, there are happenings on the shore, there's no time to explain, here,' he sat the compass on a stand on the table, 'make drawings of this, since you couldn't recreate it, maybe one day you'll be able.'

'I have already made a sketch of that Capitan. But, may I ask, what is that banging?'

'They are making room for the machines but just copy those maps, don't stop no matter what happens.'

'If you say so Capitan.' The pilot picked up the pen and began.

'Needle, help me with this furniture, Morris, get rid of the fish – nothing from the shore remember, without permission. Argh!' he yelled out.

'What is it captain?' Needle asked, at once by his side, steadying him before he fell.

'Nothing,'

'You're hurtin' cap'n, I can see it,' Needle worried, 'shall I get a lieutenant?'

'No, Needle there's no time for me, just go out and see how everything's going then come back and report to me. Here, pass me that seat.'

The captain sat down and closed his eyes as Needle ran out and watched as the last of the supplies were brought on board and taken below, before the crew from the harbour yelled a heave ho, and the harbourmaster yelled up, 'Tell your Captain, may his journey fare well!'

*

'What do you have against this mere child?' Governor De Silva asked the king after they had dined.

'That's just it De Silva, he's just a young boy. How can I believe he's the son of St Amalric?'

'Then why did you give the supplies to him?'

'The way he spoke to me, and the statement he made. I could not contradict it, and for a moment I really believed it. But when I woke up this morning, I found that I had changed my mind about him.'

'The Avaeste still lies in the bay, would you have me make an arrest?'

'No, not yet, find some certain charge you can make, then go and arrest him. If possible, make it something so big that you have to impound his ship. I do like it, imagine it finely arrayed, it's only a toy really, look at it, such a little thing, what is he doing sailing it across the wide Ether Marine? But, Sir Rubra, for publicly making a fool of me I will, to him, do the same.'

Yvette overheard this and crept away, mounting her gentle white mare, and galloping down to the harbour.

'Morris, tell Banks and Jennings I had meant to allow them some time ashore in the end, but things are beginning to work rather faster than I had anticipated. Give them my apologies, and tell them I will make up for it, and that my cabin is ready to start altering.'

'Aye Captain,' Morris said, and went.

Soon Ashton was watching as the carpentry crew came up, cutting the back wall of his cabin, and the floor, so that the whole rear section was soon on large hinges with pulleys and ropes so that in seconds it could be opened and shut. The rest of the work had been going well, some genius had figured out the bunk pulley in half a minute. The captain guessed right that it was Jennings that had made it, so two men or one strong man alone could pull on a rope then the whole row would fold up against the wall, leaving a long open passage for the machine to start off. That was another problem they had to think about, how does one fly out of a ship in an aeroplane with no wheels? Ashton thought, a solution would eventually come to him, but for now they would have to rely on the power of men pushing manually, waxing the boards, and perhaps tilting the ship slightly up to use gravity.

The ramp, and the hardest part of the whole construction was also nearing completion, they had used the walls of the lieutenants' cabin, to the curiosity of many and Banks' chagrin.

It was not long before they were able to lower the machines in down that very same access, by the captain's cabin and the lieutenants' ramp. First went in the gold one, the young captain's own, though none could see what it was for the covers bound with rope, and then came the pilot's, Gualtiero's, which he strode and fretted over as it came down, till the captain reminded him of the chart he should have been copying.

Everything was coming together so quickly, he checked on the crew, that they were all there, checked on the equipment, on Santee and Dew, then went to the upper deck and called together his men.

'You can all be proud,' he said, 'you have almost kept my requests and the laws of this land. I have only heard a few bad reports, far less than I expected. I hope you have enjoyed your stay,' a few cheered, one whispered, 'it was an eye-opener I'll say.'

'Especially you Phillips, did you enjoy your birthday?'

'Aye sir, except that I had to pour diamonds out of my pockets at the end of the day.'

The crew laughed again.

'If any of you have in your possession, something you know comes from this island, throw it overboard now, for I will not be lenient if I find it, and nor will they,' the captain nodded in the direction of the glittering bay.

The crew were still for a while, till Berens gave in and went to the rail, throwing back in one little diamond, watching its glimmering disappear as it sunk into the rippling ocean.

'Go on, the rest of you then, trust me, they'll know if we've anything on board when we go.'

Then just about the whole crew hung their heads low and emptied their pockets into the water below, tossing away handfuls of jewels, diamonds and gold.

'Thankyou,' the captain grinned, 'now, let's go.'

So the anchor was pulled up, the sails unfurled, the little ship now had some life in her and Dew the little goblin down in the engine room knew that this was time to start up again so he readied her engine.

The captain set a course then Morris took over, guiding the Avaeste still slowly over the glimmering water. Then Ashton went down again to see Gualtiero, 'Soon,' he said to him, 'it will be time for you to go.'

'I don't understand Capitan, can I not travel with you?'

'I wish it were so. Just finish the charts, I believe they will want to stop me from leaving, for the king did not really believe what I told him. And they will accuse you too I believe, if you come with me.'

'Accuse me of what?'

'You work for the king do you not?'

'Oh yes, of course, I would be leaving the island, if they have the mind to I could be charged with desertion. I see what you say.'

'Yes, I believe they will accuse me of aiding you too, all to stop me from going. There is something in the king's mind I cannot fathom, but my suspicion is it's no more than greed to have what is mine, and like a fly into this Heliamphora flew I.'

'Alright Capitan I will go as you say and save the trouble. These charts will be plenty enough for me to begin on my own way, but Capitan, I write so slow, I cannot finish them quick enough.'

'Then I'll get Santee to help you, don't worry, she won't harm you.'

'Capitan?'

'The draw, next to you,' he pointed out, which Gualtiero opened and a little head popped out.

'Ah!' the pilot exclaimed, surprised, 'a little lady fly!'

'I'm a sprite!' she defended, 'come on then, if he says so, we better finish it.'

'Very few have that map Gualtiero, so guard it.'

'Capitan, I will. And the compass sketches I took too.'

'Thankyou.'

'No, thank you, see, you see, I'm crazy of necessity too.'

'Aye, I do.'

Then there was a commotion outside, 'Let me see the captain, won't you!' demanded a young lady's voice.

'I shouldn't have let you on board!' said the deep bellow of one of the crew.

'What is this? Yvette!' the captain was amazed, 'why are you here? We're underway.'

'I had to tell you, the King is plotting a scheme against you, my father's involved.'

'I know.'

'But how?'

'Well, I thought as much, don't worry, I've planned in advance. But now there's you too, and what to do about that. Thankyou for coming to warm me in any case.'

'Captain, there are ships coming from the harbour,' yelled the lookout.

'Oh no,' Yvette worried, 'it will be them, Capitan, what will I do? I can't go back now! They'll know!'

'Trust me, if they are as clever as I think they are, they already do.

Come, you'll have to go with Gualtiero.'

'That man! What? He's here? He's crazy!'

'Hola,' said the pilot as they entered the room, 'the Governor's daughter, I presume?' He bowed over her hand and kissed it like a real gentleman.

'Oh boy,' thought Yvette, no, no, that wasn't a flutter in her heart was it? She liked the Capitan, no, she liked Armand, could it be she really liked this pilot, engineer, all along?

'Gualtiero, it's time. Quick, ready your machine. Take these sketches with you, I'm sorry I had to do this but you now have the means to get off Diamantine and go to a place of your choosing where, maybe, things will be better for you.'

'But here, this Aeloran?' he pointed to a place on the map, 'this is your home Capitan?'

'Yes.'

'Then maybe, I will see you there one day, my friend.'

'May it be,' they shook hands.

The Avaeste began speeding up, the wind catching in the sails and the engine starting to pump. The ships from the fleet of Diamantine were close and the governor was shouting for the captain to stop.

'You have broken the rules,' he shouted, 'turn back or we have no choice but to fire upon you.'

The captain was soon on deck to answer, 'What charges Governor? First tell me that.'

'You have taken something from our island, you must give it back.'

The captain laughed and turned to his crew, 'What did I tell you, they'd know.'

'But we put it all back captain, there's nothing we've kept!'

'No, I know, but I have.'

They all gasped, some were amazed, if the captain could keep jewels for himself, why couldn't they? He saw their faces and knew what they thought, so he said to them, 'It's not what you think,' then he yelled back to the governor, 'Governor, what is it?'

'My daughter, Capitan, the pilot Gualtiero, and his machine.'

'You are right, they are here, but by their own choice Governor.'

'No, she is my daughter, and he serves the king!'

'Give me one moment, I will talk to them,' so though the governor danced as his cheeks grew red, he could do nothing but wait for the outcome of the meeting between the pilot and captain.

The captain scanned the horizon before going below, if his eyes were right there wasn't far to go, if he timed it right maybe he could make it without too much trouble.

Gualtiero and Yvette had heard all that was said; now he really understood what the captain had known, why he had to leave now, why he had to go. If Gualtiero went now, out in his machine, he couldn't be charged for going against the king and neither would there be time for them to accuse the captain with some other crime before he flew out into the more equal ground of the open sky. 'I'm sorry I can't come with you Capitan,'

'So am I. Gualtiero, Yvette, thankyou, and goodbye.'

'Goodbye.'

The pilot started the engine and soon the plane crept along the passage just made for it. So immediately as the captain reached the top step the machine flew out the back of the ship, carrying in it Gualtiero and Yvette.

'There, Governor, I have had a word, now they are returned.' Then he made a motion with his hand and Lieutenant Carter let out his command, his men quickly let out more metres of sail and the little Avaeste left the water below. The wind caught up the words from the governor's throat as he waved his arms wildly and jumped up and down, and as a few cannon pops fired all around the captain just smiled as he looked down. Maybe the ships of Diamantine could fly in the sky like the Avaeste, but they were so large and bulky and the governor yelled, 'I blew it,' there was no way they could catch her now, he knew.

'Just the storm to get through now, then I can rest,' said the captain to Morris.

'I'm surprised you didn't think of that and do something about it,' said the first mate.

'I told you, you overestimate me.'

'Aye, you did say that.'

'That's why I have you. What did you come up with?'

'On the Admiral's ship, I found this,' Morris said, producing a curious implement.

'What is it?' Ashton looked at the fine metal wire cased inside a little glass cylinder.

'I don't know, something to do with the weather I think.'

'Wow,' the captain amazed as he studied it and watched as it moved as he turned and it shook or hovered or even at times changed colour. 'That way,' pointed the captain, 'I think that's where we'll fare best.'

He'd read the tool right, the crew held fast and prepared for the worst but all that met them was a light shower and rainbows arcing the ship right over. The crew all stared with their mouths wide open, touching the wispy cloud as it went right by them, and laughing at Tom as he danced in the rainbow's shining.

Gualtiero and Yvette flew to his workshop, she gave him a kiss then ran off, back to her father's house.

Ok, Yvette thought, she was so foolish now, flying with that crazy man across the ocean.

And Gualtiero, he gathered a few things together, and as he packed, wondered how he of all men could be so lucky, to have the plans for a compass that would take you into dream lands, to have maps of these, and now, even a kiss from the girl of his dreams. 'Ah! Mama, if only you could see me. Oh, but maybe that would not be good, I haven't shaved for a while, and I know you'd say I should, and I will I promise.' Then he left before the ships had returned.

'Now then Santee, I don't think I even need you to put me to sleep,' the captain fell back on his couch and he dreamed of nothing much at all, which was just what he needed after such a long trial. Carter came in, and seeing the captain there once again felt like a father and pulled a blanket up over him, tucking him in.

Chapter 5:
LIEUTENANT BANKS' TREACHEROUS SCHEME

'So has he told you where we're going then Carter?' Banks asked, 'you seem to be becoming his favourite pretty fast.'

'I just did what he asked and what I thought right.'

'So he didn't tell you anything about where we're going?'

'No, he has told me nothing.'

'All those diamonds,' Banks moaned, 'so many diamonds, why couldn't we take any home?'

'And you didn't even go to shore, it was like a dream,' Phillips put in.

'Who said I didn't go? Jennings?'

'Well, no. You was under the Cap'n's orders Banks, to stay on the ship.'

'What Captain? He's no more than a kid. Look, he brought something off the island himself, didn't he?' said Banks, motioning to the covers over the machine.

'Yeah, along with supplies with a grant from the king, he wasn't stealing diamonds or pearls or anything like.'

'I suppose you're right. You're not telling me you didn't keep anything?'

'How do you mean?' asked Jennings.

'To take home, just a souvenir of course.'

'Banks you didn't?'

'Just a few little gems, it's nothing really, nothing they'll miss.'

The others, even Jennings, just shook their heads.

The captain woke again that evening as the surgeons apprentice checked on his leg, he shook his kind head and said scoldingly, 'I told you, you should stay off of it, didn't I, isn't that what I said?'

'Aye sir, it is,' the boy said.

'Will you keep it up for me Captain, please do as I say, else there's no saying how bad it might get.'

'I'll do my best,' he smiled, and the surgeon was satisfied that indeed, he would try, and then left him to carry out the rest of his duty.

'Morris, would you pass me that book.'

'Which Captain? The red leather?'

'No, next to it, the green.'

Morris jumped onto his box then leapt up to the higher shelves, holding the shelf above with one hand, the shelf below with his feet, he took the heavy volume out with his free hand then jumped down to the ground.

'Here you are Captain,' Morris handed it to him.

'Thankyou.'

'Anything else I can do while I'm here?'

'No, thankyou Morris, the morning is your own, do with it what you will.'

'Just say my name if there's anything you need,' Morris reminded him.

Santee was outside watching the men in the sun, Dew was humming as the engine drummed. Morris didn't want to leave his captain alone, there was something he couldn't put his finger on, something that worried him like he'd seen before, when they had found the town of Althorn and the captain had contrived to get all these men on board. Was the seed of some sudden move again growing in the boy's mind? He'd become silent and contemplative again, what would it be this time?

'Is something the matter Morris?' the boy captain looked up from the text.

'No, nothing Captain, I'll go see how the men are doing.'

The captain nodded, then turned back to the book he'd sat on his chest.

If Morris had been able to read the book he'd pulled down he would have seen it was titled *Encyclopaedeae de Floradae cum Medicus in Orbis Terra Antiquituus*. And if he had been able to read that language he would have known that the captain was looking intently at a well worn page in the Encyclopaedia of Medicinal Plants of the Old World.

Despite tedious hours beyond boredom in the days of his language schooling the captain was grateful now that he had had that learning. For it served him well now as he reread the passage, about this plant titled *Carex Argentius*, or rather, the Silvertip Sedge.

There were no pictures, not even one little sketch, but only a description that was hazy at best. Telling of a plant that grew in a far distant place that could cure any illness, disease, and even, some say, pull a dying man out of the clutches of death. It sounded farfetched, but with no other hope the captain made up his mind to seek it with all his might, then he could never say that he had sat by while his father had given in to this disease and then died. No he couldn't sit by, no, he would find it at any price and take back to his father this prize.

He only had a few clues, not much to go on, but he had to find it, of that he was certain. It had taken him months even to locate this book, sitting in the great library, on Mirathan alone, on a shelf right down the back where no one ever cared to look. It had been covered in a thick gathering of dust and fine grime, and as he pulled it out a spider had run out from the arc of its spine. All around the edges the pages had dimmed with age and faded but the writing inside must have been very rarely read, for barely a page was torn, and barely a page was tattered, and after many more days the captain had come across this one page, the one that had mattered.

One day and two, three days and four, five days, now six, now even more and the captain still studied the maps and the charts and read and reread the encyclopaedia of plants. Carex Argentius is a plant found in the island group of Sho'Orakai. Where exactly it was once you got there this book didn't say. It frustrated the captain that so many things stood in his way; he'd have to find these islands first, find out just where this plant grew, find it, identify it, and somehow take it alive all the way back to his father. It was so far, and it would be hard, that he knew.

There were other things too that stood in his way; the tides of the air, the seasonal change, the nights the moon was hidden, the intemperate days. And how his crew would go on from now until then, would they pull through to advantage, would he be proud of them in the end?

And then of course, he'd have to return them, he'd have to navigate all the way back to Althorn when he'd rather just make his way straight home, but that was alright, they'd been good to him and after all, he had practically stolen them, it was only right that he return them in better condition than when he found them. That was the other thing, how would he reward them? Could he reward them from his father's treasury? Probably. But he set his proud mouth against that notion. He would find a way through his own cunning, he'd managed before, he'd manage once more.

The cheeky little sprite sat out in the sun, her eyes bright and sparkling, her head in her hand as she looked down at the men walking about on the deck, particularly the one that was at this time in command. Not Captain Ashton, no he was still inside, and not Morris, he wasn't a man and besides he was nowhere in sight, no, she was looking at Carter, Lieutenant that is, with his shiny gold buttons, tassels, and his grinning wide smile.

Santee sighed, then she let herself fall all the way from the sail where she sat to the floor, a flutter, a barely visible glittering puff that then disappeared as she darted into more shadowy stuff and went back inside, and landed on Ashton's desk with a miserable huff.

She lay back on the map that was spread over the table, her little wings touching on several countries, and she folded her arms behind her head and dreamt that she was somewhere in one of them, before turning over onto her stomach and taking a closer look at this map and the captain's markings.

'Where are we going?' she asked, screwing her lips in a strange twist as she waited for the captain to reply.

'You've never asked that before,' he said, evading the answer rather as she had expected.

'I've never wanted to know.'

'What's changed?'

'Now I do,' she answered vaguely, looking down at her toes.

'I see.'

'So...?'

'Something is on your mind my sprite, you know I'll get to the bottom of it,' the captain grinned, then changed the subject. 'You know, I think it would be good for me to get the men to make a place for me so I can lie outside for a bit, doesn't do me any good sitting in here all this time like this. Morris,' he called.

'Ha!' Santee huffed, feeling brushed aside by this boy captain, 'No, listen, you introduced Gualtiero to me, you, you made Morris known to me, you,'

'Santee,' Ashton tried to calm her as her anxiety and ire increased.

'I let you see me, don't you think boy, do you think that I could, just, maybe, maybe let-'

'Santee,' the captain stopped her softly as Morris came in.

'Aye Captain, what is it?'

'Morris, would you be good enough to send Lieutenant Carter in.'

'Right away Captain.'

'Thankyou.'

Santee sat where she was in the middle of the map of The Greater Principality of Sho'Oraki and Loi'Arinn. Her lips fell open wide and her eyes stared at the captain she called boy.

'Boy, what are you doing?'

'You want to talk to him, don't you? You've been longing to since the day you saw him.'

'I do but-'

'Now you're not so sure? And I thought you were a courageous sprite.'

'I am, but-'

'But what?'

'He's a man! A man with two little boys and one little girl who all live with their grandmother and papa. I don't like-him, like-him, I just think he's nice,' she whispered, 'if he was just boy it might be alright, but sprites don't talk to men.'

'But you are not any ordinary sprite Santee,'

'No, indeed, you're right.'

There were two taps on the door and Lieutenant Carter's shoulders appeared before the rest of him entered and strolled over to where the captain had been reading, with his head propped up on pillows and his broken leg raised on cushions.

'How are you holding up Cap'n? I asked the saw-bones how you fared, he said it was still mighty bad, he did. Boy, you got spirit Cap'n I got to hand it to you, and you rushing around on Diamantine like you did, you know you could have just told me what to do.'

'Thankyou Lieutenant, I know,' Ashton said, 'but tell me how goes the crew?'

'Well Cap'n, in high spirits they are, what with the weather so fine and the stories still fresh from Diamantine Isle.'

'That's good to hear.' Then there was silence. The captain looked past Carter's large frame to the little thing shivering on the desk, shaking her head fiercely at him; now it came to the point Santee did not want to do it, she did not want to be introduced to this giant here. She shot up at once into the lantern hanging on the hook right above and curled up tight next to the candle inside.

'Was there anything else Cap'n?' Carter enquired, wondering what to do with so much silence.

'Actually, yes,' Captain Ashton admitted, as Carter noticed he did look quite pale, 'I'd be very grateful if you could somehow conjure me a way out of here,' the boy smiled, but seemed rather shaky, 'to somewhere out on the deck.'

'Consider it done,' Carter gave a little nod then went out at once to make a place for the captain to lie.

Santee lifted her little head and peeped over the edge of the golden-glassed lantern. 'I'm sorry,' she whimpered, 'I just couldn't.'

'When you're ready Santee, it's alright.'

'But I shouldn't have been angry with you, I had no reason. It was silly, I'm sorry.'

'So when you're ready you'll tell me, won't you Santee?'

She ummd and arrd, 'Maybe I shouldn't, after all boy, what good could come of it?'

'Do you want me to search him for you a bit?'

'Would you?' she looked hopeful.

'Why not?'

Santee let out a joyful sigh and then tumbled down to the captain's side, dropping a light kiss to his fevered cheek then went whizzing away to make mischief outside.

'Oh, by the way Santee,' the captain said as she went, 'we're going to the Isle of Meridian.'

She didn't notice the droplets of sweat on his cheek, his cold, clammy hands, his pulse which was weak, or the fever which had begun to rage in his bones from a throbbing in his skull to the grating of his toes. 'Sunshine and fresh air, that's all I need,' the captain thought to himself hopefully.

Lieutenant Carter and crewman Berens came and together they took the captain gently outside where Carter had had a light construction made, a couple of barrels a few timber planks and there, mid-ship, was the bench placed in the shade. They put Ashton down with the gentlest of hands, Needle came running with pillows behind them, shoving them in roughly where he thought they'd be wanted.

'Thankyou all,' the captain said, 'but really was the surgeon so insistent that you wouldn't let me walk here on my own feet with the crutches?'

'Indeed Cap'n, insistent he was.'

'Well so be it, you may go, do what you were before I interrupted you.'

'Aye Cap'n.'

'Oh Carter, one thing,' the captain said as he eased himself back to the pillow and tried to move his pained leg to a comfortable position, 'when you were young did you, well, did you imagine?'

'Are you alright sir?'

'Aye, just answer the question.'

'Of course I imagined sir, everyone imagines things, be it good or bad sir is another question.'

'What did you imagine?'

'I imagined what life would be like if we'd more dough Cap'n, wondered what it'd be like if I'd got a proper schooling, if my folks didn't fight, and such like.'

'What about, I don't know, like what you're doing now?'

'Lieutenant on a flying ship in a sky I'd never known, my word no.'

'Oh.'

'Although,' Carter laughed, 'I did once wish I had a pet dragon so we could go and together leave Althorn. I imagined we'd fly over the fields and find a quiet place beyond the grim town. Where we could eat wild berries and play fight without no one telling us to put the sticks down.'

'There see, you did dream,' the boy smiled.

'Why Captain?'

'Oh nothing, nothing really,' he said so softly. His eyes were closed and then his head tilted to one side, like one asleep might lie.

'Are you sure you're alright? Cap'n?' Carter touched his arm, 'Captain?'

Carter lifted a hand to the boy's face, 'Why he's burning up! Morris! Needle – fetch the surgeon's apprentice. Captain?'

The crewmen were gathering round, their worried faces looking wonderingly down at this captain boy with his splinted leg, lying unconscious, in a daze in front of them.

Banks made his way to the front of the crowd and issued a thought to everyone out loud. 'We'll, the kid is out of action it seems, where is that imp that guards his hide, where is he now that it seems the captain might die? We've got to have a man in charge, a man that can lead and take command and take this cursed vessel back to our land, back to our Althorn where our families are, I suggest a vote, a vote I tell you, between us lieutenants the crew has to choose.'

'Now wait on, wait on, you usurper,' Carter vied, 'he's just got a fever, other than that he's young and he's strong and he'll make it too, so step back and let the surgeon get through!'

'Aye, and in the meantime? Till he's fit enough again to take charge, till then, what'll we do?'

'Morris is here now, he's first mate, he's in charge till the captain's through.'

'What's going on?' Morris enquired.

'The lieutenant here thought he'd make a line for up higher.'

'I see.'

'Well someone has to be in charge,' Banks defended, 'I mean, does anyone even know where we're headed?'

Suddenly it struck them, just what Banks had considered, the captain had given none the direction they were going, no word, no name, no navigational instruction, they were just one little ship, one helpless crew of men in an empty sky where none could fathom exactly where they were in any direction.

'Captain,' Morris tried to wake him as Lieutenant Carter had tried, he tapped his cheek, shook his arm but nothing he did made the captain so much as lift the lid of one eye.

'Leave him be,' the surgeon said, 'the lad needs rest, and lots of it, you lot get yourselves gone, would you go and fetch me some blankets now Tom. Berens, the galley, fetch a warm brick, we'll chase this infection out of him yet.'

Morris saw his friend and captain was in good hands so he left them and made his way behind the stairs, into the little cabin at the back, where the captain had made his quarters and Santee now sat, waiting for Morris to come in and explain to her what had just happened.

'But it happened so quick!' Santee said, bewildered, 'I was talking to him just now, he seemed a little pale, nothing really the matter, nothing I could tell.'

'The surgeon's apprentice seems to know what to do, right now Santee, we're in much bigger trouble; no-one knows where we're going, if we don't do something we'll have a rebellious crew.'

Morris bent his head to the maps on the desk, the drawings of man never had made much sense to his race, much less now as he stressed and wondered just what all these lines meant. He'd have to ask for help from the men, something that would take all his courage and shatter his self esteem, unless, 'You can't read, can you Santee?'

'Me?' she laughed dismally, 'No, sorry, but I can tell you he adds a red dot to that line each time he checks it.'

Morris took a deep breath then went back out, 'Carter and Phillips,' he was about to shout when they turned up just then, followed by none other than Lieutenants Banks and Jennings.

'We need to have a meeting,' Phillips began, 'the crew are quite worried what with the captain down and this being a strange place with no sight of land.'

'Come in gentlemen, I was just on my way to find you, you might make some sense of his maps and his scribbles.'

So the four lieutenants the captain had picked all those days ago were ushered in to the little cabin where they all stood around the captain's desk, littered with writing equipment, measurement apparatus, books open and books closed strewn all over his precious maps.

As much as they tried they could not understand the little things the boy had written but Phillips was certain he had the gist of the map, the one with the islands dotted across it.

'But what help is that?' Jennings said, 'if we don't know the way that was planned, even if these islands were all like Diamantine I'm not so sure I'd like to stop at them. The authorities did not seem so happy that we were there in the end, who knows what kind of places these are. This place for example,' Jennings put his finger on an island on the map, one he thought, if they were where Phillips had figured, would be one of the closest places to where they were sailing. 'The Atoll of Arinn, how do we know if the locals are friendly, how do we now if it's a safe passage in?'

'Should we just stop the ship and wait for the captain?' Carter asked Morris, who just shook his large, swamp coloured head. 'No, we must keep moving, till we find an ocean at least.' Morris said.

'Then what? Hey? Then what?' Banks demanded, 'some first mate you are, you Marsh Walump, your captain doesn't even trust you with a simple thing like where we're going, look at you, you pathetic little-'

'He put me in charge over the ship,' Morris countered quietly, looking angrily up at his foe 'or do I have to remind you?' his little claws cracked as he made fists with his fingers, only waiting for Banks to give him a reason.

Carter quickly stepped in, 'Hey, can we calm down, none of this will do any good, Banks is just worried like the rest of us Morris, he just has a different way of showing it.'

Santee watched them from up in the lantern, those silly men didn't know what they were doing. But, Banks had found a book which detailed some countries and right now he was reading through it while the others tried to determine more definitely where they were now. A devious smile alit on his lips and a greedy gleam awoke in his eyes, he shut the book silently then went back to the map, he would get what he wanted and that was that.

'An idea gentlemen, has crossed my mind, I suggest we make our way to this Atoll of Arinn. It is the closest, is it, is it not, from all we can discover, and after all, we need not go ashore if it doesn't seem safe. There we can wait for the captain to recover.'

Then Santee remembered what the captain had said, he had told her they were going to the Isle of Meridian, not to this Atoll of

Arinn. So behind their backs she cautiously floated down, and in Morris's large ear, amongst the wax and the hair, she found out a temporary chair. 'Morris,' she whispered, 'the captain said we were going to the Isle of Meridian,'

Morris looked up, 'Lieutenants, the captain did mention one thing, the Isle of Meridian, can you point it out to me.'

They perused the map for many a minute, from one corner to the other, but they couldn't find it.

'Sorry Morris, it's just not there.'

'Oh, is there nothing similar, or nearly the same?'

'Nothing my friend, I'm afraid,' Phillips answered.

'I suppose,' Morris studied Banks for a moment, then gave in, 'we best make for the Atoll of Arinn.'

'Wait!' Carter said as Banks moved his hand from the place where it lay, when the others had turned away, 'I'm not good with letters, but I have been learning, to me that looks like something that might read Meridian.' He read, 'Mm-eh-ar-ay-de-ay-an, Me-rid-ee-an, Meridian!'

'Why yes,' said Phillips and Jennings, 'That's it! It's here. Not too much further than the Atoll in any case.'

Now Carter was a good and simple man and he did not think that maybe it had been Banks' plan, since he'd read what he'd read, to thwart them from finding that island. So now Banks fumed internally that this simpleton Carter had not been such a fool. So he'd go along with it for the time being and while they made their plans he would do his own scheming, somehow he would get to the Atoll of Arinn, according to the book, it was just the place for a man such as him.

'Look at that, so it is,' he said, 'well spotted Carter, just think, we all missed it.'

Morris's shrewd mind put Banks in his place but what was the point of making a fuss? The swamp monster thought, right now it wouldn't do any good for any of them.

'Alright,' he said, 'let's get going, we'll make our way to the Isle of Meridian.'

The captain shivered in his sleep. The sun was beating down upon the sparkling deck of the little Avaeste. Her timbers and her cordage were humming under the skilled hands of the crew and the beauty of this glorious day. It was many days now after the captain had taken so violently ill. Many days, with no sight of land still. In and out of wakefulness he came, but never long enough nor alert enough for any to make him understand that they'd like his attention, to ask him if they were right in making their way to the isle of Meridian and if they were right in what they had been assuming was their point on the map and their direction upon it.

The night came and went, and as it did, Banks made a few minor adjustments to the course, surreptitiously so that nobody noticed.

With the dawn an island appeared on the horizon, then another and another, a tiny cluster of them. The nearer they flew the more they could see, of the islands, the reef and the surrounding sea. The sea was blue as blue and the islands green as green, bordered by the whitest sand in between. As they got even closer they could see many a ship resting by the shore or out in the ocean. Great ships, big galleons, sloops and corsairs, schooners, square-riggers and cutters all there, right down to the jolly-boats and yawls making their way from the great ships to the shore.

The crew on the Avaeste shook inwardly, who knows what kind of place this was, what people they would meet.

'Excited lads?' Banks rubbed his hands, if no one else was, he was indeed.

The ship sank safely down to the sea, just as the captain had showed them all those days ago on the isle of Diamantine. Below them, in the water so clear, were creatures like they had never seen.

The crew hung over the rails to peer down, fishes of every colour they could imagine, corals and swaying seaweeds, starfish, eels and sharks all together below them.

But Tom Needle had out the captain's telescope and was eyeing the shore and gave Morris a poke. 'Hey,' he said worried, 'look at that there crew, I don't like the look of them much, do you?'

Morris took the glass and surveyed the scene, 'Aye Needle, I see what you mean.'

The crew Needle had spotted on the biggest of ships was a rough looking bunch with a leader quite gruff, they could hear his voice now carried over the sea, they wouldn't want a run in with those men, and that was a certainty.

Jennings gathered the other lieutenants, 'Friends,' he said, 'I'm not liking the look of this, but I have an idea.'

'What do you suggest?' Phillips said.

'Well, there's no ship in the bay flying a flag, so let's not have one raised.'

'I agree,' Banks said.

'And I suggest we stay in our old gear, no new coats at this port,' Jennings mentioned the neat uniforms they might have worn, 'by the look of that lot it would be best if we not draw attention. After all the rank of lieutenant might imply that we're attached to some kind of military regiment, and I don't know about you but I don't think it I good idea to send out that message.'

'I see your point. Let's pass that on to the men, and let's keep the kid inside, and the monster out of sight, if anyone wants the captain I say let's give Phillips a try.'

'Alright.'

'Carter – it's best for all of us.'

'I know, it's just, something doesn't feel right,' Carter said, then shook his head, 'well, never mind.'

So they sailed into this unknown harbour, a lost and nameless crew, in a little ship that had travelled so far from where it had begun, so far that none really knew.

The boy captain opened his eyes as they came to a halt, he smelt the salt air, the fresh sunshine and he became a little revived. He lifted his weak arm quite slowly but managed to find the window and unlock its frame and push it out so he could get more of the freshness and more if the view, just for a moment, then he lay back down, he was so weak he had to.

'I am so tired,' he whispered, he touched his throat, 'so dry,' he held his head as the throbbing came again, 'ow, my head, my eyes.'

He closed his eyes. He could hear the activities of a busy port, hear the plank go down on the pier, hear his men coming and going, their excited chatter, the cheers. He heard someone call for the captain, something in his dulled mind told him to get ready to receive a visitor but his body slept on in a daze, and besides which, nobody came.

Carter waited anxiously on board while some of the crew went out, and then that man had come from the town and demanded the captain, demanded to see him, not later, but now.

Phillips had fronted with his giant sized frame, which overshadowed this man like a cloud full of rain, and Phillips asked what he could do for him and the man said he just wanted to know how long they'd be staying and that it was a silver coin for every day they remained at this pier, owned by him, as they could see here.

Phillips gave him the day's fee from his own pocket, it was the least he could do for the captain, he thought.

When some of the crew returned from the shore they were grinning and laughing at the good time they'd been having, they saluted Carter as they went by, but then one said, 'Oh, by the by, this isn't the Meridian Isle.'

'What? Then what is it? Where are we?'

'I don't know Carter, something about a coral atoll, Atoll, something.'

'Arinn?'

'Aye sir, that's him,' he laughed and went off with his friends to sleep the rest of the day away till they could go and begin again.

Carter went straight to check on the boy, opened the door and quietly looked in. To all appearances he was still sleeping, but at least it was easy, not like all those other days when his body had been fighting, fighting so hard against the fever inside him. But it was over now, Carter reassured himself, at least that was something, soon the boy would be back to his usual self again.

Carter decided to check out this place for himself. Phillips and Banks had already gone, but there was still Jennings to look after the crew and the Avaeste. But first he found Morris sulking in the galley, and let him know of his plans and that he'd checked in on the captain and he seemed to be mending. The swamp monster was thankful for Carter's news but just remained staring blankly down at his stew. Everyone had betrayed him, the captain too. Morris had discovered the engine room, and the white eyed goblin the captain called Dew, who when he had seen Morris promptly shut the door and locked it. Not to speak of the men who didn't care a gram for his thoughts or his plans. He was just a marsh walump like they all said, a poor monster with no prospects far from his swamp. Morris sipped his stew and wondered, just how was he going to get rid of that goblin?

On the shore Carter found that it was a spicy melting pot for everything, this town. Every building was different, every man had his own style, there was no prevailing fashion, and it seemed, no order either. There were goats and pigs at the harbour, penned in only by barking hounds with their herders yelling out sale prices to all around. Women walked by him with trays or baskets on their heads, selling fish or spices or a flat variety of bread. Carter bought one of these loaves, it was warm and delicious, tasting of a buttery oil and a hint of, what was it, sesame and olive?

Crates were coming in and crates where going out, there was no doubt about it, it was a very busy port. Barrels were stacked up at several docks, ships came and went even as he watched. Some men watched, some worked, some commanded. Many lazed, many drank, many went this way and the other.

Nearly every man had a sword at his side, a ready smile but a searching eye. Many had pistols tucked in their belts, even the kids he saw ran around with wooden ones in their hands. Needless to say Carter was becoming a little overwhelmed, but he kept on, telling himself he was a brave man. Yes he'd been to places like this in his travels, back in the world he had known, but he never liked it when he'd been crewman on a ship that had to go those ways, and if they had to leave this place in a hurry where would they go? He did not know this world at all.

Then there was a crack of gunfire somewhere ahead, a shout, and hollow laughter, a cloud of dust as a man was kicked to the ground as he ran. Was that Banks? Carter started to run in that direction, up the hill past the inns and ale houses. He pushed his way through the gathering crowd, in a heap on the rocks and the dirt sat Banks, formerly Lieutenant, grovelling for mercy, his neck being at the point of a sword, or rather, a scimitar, that is, a sword with a curve.

The man in whose hand the scimitar was held tight, was tall and lanky with a tattered tricorn for a hat, sitting over a tight bandana. His jacket, like his hat, was tattered and patched and his beard and moustache was crafted just in a way that made Carter think at once that this man must be a bandit, a brigand, a wanted man, in other words what Carter thought was that this man must be a pirate.

But he spoke, that man, 'Gentlemen,' he says, 'I think we have here a thief in our midst.'

Laughter ensued for many a minute, they were all of them thieves here and they knew it. Carter breathed in and stepped forward, he didn't like Banks over much, but after all they were compatriots.

'What has he done?' Carter asked of the man who held Banks in his power.

'What has he done?' that man laughed again, 'What has he done? And who might you be to be asking?'

Carter thought about his answer, 'We are both crew on the Avaeste.'

'Ah, so you know him?'

'A little.'

'Oh, conspirators?'

'Not at all. May I ask sir, who you are?'

Again the crowd exploded into uproarious laughter, 'Who am I?' the man smiled, 'why Dugan enlighten him.'

'My man,' an old, nearly toothless companion sniggered as he leaned upon Carter's shoulder and patted, 'my man, he's the Guv'na.'

Carter swallowed but the lump remained; this was going to be worse than Diamantine.

'Your friend here just tried to get away with a treasure of great renown.'

'Banks? Is it true?' Bank's head just hung down. 'What was it?' Carter asked these men, 'Gold? Silver?'

'A jewel, worn by the lady who looks out over the atoll,' the governor told him, 'Lady Arinn.'

'A woman!' Carter exclaimed looking shamefully at Banks.

'A statue,' the governor explained, 'it was a beautiful red diamond, as big as well -' he lifted Banks' head and forced open his lips, poking his fingers around in the lieutenants teeth, 'this.' With that he produced a sizeable gem, about the same circumference as the yolk of an egg.

'What have you done!' Carter said through his teeth, 'and what will I say to the captain? How will I explain,' then to the strange governor, 'Sir, you have your diamond, I'll take this man back to the ship, you can be assured the captain will deal with him as is fit.'

'No need for that,' the governor said grinning, 'I've a notion what to do with him, and you too.'

'What's that?'

'Bring them lads, here's some fun to be had.'

The governor bandit put his scimitar away and his men grabbed Banks and Carter, tying them up by their wrists then dragging them along behind as the governor marched back up the hill, lighting his pipe from a baker-woman's fire.

Carter and Banks sat in a cold and damp cave overnight, other prisoners were there, and with the rocks and the bars Carter could find no way to escape.

'What have you done Banks,' he repeated, 'you knew about this somehow didn't you? You misguided us so we'd come here for this, but how did you know of it?'

'A book of the kid's.'

'Now look at us.'

'I'm sorry Carter, really I am, I'd no idea it'd turn out like this.'

'You should have thought of that! Your actions jeopardise us all don't you see, and you all think I'm the fool!' Carter put his head in his hands, 'What are we going to do? What if hanging is a punishment for crimes like this Banks, did you think about that? I saw a scaffold down in the square, I'm sure it's not there just for show.'

'Stop it Carter, I said I'm sorry, what more can I do?'

A faint light could be seen on the moist stones as the morning sun warmed as it rose. Through the bars looking out over the sea Banks saw another ship coming in. It was built on a scale that dwarfed all the rest, her crew must number at least five times that of the Avaeste, her masts were taller than any he'd ever seen, her sails immense, and even the figurehead at her prow was the size of a small ship in itself. Banks didn't like the look of it, but he didn't tell Carter, who hadn't seen it yet; it was more bad news and he wasn't sure if Carter was up to it.

A few hours more and a familiar laugh met their ears, not the

governor but one of his comrades. 'Sleep well boys?' he sniggered as
the jailor pulled them out with the rest of the crowd and began to
lead them, all roped together, down the gravelly slope to the town.

A crowd was growing by the minute in the square, many of the
crew from the Avaeste were there, along with the crew from several
other ships, and many of the townsfolk on top of that. There were
prisoners being brought down from the jail on the rocky mountain,
and the hum going round was that they were in for some fun.

'Oy! Let us through,' a gruff voice yelled above the hum. It came
from the mouth of an aide to an aging captain. He too had the
bearing of a pirate of long years, he must have been known here for
they pulled a barrel up for him and promptly he sat, with probably
the best view of the scaffold in town. Several other men and women
with prominent bearings made their way to the front of the group
and found for themselves a good outlook. One man was even
brought on a jhampan chair, a seat on poles which was carried on the
shoulders of two dwarves with rings jingling in their beards, and
through the middle of their noses.

Then the prisoners came, Carter's head was hung low with shame,
Banks was looking around for any chance of escape.

They were marched up onto the scaffold's planks, the whole row
of prisoners stood before the crowd. 'You're lucky really my friends,'
the governor came up and said quietly between Carter and Banks,
'this only happens once a six month see, and you've only had to wait
a day, whereas those fellows,' he motioned to some other captives,
'they've been dreading this day for half a year, see last time they just
missed.'

Then he turned and faced the large crowd, spreading his arms out
to quieten them down. Now Carter looked around, he could see
there were many more prisoners than he thought there had been, and
down in the crowd when he looked that way he saw his friends, the
crew of the Avaeste, among them were Phillips and Berens, men
who were almost family really, when it came to it, now, so near the
end, oh! how his heart pounded!

Chapter 6

HOW OUR CAPTAIN INTERVENES

'Friends,' said the governor, 'the day for which you've all been waiting so patiently for, thieves and murderers the lot of them, so I'll not keep you more, the bidding's all yours.'

'Bidding?' the word hit Carter's mind and he and Banks looked to each other, confusion in their eyes, 'bidding?' Carter stopped the governor as he intended to pass, 'you mean we're not being hanged?'

'Hanged lad?' the pirate laughed, 'now why spoil a good life?' and with that he jumped down from the scaffold and turned to watch as the business went on.

One by one the prisoners were sold as the captains or their men did their bidding and cajoled. Every so often a fight would ensue as two captains wanted the same man but didn't want to pay higher dues.

When it came to Carter's turn, a swarthy brigand got up and cut him free, turning him around for everyone to see. He had muscle and a good frame, all his teeth and a roughly handsome face, he'd fetch a high price it was sure. Carter's heart beat hard in his chest, to say he was scared would be an understatement. Of everything that could have happened, it was certain he never imagined being sold into piracy!

The old pirate captain sitting on the barrel and a determined Madam Corsair standing to the side were both after Carter and for a long while they vied until the man who had come in the chair with the dwarves raised his hand.

The man was unlike anyone else in the crowd, he wore a rich purple fabric about his head with a blue feather falling over it. He had hoops of gold in his ears that reached down to his shoulders and all around his eyes was a dark malachite, dark like his black hair that hung around his neck and the moustache and beard that held in it another gold ring yet.

More gold still hung around his neck and dripped down his tanned chest, with coins from many a country and trade beads from places still further away. He played with these jewels lazily as he lay, fingering them as he smiled and waited patiently for things to come into play. Banks noticed that this man had a sword, a wide sabre with fine etchings down its spine, tucked negligently into the belt by his side. He noticed too, more gold still, in bangles pushed up past his elbow whose glittering curves caught the sun. All this gold and riches and yet all the man wore was a rough leather vest, a pair of loose breeches tied at the ankles and held up at the waist by a tattered red sash. Carter meanwhile had noticed his shoes, sitting on the end of this man's lazily crossed legs, like little slippers they were, with pointed toes that curled around with bells jingling from the tips, of course the bells were golden as well.

He spoke so assuredly and yet so softly but everyone heard what he said, but Carter could hardly believe.

'This man shall go free,' he said in his strange accent, it sounded so grand though he said it quite simply. And just as the two bidders were about to start arguing the man in the chair snapped his fingers and waved and at once the two dwarves left him in either direction, handing to the captain and the mistress a fine ring each and the man himself turned to the governor, who was not far away, handing him a fine piece. 'A fair fee I believe,' the man said.

The pirate governor raised his eyebrows, 'Fair indeed,' he said then waved to the swarthy lad, 'Alright, set him free.'

Carter, once he had recovered from being shoved off the platform and onto the ground, went straight to the man who had engineered his freedom somehow.

'Sir,' he knelt before him and hung his head low, 'sir I don't know how to thankyou, but you have my allegiance.'

'Yes Carter, I know.'

Carter looked up as this man spoke his name. How did he know it when Carter didn't know him. 'Sir, how?'

'Just stand by a minute lieutenant, there's more to do yet.'

Then lieutenant Banks was brought out on show, his hands unbound and shirt pulled off for his physique to be seen by all. Not bad, most thought, he should be able to do well in a fight or a raid by night, or down in the engines keeping them going. The old captain looked at the man to whom Carter had kneeled, did he want to save this one? The man just motioned that he didn't really want him, so please, they were to go right ahead. Banks eyes saw it all, and they pleaded with the man who had bought freedom for Carter just ahead of him. Then the bidding was over nearly as soon as it had begun, the old captain's mouth in a twisted grin as he paid the governor and sent his men to fetch Banks from the stand.

Banks saw the other prisoners the old captain had purchased, a miserable, sorry lot, with whom he'd be sharing. Some were already being taken on board, his was the large ship that had come in that morning, the hulk, the immense and festering ship, oh no! Banks turned back to try and see Carter.

'Carter, help me!' he cried and though the words couldn't be heard Carter knew what he meant.

'What can I do?' Carter raised his hands and shook his head distressed, 'I can't do anything.'

Banks looked around, searching for some hope in all this, not even all the men on the Avaeste, his companions, would be able to get enough together to get him out of this and he saw their sad faces as he was led past them, down to the pier with the line of other captured men.

Banks was desperate now, and he broke free from the line and ran back to the spot and with his hands still tied he fell at the feet of the old captain.

'Please, sir, I have diamonds on my ship, I will give them over if you just release me!'

The old captain laughed, and the governor explained, 'Some of your crew already tried to use those to get your freedom yesterday, but they were just glass I'm afraid.'

'No!' Banks cried, 'It could not be! Then utterly distraught he collapsed by the unknown foreigner and got to his knees.

'Please,' he begged, 'please help me, please, that will surely be my death, I have a family sir, far away, I was wrong, I did commit this crime, but please sir, have mercy, as you did with my friend sir, please, set me free!'

The old captain's men came to take Banks away but with a slight gesture the foreigner kept them at bay. He smiled at the old captain and held up a finger, he'd just be one moment with his new slave here.

'I will not set you free.'

'I'm begging you please, you had my friend released.'

'He was not guilty.'

Banks hung his head again, 'Sir, would you at least consider to buy me.'

'You think my ship and my command will be kinder than that of this captain, you do not know what you are saying.'

'Anything would be better than going with him, please sir, I'm begging.'

'Sir,' Carter put in bravely, 'he has his faults, but he is my friend.'

The foreigner shrugged and thought, 'What was your crime?'

'I, I stole a diamond sir,'

'That's all? I think you are lying, and so wasting my time,' he clapped his hands and the dwarves made ready to carry him off.

'Wait, there is more, as you say, I regret all of it believe me, I do, so sincerely wish I had not gone through with it, I went against my friends, my fellow crewmen and,' Banks looked down,

'Go on,' said the man.

'And against my Captain, when he could do nothing to prevent it. Now look where I am, and I know I deserve it, but,'

'I will tell you a secret,' the man said, loud enough that those around could hear if they were inclined to, 'the diamond you stole, the one you took from Lady Arinn's hold,'

'Yes?'

'They put it there to catch men like you.'

Banks' jaw dropped and Carter's did too, and the man continued, 'How else would they legitimately keep their slave trade afloat, but by putting a diamond in broad daylight on the edge of a cliff, a diamond that is really no more precious than quartz. Its beauty lies in that it catches the sun and you can see it glimmer from miles afar, isn't that right Governor?'

The shrewd pirate nodded, 'Aye, that is so. Truth is I would miss it if it were ever really stolen, I would, I would so miss having a laugh at the expense of fools.'

'I am shamed sir, that's enough, I am shamed through and through, I'll change my ways sir, please, just take me with you.'

'Oh but we're not done yet,' the foreigner looked down at him with such piercing eyes, Banks thought at the time.

'I've another question.'

Banks didn't reply.

'Would it have been worth it, if the diamond had been real, to have fooled your friends like that, to hide and conceal this thing that you'd done until you reached home? To become wealthy from its sale, had it had value, to buy an estate and a seat on the council.'

'If I'd have pulled it off, I'd have been a rich man, life would have been so much easier,' he tried to explain.

'You haven't changed!'

'I have sir, indeed I have, I'll never try anything like this again, I-'

'Why should I free you, or buy you even as you ask, when there are worthier men still up on the stand, and that isn't all anyway, is it? There are more crimes tucked away in your chest I'm sure.'

'No, only as much as any other man, and besides which, who are you to condemn, you come here with your gold and your slaves to buy up more men,'

'Banks wait!' Carter stopped him, but the foreigner pushed him back with a wave.

'Who am I to condemn? You are the one asking me for freedom. The gold you see I have made in self sacrifice and fair trade, the men who serve me serve me freely, they are not my slaves and I don't know but I didn't think I bought any slaves either, today.'

Banks bit back the words on his tongue. There was a lot in his history he could be ashamed of, but that's just it, this man knew that he wasn't.

'You still have no remorse,' the foreigner said, 'until the day you do you shall be a slave.'

'No, oh please sir, no!'

The man drew out his knife and gave it to Carter, saying 'Cut your friend free,' then turning to Banks and placing his fee in his hands, 'give this to that captain and then follow me.' He clapped and the dwarves put the chair back up on their strong shoulders and went through the crowd and down to the pier. Banks and Carter followed behind and many of the Avaeste's crew hung to the side as the bidding continued for the other prisoners.

Banks jogged to catch up with the jhampan as he saw where it was headed. It had now reached the boarding plank of the fair

Avaeste, the first dwarf had in fact just set his foot on it.

'Wait,' Banks hesitated, 'my captain was fevered when I last left him, he probably won't be in a fit state to see you, let me leave a note for him, he'll understand why I have to go with you.'

'Fevered?'

'Aye sir.'

'You are right Banks, he still is.'

'Sir?'

The lieutenant remained confused as the dwarves took the chair over the plank and were helped onto the ship by the crew who had remained. It was not until Banks had followed them onboard that all became clear. As the rest of the crew tumbled in from the shore and sails were set straight away at this man's command, and as the flag went up, the flag of Aeloran, and off came the man's beard. Banks couldn't speak, everything that had passed became blurred.

They sailed away from the Atoll of Arinn, not much worse for wear than when they'd gone in which is more than could be said of many a vessel, many a crew and many a soul.

The captain stripped himself of all the trinkets of gold saying, 'Melt it back down into plate and replace the sheets we stripped from the plane. Morris, Dew, you can go find Santee and get yourselves changed back into your proper shapes but don't you start your brawling again until I've had a word with you two, then you'll need to go down and take back over from Needle, Dew.'

'Aye Captain,' they both said and went off to his cabin where they'd find the sprite waiting for them.

'Berens bring me some vinegar and water, I've got to get off this yellow colour somehow. Not much I can do about the hair though I suppose,' the boy sighed.

'Don't worry Cap'n,' Berens tried to cheer him, 'it'll soon grow, but I don't know, the black suits you too.'

The captain eased his leg down from the chair, it throbbed as he did and his face showed a grimace. Another of the crew brought his crutches by, and Carter was up quickly by his side, 'Let me help you captain, take my arm.'

'Captain,' Banks said finally, 'Captain, I, I, I don't know what to say, you risked your life, the ship, why, everything, dealing with those pirates…..everything, all for my sorry life!'

The captain said nothing, the lieutenant continued, 'I, you're right, I stole the gems from Diamantine, I snuck off the ship I swore the others to secrecy, I plotted behind your back and I schemed, I used harsh words against your first mate and my own men, and so many other things, I am rotten, completely rotten, captain, forgive me.' And with that a salty tear crossed the lieutenant's proud cheek.

'Banks,' the boy captain said, as he smiled wearily, putting his hand on the lieutenant's shoulder, 'now you're free.'

Banks couldn't keep standing but sank to his knees in his happy grief, the great galleon he could have been on still sat large in the distance, but he found warmth now, in the familiar timbers of the Avaeste, and returning to his heart, and he breathed in such relief.

'Come on Carter, after all that I think I need to go back to sleep,' said the captain.

'I don't know how you did it, you still being so weak. Last I saw you before I went ashore you were like a babe asleep.'

They reached the cabin were Morris and Dew were their old selves, the Goblin and the Monster were staring each other out.

'Carter, this is Dew, he lives down in the engine room. Dew this is Lieutenant Carter, and who's that behind you? Oh, Carter, this is a good friend of mine, Santee, she's a sprite.'

For a second Carter was bemused, they knew of swamp monsters where he came from, and in legend he'd heard of goblins too, but sprites? Well now, that was something new.

'Nice to meet you,' he said looking at the shimmering thing on the captain's desk. Then poof! She disappeared, taking Carter aback, he looked at the captain who just said, 'She'll come back.' And just then she did, human sized, in front of Carter, barefooted and real with her eyes glittering like her whole body had just been, looking at this man she had been longing to meet. She pushed her hair back then firmly shook his hand, 'Yes,' she said smiling at him, 'it's nice to meet.'

The captain drew the two enemies aside, the Goblin of Kebaticus and the Monster of Swamp. 'Do you think it's possible for you two to survive on the same ship? And if not that, is it possible for you to pretend that the other one of you does not exist?'

'It's alright captain,' they both said, almost at once, Dew continued,

'We've decided for your sake to put aside,'

Morris went on, 'our differences, and for the sake of your voyage. You see, when I was about to rip Dew's throat out Santee came down with your message for Dew,'

'And she told us why you'd set out, and why you continue,'

'I see.'

'So we decided to put our differences aside, for you.'

'You know I'm so grateful for both of you, I'm so proud of you for what you do always, and especially today, I thankyou.'

'And we're proud of you Captain, but you just lie yourself down now, you're nearly falling over as it is.'

The boy captain did as they said, they took off his strange clothes and his feathered hat and pulled up the blankets over his shoulders, tucking him in with a nod and a pat. Then Dew went back down to take over from Needle and Morris went out to set the course and check on the crew. So the captain fell asleep to the soft, lulling voices of Lieutenant Carter, and Santee, the sprite, as they sat at his desk as they watched over him and conversed about anything and everything till it was nearly night.

Chapter 7:
THE MERIDIAN ISLE AND ITS QUEEN

A smile grew on the young captain's face as he lay and a scent came on the afternoon breeze, unhesitating through the window, a scent crisp and clean and laced with an earthy sweetness that told him of beautiful mountains covered in pine trees and ferns and a coastline of grey stone and freshwater rivers running right down into the sea. 'Meridian at last!' he whispered, 'at last we're here.'

'There it is!' Needle shouted, 'the Isle of Meridian, it has to be!'

The crew came up and once again cheered, but this time with more vigour as they knew that now they were where the captain wanted them to be.

'Carter, can you bring the ship down,' the captain requested.

'Aye Cap'n,' he said, then as Carter exited he took Santee's hand and, smiling broadly, said goodbye, and that he was glad they had met. She disappeared as he went, in a glimmering pop! As she gasped, then appeared once he'd gone, a bright light in the lantern above, peeking down at Ashton, then sparkling down to him, whispering in his ear, 'Oh no, you know what boy? I think I'm in love!'

Ashton laughed, 'Really Santee? I wouldn't have guessed it.'

'You tease!' she laughed. 'Don't be mean or I'll make you go to sleep again,' she threatened.

'You wouldn't!'

'Wouldn't I?' she glanced cheekily at him.

Ashton grew serious, 'Santee, I know you think well of Carter, but don't pin your hopes in him.'

'But he is still young, and he dreams.'

'But he is older than you, and he is a man Santee and I'm not sure he has the same feelings.'

Before Santee could protest, there was a knock on the door, it was Swamp Morris. Even as he came in the Avaeste touched the sea, Carter was really getting the hang of it, she came in so smoothly.

'Captain,' Morris said, 'there are lights in the harbour, we're making our way in. From what we can see there is an assembling of men at the dock. Do you want to send in a shore party this evening or wait till the morning?'

'Oh, we're going in now,' Ashton said, with growing excitement, 'ready the boat Morris, I'll be going, you too if you want.'

'Can I come?' Santee asked from her room back up in the light, tinkering with her things to find a dress of the right kind.

'Of course,' Ashton answered, 'like I always tell you, you're a free sprite, you can do as you like.'

'Yes but I don't want to ruin some grand scheme of yours by doing something silly now do I?'

'You won't,' Ashton said as he slowly stood up from his bed, gingerly testing his leg with a little of his weight, waiting for the throbbing to return on a larger scale. He found his best trousers and eventually got into them, his best shirt, his best jacket, the one with the sparkling gilded buttons, took out his hat and held it under his arm, the one not leaning on the crutch.

'Santee, a mirror, would you?' he asked. Immediately she snapped her fingers and the wooden door of his closet became reflective glass. Ashton sighed, 'Well, it will have to do I suppose.'

'You know,' Santee said, trying to be encouraging, 'I agree with Berens when he said what he said about black hair suiting you.'

'Do you think?'

'Yes I do,' she turned away and the glass became wood, 'black or blonde hair, you're the best boy I know.'

The captain smiled then went out to meet his crew. The flag of St Amalric had been strung up high as he'd asked them to do, and as it flew in the sky, the blue and the white stars shining out against the evening light, the captain smiled, he could not help but be filled with pride at the sight.

The city of Meridian was set around the harbour, rising gently up the slope of the hills beyond, with white washed houses, wooden houses, houses of stone all nestled in amongst a great forest of pine and throughout the heath land of the ocean side. Their lights and their music were glimmering out across the sea, such a joyful sight and sound to those coming in, captain included.

He picked out a few to go with him to shore, Tom Needle, Berens, Gragan the elder, Lieutenant Banks and Lieutenant Jennings, a man called McGregor who had once been a bosun, another called Patrick who came from beyond Althorn, from a land he called Aiyr, and there were others beside them, and of course, Santee and Morris.

The row to shore was over quickly, they were hailed kindly and brought in by the waiting party. Such a homely, welcoming place it seemed, and so it turned out to be. They dragged the boat up on the beach and exchanged greetings like friends of old once again reuniting.

Then the young captain bowed to her majesty's representatives, 'Captain Ashton St Amalric, come to pay my respects to the queen.' They bowed in return.

'She awaits you son of Mathis, Prince of Aeloran and the surrounding Aethermarinus.'

The accompanying crew were amazed by this greeting, their young captain, royalty? How could it be? But then again, knowing him, it wasn't hard to believe.

The procession became grander and more grand as they went, through the streets of Meridian and up to the royal residence. They had sent for the royal carriage, her majesty's own, to make the way easy for the young captain. They brought horses for his men, but the captain had his first mate beside him as Morris didn't like horses and they didn't much like him.

The way was lit with small moon-like lights held within sculptured columns that looked like nature had forced itself up out of the ground just to hold them in their subtle brilliance.

The citizens of Meridian came out to see, to wave at this prince and his company, they had seen many far grander receptions before but there was a difference about this. This prince had brought none of his own grandeur, it was all given to him by them, and freely done. Their love for his father, the wise king, was genuine.

They came to the palace, gladly, for the captain had not been expecting such a public reception. Then came him to the queen, the lovely Annabella Bien. She sat waiting, holding her baby, rocking it gently in her slender arms. Her aides took it from her and left as he entered alone.

'I hope your men will enjoy the repast prepared for them,' she said.

'Thankyou, I am certain they will,' he answered. She was so beautiful, her dark hair gathered up loosely, hung with roses and pearls, pearls also glimmered at her ears and around her neck, so stately, her creamy white dress held her torso close and upright but the skirt of it flowed gently down and over the floor where she sat. Her eyes were dark and penetrating, her features firm but kind.

'I considered that it may be you wished to speak with me about important matters, easier discussed without the presence of others.'

'I thank you. Do forgive me your majesty, I would kneel but,' he motioned to the splint.

'Forgive me, it is I who should ask you to sit, please,' she beckoned.

She sat at the far end of the chamber, a hall whose architects could not decide if it were to be in indoor or an outdoor room and so had come to a rather lovely compromise. It was complete with a long empty dining table to one side and a garden on the other. The table was made of a white timber, so too the woodwork throughout the garden. The floor was white slate tiles, moss grew in between each one, a break in the roof half way down showed a broken canopy of trailing vines, softly scented climbing roses and white wisteria hung down.

He took a seat near her as she desired.

'I am glad that I have this opportunity to meet you,' she began kindly, 'Edward told me about you. You are very young, Ashton, to be captain,' she observed.

'Edward! My brother?!' he said, happily surprised.

'Yes, he was here not a week since, returning home to your father. He told us,' she thought, then changed her tack, 'I sent with him gifts for your father, and my wishes for him to regain his strength. The hearts of our nation are with him.'

'Had Edward found a cure for the illness?' Ashton asked with eagerness.

'He did not discuss it if he had. He told me there was little hope and that he was heading home, prepared for the worst. You should return too Prince Ashton, little one, but first, tell me why you've come.'

'I will not return until I have found what I came for. I have made it here to Meridian, I am so close. Can you tell me of a plant, they call it the Silvertip Sedge? I have read it grows somewhere here in the isles of Sho'Orakai, it has healing properties. I would take some to my father.'

'I have not heard of it,' she gazed at him searchingly, through the aspect of being aloof.

'Perhaps you have a botanist?' the captain asked, 'direct me to him, lives he on the other side of nowhere I'll go there to see if he knows.'

'I will have him come here to meet you,' she called in an aide then spoke the words and they went again. 'Tell me, eighth prince, what drives you, so young, to take this journey and not leave it to your older, well able brothers?'

'I have a great love for the king, my father,' the captain answered, then saw his mistake.

'And your brothers don't?' she searched him, smiling.

'I meant not that,' he corrected, 'but I could not sit by and watch this illness take him. I love him more than just a father, more than my king,'

'As your rescuer?' she suggested. He looked at her intently, questioningly. She explained herself, 'Edward told me of your adoption, he spoke well of you, but we had little time to say more.'

'I see.'

'Don't worry,' she assured him, 'if Mathis has made you his son, I will favour you as I do all his sons. Tell me, was your family in his service?'

'No, I am not of Aeloran.'

'But you look to me as much from Aeloran as Edward. Where did Mathis find you?'

'It was years ago, I was very young,' the captain looked aside, 'does my name not say enough?'

'Ashton?' she repeated, 'No, I don't understand?'

He had hoped she would just say some general place and he could evade a proper answer, but it wasn't to be. So he answered the beautiful Annabella dutifully.

'Ashton he calls me, for my name was burnt up along with

everything else, there is none left who can speak it. My race was destroyed in a terrible fire; there was a great war, over so quickly, everyone and everything, the entire isle was burnt to a floating cinder. St Amalric and his army were too late to stop it, but he saved me.'

'I am sorry,' she said, she seemed sincerely moved by the story, 'was it Calegra who brought the war upon you?' she asked.

'Yes.'

She was near tears as she explained, 'The tyrant Calegra destroyed several isles before Meridian and her allies even knew what he was doing, before we could get to him with a large enough force. He was clever, he began beyond the limits of the charted Aethermarinus, in the hidden territories, there was nothing we could do, until Mathis came. I am sorry Ashton, truly, do tell me, who were your people?'

The captain did not wish to have this conversation, but she was the queen of the Meridian Isle and all the rest of Sho'Orakai, the beloved Annabella. Who was he to refuse her? Especially as it was he who came to her with his request.

'You wouldn't believe me if I told you,' he said, standing and stepping away from the table, 'but I trust you and I feel safe here within these walls,' he looked around him. 'So I will show you. I haven't done this for quite a while, so it might not be as refined as it was, but perhaps if I-'

Ashton put his hand across his face, then looked up at the starlit sky through the flowers in the arbour above them then suddenly he wasn't there but doves flew from where he stood, dozens of white doves, up into the air. The queen stood up, amazed, wondering, watching as the doves disappeared and petals of delicate whites and creams fell from the vines above onto the floor around her, a gentle breeze drew them together, away from her, and Ashton stood there again.

'Ile de Novo!?' she exclaimed, 'you are from the Ile de Novo?! Oh Novania! You are Novanian?!'

'Yes.'

'You are right, I would not have believed you had you told me. Oh dear boy! You lost paradise, we all did that day, such mourning there was, there were so few who had ever seen it, it being at the far edge of the world, but those that knew of it, my boy, such mourning.'

'No one must know I exist for my race was thought to be completely wiped out, and Calegra, and his hate, still exist.'

'I understand why your love is so great for the king that you risk your life for his, but there is more still, I feel it, more that drives you on, tell me Ashton,' she asked him gently, 'what is this burden you carry?'

He looked down, 'Burden, your majesty?' he tried to evade.

'Ashton,' she soothed, 'it is as obvious to me as daylight is to your eyes.'

He relented, 'What I showed you now was beautiful, was it not?'

'An understatement!'

'The Novanian celebrate everything beautiful. But as much as we can be lovely, we have within us the potential to be anything that existed on our island, the good and the bad. I was dying, you understand, I had seen so much war and suffering in those last days, and I was young, there was so little left of me. As I lay dying beauty and horror poured from me, flowers and thorns, birds and serpents, life and decay, all flowing from me, living a moment, then dying and fading into the ash.

'St Amalric said he saw a little blue swift from where he stood on the ship, flapping, caught there in the rubble, amongst thorns and fire and the greasy, ashen sludge, when he got out his spyglass he realised there was one of us still alive.'

The beautiful queen shook her head as she listened, 'Go on,' she begged him.

'St Amalric stepped down from his great ship and picked me out of the miring ashes, but even as he lifted me I could see his face change, though I was fading I knew, I could see a sadness come into his countenance. Soon after is when the illness started and he began to die, though it grew only slowly upon him. He must know it was because of me, because of the terrible things I was in my death, but he never said anything, and then he made me his son.' A tear fell down Ashton's face, turning to powder even as it did, black like the ash of that day, it fell and scattered across her majesty's white slate floor.

'And your brothers, do they know?'

91

'No, no, please that they never will. They were younger then and he forbade them go with him to war, they did not see, they have never, for I have never shown them what you have just seen, only a few crew, and the king, knew where I was from. How could they ever forgive me did they find out? Besides which, what does it matter now? I am afraid to show myself as a Novanian, I have rarely done so since I was rescued.'

'Thankyou for trusting me, now I understand you, and though I think you should still return home to the king, I will do everything I can to aid you. Ashton,' she knelt before him, looking up into his face and taking his hands, 'remember my boy, remember this whatever happens, Mathis St Amalric is the wisest king that has ever lived, he would have known he was risking his life to save yours before he did it.' She nodded to him, her face searching his to make sure he understood, 'and even if he didn't he would say now that it was worth it, I'm sure of that. Now come,' she stood and smoothed herself out, 'here is the botanist, I'm sure you will wish to talk things through with him in more detail, I must leave you to attend my son Kielan.'

The captain felt strange, in one way lifted of a weight, in another way burdened again. But he soon became himself while talking to the botanist, asking of the plant and just where he might find it. The old man thought he knew a spot where the Carex Argentius might be found but asked Ashton to follow him first though and search some of the archives in the library in case there was a picture or locality to be found more easily than just covering the ground, not that they could do anything until morning in any case.

'And I have a suspicion,' the botanist said, while turning a page and scratching his head, 'that the silvertip sedge is a rather rare specimen, grows in damp areas, if I'm not mistaken, almost a marsh plant it would be, but restricted to higher altitudes. Now let me see, there's few enough places of that description in this part, but of other isles I'm not an expert.'

'Who is?' the young captain asked.

'Well, let's see, there's Highbury, he's a good sort, her majesty's cartographer, here he is now would you believe.'

'Evening all,' the burly man greeted as he entered the musty room where they were seated in the library, rolls of parchment under his arms. 'Her majesty sent me, how can I aide ye?'

'Highlands Highbury,' the botanist said, 'we are looking for a plant called the Silvertip Sedge. Here it is.' He tapped the book and handed it to the captain, 'Not much of a picture there, but a fairly good description. And how about that, we're only the fifth book in.'

'It says it used to grow on the Ile De Merle,' Ashton read, 'it says it has died out.'

'Oh,' the old botanist put his hand up to his chin, 'oh dear, I didn't read up to that.'

'The maps, may I see the maps,' the captain hurried them.

'Certainly,' Highbury spread the sheets out across the table, 'here, this is the one you want, Ile de Merle, Blackbird Island. It's only very small, and unpopulated, west from here and down towards the islands of Loi'Arinn. There is a mountain of some size there, multiple habitats, perhaps you may still find this plant, somewhere hidden.'

Ashton studied the map. 'May I draw up copies of these maps?' he asked the worthy Highbury. 'I have maps on board of the island here, but none so well drawn, none with detail so great.'

'Certainly, yes,' the mapmaker laughed, enjoying this compliment on his work. 'Give me just a moment, I'll bring the equipment and help you myself.'

So the mapmaker returned and the maps were redrawn, the botanist left them to their work, and so came the dawn.

Highbury slept with his head leant back on his seat, his throat shaking as he snored, his nose facing the ceiling. The captain's head was sunk on a map, his black hair across it, his fingers still clasping the quill, and covered with ink. He was a picture to look at, Annabella thought, and she hoped the baby in her arms would grow as noble as what lay inside that boy's heart.

His jacket was hanging on the back of his chair, his neat white shirt had become untied at the wrists and the neck and hung loosely on him like a night shirt, yet he wore his black boots, all polished and new, one straight out with the splint on it still. She whispered, 'Wake up Ashton, it's morning,' to him, but left before he woke so he wouldn't be embarrassed that she had seen him like that.

He woke, his eyes seeing the glimmering dawn through a window ajar opposite them. He looked at the maps, had they finished them? Yes, the particularly important ones in any case. He gathered them together and rolled them up tight, 'Goodbye Highbury,' he said 'for your great help I thankyou kindly.'

Highbury still snored but he mumbled, 'My pleasure, quite alright.' So the captain went out, jacket in hand, 'down to the shore,' was his first command. His crew had returned late last night without him, they worried but they had been assured he was quite alright. Now they rowed in to meet him as they saw the carriage come; down from the palace they had first seen it, the very first to see it, of course, was Tom.

Needle had begged them to be in the boat that went to the shore to meet the captain and tell him of all the things that had befallen. Good things they were, that was for certain, for what but good was there? said the crew, on the isle of Meridian.

The captain just smiled as he sat in the boat, as his crew heaved on the oars and young Thomas spoke. He told of the dinner, the feast they had had, with uncountable fruits and delicious breads, of the beauty of the queen as she had entertained them, when she came, and of her staff who once had served them, sat down to eat with them! 'Oh!' exclaimed Tom, 'Oh, if that had happened on Althorn the governor would have had to order a whole week of floggings! And we being just sailors, who are we anyway to sit at her table? She didn't even care that I et me bread with me fingers!'

'That is why her people call her beloved,' Ashton said quietly, more to himself.

'That is why you feel like you know her, like a cousin, or even a sister,' Tom mused, 'all the crew thought it, she's just wonderful, before you answer her question it's like she already knows it.'

'Like she's read your heart,' Ashton said, watching the way the waves rolled gently across the bay.

'So Captain,' Tom continued, 'are we leaving?'

'Only on a short trip for now.'

'Where are we heading?'

'Ile de Merle. We'll be there before long.'

Ashton handed the maps up to Swamp Morris, who took them and laid them out with the others.

'Prepare to set sail Phillips,' ordered the captain, 'then head her westwards following the islands.'

Then Ashton went back to change his fine raiment to a more suitable outfit for the stalking through grasses and the climbing of mountains.

'So,' there was a little voice floating down from above him, 'you were a while on the island,'

'Not really, only an evening,' he said, as he did up his buttons.

'A whole entire night to be precise,' Santee corrected him, then simpered, 'I was beginning to think that you might like it so much you forgot about us.'

'Meridian is beautiful I must admit, but it's so good to be back on the Avaeste,' the captain smiled up at her, tired but determined to go on despite it. He sat at the desk and ran his hand over the map, then began making some small, simple copies of it. 'Did you have fun then Santee while you were there?'

'Oh indeed Captain, I didn't know it but other sprites live here.'

'Oh, really? And were they kind to you?'

'They were the best of sprites I've ever met,'

'You don't want to stay with them?'

'Oh no, they were not like me, they were so very different, and besides, I'd rather stay here on the Avaeste, and I know you don't mind.'

The captain looked at her as she walked across the map, and smiled, 'You and me Santee we're two of a kind.'

'Is this where we're going?' she stood on the island he was studying.

'Yes.'

'What are we going to do there?'

'Looking for a plant, do you want to help us find it?'

'Yes, alright,'

'By the way Santee, have you seen Morris?'

'No,' she shook her shimmering head.

'Strange, he usually hangs around till I give him his orders,' the captain said.

Then there was a great laugh coming up from below, not a giggle or burble, or big belly bellow, but an oddly loud chuckle and a swampish gurgle.

Santee looked at the captain and the captain looked at Santee, then he got up from his desk immediately and went out and down to the engine room in a hurry.

As they were still sailing along on the sea and not across the Ether Marine, the little goblin had sat down to tea after scrubbing and scrubbing and making himself clean. So now he sat, with his albino white skin, offering his friend, Swamp Morris, a muffin, and there they were, laughing together, wondering why their families were feuding.

The young captain joined in the laughter, as he leaned on the door and took the scene in. He had thought the worst, that something had come over Morris to make him want to start this war with the Goblin again, but it was just the opposite of what he had imagined.

'Join us!' beckoned Dew with a grin full of tea leaves.

'Yes, do, please,' added Morris, swatting a fly with his muffin, then pulling out a seat.

'Well, I would, thankyou,' Ashton said, 'but I really must go and direct the crew, but please, continue you two.'

'Do you need me Captain?' Morris asked him.

'Well, I will, yes, but you've time enough to finish.'

The captain left them to it and went up to the deck, calling to his men as he saw they were fast approaching Blackbird Island.

'Pull closer in,' he directed, 'now lower anchor, set down the boats, Banks, stay on board with your men, you will be captain of the Avaeste while I'm gone. The rest of you into the boats, we go ashore.'

'To that island Captain?' Berens dared to ask.

'Yes.'

'It's so bleak,' he commented, and Berens was correct.

No sand on the beach, just a black rocky shore meeting tortured old trees, that swayed and creaked with the breeze. It was hot, and pungent as of sulphur, as it swept across from the isles of Loi'Arinn. They could see it now, on a far distant island, a tall black mountain, a volcano erupting, but they entered the forest and soon the sight and smell of it was gone, replaced by the all surrounding dense trunks and bracken.

'We have come here to search out a particular plant,' the captain began, 'I want you to split up into a few groups men, we will cover the island from bottom to top till we find it. I'm afraid I don't have a very precise description, but here's what I have.

'We are looking for a type of grass like thing, or maybe even a reed, a marsh plant it's likely, it goes by the name of the Silvertip Sedge. One book says that its leaves are narrow and flat, but it also said we wouldn't be able to find the plant. So here's my plan.'

He laid it out to them as he handed them maps, what they were to do, go inch by inch and collect what they found, any grass any leaf that grew around they were to take a sample of and write down exactly where they'd found it, what kind of plant it was and go on and keep going till they had covered the island.

They formed groups and split up, setting off in different directions, he hadn't told them what it was for but they could see it was important to him, and so, that being known, it was important to them.

The captain had with him Carter and Berens, Morris and Santee, Tom Needle and old Gragan. He took the high path, straight up the mountain, even with his leg as it was they had to walk fast to keep up as he was so determined. Then they reached the place he had marked out for this team, and so they began sampling everything and cataloguing.

The captain looked around him at this strange land, so desolate, trees all blackened and rocks and so little else to it. Even the blackbirds of its name couldn't be seen, only the odd lizards, bright red dragonflies and other insects. Where would there be a marsh on an island like this?

Higher and higher and higher they went, the sun went up then the shadows leant, they found so many grasses, so many flat pointed leaves, some that grew tall and some that could only be found if you bent down and peered at the ground. Some were red, like a deep burgundy, and many were green, bright, dark and every shade in between, there were even some ochre strands, that showed hints of orange, but nothing they found could be called silver, not even grey, or in between. Nor had they come across any trace of a marsh, small streams, yes, but none of them were bordered by this silvertip grass. But then, as they scaled the very peak of the mountain, as they came to the top where the land flattened out, they saw here a sunken portion, a sort of a basin surrounded by trees and the sound of many cicadas. The hope in their hearts rose for a moment, as they saw this marsh was covered with grasses.

'I'll go out first,' said Swamp Morris, checking the way was safe for the others to follow. He found no quick-mud, no pot-holes or hidden creatures and so, he told them, they were alright to follow.

The grass all around them was quite tall, it came up to their knees, sometimes even more, and it had firm dark leaves of an olivary green, and as they went further into the marsh they realised it was the only thing here, this grass, and some snails. So the little hope gathered by seeing this place, soon melted away just as fast. And then as they neared the middle of the place, wading through the mud, it started to rain.

Morris snapped a snail up from where it crawled, the captain looked up to the sky above, the light grey clouds had brought quite a downpour.

'Let's head back Captain,' shouted Carter, above the rain, 'or at least let's find some shelter, and fast, those clouds coming show lightning.'

Even as they went to the trees at the side thunderous rumblings rattled the sky. They sat on the bank under the boughs, getting wet still, but not as wet as they would have been if they'd stayed out there, where Morris still was, catching snails with his rather long tongue and having other such fun in this hidden bog.

As they waited the evening grew and then came the night, they thought of going back down to the ship but the captain said they could return but he wouldn't be leaving till he'd finished searching the very last corner of this place and he wasn't going down only to have to come up again tomorrow when it was so far to come and such little area left to examine. And so they all continued to sit, the rain kept on, but then the clouds dispersed little by little, the stars were coming out, and then a little moonlight.

The captain gasped, and before the others all saw it he was out in the marsh again with Swamp Morris, looking around him with so much excitement, and all of a suddenly that's when they saw it, the olive green leaves of the grass in the marsh gleamed and then shone as the moon reflected upon them, a silvery shimmer ran across their tips as they were blown by the gusts. 'The Silvertip Sedge at last,' cried the captain, 'the Carex Argentius!'

'Are you sure?' asked old Gragan, still sitting on the bank, squinting his eyes up to emphasise his question.

'Yes,' answered the captain, 'well, that is, I will take it to the botanist back on Meridian and seek his opinion, but as far as I can ascertain, this has to be it. What else have we found that's anything like it?'

'It's just that I was young once,' old Gragan said, leaving the rest to wonder just what he meant, but then he continued, 'yes, young I was, and we lived near a pond, or rather, a swamp, so I'm familiar with sedges, you see, Captain, and this plant, I don't know but it doesn't look like a sedge to me, it seems more like a diminutive neoregelia or similar relative.'

'Well,' said the captain, 'there's a book in the library has an old drawing so I'll make sure to compare it.'

'Yes, do that,' the old man said, then looked at the stars, rather blinking.

Chapter 8:
THE EVERLAST ENTERS THE SCENE

By noon time the following day the Avaeste had returned to Meridian bay, but it was not the only foreign ship to let down its anchor, besides them, moored in the deep was a grand looking galleon.

Pristine white flags flew from its tall masts, its timbers shone with that rich varnished blush, and proudly painted in a golden shade across its stern was a name.

'The Everlast,' Ashton thought as he read it, 'now who captains that?'

A well dressed crew looked down from their great height laughing at the little Avaeste as it went slowly by, till they sailed closer in and let down the chain.

'Do you know them Captain?' asked Berens as they studied the galleon.

'I don't think I do,' answered the captain, 'I'll have to check the ship register in my cabin, a ship of this nature is sure to be listed. Come Berens, let's check it.'

Ashton pulled out a very large book, bound in red leather and embossed with a ship, he flipped through the pages till he came to the one with a picture of that ship and a detailed description.

'The Everlast is a ship built by the Brothers McAllen for the king of Aeloran, finished on the 5th Februarius '76. How come I've never heard of it?' Ashton asked, but kept reading, there was more to find out. 'Ah, it was given as a gift to the king of Meridian, then captured in battle, disappeared. And that's the end.' Ashton looked at Berens, who said

'But there she is.'

'Crewed and captained,' Ashton added as they went out to look on her again. Even as they did he observed a lady dressed in white sitting in a boat on its way to the great ship. The queen waved to him and was soon alongside.

'My young captain!' she called up, 'I cannot stop, but tell me, how went your expedition?'

'Nothing certain, but a few possibilities we shall compare, may I ask for the use of your library once more?'

'Of course, I expect it, and would be hurt if you didn't,' she said as she held her white hat so it didn't blow off with the wind, waved to him then signalled her men to start rowing again.

'One question my lady, before you go on – this ship,' he pointed to the very big one, 'she is yours?'

'Yes,' she smiled broadly, 'returned to me this day after so many years of service under a foreign name.'

'Who's her captain?'

'Would you believe it's Carramar Von Marax, once a former general of Calegra, now bearing allegiance with us, it's wonderful isn't it my young Captain, I go to inspect the ship now, at his request.'

Her face smiled broadly and her words sounded true, but he detected a certain sadness in her eyes, a faint worried look, no one else would have seen it, of that he was almost sure, no, that troubled expression was for him, and for him to act on.

Ashton stepped back into his cabin and opened the lantern where his little sprite slumbered. 'Santee, wake up,' he whispered, 'come on, I need you.'

'Boy, I was rained on and rained on and didn't sleep a wink, don't you think I could finish this one little sleep?'

'Not now, sorry Santee, I haven't slept either, I only caught a few moments as we made our way back here, but Santee please, it's really important.'

'Is it?' she giggled as she lay there, 'then you shouldn't ask it of *me*.'

'You'll do fine, you underestimate your ability. All I need you to do is follow the queen and report back to me.'

'Follow the queen?' she sat up, 'the queen of Meridian?'

'Aye Santee, that queen. I leave now for the island, taking the samples. The queen will be on the galleon, The Everlast, if anything happens get to me at once, I'll be in the library in the palace, most likely.'

'The Everlast. But isn't she your friend boy, why must I be a spy?'

'A very dear friend Santee, that's why, and because only you can.'

'I don't understand.'

'Nor yet do I. So will you do it?'

'Well,' she thought, 'yes. But only because I too am a very dear friend. I'm I not?'

The young captain smiled, 'The dearest and best.'

So the dear little sprite braved the gusts in the bay to get to the queen as she toured the galleon, and Ashton took his samples, and those collected by all of his men from every inch of Blackbird Island to her majesty's botanist, and together they compared the samples with the books and the drawings they had.

'I'm sorry to disappoint you,' the botanist said, as he looked through his spectacles and studied the plant, 'but this broad green grass that you found is just that, a grass, it shimmered silver you said?'

'Yes, in the light, here,' Ashton took it and showed the botanist how, with just a little reflection the silveriness showed.

'Yes, yes, quite amazing, but it's definitely not your sedge I'm afraid. But don't despair, look at this lovely collection,' the botanist said, he was quite excited, 'we've quite a lot of samples here, so well collated, by the end of this I will be in your debt, it's a while since we've sent out a botanical expedition, as these books certainly show, this will make it well up to date.'

'Right, let's get to it.'

So they set about with their heads down, going through the samples one by one, Ashton of course finding the silvertip sedge in every second leaf that he studied. But the botanist would only shake his head and so on they went.

'So do you know anything about this new galleon?' Ashton asked as they continued sorting.

'Oh, she's an old ship,' the botanist answered.

'Newly arrived, I should have said,' corrected Ashton, 'or anything about this General Von Marax?'

'No, not really. He sailed in last night I'm told, with the sunset far behind him. He sent a group of emissaries up to the queen this morning with letters and gifts and other such things, said he's returning the ship, transformed once again to her former greatness and would her majesty care to inspect.'

'Strange isn't it.'

'Well, I suppose it is, but the war is no longer, it has been over for many years now, there is no reason why things shouldn't happen like this.'

'And the queen, she was happy?'

'Indeed, she was quite overwhelmed, so I am told, she immediately accepted his offer to go on board.'

'I see. Would you excuse me a minute,' Ashton said, and then left.

Just as Ashton walked out the door he was met by a puffing, red faced little Tom.

'There you are Captain!' he bent over to catch his breath, 'I was sent up by Jennings, he says some men from The Everlast wanted to come aboard the Avaeste, but just like you told him, we was careful and said Cap'n's orders no-one was to board us. They left soon enough, friendly sure, but we could see they was in a huff.'

'Did they say what they wanted?'

'Not exactly, no, that's why Jennings sent me, he didn't like the look of them Cap'n and neither did we. They was eyeing our ship cap'n, that's what Banks said, said he knew the look of thieving scoundrels when he saw them, cause he was one himself.'

'You're sure they were from The Everlast?'

'No mistake Cap'n, we saw 'em go back. And Captain, after they'd left, Morris found a keg of gunpowder, when he went to catch a fish, set to ignite under the stern of the ship, with a slow burning cord it was, Jennings reckons we had an hour, maybe more.'

'Right, well, you're here now so make yourself useful, go in and help Henry, I might be a little while.'

'Henry?'

'The botanist.'

'Oh, alright, can't I help you Captain?'

'Trust me, you are,' the captain smiled then set off in another direction.

He walked through the palace till he found a place he thought would be just right for what he desired. He knocked on the wall, soon the curtain was opened. 'Prince Ashton!' a young man greeted him, 'how can I help?'

103

'What's your name?'

'Bastien, I'm her majesty's secretary, do you need something writ?'

'No, thankyou, but tell me, does this room have an ocean view?'

'Why, yes of course, one of the best.'

'May I?'

'Why yes, do come in,' Bastien pushed the curtain aside and followed the captain across to the window and admired, 'isn't she something, The Everlast, such a grand ship. A gift from your father I believe, back in the years before I worked here, is it so?'

'Yes, tell me, do you have a 'scope?'

'Of course, yes, when I'm not busy, which is very rarely. I like to watch the happenings out there, sometimes I like to think I'm a captain, imagine things, but anyway, here we are, not an expensive glass,' the secretary apologised, 'but it's what I use.'

'As long as it does the job,' Ashton took it and pulled it out to look through.

'So,' continued the secretary, 'ah, wow! Here I am with Ashton, son of Mathis St Amalric of Aeloran! We missed you at our meal two nights past, we were all of us expecting you to join us.'

'Yes, I must apologise, I had urgent business and still do. Bastien, do you know if your defences along this side of the mountain are operational?'

'Our defences?'

'The cannons?'

'Well, I assume so.'

'And manned?'

'I do not know.'

'Can you find me someone who would?'

'Most gladly Captain, I shall-'

'Bastien, it's urgent.'

The secretary nodded then hurried away.

Ashton looked out to the sea, to the galleon. He agreed with Banks, there was something not quite right about them. But what was it? What was going on? What was this something? His fear of Calegra, his hate of him clouding his judgement? Making him suspicious of a good man come in peace? Ashton paced and searched himself, no, that wasn't it, this was more than a feeling, though the fear and hate did exist there were other things too, but as yet they were just not quite so obvious, there was that gunpowder yes, but couldn't someone else have done that? After all the men hadn't actually seen anyone do it. The pirates from the Atoll perhaps? Oh that he could be back searching for his Silvertip Sedge instead of worrying about this!

Then came in the general of her majesty's forces, a solid man, tall, and by his scars it was obvious he'd been through many a battle.

'General Angaston,' he held out his hand, 'it is my pleasure to meet you, son of Mathis of Aeloran.'

'You might not be so pleased when you hear my suspicions,' said Ashton, getting right to it. He knew there wasn't time, if his suspicions were right, to wait another moment in getting Angaston's advice. He didn't wait for that man to answer him either, though with such an abrupt introduction the general was speechless so it wasn't hard for Ashton to say what he needed.

'I am afraid there is an underhanded game at play, General, I do not trust this Marax, or his men for that matter. My crew have informed me our ship was being studied by men of dubious character reporting to Marax.'

'Of course, none of us trust him!' the general laughed, 'heavens lad, I've fought against him, do you think it's easy for me to get alongside him? But it is peace lad, you can't go accusing.'

'There's more,' Ashton continued, 'they have also found a cask of gunpowder by the Avaeste, set to explode, put there by those men, it is supposed, and also before the queen reached The Everlast we talked, she and I, and I could sense a sadness in her, a fear, something great, but there was nothing in any of the words she said.'

'Nothing you've told me is the basis for anything, all supposition.'

'May I ask, was it just the crew of her boat went aboard with her?'

'Aye, her personal guard.'

'I see. She has been a while away now, hasn't she,' the young captain commented, 'surely, she wouldn't be long, what with her baby. She didn't have him with her so she would have to come back.'

'Well, that's true.'

'And how long has it been now?' Ashton checked the time, 'three hours at least, any baby so young would soon need his mother, else he'd be crying, you'd hear him the palace over.'

'Yes, oh and we do,' Bastien laughed, 'but none of us mind, Kielan is her first child. Come to think of it now, I haven't heard him cry for a while.'

'General, we must act, send out more men and escort her back.'

'You've no proof of anything,' the general calmed, 'Prince Ashton relax, if something is amiss my men will soon notify me. I thankyou for you concern, but really my lad, it's not your problem, the cask was probably just a prank set up by your men, something silly to just make a bang, fireworks perhaps.'

'No, Angaston, this is a serious thing, by the time you have further proof there'll be no time to act!' Ashton said frustrated and even as he did another man entered, saluting the general and bowing to him.

'Sorry to concern you,' the soldier began, 'but I'm afraid there's been a disturbance, her majesty's maid was found just this minute, unconscious and bound behind the cradle – the babe, Kielan is missing.'

All hearers were silent, then Bastien gasped, 'My friends, look at that!'

Even as they watched, high up in the palace where they could do nothing but stare, amazed, the crisp white sails of The Everlast were freed, the anchor was up and the ship underway.

'The cannons!' yelled general Angaston, 'to the cannons, I'll not let them get away!'

'No!' Ashton stopped him, 'you would fire on the queen!'

'Corporal, notify the admiral, send out the ships,' he said to the soldier then turned back to Ashton, 'but our fleet is idle, it will take too long to mobilize even one ship, Prince Ashton, your little Avaeste?'

'She is fast, but even she, what with their head start what chance have we?'

'Whatever it is, it's greater than ours.'

'I have not the men to take The Everlast! Tell me, if the queen knew of this, as her sadness would seem to say, why did she tell no one? Do you have the letters they brought her today?'

'It should be possible to get them, they'd be in her safe.'

Another soldier ran to the door, 'The maid is awake, she says early this morning, just before the first session, is when they bound her.'

'Just before the emissaries arrived,' the General thought, 'yes, after she received the letters and gifts the queen did step out for a moment to check on the child,'

'The maid said they waited till the queen had fed him once more and returned to the court, then they left with the child and knocked her to the floor.'

'But why not do anything? After all this is her kingdom, what did the letters contain?'

'I have a key to that safe,' said Bastien, shaking with grief and fear for his beloved queen.

So the group of them hurried along to the place, but Ashton had seen a sparkle at the window and for a moment remained, opening the latch and letting her in, that cheeky little sprite at once flew to him and he caught her gently in the palm of his hand, she was all tired from battling the wind.

'They're leaving,' she puffed, 'with Annabella Bien.'

'Yes, we know that,' he said.

'Then why aren't you doing anything?'

'We only just realised it. What is the situation on the ship?'

'She is locked in Marax's cabin. Her guards are locked up below deck.'

'And her baby, Kielan?'

'I saw no babies on board at all.'

'He must still be here, her life a ransom for his perhaps? Such a prize, Annabella Bien, what do they want to do, start the war again?'

'No, I overheard them, that General said that they were well on the way to taking Meridian. Boy, I don't think they're very nice men.'

'Taking Meridian?!' Ashton gasped, thinking for a moment, then Marax's plan became clear to him. 'Did they see you?'

'No, I'm a very clever sprite, like you said.'

'Did the queen?'

'No, I don't think she did. But what does it mean boy, tell me, are we going to rescue the queen?'

'You'll hear soon enough Santee,' Ashton said, putting the tired little sprite in his pocket gently, as it was clear she couldn't possibly fly for a while. He took one last glance down to the bay before running after the general and the soldiers, calling as he went to any he passed, telling them to follow him to the court, for Meridian was in danger and they must make haste.

'General!' Ashton called as he made it, 'the contents of the letters, what of them?'

'Blackmail young Prince, clearly writ; she was to go with them, not saying a word or they would have the life of her child for it.' The general sighed, 'It's our fault, we became too complacent, too quick to see the good around us, who would have thought this would become of it?'

'That's not all,' Prince Ashton informed him, then turned to the palace employees who had been congregating, 'I believe this whole thing is just a distraction while the men of The Everlast scale the mountain. General, don't send all your soldiers out with the fleet after the queen, they will be required here, any moment, we must fast prepare for an assault from your own batteries for I am almost certain they've been overtaken or if they haven't been already, they will be.'

The general took a moment to think it all through, then with sudden clarity he saw it all too, the blackmail here wasn't the final intent of General Carramar Von Marax and his shipmen, how could it have been, what good would it have done them to sail away with Meridian's queen? Young Prince Ashton was correct indeed, it must be a distraction to draw out his army, to make them focus on a diminishing target while all around them the soldiers of Calegra lay biding their time, waiting to strike.

'I will go after the queen,' Ashton offered, 'send out your ships with me but only minimally crewed, the rest of the men must stay here and assist you. Send only enough to make them think we still haven't a clue but are going after them and the queen with everything, like they expect us to do.'

'But your men – they are not soldiers?'

'No, they will not need to be, if the enemy is taking Meridian the Everlast will now be only poorly crewed, General I go,' the young captain saluted.

Angaston returned the salute, 'May victory be with you.'

'Thankyou General, and you.'

Ashton didn't wait to hear anymore but ran out of the room and straight down the hall, pulled Needle and the botanist out of the library, urging them to get to a safe place, and rather quickly. Tom was adamant he would go with the captain but surprised by his stern face he did just as Ashton asked him. Then Ashton borrowed a horse from those waiting at the palace gate and not heeding his mending leg galloped down to the bay.

'Up anchor!' he yelled, even though the boat that brought him hadn't yet reached the Avaeste. 'Let out the sails!' he bellowed. 'Everyone on deck!'

The crew assembled, their mission was explained, they may face cannon fire soon, Ashton told them, so they must get fast underway.

'You didn't ask to be here,' the captain said, 'so it's not lightly I take you out on this mission, and I will not expect you to stand and fight if it comes to that.'

'Oh but we will Captain,' said Phillips.

'And I second that,' added Banks, 'we'll show them they underestimated us and the brave Avaeste.'

'Hopefully it won't come to that,' Ashton said, 'for I have another plan.'

So as the Avaeste skimmed lightly through the sea, they heard of Ashton's plan to bring back the queen.

The covers were pulled off the captain's aeroplane, the one Gualtiero had finished off with gold plate, the ramp at the rear of the ship was lowered down and the captain prepared to take the thing out.

After tucking dear little Santee into her bed, he ran down to the goblin, idling in the engine room and called him out, 'Dew, I've got another job for you!'

'I'm only good with engines Captain, as you know,' Dew excused.

'Then this is perfect for you!' he grinned and pulled the little goblin along, taking him to the place where the plane was.

'Here, look, it has an engine Dew, do you think you can fly it? I'm counting on you.'

'Well, the Avaeste's engine isn't anything like it, but I suppose,' Dew said as he ran his hand over it, 'I could try it.'

'You'll need your goggles, it'll be windy up there, and maybe a vest.'

'Up there?' Dew scratched his head.

Ashton explained, 'It's a plane, it flies in the air!'

Dew stepped back, 'Don't you think, maybe Morris?'

'He doesn't know engines, not the first thing about them, you know controls, Dew, and about things like fuel, water and overheating, don't you?'

'Well, yes, I suppose I do,' he agreed.

'Get in then Dew, and help me save the queen.'

'The Queen? Why didn't you just say so.' He pulled on his goggles and then he and Ashton hopped in.

Ashton encouraged, 'And Dew,' he said, 'just think, you'll be the first aeroplane-flying goblin!'

Chapter 9:
THE ENGINE GOBLIN LEARNS TO FLY

The engine started perfectly, and Dew ran over the controls, seems easy enough, he thought as he started them going, then faster and faster along the special tracks they'd made, till they reached the ramp and then the goblin really laughed as out of the darkness and the closeness of the little ship they were suddenly up in the vast openness. The blue all around them, the clouds so nearby, the gliding gulls surprised to find something so big and loud in their sky, and startled by the little goblin's wide smile.

From the little gold plane Ashton scanned the sea, so far below them. At the speed they were going it wasn't long before he spotted the Everlast and tapped the shoulder of the brave goblin.

'There she is, let's go down and take a better look, but not so low they think anything of us.'

So the goblin steered her down till he thought they'd be about where the men below might make them out for a rather large bird, or perhaps a kite, though what a large kite would be doing here out over the ocean Dew couldn't surmise, and besides neither of those things shined like this aeroplane shined, no, even if they went lower none could see what it was for the brightness of the gold in the sun just blinded.

Looking back in the distance they could see the Avaeste following along with several of her majesty's ships, and then a pop, a gunshot, echoed up to them. Ashton pulled out his spyglass, it was just as he thought it would happen; he hadn't been in one of Calegra's battles for nothing! The defences on the mountain were being overrun, men in Calegra's black tunics had taken the cannons!

At once the resounding sound of the cannons sickened those in the ships as shots were fired all around, the water splashed up as shot came near and with every pound the ships shuddered in all of their timber.

Ashton studied the way things were proceeding, and knew if he was going to act he was going to have to act soon, for the edge of the ocean was coming up fast, it would have to work; he'd have no second chance.

He nodded to Dew, and then disappeared into a flurry of feathers, and flew down to the ship, numerous fast, darting, dark swifts.

The window at the stern was open a fraction, this was it, the general's cabin, the queen was alone, sitting on his chair, then suddenly, even as she looked up, a flurry of swifts then Ashton was there.

'My young prince!' she whispered then fell to her knees, taking his hand and kissing it softly, 'I knew you'd understand, I knew you'd come to me.' She'd tears in her eyes and flowing down her cheeks, and in her hand a sodden handkerchief.

'Your Majesty, we haven't much time, come with me,' he pushed the window wide open,

'No, I can't go, they'll kill Kielan.'

'Your majesty, they will do more than that if they fulfil their plan, right at this moment, they're taking Meridian!'

'What? No, they told me their plan, they just wanted me, I wanted you to come so that I could get you to go back and tell those exactly what happened, and why I couldn't return.'

'Listen,' Ashton urged her, 'don't you know that sound?'

She shuddered, 'The cannons!'

'Yes, they fire on your ships, and my Avaeste! Calegra's men have the guns, somehow they must have snuck men onto the island, unsuspected, I suggest, in the bottom of this galleon that first night they arrived. But no time to dwell further, Queen Annabella, come.'

'Are you sure that is what's going on?'

'I have seen it begin, I have seen the black coats of Calegra's men.'

'Do you think the tyrant himself is here?'

'It's a strong possibility, if not right on the island, he'll be somewhere quite near.'

She put her hand to her mouth, 'How blind I have been! How naïve!'

'Your majesty, this can all wait, right now we have to get you to safety, please, take my hand, jump with me, we cannot hesitate.'

'Jump? But the sea is so far.'

'I'll jump with you, we'll be alright.'

'But surely we're near the end of the sea, we'll be washed out into the open Ether Marine!'

'The longer we wait my lady, the closer we'll be, please, take my hand, trust me,'

Her hands were quite shaking but she took his and they jumped.

The Everlast kept on, for the moment unaware that its royal captive had dared to escape, over the side, swallowed up in the great ship's foamy wake. Ashton held her hand tight and finally together they came up again, through the bubbling ocean back into the glorious light.

'Your Majesty, don't be alarmed at this, it is a contraption of mine,' he said between gulps as he caught his breath, as the gold aeroplane came into sight, 'flown by a friend of mine, a goblin, named Dew. As soon as he nears he'll throw down a rope, quickly get your foot in the hold and he'll fly us back to the Avaeste, as she will have come out of the range of the cannons, but as soon as he comes remember the men on the Everlast will know you've escaped at once, who knows what they will do, be prepared for the worst.'

So Dew came and let down the rope and the queen did as she had been advised, Ashton stayed with her till she was certain she had a good hold, then he found a notch and hung on just below her, and the goblin turned around even as the waves from the churning water grew larger, they had only just made it in time, before the sea ran out and there would have been only the wind and the sky.

The men on The Everlast saw the little plane and wondered at it till they saw the queen and the young captain escaping from them, by now The Everlast had gone out into the sky, but they picked up their guns and they started to fire.

They fired at the plane and Dew tried to manoeuvre in such a way that would make them miss him but he had to think of his charges below, and pretty soon he was hit, well, not him but the plane that is, and though little Dew is an expert in engines there was nothing he could do, mid-air, when one of the shots hit the main fuel tank.

He steered the plane over and they reached the Avaeste, Ashton and the queen disembarked but then Ashton caught the rope again as Dew kept on going and he climbed up to him, what was the goblin doing?

'Dew, we have to jump, leave the plane or you'll crash with it!' he pressed, even as the engine began to sputter far worse, then cut off, the propeller stopped and they glided for a moment, then rapidly lost height.

The crew of the Avaeste and the queen Annabella Bien watched in horror as the plane went down, smoke flowing from it as it went down near one of the small islands.

Annabella gasped, the crew stood stunned, looking out, wondering what had happened to Dew and their captain.

'Turn around!' Carter yelled, 'let's get to that island!'

So the men jumped to action, running everywhere, Morris took the wheel and spun her as the work of the sailors allowed and they made their way with more speed than they had ever before achieved.

They followed the smoke till they found the tail of the plane sticking up sickly out of the water, worrying now as they looked around. There were no signs of life at all just an oily silt bubbling out.

But then they heard a cough and spluttering, they were stunned as their little engine goblin climbed back over the side of the deck.

He coughed and pulled a little fish out of his mouth, throwing it over the side then spluttering as more water came out, out of his mouth and out of his ears, out of his nose and everywhere. His skin was a little blacked from the smoke from the engine, and his goggles were cracked and hanging around his neck and his vest somewhat tattered.

'You're alive!' the crew shouted, all so amazed.

'Yes,' said Dew calmly, looking over himself, 'it seems that way doesn't it?'

'Ashton?' asked the queen, her eyes pleading.

'The captain?' asked the crew, 'what happened to him?'

'Well,' the goblin began, looking at the floor, wondering how to put it, 'well, what happened is, I really can't say, it all happened so quickly I don't know how to explain.'

Then everyone turned, as casually stepping out of his cabin, doing up the last button on his tunic, stepped Ashton.

'Miss me?' he grinned.

'Captain!' they gasped, 'how on earth? Who? But? Where?'

'You lads came in so fast you nearly went right over the top of us!' Ashton laughed

'But what happened?' they all begged to know.

'Well, what with the speed we were falling we're quite lucky really, Dew managed it well, but in the end there was nothing could be done about it, we jumped out then she hit so hard coming in the pontoons snapped off, and the rest of the aeroplane was soon engulfed by the sea, it might be possible to salvage it, what do you think?'

'We can sure do that Captain, a few ropes around her tail and we'll pull it back in.'

'Good,' the captain nodded, 'then Dew, do whatever you need to do to get her flying again.'

'Aye Captain.'

'Thankyou,' Ashton patted Dew on the head then turned to Annabella, 'your Majesty, please, accept the use of my cabin, you'll want to change out of your wet garments I imagine, there are some clothes laid out for your inspection.'

'Oh Ashton!' she smiled, but still with that worry in her eyes, her home was still under siege and she still didn't know the whereabouts or safety of her child. 'Indeed, I thank thee,' she said, then went back to his cabin.

'Your orders Captain,' the lieutenants asked, but for the first time they saw the young captain stumped.

'Ah,' he sighed, sitting down on the stairs, he'd been so long awake, so long without rest spending so much adrenalin, indeed it was spent. 'What do you think we should do men? We cannot head after the Everlast, we don't have the weapons or the men, we have to take the queen back to Meridian but we can't, not if the place is overrun and in the middle of intense fighting, and going back we'd have to face the cannons again, such a risk. Your thoughts, men?'

It occurred to them that they didn't know either, what would be the best way to proceed.

'We could of course take the queen somewhere safe, like Diamantine,' Ashton continued, 'or further, but she'd not go without

Kielan, I know it, and we can't abandon our friends here on Meridian.'

'No, we can't,' they agreed.

'And,' Ashton rubbed his face as he worried, 'I still have to find that silver-sedge-weed.'

'Didn't we find it?' the crew asked, rather stunned as they'd thought they'd done a good job collecting so many specimens from the island.

'Well, maybe, but the botanist didn't give me much hope; even the one I found that I thought must be the one, he said no, that it wasn't and there was no way that it was.'

Carter came forward, 'Captain, before you came back from Meridian, did you see Tom?'

'Yes, I did, I left him with the botanist.'

'Well, that makes it easy,' Carter said, 'we've got to go back for him, we've got to sort out these black jacket men, got to take the queen home, give her safe passage, sort it all out so we can get on with finding your Silvertip Sedge, don't you see, it's simple really, we go back to Meridian. Men, are you with me?'

'Aye,' they all said.

'Yes Captain, we're with Carter,' said Jennings.

'And I'm with your men,' said Annabella Bien, coming out from his cabin in a lovely but practical dress. Thanks to Santee of course for the provision of that.

'We're hardly more than twenty,' Ashton reminded them, 'Meridian is a large island, a great city, and I don't know if you've thought of it but this is not all of the enemy, more are coming it is certain, they will want to take Meridian properly, this was just the first gasp, set to take the main defences out and make it easy for the rest of them.'

The crew hung their heads, they hadn't thought about that.

Ashton continued, 'General Angaston has the army and navy in his command, he's had more notice than they expected him to have, what difference will us twenty make, I have something else to suggest.' The young captain studied his hands for a moment, thinking through a plan. Morris didn't know what the others thought, but to him the captain looked sad.

'Let me ask the governor of the Atoll of Arinn for his aid,' the captain asked the queen, explaining, 'he has a great many men and ships at his command.'

'He will never come,' Annabella sighed, 'he is generally a good man, though a rogue, but he wouldn't risk his life for this island, unless it were to be his when he was done.'

'I think I can persuade him,' Ashton replied.

'Well, if you can, there's no harm in trying.'

'Shall I set course for the Atoll of Arinn Captain?' Banks asked, gingerly, he didn't really want to see that shore again if it was a possibility.

'No, it will take too long and we could be caught out if Calegra has more ships on the way, wait here and stay safe, all of you help Dew, we must get the aeroplane flying again.' The captain stood and stepped back to his cabin, closing the door firmly behind him.

The golden aeroplane was quickly hauled in, over the ramp they had built at the back while on Diamantine, and down into the ship's belly. It still shone with a smoky golden gleam.

Those not working on the plane worked at getting the ship all ready, ready for anything that could eventuate, priming their pistols and checking that their cutlasses were strapped on and that they were ready to fight.

Had they heard, back in their home of Althorn, of this tyrant Calegra and what he had done? No, this was all new to them, but they could see instantly the good men, the people of Meridian, their Captain Ashton, they were set apart from this General Marax and his men, they were worth fighting for, and if it came to it, dying.

The very young captain sat down on his bed, putting his tired head into his hands. He sighed, he knew what he had to do, he just didn't like the thought of doing it, what would he tell his crew? He lay back and stroked the wood of the Avaeste, the fine little ship seemed to know his hand and it swayed on the swell of the sea gently in return. Ashton pulled his sore leg up onto the bed and rested while he could, while he waited for the aeroplane to be fixed, but it was so hard to wait with the distant cannons still firing and the memory of Ile de Novo playing on his mind. Despite it all, he was still a just boy, and he was very tired, and so it is he fell asleep without trying.

The men who knew how beat the plane's twisted metal back into shape, while some soaked up the water from around the engine as Dew had told them to do, some reattached the pontoons with wood and with rope and others cleaned the seaweed from the nooks it had become stuck in and Dew himself patched the hole in the tank up.

They were doing such a fine job and when all was nearly finished Dew tested the engine. It wanted to start, it really did, but it coughed and died and Dew scratched his head.

Then, 'of course!' he exclaimed, 'of course, what was I thinking, we lost all the fuel, I've got to fill up the tank!'

So Dew ran down and soon was back with a flask of blackcurrant juice which he poured into the tank till it couldn't take anymore. And then he tried the engine, and the engine gave a click, then a few more and then she turned over and began to purr.

The men and the monsters jumped up and down, dirty from their efforts and apprehensive at their situation but happy at this wonderful little success.

Morris ran up and informed the captain who picked himself up with effort and neatened his appearance before going downstairs, climbing into the seat once more, with Dew at the controls and the men pushing them to start off, then they flew out the door and towards the pirate islands once more.

Ashton found the governor pirate about to sit down to smoke a pipe after his lunch.

'Hey, how'd you get in here past my men? Do I know you?' the governor asked as he leaned back on his couch, lighting his pipe. 'Ah yes I do,' he laughed, 'you're the captain of the little Avaeste, aren't you?'

'Yes'

'You know,' he smiled in his cunning kind of way, 'your men weren't worth what you paid,' he laughed, 'you didn't have to put on that charade, I would have returned them to you if you wished me to, provided you had something to trade. I always welcome new business partners with open arms.'

'Good, as that's why I'm here governor Renardo,' Ashton began, 'may I sit?' he said, overtired.

'Be my guest, and help yourself to some bread.'

Ashton did, then said what he'd come all this way to say, 'I want you to help me save Meridian.'

The pirate put both eyebrows up very high in surprise, 'Last I knew Meridian was as it always has been, not needing saving, and not the very place for someone such as I.'

'She is under attack at this very moment, from the forces of Calegra, under command of a General Von Marax. I would have thought someone in your position would have heard rumours and plans of these things.'

The pirate laughed, 'I suppose I might have, but what is this, you think I should attend?'

'You have the ships, and the men.'

'What makes you think I'll agree? I've no allegiance with them and them none with me, why should I do it, tell me?'

'If Marax or Calegra took control, you might lose your sway here.'

'No, unless I threatened them I'm convinced they wouldn't bother me, but that wasn't the answer you had for me was it?'

'Well, naturally I assumed you'd require a fee, so if you should aid us, and then if we win, I will give you in return the Avaeste, a good ship.'

The governor bellowed loudly, a guffaw of laughter shook his whole body, his eyes wrinkled up, his moustache shivered and tears rolled down his cheeks as he tried to overcome the mirth that overtook him.

'Oh,' he held his stomach, 'oh my boy, you shouldn't be a captain, oh no, your employment should be in comedy.'

Ashton just waited for the governor to calm down then said, 'Well, if that's how you feel, I'll be going then,' and was about to get up but the pirate stopped him.

'Wait, wait, finish your bread,' he begged, 'I shouldn't laugh so, but you must admit, it is funny, isn't it?'

Ashton grinned, 'I saw you eyeing my ship, you know her worth, though she was a wreck when I found her, she hadn't lost any of her spirit.'

The pirate thought, and Ashton kept on.

'And you know who once owned her.'

The pirate relented, 'Aye, I know.'

'The explorer, Trevallian Valentin. The only ship like it, built by the famous Phineas Tuck, she's fast, she's able and though others may laugh she's manoeuvrable,' he praised her, 'and tough.'

'Stop, stop, you are right. I did have my eye on her even while my men mocked. But do I like her enough to risk losing some of mine?'

'I think you do, yes.'

'You're a rascal lad,' the governor said, 'if only I'd found you before you gained some respect, you'd have been a fine pirate, and coming from me, that's saying something.'

Ashton grinned but kept on with his argument, 'You will also gain some esteem of those on Meridian, which I assume, at the moment you lack.'

'We have an understanding, I don't need their good opinion. But the general there does harass my traders, now and again, but mostly they avoid him,'

'I could have a word.'

'No boy,' he said seriously, 'don't you go making deals like that, I know what I do isn't quite correct, it's only right that the general makes his threats.' He thought another moment, scratching his chin, then he answered. 'Alright, I'll come, on your word that when it's over I'll have the Avaeste, and that you'll do as I signal you to do during the attack.'

The young captain was sad but he took the governor's hand and shook it firm. 'You have my word. I will see you when you arrive, and if not then, when we've won back Meridian.'

'Oh and lad, what's your name?'

'Ashton.'

Ashton left him, then when he'd finished his pipe he went outside to where his cronies were playing chess in the sunlight. They looked up surprised, 'we thought you was going to rest a while guvna, can't you sleep?'

'Well, that's hardly possible when you let boys in to harass me, is it now men?'

'Boys guvna? We haven't seen no one.'

The governor looked confused, then looked out to the harbour, no ship he didn't know, no ship was leaving. Strange, how perplexing, but he dare not say anything to his men or they'd think he was going a little mad, which he was, possibly.

'Pick up your legs men, we're going to Meridian, all ships ready manned, all cannons full stocked, bring your pistols and muskets and sabres and swords, well, come on!' he yelled, 'I just want to go there, set off a few pops, scare off Calegra's army then be back tomorrow before the sun drops.'

It took them the afternoon to prepare, then they were sailing off as the evening set.

Ashton ran down to the quiet side of the island where Dew waited in hiding with the plane, climbed back in and they were off once again.

This time the landing was a simple thing, Dew let the plane down slowly and gently till it touched the ocean. They neared the Avaeste with the crew leaning over the edge cheering at their return. They helped Dew and Ashton back on board and hauled in the golden plane.

Queen Annabella's eyes implored him to speak to her of the outcome of his talks.

'Success your majesty, Vasco Renardo is going to come to your aid. He is readying his men as we speak.'

She gasped and her face showed such relief and happiness, Ashton was glad of the deal he had made, Meridian's freedom and Anna Bien's happiness were worth much more than his ownership of the Avaeste.

'I will wait until he arrives before I take any action, it will take him a few hours to get here, I suggest you get some sleep while you can your majesty, please, use my cabin.'

'Thankyou.'

'And your majesty,' Ashton added.

'Yes?'

'I'm sure Kielan is safe.'

'Thankyou Ashton,' she said, then closed herself in his cabin.

Ashton sat down in the shade beside the stairs, Carter, Berens, all of them were there.

'Feels so empty don't it, without little Tom's endless chatter,' one of the men said.

'It's too quiet,' another agreed.

'The cannons have stopped,' Ashton said, 'listen.'

Jennings had the telescope out and was looking across to the Meridian harbour, 'Can't see what's happening.'

'Get some rest men, there'll be plenty to do tonight.'

Eventually the men dispersed to their own musings, some went below out of the sun and played cards or other games, some read, some sharpened their swords. The lieutenants came and went, keeping a watch on the goings on over in the harbour, watching to see if they could make out the state of things.

Morris sat down by the captain in the shade and scratched his head. Every so often he'd catch a fly out of the air and eat it, thinking between times of what to say to the captain, how to best help him through this time. But Morris could think of nothing and so just kept sitting beside him and catching flies. It was handy having a swamp monster around when there were flies, Ashton thought.

The breeze began to cool as the day wore on, it would have been a most pleasant day without the terrible things that had and were still going on.

Chapter 10:
AGAINST THE TRAITOROUS TURNCOAT AND THE TYRANT

Harrick called down from where he sat high up the mast, 'Ships coming in, big ones, can't see their flags yet.'

'Lieutenant Phillips, your glass,' Ashton asked, standing and leaning against the side railing. 'Thankyou,' he took it, analysed what he saw and then handed it back.

'Captain, what is it?' Phillips asked, he saw immediately something was wrong, the captain's face was ghostly white, his hands shaking though he tried to control them.

Men were coming back on deck after hearing Harrick's call, the queen too showed herself, smiling, 'Governor Renardo! He has come!'

Ashton shook his head, 'No, those ships don't belong to Vasco, nor any aligned to him.'

Annabella took Phillips' glass and put her eye to it, they were close enough now for her to just make out.

'Calegra Camba Descada!' the queen drew in her breath quickly, 'with his whole fleet! Rebuilt! Why is he doing this?'

Even with Renardo's help, there's little hope now, Ashton thought. This army, this fleet, was immense and it would be well equipped. At least Meridian was much more capable of defence than Ile de Novo had been. He had never even seen a gun before that day, never had seen gunpowder, cannons, explosions. Never had seen great galleons fighting each other till they were ruined.

Why had they fought over his homeland? When their dead fell to the earth and the ships sank burning into the land. What did Calegra have against his people, the least of his enemies, were they just easy? Now Calegra was here after one of the greatest of his enemies.

'Ashton!' Anna Bien gasped, 'Edward's ship!'

'What?! Are you sure?' he took back the glass, in the fading light it was getting harder to make out, but there could be no mistaking the trim topsail schooner that was captained by Frederick Gifford on Edward's behalf. Edward preferred to let that capable man do the captaining and just be Prince Edward as always while he was on board. But why were they here? They were flying the flag of St

Amalric and of Calegra together, but that couldn't be right, they must have been captured.

'Who's Edward?' Phillips asked as Ashton handed the telescope back.

'My brother,' Ashton replied, 'first in line to be king, they must have been captured on the way back to Aeloran. Call the men together Phillips, I can't wait for the pirate any longer. We have to go in.'

'But Ashton!' the queen exclaimed, Phillips too and all who heard, it was an insane proposition when one looked out at the scene as it sat now before them.

There was The Everlast, the first galleon, now returning with Marax and his men, however many more men he had smuggled ashore, plus those men, having overtaken part of the mountain the enemy wouldn't have to look out for the cannon fire from the hillside. And now of course there was the fleet of Calegra, his ship, two other frigates plus another galleon, and multiple smaller ships, including Edwards's schooner. It was also getting darker by the minute. There was in their favour the three large vessels of Meridian, but they had been damaged from the fire of the cannons and it could not be seen what state they were in, but that they had ceased chasing Marax and now sat between this fleet and the stretch of water before the range of the cannons.

'We can use the darkness,' Ashton explained, 'that's probably what they're planning, so while they're doing whatever they've planned we can sneak up and find out what's going on. As soon as the light has gone from the sky I want no light to be seen on this ship, I want nothing shiny or reflective to be on deck. If your buttons are too bright turn your jacket inside out. Do you understand lieutenants?'

'Aye captain,' was the shout.

He could see the worry and doubt in their eyes, 'You have trusted me this far,' he sincerely added, 'I would like to say there is no reason not to trust me tonight, but the truth is I don't know what will happen, there are too many factors at play for me to see the best way to go on. If you don't want to do this I give you leave to stay here on this quiet island.'

'We're going with you, like we've said before.'

'If you come, you must come prepared to give your all, for I will demand it of you.'

'I am prepared,' Carter said, stepping forward.

'And I,' said Berens, then Phillips and Jennings, Banks followed them, then the rest of the crew, it goes without saying the same decision was made by Morris and Dew.

'But what is your plan?' asked the queen.

'You cannot stay on board the Avaeste any longer your majesty, for I do not know what we will face.'

'No, I will stay, I must.'

'This is my ship your majesty and she is not the property of Meridian, I ask that you let me do what I can to assist your kingdom and your son, that includes going now to this island where you will be safe away from the battles that will take place.'

'But Ashton, how can you?' she begged him as two of his men followed his direction and ushered her to the little boat to be rowed ashore.

'It is for you.'

'You would leave me here alone while you go fighting for my country!?'

'Yes.'

And he did, but not quite alone. He sent Santee to stay with her and protect her.

'He sent a sprite to look after me!?' Annabella asked in surprise as the sound of the oars died into the night.

'Oh yes, and keep you company,' Santee replied, 'but if the boy was here he'd tell you, I'm no ordinary sprite.'

'He's just a boy, what can he do?' Annabella sighed, 'what can he do against all this!'

'You'd be surprised,' Santee replied, 'he's no ordinary boy.'

'No, I know, but still.'

'And he is very proud. And stubborn sometimes,' Santee sighed, 'but very, very kind.'

'Just like all Novanian's I ever met of his type, but being alone now and untrained his traits are less refined.'

'Novanian?'

'Oh, I'm sorry, I thought you would have known, if he has not told you, you must not let on you know,' the queen explained, 'oh I did not mean to betray him, but you did say he was no ordinary boy and I assumed you knew.'

'What? I don't know what is Novanian? It means nothing to me.'

'Well then,' the queen said relieved, 'it doesn't matter then does it. Please, Santee will you help me? I must get back to Meridian, I must find my son.'

'Well,' mused the sprite with a cheeky little grin, 'he didn't say we had to stay here, so I guess, if we can find a way, we can go to Meridian.'

The gentle wind caught the sails of the Avaeste and the men whispered commands as they ran over the deck, and silently, so silently she made her way to the convoy of great ships, a tiny little craft into the enemy fleet. The moon was out but slightly disguised by a thickening cloud that moved across the sky and so for the moment the little ship went unnoticed by those invading.

Before they were spotted a few of the crew had made their way on board the Concordor, that is, Edward St Amalric's schooner. Ashton was amongst them of course, and they snuck along the deck, around the empty cabin, then down the hatch and below, but then in the darkness a cold metal object met Ashton's face, someone held a pistol to his forehead then he heard the sound of a latch being drawn into place.

'Now what's this?' said the voice, Ashton couldn't see who it was, as it was so much blacker down here than it was up above, but the voice was so familiar, familiar yes, like no one else but that brother of his, Edward!

'Edward?! It's me, it's Ashton,' the young prince whispered, he was astounded at this meeting but very happy indeed that it was his brother and not an enemy. Prince Edward smiled then lowered his gun.

'What?! Someone a light!' the command was given, a lantern lit and held aloft. 'Ashton! I can't think what you're doing here or how it is you came to be, but now I see - you it is!' he replied laughing, but slightly angry, maybe? Still he embraced his adopted brother warmly.

'What are you doing here?' Ashton went on, 'the queen told me you were on your way home a week since, across the Ether Marine?'

'Aye, well I was.'

'I have the Avaeste very close by,' Ashton informed him in excited voice.

'The Avaeste?'

'A beautiful little ship. Edward, so much has happened since I saw you last, but never mind I'll tell you all later, right now I've twenty men ready to fight, I can help you take The Everlast and free the queen's guard, and then, well, isn't this meeting a blessed chance, together we might –'

'Take The Everlast?' Edward laughed, 'The Everlast!' he said again. 'Do you think I'm daft?'

'Well, what are you doing here otherwise, but to turn and take Marax by surprise, with your men and mine that's fifty of us surely we can put up a good fight, and how were you captured Edward? How did you escape?'

'Captured?' he laughed again, 'I was never captured by any means, I'm here fighting with Marax against the queen!'

'What? Edward, I don't understand,' Ashton said shaken, 'you mean you're sailing in Calegra's fleet?'

'Aye, I am.'

'But Edward, Meridian is our ally, has not the queen always been a friend of our father, the king.'

'No Ashton, you are mistaken,' Prince Edward informed him, 'Queen Annabella is not as she seems, she may be beautiful and gracious and give us the honour we are due as sons of the king, but-'

'She aided Aeloran and others against this man,' Ashton defended, 'her armies fought alongside ours in the recent wars, and the wars before-'

'That may be, but what does she do now, for our father at his most desperate hour? Ha! She sends her best wishes, gifts of spices, and gifts of books and fabric; what does a dying king need of those, I ask? When I am king, Ashton, and that will be soon, I want alongside me powerful friends, and that's what I do. I am forging such an alliance with Calegra, he is more powerful an ally than Meridian could ever be.'

'But at what expense? Edward you deal with very bad men!'

'No expense, no, already there are benefits, you couldn't understand little brother, but here! Some ally is Annabella Bien, where was Meridian when the outer realms where falling? How can she sleep, how can she call our father her friend.'

Though Ashton's heart bled, for Novania lay in the outer realms, he defended the queen, 'No Edward, that's not how it was, you know it! I came to these islands searching for a cure, she has done everything to aid me, everything she could, and I was making some progress before the Everlast turned up.'

'Searching? Progress? What cure?!'

'Aye, for the flower of a silvertip grass, they make the cure from it apparently, somehow, but it's rarer than rare and not even her botanist nor her cartographer could tell me exactly where it might grow, if indeed it exists, we have searched and searched and were going through what we had found when-'

'Of course she would send you on wild goose hunt.'

'No Edward, it wasn't like that.'

'Wasn't it?'

Argue and argue they would have done about the merits or demerits of the queen of Meridian, but at that moment was the sound of a cannon, followed by a crack of timber of a ship quite near them.

'General Angaston must have retaken some guns!' Ashton said excitedly, 'I wonder which was hit, Calegra's Descalabro, the Zamparda, or the Everlast?'

'They were not from the shore defences Ashton,' Edward observed, 'that shot came from behind us, from another ship, I'm sure of it.'

'Vasco Renardo, he's finally come!'

'The pirate?!'

'The governor.'

'One and the same. What has any of this to do with him?'

'There's no time to explain,' Ashton stood bravely and held his sword high, 'we're wasting time here like this, I'm still for the queen,

Edward despite all you say, so either fight with me or get out of my way!'

Ashton's men waited for a sign from him, eyeing Edward's crew up as they eyed back in return. Swords were ready and muscles were tensed, eyes searching the dark in case the other moved first. Edward would not move, Ashton stepped closer with his sword and held its shining blade forward.

Edward laughed, 'This is ridiculous, what do you expect to do with that!?'

'Brother, I'm in earnest,' young Ashton said.

'As am I Ashton, put down your weapons, we have you surrounded. I don't want to have to fight you brother, not like this.'

Ashton turned his eyes and gathered, that yes, Edward spoke true – his men were surrounding the few Avaeste crew who'd boarded with him onto Edward's schooner, and they'd guns too. So the young captain put down his sword, and one by one his men sadly followed.

Meanwhile, Queen Annabella and Santee the sprite had walked across to the other side of the small isle where Captain Ashton had left them to be safe for the while. And there in a clearing on top of a cliff was a neat little gazebo etched all around with an archaic script. It was a delicate frame, all painted with white as was most of the architecture of Meridian at this time, and all across the timber was moss and was vines, as if no one had used this place for quite a while.

'Oh! Of course!' exclaimed lady Bien, 'now I know where I am. This was once our private escape, when my Josef was still alive.' And as she said it she wanly smiled, 'Oh my Josef, that he was here now, by my side.'

'What happened to him? How did he die?' asked Santee, she was always known to be a very direct sort of sprite, but Annabella didn't mind, no, she only sighed.

'Josef went to war, like so many men, battled that tyrant, inspired our army, till he'd nothing left to give. After our small victory, and the cede, he returned to us, but though time passed he never

129

regained his strength. Then he contracted a fever, such a minor thing, a trifling thing a child could easily beat, but Josef had nothing left to fight it, no matter what we did. To think that we may have saved him, had we known of this thing of which Prince Ashton is seeking, this flower which our own physicians and scholars, and this land, have long since forgotten. But come Santee, enough reminiscing, we must make haste to find my Kielan. Come.'

The queen followed a narrow path, from beside the gazebo to the edge of the cliff, then around the side and into the rock face seemingly as she entered a cave. Santee followed as she went on and on, through the twists and turns of this long cavern. Water could be heard as the ocean moved somewhere above the path were she trod and Santee flew.

'Where does this lead' Santee whispered, as if there were things in the unknown ahead that would hear her.

'Back to Meridian,' answered the queen. 'I might need your help Santee, are you a sprite that can do disguises?'

'Why yes, that I am.'

'Good, then may I kindly request your assistance.'

'I will gladly give it,' she said, 'but only, well, the thing is,' Santee confessed, 'I'm not yet that good at it. You see I can make goblins look like men and swamp monsters look like anything, and I can even turn them back, but, well, the last time I tried Ashton – well, let's just say he won't let me do it again, well, he did, but that was only to turn him back.'

'But Ashton is different,' Annabella informed, 'you will have no trouble with me, I am certain.'

'Oh, but if I make a mistake!'

'Don't you worry now dear Santee, I'm sure you can do it.'

Captain Ashton sat in the dark, along with his men; all of them had been taken across to the Everlast and locked up in the very same cell as the queen's guards. They shook the iron grate above their heads, they cursed at Edward's men but soon they were alone in the gloom and thick air below deck.

The young captain had his head in his hands, he really could not make any sense of it; it wasn't like Edward at all to be so quick to judge, so quick to leave loyalties, to so heavily begrudge. No it wasn't like Edward at all to be rash, he was the eldest son after all, he knew the kind of man Calegra was, he had seen the outcomes of his wars. Oh, could it be that he never really knew Edward at all?

'Right then men,' Ashton stood up with determination, 'what are we doing lounging down here when we're supposed to be out there saving Meridian! Berens, give me your leg.'

'My leg Cap?'

'Aye sir, your leg, stand you here. I wish to take a look and see what I can.'

'Pitch dark out there sir, I'd say. Just like it is in here,' Berens said as Ashton stood on his leg and peered out through the corner of the grating. He was indeed correct, the outlook and predicament was very black.

'Ah,' sighed Captain Ashton, stepping down, 'ah,' he said again, not so loud. Wondering, racking his brain, for a solution to this situation, with Edward out there, Kielan lost somewhere, General Vasco Renardo on the advance, not knowing that here sat Captain and crew of the Avaeste, and back on the island the lovely young queen who must be fretting in worry, so must Santee.

There was, of course, one way to escape, for Ashton at least. He could be the Novanian he was and fly out of here, but what good would that do if still down below were stuck these fine men of his crew? He could perhaps find a way to release them but how? He must think it through, and besides which, young Ashton was afraid for this was Marax's ship, Calegra's men, and Calegra himself would be somewhere near at hand, the very man who had destroyed Ashton's home and burnt and blown to the ground everything and everyone he had known.

The men threw ideas for escape at him, none of them sane, for they had no gun powder, no charge, nor any hidden blade. But then when their ideas were almost caput, a man in the darkest of the corners spoke up. No one had noticed his presence before, but they took notice now for his voice was strong and was proud.

'Don't you worry now lads, Edward put me in here too, with a key and a pistol, at the same time as you,' then he chuckled, 'oh though I did enjoy watching you all trying to get out.'

'Who is that?' the young captain asked with a grin, 'I know that voice don't I – why it's, it's Captain Frederick!'

'Aye, it is I,' they took hands and shook, Ashton turned around to his men,

'Men, this is a good friend, Captain of The Concordor, Captain Frederick Gifford, of his majesty's fleet. How are you my friend, and what possessed you to be led into this mess?! Oh and how do you propose we get out of this?'

'Well, I am very well lad, there's much to explain, all I will say for now is that on our way home from Meridian we spotted The Everlast, Marax's ship, and wondered just what was happening with it, for from its course we assumed it must be heading this way but we steered well clear of it. Then further on we sighted the rest of Calegra's fleet, and we noted their bearing, and what do you think?'

'They were heading here too.'

'Aye, so Prince Edward, bless him, takes his courage in hand he desires me to take us on a course that will force us and them to meet. Then when we do he boldly goes aboard, after receiving an invitation from the curious warlord, taking me with him to tea, shivering in my boots, surrounded by those thuggish sailors and Descada's cohorts.

'I did not think we would ever get aboard, but now then - who wouldn't want to meet the eldest son of King Mathis, who will inherit the crown, and sound him out? For Calegra had never met any of you, and that's just what he did do, he sounded Edward through and through. Oh and I tell you never did Edward put on such a show, from the moment we boarded he wasn't the Edward we know, he was arrogant and pompous and callous, and he utterly fooled Descada into thinking he was impatient to be king, impatient for the power and keen to make new friends. And so, that's how we find ourselves here, 'helping' Calegra against Meridian. So don't you worry Prince Ashton, Edward has many plans, and I, dear friends, have a way out.'

With that Captain Frederick produced a key from his pocket and put up his hand, 'But before we go out there fellows, I'll tell you the plan.'

Chapter 11

IT SMELLS OF ASPEN
& SOUNDS LIKE GUNFIRE

Far from what young Ashton expected Queen Annabella was not in a fret, but was working as fast and as fiercely as she could to get back to Meridian and find her young son. Santee on the other hand was fretting a lot, for back down now the queen would not, and so the little sprite had bowed to her will and at her wish caused Queen Annabella to look much older, and far less stylish. Yes, no one would recognise the bent old lady, with hairs growing from the warts on her chin, gnarled fingers bent around a short walking stick, old tattered clothes and an unravelling shawl wrapped around her shoulders and her grey hair. No, no one would want to look at her, let alone think that this old woman was indeed the queen.

'You did it Santee!' old Anna smiled, much pleased, but Santee shivered to think that she had done this, and shook to think of the outcome if she could not change the queen back. So she slunk into one of old Anna's pockets and there she sat as Anna kept on, down the hidden track back to Meridian.

Eventually they came to the opening, low in a cove behind a deserted cliff, but not many a pace did they have to continue before they came to the rows of fishermen's homes. Then down the empty streets they went on and on, all the time in the distance the sound of the ships cannons. The further they went the higher the ground, the closer they came to the heart of her beloved town.

They passed groups of soldiers, many of whom stopped her and told her to get herself home, for this was not a night for any to roam outside, but she just agreed and kept on till she reached the home of her maid, well, of her maid's mother that is, for the maid herself had a room in the palace.

Anna now knocked on the weathered wooden door, soon there came a hullo from within, a clunk of a lock, a creak of the hinges and an inch opened up, 'Who are you there, and what do you want?'

The woman inside was an kindly woman too and when she saw old Anna she softened, 'Oh, how can I help you?'

'I know it is very late in the night, but I heard the news from the palace,' old Anna croaked, 'I was concerned for your daughter, has she come home?'

And though the lady inside couldn't quite say if she remembered this old woman or nay, but she seemed familiar, so she was invited inside.

'My daughter is here,' the lady confessed, 'oh she is so distraught, she is oh so distressed, they sent her home after what happened, and what is happening, but come in, have a seat. Can I get you anything?'

'No, no, I'm quite alright, or perhaps a warm tea if you're having one dear.'

While the mother busied to make the tea, Anna spotted the maid, she sat shivering by the empty fire, staring at it with her tear stained eyes.

'Come child, what happened now?' old Anna asked, with concern on her brow.

The maid sniffed her nose and wiped her eyes, it was all she could do to stop herself from a new burst of crying, but she answered old Anna, and that most sincerely, in a torrent of words that came flowing out, that it was all of a suddenly, all of an instant the men came upon her and forced Kielan from her, when she went to scream it was all she knew of it, and then when she woke the dear queen was gone, taken by their enemies along with her son, and now, they had heard, parts of Meridian were overrun. Oh if she could have known what was to come and oh if only she could have saved Kielan!

'Child,' said Anna, 'oh child it was not your fault, don't be distressed, we will make sure some good comes out of all this. But tell me, did you hear, did you perchance catch what any of them said, these soldiers of Calegra disguised as good men?'

'No, there was nothing, nothing at all, as I told the general.'

'No clue to where they might take her young son – for I myself have heard that the queen has been saved, but still Kielan has not been found.'

'Oh saved! Please that be true, and pray the same soon for Kielan too! But no clue did I see, oh but there was one particularly horrible man that the others let in, with horrible clothes, and a horrible grin, strange though – he smelt like aspen.'

'Aspen?'

'Yes!' the maid gasped excited as she saw the clue that she'd missed, 'like that crisp smell of the forest on Monte Caliche.'

'Or the woods behind the palace where the sanctuary sits!' old Anna put in.

'Yes, yes that's it!' clapped the maid.

'Ah,' Anna smiled as she stood up slowly to go.

'You should find the palace guards and let them know,' her mother put in.

'Yes,' said the maid, 'yes I should indeed, dear Kielan's life could depend upon it!' and so the young thing grabbed her coat and ran out the door, in her ears the yells of her mother not to do anything foolish, but to keep herself safe and well out of trouble.

'Well, I best be off too,' Anna excused, 'thankyou for the tea, you've such a good daughter.'

'I thankyou too, without your questions she might never have thought about it like that.'

'I will see you later now.'

'Yes, yes, see you.'

And so old Anna continued her walk through the streets, on and up towards the sanctuary, while the mother of her maid was left to wonder just who was that old lady that was oh so familiar, surely she must be the mother of one of the neighbours.

'Oh my heart is restless within me Santee,' Anna whispered as she went, 'I am much afraid for my son, much afraid, I can't help it; though I don't believe for a moment that they will have harmed him.'

'No indeed, he will just be their insurance.'

'But he is so young Santee, and I have been gone so long, and no babe young as he should remain away from his mother.'

'No indeed, I'm sure he won't be for much longer, we'll soon have him back.'

'Yes we will,' she determined, and when Anna made her mind up, well, that was that.

Now the governor pirate, the infamous Vasco Renardo, came in suddenly with three of his ships, over the horizon and directly in as soon as the sky had become darker than dark, and behind those three great ships several smaller vessels came, all eager to have this over as quickly as it had got underway.

They came straight and begun working the guns, his uproarious men laughing and jeering as they let out the pops. Soon all Calegra's fleet had felt some of the blasts, not that they didn't hit back, but as they were unprepared they didn't hit back fast. They were not expecting this pirate king to come to the aid of those neighbouring, and they hadn't counted on one young boy with the courage of a knight hidden inside. But nor did Renardo think that he was, in all this fight, firing at the ship that Ashton was on! But that was the case, The Everlast shuddered, they all felt it shake, they all felt the splintering, sickening quake, and as they ran to make their escape they all felt the second and third shots down her face. And then, and then, when they were almost to the point where they could descend to the long boats waiting alongside, who but Carramar von Marax himself should sneak around a corner and wish to bid them goodbye, along with many of his men, so the crew of the Avaeste along with this Captain Frederick and the guards of Annabella Bien, found themselves at gunpoint again.

The lot of them stopped, and though they had re-armed themselves with their swords and their guns, and could have battled right then, they were stunned by the sudden sight of this daunting one who now aimed at Ashton direct and for sure with the trigger half pulled, the bullet so ready to come.

But then what should occur but another fair blast, straight from Vasco's proud ship to The Everlast's main mast. With the tremor of agony the timbers received Marax lost his balance, so the good men of Althorn, Captain's Ashton and Frederick, were at last able to open arms with the enemy.

To Ashton's relief Frederick stood up to Marax, after all he had the most experience, Ashton should have fallen straight away he was sure, under the blows of the superior soldier, for even Frederick was finding it hard to maintain his defence against this man of Calegra's. So though the force with Ashton was only small they stood up and fought, and they fought well, but the men of this Calegra's general, this Marax, were more than they and well versed in the worst fighting methods, and the bigger battle raged around them still, this unannounced war, these ships all together blasting still at each other, the men on opposing ships trading bullets and insults, the enemy on shore making it hard for Angaston to know how to go on.

What were they aiming to do? From which way were they coming? He was doing his best but only morning would tell if his best had been enough to save their beloved Meridian. The moon had shown him more ships in the bay, some that had come to Meridian's aid, firing across at this bold enemy, but none could tell yet just who was winning this multi-faceted fray.

And just as the men of the Avaeste faltered, as they fought with all courage against these men of von Marax, men from Renardo's vessel, El Torero, made it across and joined in the tussle with joyous curses and their strong, ready muscle.

'I believe we're friends today,' one of the pirates laughed as he saw Banks in the fray, and with much surprise Banks saw it was one of the ones that had jailed him, days ago on the Atoll of Arinn.

'Of that I am glad,' Banks laughed, 'let's keep it that way.'

*

Mathis St Amalric, King of the Isle of Aeloran and surrounding Aethermarinus, lay still and calm between the finest linen sheets.

He was not an old man, he should have been hale and strong, not lying here on his deathbed as he was. His eyes were still bright, when the energy came enough for a thought to cause him to open them, however slight.

'Where are my sons?' he would ask those that waited on him, those that watched him around the clock, waiting by to offer any little service that the dying king could possibly want. 'Where is Edward? Where is Lucas, Simon, Ambrose? where is Marcus, Sebastian and Phillip?'

'Some are nearby sire,' they would answer, 'others have gone in separate ways across the known world to find a cure for you.'

'And Ashton? Where is my Ashton?' he would whisper with what voice he had left.

They would shake their heads, they could not say, none quite knew just where he lay, and they would hope and wait for the king to sleep again, and pray for all the sons to return before it was too late.

*

Now old Anna, with her arched back, trembling hand on her walking stick, and that old age grimace, made it by and by up the way towards the sanctuary in the woods behind the palace, to that hill which smelled of aspen, where she hoped that she would find her dear baby Kielan.

It took quite some time to make the way, with old legs and an old body, and Santee sitting on Annabella's shoulder was begging to change back the queen to herself or some other being that would make the way faster, but Anna was certain, and Anna was wise, she might go a little slowly but she could go far in this disguise, for though they passed many a soldier, and many a person running helter skelter, barely a one cared to stop her or mind her for what danger was an old woman? And when she passed those who stopped and begged her to find some shelter, she just nodded and went on and they ran off lightly cursing that stupid old woman, she'd get herself killed but they had to keep going. And so it was that Anna made the top, it was quiet up here out the way of the shore, and the sight of the sea, up from the lower hills where the fight continued, and she hurried on now to the high little hall, the white wooden frame could be easily seen, as filtering now through the trees was the first grey light of dawn.

Anna snuck closer, and with Santee peered through the low bushes and around the tall trees, and little by little they neared. Then, oh then, their suspicions were confirmed, the dear little hall was surrounded by the enemy's men, they'd rifles in their hands and a sharp look in their eye – oh how would they get in! It was just as she feared.

'Santee,' the queen said, 'I don't suppose you could transfigure those men?'

'What a suggestion!' Santee huffed, much horrified, 'now I am a good sprite Queen Annabella, I understand the situation is dire but it goes against my principles to change a person against their will. Why, in sprite law it's downright illegal.'

'Even in war?'

'In war especially so!'

'Oh,' said the queen, she hadn't realised it was such a sensitive issue.

'But,' Santee said, 'I suppose the case is peculiar, I might just be able to do something other.'

Do something other? What did she mean? What would she do? The queen thought as Santee sped off through the trees.

Santee picked a tired looking fellow that was one of two guarding the entrance to the little white hall, and she snuck very close without being seen and she said to the man, 'Hm, now, how nice would it be to be a soldier here, calm and quiet most of the time, and such a nice island.'

'It would be something wouldn't it,' the man said, not hearing it was a sprite talking but the voice of his friend.

The other soldier said, 'What?'

'To be a soldier here, would be nice.'

'I suppose.'

'Isn't that what you just said?'

'What?'

'About the peace and quiet. I'd like to be a solider here any day, just think of the mess we'd be in if we were in the troop down in the bay. And you know when we got here I thought the people of Meridian were quite nice, and friendly like.'

Santee chuckled, her work had begun, and when the other soldier looked back at his friend he raised his rifle, and the words on his lips couldn't quite come out, he was indeed speechless, not to say startled.

'What?' said his friend.

'You're, well look!'

'What?' said the soldier, utterly bewildered, then he saw what his friend saw, that something had changed, no longer was his uniform that of Calegra's but with all of the glory of a proud soldier of Meridian, his uniform now shone with bright colour and gleamed.

'Traitor!' said the other.

'No I never was!' but at this strange confrontation the friend also raised his gun, 'I didn't put this on, believe me I don't know how this happened!'

'What, have you been a spy all along?'

'No! I never!'

'I called you a friend!'

'No, you know me – I wouldn't do this!'

'I know you are a liar, I know you are a thief, now, tell me what's to stop you doing something like this?'

'I wouldn't, and if I did, showing you now would be insane wouldn't it?'

'Aye, I've always thought you a little daft to begin with,' said the other, tapping his head.

Then from the commotion other men came, other soldiers of Calegra to this one's aid, but by the time they had got there another few had agreed, from Santee's schemes, one thought it would be nice to be an officer, and the other a chef, and another admitted that to be a violinist was always his wish.

So when they all appeared at the front of the hall, what a strange sight for them all. At first they went to apprehend this one soldier, the soldier of Calegra wearing Meridian's colours, but then they all faltered, as one saw his gun, well, that it was not a gun but a rather large soup ladle, and the others thought there was another traitor, that one who'd longed to be officer, he too was now wearing Meridian's attire, and the violinist, well, he couldn't really do anything but wave wildly at the others with his bow and his instrument.

Soon they all dropped everything and ran from the place, saying it was haunted and cursed, and there was nothing on earth could make them stay. So they ran on and as they did they passed a little old lady who grinned at them so wryly and with such a devious eye they thought maybe she was a wicked one and maybe she was behind it so they were jolted more and ran with all speed to leave this forest and make for the city and then for the shore and back to their ships, throwing off this strange clothing as they did.

'You were brilliant Santee,' old Anna chuckled as the little sprite fell onto her shoulder.

'It was funny wasn't it?'

'It was indeed.'

'Would I could do more,' Santee sighed, 'would I could end this war, but I'm afraid small forays are the limit of my ability, more than that and I would whittle myself away and there would be nothing left of me.'

'No, you did well dear Santee, I am very proud of you. Now, let us see if there are more of them inside, and let us see if it is that here they hold my babe.'

Boldly old Anna went straight up the three steps of the little white hall that sat in the woods and she pushed the doors open and walked straight in.

Soft light came through the tall windows and in through the door, showing the dusty interior unmoved, no one could be seen, nothing but emptiness, and at once beloved Annabella's heart sank. 'Oh Santee, do turn me back!' she said, she could bear it no longer, and Santee did as she said.

And beautiful and herself once more the queen sank to the bench, tears on her cheeks and woe in her eyes. She had been so certain, she had been so sure, but the hall was so empty, so untouched inside.

'Oh Josef!' she cried to her departed king, 'oh Josef, you would know what to do, you would know where to look, oh how I have failed! Oh how to go on!' For a moment she despaired, she let herself cry, she let herself sit for a while and regather her mind. Then she stood, wiped her face and smoothed out her dress, then,

'Wait, what was that?' Santee said.

They waited more and listened, and then it came again, that low little whimper, that quiet little bang.

At once Annabella hurried to the other end of the hall, which it seems now they had not thoroughly explored, and she threw off the covers of the sleeping furniture, off the tables and chairs and the big old lectern, and there in the hollow under the stand was her waking baby and a young wet-nurse, all bound and gagged, but thankfully not hurt.

Annabella stood the young woman up and undid her bonds, embraced her as she stammered explanations and apologies to the queen, but the queen's eyes just overflowed with the happiest of tears, 'Oh no dear girl, I know you were forced into it, how can I thankyou, oh with all my heart I thank you for looking after my Kielan.'

Kielan even then, began to cry properly, he must know those sweet tones of his mother's voice, and so Annabella took him out and at once sat down with him.

'I missed you too,' she said, and Santee sighed at the sight, no wonder they all call her Annabella the Beloved.

*

By this time the general, Angaston that is, first in command of her majesty's men, had pushed back the enemy down to the sea, he'd retaken the cannons, retaken the town, retaken the shore and now Calegra's men were swimming back out to their ships, but they were not really sure if that was such a good idea, for it seems the ships in Calegra's fleet were now heading away, heading so fast it could be assumed they had forgotten the brave men who had done the hard work on shore, they wouldn't just leave them would they? Oh but they did, yes, with the arrival of the pirate-governor Renardo, and with the event of Angaston retaking the guns, Calegra's fleet fled; to stay would be certain defeat, and there was no way Descada would accept that outcome.

But one great ship of Calegra's remained, The Everlast sat swaying gently on the rise and fall of the sea. She was in a bad way, splintered and smoky, but she still told of the great ship she was and could be. And on her boards, across her deck, a weary, wounded group remained, a mottled crew it was indeed, pirates and sailors all together, lying where they could, swords still in hand, half asleep from their weariness but smiling, as victory was theirs.

The young captain leaned upon her rails, looking across the bay, at this chance fleet that had come, those ships of Meridian, of the Atoll of Arinn, The Everlast, The Concordor and The Avaeste, all together under this soaking sun. He gazed at his Avaeste, the dear little ship, half the crew still there now, wondering what to do. Then he looked across to El Torero, the pirate-governor's ship, and there Renardo waved to him as he smoked a pipe in the early morning.

'My thanks Renardo,' Ashton called, then pointed to his fair ship, 'a bargain is a bargain friend.'

Vasco blew out a circle of smoke and grinned, 'Yes, a bargain is a bargain, but no hurry my young capitan, I give you time to collect your things and say your goodbye, I'll collect my due this afternoon if you don't mind.'

Ashton nodded, then sat in the shade and was still for a moment, collecting himself and waiting for his men to wake up, wondering how he was going to proceed with a crew but no ship and all the things before him he still had to do. And he wondered as he sat of his brother Edward, his schooner was still there, but where was he? and how had faired Annabella Bien and what had become of baby Kielan? He must get back to the island at once and see just how the queen and Santee were going.

So he raised his weary body and rallied his men, and soon they had found a long boat and were away, back across to the Avaeste, and back to their friends who waited there, desperate for news of them, and though he thought he should, he couldn't quite tell them yet that this may be the last time they embarked however much he desperately wished it wasn't.

The lookout Harrick called, 'It's the captain!' and soon all were there, ready to help the crew back on board, asking for the stories of just what went on and how they all had faired. The captain gave orders to make for the place they had left Annabella just last night, then he went to his cabin and proceeded to pack every little thing that was his from his bookshelf, his chests and his desk.

Morris watched him curiously, but said not a word, seeing the sorrow and worry that hung on the young captain's forehead, but Morris followed his example and put everything that he owned into the little box where he slept then tied a belt around it, so when the time came to do whatever Ashton planned, he would be ready for it, yes, he would pick his bed up and carry it.

They reached the little isle, but no one could be seen, no sight of Santee and certainly none of the queen, so Ashton wondered, maybe she had found another way to get from here, perhaps signalled a

143

passing boat to take her back to Meridian. It was the next place he wished to go in any case, so he would see if she were there.

So they came in to the beautiful bay, where the green hills rolled down to the pebbled waves, but it was a sad arrival for it was grim, with so many men still here, wounded from their part in the fray. Many were surprised just how much damage was done to this fair city, in just one night, by Calegra's men. But Ashton was surprised things lay as they did, that most homes still stood, though some were in ashes, it was a much better outcome than he had expected, having seen the power of Calegra before, and his methods. And now as they rowed once more into shore, men of Meridian greeted them with cheers and with warmth, for they had stayed to aid Meridian though the fight wasn't theirs, and in so doing earned further friendship and respect.

'And what of your queen?' Ashton quickly asked, 'has anyone heard, and what of Kielan, has he been found?'

And so they told him the remarkable news, Annabella was safe and with babe in the royal residence. Even as they stood a soldier rode up, the queen's sign on his sleeve, and a message quite urgent, 'Prince Ashton, if you will, the queen requests your company, along with that of the governor of Arinn and all your men, to dine with her in informal luncheon, today, even at noon or as soon as you can.'

'I accept,' Ashton said, and his men were excited, lunch with the queen of this fair island again! What privileged men they to dine with royalty, to fight for a worthy cause, and though Banks still wondered if they would be rewarded he was still quite happy with the reward his own heart had accorded, the pride and the happiness that swelled within as he followed this boy captain, who all now knew, was the son of a king.

Even before they reached the palace steps, Tom Needle ran down and embraced the captain.

'Oh sir! I knew you could do it! What did I say, I said to old Bartle, Henry the botanist that is, I said Old Bartle you know what I think, I don't think that this Calegra man has a chance, not with my captain, I said.'

They all laughed and cheered and Ashton was too weary to do more than shake his head, and say quietly, 'It wasn't me Tom.'

'Oh but it was!' said a strong voice, though a tired one, and Prince Ashton looked up to see General Angaston.

'From what I have heard,' the general continued, 'it was you who informed Vasco Renardo, it was you who took your men and rescued our queen, it was you who returned and engaged them in hand to hand battle on ship.'

'A small part,' Ashton replied as he looked at those assembled here, the queen's soldiers, the palace attendants, Angaston, officers, Renardo! Edward! Annabella and Kielan!

Oh, how his heart overwhelmed him!

'Come,' Annabella said, 'I would speak with you before we dine with our brave men.'

Chapter 12:
BUT THERE'S A HEART OF HAPPINESS AND TROUBLE

Once more Ashton found himself in close discourse with this heart-seeing queen. She bade him to a room that overlooked the sea, white windows opening to the fresh, fresh breeze, tinted with the sweet scent of blushing wildflowers and heath. She'd a tear in her eye, Ashton now observed, a joyful tear, she said and brushed it away. She still held Kielan, sleeping with his head on her shoulder, then she sat and begged Ashton to do the same.

'I wanted to thankyou in person, sincerely dear Ashton, with all the heart I possess I am grateful to you. Angaston tells me it was you first had suspicions, you first ready to act, and I truly thankyou.'

Ashton didn't know what to say.

'Edward tells us you even stood up to him!'

The smallest smile began in the corner of the young captain's lips at the recollection, 'Yes, yes I did.'

'It is a brave man indeed that stands up to family for what he believes,' Annabella said and was going to ask what was this other thing? this sadness that consumed him now when all the rest were joyful in this victory. What was this sacrifice Ashton had made to save Meridian? She was going to ask, but decided now to wait, for she could see he would not say, so she just let it be for now, she would discover what it was some other way.

'But,' Ashton asked, 'one thing I don't understand, I had thought Calegra more powerful than this, I considered him come intent to do what he did to us on Novania, and yet, he did not.'

'No, when last your father fought him, he took that power away, so Calegra can never do what he did to Ile de Novo and those other isles again, your father destroyed those weapons of the tyrant that caused so much destruction, he destroyed them and the power behind them so infinitely that there is no possibility of them being made again.'

'But Calegra still fights on.'

'Yes, he still has power, as you saw here, power to deceive and trick us, power to persuade those men to serve him, and the power of doubt,' she paused and looked within Ashton's mind, adding, 'and of fear.'

Ashton turned away from Annabella's lovely face, how acute she could be in her perception!

She saw she was right, that this boy's heart, though brave, was quaked at the thought of Calegra being anywhere near.

'Ashton, if you meet him he will use it against you. If you meet him, remember your father the king. Calegra thinks he has power, and he thinks he can win, and he likes making flurries and upsetting us like this, but he has already been defeated! Even if we had been overwhelmed here, and he had overtaken Meridian, he couldn't take what's in here,' she pointed to his heart and said, 'and that's where true peace really is.'

Ashton nodded and tried to understand her words, tried to take them all in, and then as he thought he came to another thing and asked, 'my queen, what of Santee?'

'Sleeping,' Annabella said, and bent so Ashton could see his friend lying hidden in the roses that were made up in her hair. 'Though I believe she likes your pocket better, perhaps, you should take her now. Be careful Ashton, she quite wore herself out.'

With fingers so light and careful, as only a Novanian's can be, Aston took the little sprite, sleeping so soundly and placed her in his pocket ever so gently.

'Now I think we better not disappoint our people,' Annabella said, and together they walked back to the great hall where lunch was being held, and where all manner of man sat waiting to begin. Pirate, sailor, soldier, officer, captain, governor and prince all waited with much talk and laughter, but as soon as beloved Annabella appeared they were silenced. She said the words a good hostess should say and thanked them all for their service, then sat down with them and the covers were lifted.

But more the queen had in store for them, more than just a fine luncheon, she wished to give these men what they deserved, recognition that is, reward and honour. She had arranged a parade that would presently end up here, they could hear it now coming, with the pipes and the drumming, even now entering the palace. The good people of Meridian came in to the hall where they were dining, with all colour and pomp, music and dance, much waving of banners and streamers, and amongst all the various flags Ashton could see that of Aeloran gleaming, alongside that of the pirate isle, Sho'Orakai and Meridian. His heart swelled and even more it did as his men where called up, and all of them received the Silver Star of Meridian, beloved Annabella herself pinned to their tunics each one. Even old Gragan received the medal and he smiled with a teary eye saying it was the first medal he'd ever got in his life. Young Tom got one too, grinning proudly and standing as tall as he could.

'This,' she said, 'is the honour we give to our most courageous soldiers, we honour you and we honour them by awarding this to you today, for the way you stood to fight for us, as you did, when we were in need.'

Ashton's men could not quite believe this honour given, and quite often as they now sat back to dine, they would gaze at their medal and grin. They would look at each other and laughter would follow, oh it was the most happiest of moments.

To Ashton and Renardo Annabella gave the same reward, but she squeezed their hands as she did, for their parts in it all she was more thankful for than any award could convey.

Then the ceremonies were concluded, and all continued to eat the fine food that was before them. Ashton sat by Edward, silently at first, eating because it was the thing to do, not because he felt much hungry. He should have been, but what could he do, the Avaeste was so much part of him the thought of losing it made him feel quite unwell.

'I didn't know you had it in you,' Edward said at last, smiling proudly at his little adopted brother. 'You did good out there you know, to tell you the truth, better than I could do. To think we all thought you'd die within a week when father brought you home, he told us you had died already once, but he had pulled you back to life. He's done that a few times father has, he's got the touch you know. He'd be proud of you Ashton, I'm sure he would, and I am too, proud to call you my brother.'

Ashton smiled, but sadly inside, he thought Edward would not be so kind if he knew the truth, that it was he who caused his father to lie now near death himself.

Edward couldn't understand the look on Ashton's face, so he just gave him a brotherly smile and pat across the back, then got into the general conversations that were rounding round the reception.

Ashton slipped away when no one was taking notice, leaving the palace and climbing up the rocks to a spot on the high hill that was deserted and silent. The wind was precious here, like wind out on the sea, and it caressed the prince's cheeks with tender fingers, it filled his lungs with hope, his mind with ease. He relaxed at last and leaned back, then he heard a little cough, a little shiver in his pocket. Then the head of Santee peering up at him appeared.

She smiled when she saw his face. 'I know you,' she said, 'I thought this smelt like your pocket and it is!'

She flew up and hugged his neck. 'Don't you leave me again boy,' she almost cried, to Ashton's surprise, 'best boy I have ever met.'

She sat on his shoulder and leaned on his neck. Then sighed, 'Can we go back to the Avaeste?'

Ashton rubbed his nose and turned his face away. What could he say to Santee, or to the men – what could he say?

'I ah, I am not captain of the Avaeste anymore.'

'What! I don't understand?'

'All that remains is for us to remove our belongings and our stores, and tell the men, but I don't know quite how I can do that.'

'Was the Avaeste damaged in the fight – damaged beyond repair?'

'No, she is fine.'

'But how did you lose the Avaeste boy, why?'

'It doesn't matter, it is done and we will go on.'

'How? You can't go anywhere without a ship.'

'We will get one.'

'One that can traverse the Aethermarinus as she does? I doubt it.'

'There is doubt, but it must be done.'

'Won't you tell me why boy? Why aren't you captain of the Avaeste anymore?'

Ashton relented with a sigh, 'It was the pirate's fee.'

'Fee? What for?'

'Do you think the pirate really cares if Meridian holds or falls? So I made him a bargain, if he came and we won, he could have the ship.'

'Oh,' said Santee, not expecting that answer, 'oh,' she said again seeing it now, Ashton's plan and how he had carried it out, 'oh' she said again, as she saw if he hadn't, Meridian may now be in the hands of the tyrant. 'Oh,' she said, 'Ashton, you're the best boy I know.'

'So you've said before.'

And with that she flew up and placed on his cheek a little sprite kiss, which tingled all warm and icy at once. He blushed, and she smiled, and then together they laughed, why were they so worried? They had got through worse than this before hadn't they? and they had always pulled through it.

So Ashton strode back down to the bay, to a street where there were houses which you could rent rooms or the entire place, if you could pay, and he counted the number of rooms he would need for all his men, Morris, Dew and Santee, and tallied the total amount that was required and counted the amount he had with which to bargain and realised it would not be that many nights before they would be kicked out, unless they found work, of course, but, there was so much else to do in looking for that curative grass. How could they contrive to do it? So he turned to the host and tried to negotiate a better price, after all, it was not so often he'd have so many rooms hired.

And so with one night's board already paid, Ashton went to gather his men, to try to tell them the sad news about the Avaeste.

As they rowed back out for the last time, Ashton thought, and his heart heaved with sadness, his brow knotted, distraught; he surveyed the fine ship, the grand little barque, how he loved her clean lines, her dear and determined will to do anything he asked. How he felt a traitor to have used her as a bargain, but he looked back at Meridian, wasn't it worth it? So many lives saved, so many friends, and the good coming out winning. The Avaeste understood, Ashton knew as they neared and he touched her fine timbers, yes, she understood, she knew why he'd done what he did.

'Jennings!' he yelled as soon as he was aboard, 'Phillips, Carter and Banks, if you would lieutenants, gather your men.'

Soon it was done and the fine sailors of Althorn stood tall, all at attention, ready to do anything this young captain would tell them to do, for any call, any action. Ashton stood before them, looking them over, he was so proud of his men. That rabble of sailors he'd pulled from the bar, had become the best crew he could have asked for. There was still a way to go with many of them, but all of them would agree, they were changed men, and changed for the better, it was certain.

Ashton cleared his throat, 'I want to thank you all for coming this far and staying the course with me, even though we faced such danger and though it grew very difficult, and very hard, even though I expected so much of you but gave you nothing, not even my reasons, nor my regard. You have strong arms, I couldn't ask for better, and such staunch hearts.'

They cheered, but Ashton hung his head, and a little of his pride seemed to fall from his shoulders even then.

'But I am no longer your captain, and the Avaeste is no longer our ship.' The men were silent, Ashton had expected an uproar, but there was only quiet, all waiting to hear more.

'I have rooms for us in the bay for tonight, we must have ourselves and all our belongings off the Avaeste in the next few hours. I'm sorry. I truly am.'

'But Captain, how'd you lose the ship? You're not a gambling man, what happened?'

'Never mind, what's done is done, you don't answer to me anymore, if you wish to find another berth you're welcome, but you might be lost out here in the Ether Marine for ever. I'm sure that wouldn't worry some of you, but others it might, if you stay I will get you back to Althorn, somehow, eventually.'

'But Captain-'

He put up his hand, 'Questions can wait, we must move now or our belongings will share the ship's fate.'

Dew had been listening to the captain's speech, and now the little white goblin poked his head out and ran to the boy as he entered his cabin, 'But, excuse me cap-tin,' the little goblin said, 'what of the aeroplane?'

'Oh Dew I'm sorry, I hadn't even thought about that.'

'Could I perhaps take it out, and anchor it in the bay? That is, could I sleep in it so I don't have to go in to the human's place?'

'Of course Dew, of course, I had quite forgotten, that is, that you wouldn't like it, that is, that you were a goblin. What I mean is, you're such a friend Dew, do what you like with the aeroplane, I trust you.'

'Thankyou cap-tin,' said the goblin and he was off to do as he'd said.

Annabella and her council saw the pirates away as friends, and with much thanks, but having mutually agreed that they would go on just as they had been, each eyeing the other with disdain and suspicion, unless Calegra came back, in which case, Meridian would aid the Atoll of Arinn, and the Atoll would aid Meridian, depending on whom Calegra attacked, if indeed he did.

So all being settled and the pirates returning, Vasco Renardo and his closest posse turned up to collect his fine prize. The men had all gone and the ship was quite sad as it sat so empty, and tugged on its anchor, yearning to follow the flowing tide and beach itself on the shore. But the governor took the wheel, and her anchor was raised, her sails unfurled and quickly she was away, and Renardo felt the fine movement she could achieve, the quick speed, her smooth wake, and he saw that all he had heard, and what Ashton had said of this Avaeste, all was true, she was a fine little ship, his eyes gleamed. And now, she was his!

Ashton watched on from the shore, only turning away when he could see her no more. His heart sank, but his will continued. Tonight he would rest, and then tomorrow he would begin the search for the Carex Argentius again.

After all his books, his charts and his equipment was brought in, there was not much space in Ashton's small room, but he could still walk from the door to his bed, so it would do. He hung the blue flag of Aeloran up and gazed at it, falling asleep as he did. Morris put his chest down in the corner and crept in, and Santee blew out the candle, hopped into the drawer and she too slept, in that room in the inn, on the road which ran away from the bay, but where the waves could still be heard, their gentle ebb and return.

When morning came and the men of Althorn rose, they found

Ashton up and sitting to breakfast, and breakfast was also ready for them. When they voiced their surprise Ashton just replied, 'I said I would look after your interests when we began, and so I will, as long as I can.'

So they sat down to eat and filled their bellies, it wasn't a large meal but it was quite satisfactory. And before Ashton could even get out the door, he was met by Tom who held up his hand, revealing a silver leaf in his palm.

'Is this it?' he said, eager to please.

Ashton shook his head, 'No, that's from an olive tree,' but thanked him sincerely. Then Carter and Jennings came up.

'There's a ship in the bay captain, lovely lines, just the size to suit us, shall we ask the captain who owns her so we can ask a price to lease?'

'No,' said Ashton, though he was surprised and overwhelmed by the kindness of his men, when he had thought they may be full of anger, and quick to rebellion, but he told them, 'There is no ship in this bay can carry us safely back the way we came, they may reach Aeloran by the usual ways, but none here can traverse the unstable planes, where we needs must go if you are to get home. Although, I suppose with alteration some might make it, but they were not so designed, so I'd rather not take the risk.'

The men were not quite sure what he meant, but they got the gist of it, what they needed to find was an extra special ship.

'But,' he said, as though reading their minds, 'the ship is not as important as finding the Silvertip Sedge,' he added, 'I don't expect it, but if you've nothing better to do I would appreciate your help.'

Of course they were only too willing to continue to call him captain and do as he commanded. And so Ashton was just about to go again when who but Prince Edward walked past, then stopped and said how fortunate it was to have stumbled upon him for everyone was looking for him, and indeed, so was he.

'For those of you who do not know, this is my brother Edward,' Ashton explained, 'next in line to be king on Aeloran,' and his men greeted Edward with due respect.

'What is it Edward? I was just on my way up to see Bartle and Highbury again, that is, if they'll see me.'

'Well, back on the ship, last night in the dark, you said something about a cure Ashton, did you not, when I was going on so, acting my part. Was it true what you said, that a cure might exist? Is it a real living thing and not just a myth?'

'Aye Edward, I think so, at least, with everything I am I hope. Bartle, the botanist, certainly thinks that such a thing did once exist, for its record is found in many a book, only, old books they are, and all of them unclear. We have searched an entire island where it is said to have been, the Ile de Merle, not far from here, and we were going through our finds when it became clear that Von Marax had not come with his apparent repentance, but in fact quite the opposite. So we had to halt our progress, I go now to continue where we left off.'

'Indeed Ashton I wish you all luck, but believe you will find none. I myself am returning from afar, we searched out a rumour under southern stars, a rumour of a man who could heal all ills, but he was just a fraud with pretend potions and stuffs I'm sure did no good to anyone but those who weren't ill to begin with. I would stay and help you Ashton, I would, but I am done. I fear for our father, I fear even as it is I may be too late, I should never have left you all alone, never have left him in that state, I must return Ashton, you understand that I must.'

'Yes.'

'I wish you would come with me my brother.'

'Understand, I can't.'

Edward nodded, Annabella had warned him that Ashton was a determined soul, so much greater than Edward had ever known or guessed, that his quiet little brother possessed such inner strength.

'I'm leaving as soon as I can,' Edward continued, 'we are loading the supplies now, so, even this morning I go.'

'Tell father I am safe and well,' Ashton said, 'tell him I think of him with every breath. Hopefully I won't be too far behind you, though I doubt it will be soon. It is all I want to see him again, but I cannot face him if I do not follow this search through to its end.'

Edward nodded in understanding, they all dearly loved their father, the king, but sometimes it surprised Edward just how much Ashton did. They knew he'd been saved from the war, and now and then Edward wondered how bad it had been where Ashton was from, but their father had forbade them of mentioning it or asking questions of Ashton or him of just what had happened and just where it had been, so even now, though he so wished to know more, Edward just smiled and took Ashton's arm, shaking it warmly, in a brotherly fashion, 'Take care Ashton.'

'And you. What if you see Calegra's fleet? They will want to have you.'

'I can easily evade them,' Edward grinned, 'what with The Concordor and Captain Frederick. Goodbye then.'

'So long Edward, and my regards to the others, if you see them.'

'Indeed, oh and Ashton, what's with the black hair?'

'It's a long story, I'll tell you next time I see you, when the fair winds carry me back to Aeloran.'

And so he was gone, and once again Ashton was alone on this adventure so far from home. At once he continued without further interruption, up the long road to the palace. He noticed that the goblin must be off with the aeroplane, for he could not see it anywhere in the bay, and men worked repairing The Everlast with such speed and fury it might have been worrying. But that was not his concern, no, on to that library he continued to go, to that place in the palace where Bartle and Highbury were waiting. Somehow they had known that he would be coming back, wanting further study of the plants and more knowledge of the maps. But Bartle surprised him with a tidy piece of information, a tiny sentence they had missed which may just hold the key they were missing.

In one of the older, seldom read books, with dust collected on its top and a much faded edge, he pointed to the phrase, at the bottom of the page about the Carex Argentius and without further prologue his find was announced.

'Indeed the Carex Argentius could not possibly be here on Meridian, well, at least, not flowering at this time of year, and flowering it must be to be of any use. The whole plant changes you see, when it comes out of winter, and we have just passed spring, haven't we Highbury, so I'm afraid, unless you want to wait another year until then, when you may or may not find anything, may I suggest you look for a place that is now in winter, and catch the Carex flower if you can, as it comes out of the snow in the early spring.'

'But that would mean going to the other side of the world, or at least quite some distance,' Ashton told them, 'and far I have already come. It would take so long.'

'And you haven't a ship,' reminded Tom, looking glum and quite worried at this new hurdle they'd stumbled upon.

Ashton paced, though his newly mended leg still gave him pain, and he read and re-read this page Bartle had found, then he turned to Highbury and asked, 'Do you have a place in mind sir, where I might start?'

'Well, let's see.' Highbury fumbled with his charts, he hadn't really expected the boy to go through with it or even think to take it as far as this, not that he wasn't happy to help he just wasn't quite ready.

'Somewhere like Meridian,' Ashton said, thinking aloud, 'somewhere with the same sort of geography, but a place that lies now in winter, maybe under snow.'

They thought and they thought and pulled out many a chart, many a place where perhaps Ashton could start, but all were so far, and all so unsure, then thinking on it Ashton shook his head; he was not sure it could be done, was not sure he could do it, but then as Highbury searched through the maps Ashton stopped him, pulling out a map he had gone past, saying unthinking, 'Why, it's home!'

'Aeloran?'

'No,' Ashton held it out and ran his hands over the land, that beautiful country, her shores, her mountains and valleys, her glorious rivers and natural abundance. Ashton had started to forget all these names, of the curves in her coast, of her magnificent lakes.

'Ah, Ile de Novo?' observed Highbury, 'paradise they say. But no one can get close, though it has been years, we wanted to remake the maps but she still burns, yes, and the waters now mires that still simmer, oh the blackness that fell on that land still lingers, and nothing lives there my boy, it is all ash and stone, nothing survives.' Even as he talked a tear fell unnoticed from Ashton's face to the map below him, but Highbury continued, 'Here, this is the one you meant isn't it,' Highbury pulled out the map of Aeloran and spread it out, he did not know what very few knew, but as all assumed, he assumed too, that Ashton was from Aeloran, and looking at him, who would have not thought it true?

'Yes,' Ashton said, and tried to smile, 'yes, that is home too.'

'Ah but here is a place you might want to go, it will be coming into autumn now, here Ashton see, the Isle of Wye.'

'Where does it lie? How far?'

'Two months or so on a favourable wind, that's what it says here, but I couldn't say, I am no sailor Ashton and I haven't made the journey myself. I might be able to search out a captain that may know, or at the very least a captain's transcripts perhaps.'

'Do you know anything of it?'

'Not much at all, but it sounds fair from the description there.'

'So does Ile de Novo, but it is no more.'

'Too true, too true, Ashton, I will search out some more information for you.'

'I thank you. Bartle, are you certain that none of the samples we brought is this plant, or even close?'

'I'm sorry Ashton,' the botanist said with a shake of his head, 'I checked all the samples and checked them again, though I wish it were so, it was not I'm afraid.'

'But how will I tell the Carex Argentius apart when we get to this isle, if all I have found so far have failed? Would you like to come with us Bartle so you can tell me if I have the right plant, when and if we find it?'

'No, no I'm too old for this kind of adventure, but you've no need of me, you will not mistake it in the spring, for as it comes out the snow and then as it flowers and grows, I read it is quite unique.'

Just then Lieutenant Carter ran in, with a bright flash in his eye and a jump in his step, 'Captain, come quick, oh you must see it, you won't believe it I know, Captain, but the Avaeste has come back!'

They all ran out to a place where they could see the view of the bay and the sparkling sea. Carter was right, the Avaeste was there, sitting lovely as she did, as if waiting for him. Then he noticed The Everlast now making way, and the pirate-governor Renardo giving him a wave from her deck. Then queen Annabella drew alongside him, and whispered in his ear, 'You've a brave little goblin in your crew, we made a trade with Renardo, your Avaeste, for my Everlast, I have to say it was harder than I thought, she must be some ship, your brave little barque.'

'Aye, that she is,' Ashton said proudly, 'I don't know how you did it, I don't know how to thankyou.'

'It is I who was at a loss how to thank you, Ashton, I did not know all you sacrificed for us at first, but I'm glad I discovered it. Renardo said he couldn't get the Avaeste to sing for him in any case. Seems she needs a captain with gentler hands than theirs. And you *will* accept her back Ashton, for the debt we owe you for your courage is mine to repay, and it is my will that she be yours again.'

Ashton gazed at the queen, much overcome and delighted, 'Gladly I accept!' he said, 'do you hear that men! The Avaeste is ours again!'

A cheer filled the sky, a dancing up the dirt followed and many a sailor's cry, and the young captain turned back to the queen and she was thrilled by the wild joy in his eyes, he thanked her again then ran back in to Highbury and Bartle to plot and plan his next course.

It was not just a case of getting there but of all the stops in between, of where would be friends, where would they find fair skies, and where would they find enemies. And though the maps were of the highest standard, and the men very knowledgeable and kind, it could not be helped that many a map was older than was helpful, incomplete, or mis-catalogued in a place none could find. But Ashton gathered all the knowledge he could, all the advice he could glean, and within another day the ship was restocked, with compliments of the good people of Meridian. And his men were back on board, excited and ready to go just as soon as he gave the word.

Ashton set out his cabin again, just as though he had never gone, only now there were a few extra books, extra charts, and some useful tools for more precise navigation, and also up in the hanging lantern Santee found a chair for herself, along with a bed and a table, all of a size just perfect for her, as if it had been just made so.

'Did you do this boy?' she looked down surprised, as she studied the fine sheets and the blankets.

'Aye, a small present,' he said.

'But why?'

'It occurred to me you have nowhere to sleep, nowhere that's just yours, do you like it?'

'Do I indeed! It's just perfect! Oh but where in high heaven did you find it?

'From a sprite clan on Meridian.'

'But the sprites here don't talk to men,'

'No, but they talk to swamp monsters, he was kind enough to help me find it, good old Morris.'

'Oh I must thank him too!' Santee said delighted.

'Yes, do, he would like that. Oh, I almost forgot, Annabella gave me this for you.'

Ashton took out of his pocket a neat green velvet box, he opened it up and Santee gasped – it was her very own Silver Star, and she stood beside it as Ashton held it up, it was nearly as high as she was.

Within another day the Avaeste set sail, with the people of Meridian watching, there went Prince Ashton, of Aeloran, now beloved to them for himself and not just for the wise king, for the stories had run around that fair place, the stories of what he had done, so that even his men knew what they said of all the actions of young Captain Ashton, and them.

Chapter 13:
WE'RE UNDERWAY AGAIN HURRAH!

Up went the anchor and out came the sails, on turned the engine, and the young captain took the wheel. The lieutenants ran about commanding their men who worked as they cheered, 'Here we go again!'

Soon they had left the sea of Meridian behind, and were out once more in the vast open sky. The clouds sailed past them, the sun came and went, the moon and stars looked upon them now and again, and Ashton smiled, the wind blowing back his hair, the Isle of Wye was such a way, but if things kept up like this it would not be long before they were there.

The men got to know more of Morris and Dew, and a respect seemed to grow between these two groups, no longer were they considered as Walump and Goblin, no, now they were considered esteemed comrades. And though Carter had not elaborated much, he had indeed let out, that the little sparkle they saw now and then hovering around them was a friend of the captain's, who was a very kind sprite.

But Santee was sad because though she thought she had loved the man Carter, it was clear that he hadn't even considered loving her, just went along as good friends on that day they had met and thereafter. Perhaps he thought her too young, too odd, or too impulsive, and when she thought it through again, she laughed at herself, 'Of course, you're a sprite you fool!' she said, 'it was just a passing fascination; no man would ever love you! And you were silly to think it, Santee my dear, how could you even think it? and what would they say at home if they heard that I had fallen for a great big giant!' Santee sobbed, 'But no more,' she shook her head, 'no Santee dear, no more. Your fellow sprites don't want you, others think little of you and the rest of the world is too huge! Oh Santee dear, what are you going to do?' she said to herself, then answered. 'But, haven't I been safe since I came onto this ship? Haven't I had all I needed?

Yes, that I have,' and answered herself again, 'that is when you met Ashton.' The sprite nodded and smiled, remembering the day, then darted back into his pocket, which happened to be the best place to sleep, despite her new blankets and sheets, for it was by the sound of his heart's steady beat.

Dew, with the help of Jennings, had invented several different ways which would allow him to be away from the engine, for now he had found friends he didn't much like being alone for such long times. What would his family say? he wondered, for goblins were renowned hermits, that he had become such an extraordinary extrovert by goblin standards. He thought of introducing his friends to his family, and laughed as he saw the terrified faces, on both sides that is, of the goblins and men, if they were to meet one day on Kebaticus.

And while they had tinkered, Morris was pleased to stand at the boy's knees holding his spyglass and compass as always, and feel the cooling breeze blow his whiskers and watch the Aethermarinus ahead for any small sign of the next port to which they were destined.

The lieutenants spent time down with their men in their quarters, mostly sleeping to catch up on all the energy they had expended in the journey so far and all their excitement. When they weren't sleeping they were mostly to be found on deck, in the usual, familiar employment; keeping the ship gleaming, going through their paces, or just watching their vacant surroundings, and the curious flying creatures that came and went.

Ashton sat back, and smiled now and then, but he couldn't really relax, not till this was over, not till he was home would he be able to do that. He kept his eye oft on the compass, always rechecking their course; the route they were taking was dangerous enough, without ending up someplace far worse.

With every day the warmer it got, for the closer they were to the equator, and when he was asked why it was so when they were supposed to be heading to a wintry place, Ashton replied that the way they were going it had to get hotter before it got cold.

Now when they had been sailing for several weeks with no sight of land at all, with the Ether Marine changing from fair and clear, to cloudy and sticky, with the definite chance of a storm, well, the men they began, as always happens, particularly in heat such as this, to suffer a little from being all together on one little ship, so confined and so near, and many a little issue became a big issue and the men were quicker to become frustrated, that is to say, aggravated, irritated, and well, simply bothered. And Ashton observed, as all good captains would, that it was time for him to do something.

Thankfully they were not far from the one of the isles Highbury had suggested, an ordinary place, he had said, with fair folk, not wild, where they would not be unwelcome. So Ashton altered the course just a little to sail in to this island, and he hoped that it would be as Highbury said, and hoped there would be no unwanted surprises.

But as they sailed on to that ordinary isle, written on Ashton's map as 'Baroco', a stifling heat seemed to overtake them, like a draft from a flaming fire. Sweat condensed on all their skin, washed their foreheads and dripped from their noses, so surrounding was the humidity, and they grew weary, such was its weight upon them. Many a man turned to his friend, as their knees bent and they sank to a seat, and asked the other, 'Now, I wonder, just where is this captain taking us?'

Ashton had to assure them, that though he had not anticipated being quite in this predicament, they had now passed the equator, and so it should start to get cooler, if not soon, at least it would later. And then they spotted the Isle Baroco, a bright yellow spot in the distance. Perhaps, perhaps if the wind went their way, they would make the place by sunset.

Chapter 14:
TO THE ISLE OF YELLOW SANDS

They worked and they toiled to make the way faster, carefully altering the sails to catch whatever slight bit of breeze this burning climate would offer. Dew ran around, down in the engine room, doing all he could to keep the engine running without heating-over, and they came in good time to be there well before evening. But none could imagine what befell their eyes then, what they could see of this island, for in all their travel in the low earth and the higher, they had never seen anything quite like it, except, said Patrick from Aiyr, in stories about the desert called Sahara.

'Captain?' said Jennings.

'Captain?' said Banks.

'Captain?' said Phillips and Carter, 'what shall we do? However will we land? how will we enter the harbour? For it appears that on this island here it is all sand, in fact there is no sea, no water!'

And all the crew wondered and all the crew worried as they peered down over the side, at the dunes of yellow sand that rolled from here to there – and indeed to everywhere in their sight. They worried even more when they saw Ashton's face, full of concern, and he ordered them to sail around the island again, then promptly turned and went back to his cabin, without any explanation.

Ashton restudied his charts, and all his markings of their journey, he checked the compass, he checked his bearings, then he read and reread the description given from Highbury. There was no mistake, this was the place, Ashton was sure he'd done everything right, for hadn't he sailed all this way without many a mistake, and half the way by the infallible stars of the night sky? Yes, this was the place, his course proved clearly, this was the Isle Baroco, but nothing about the isle resembled the place of which Highbury had told him.

So the young captain went back out to his men, and he called for his lieutenants to practice their geographic skills and outline the coast of this island as they rounded.

'What, *now*?' they asked.

'Yes now,' he replied, 'for it will soon be too dark.'

So though they screwed up their mouths, for they did not want to do this, what with it so hot and humid who would, but they stood on the upper deck with their equipment and did just as Ashton had asked them.

They had made a good beginning by the time it was dark and Ashton collected their drawings, then took them inside and they watched as he lined them up with his own chart of the island.

'Look at that,' he said, and they did. The maps they had drawn were nearly the same as the one he had copied on Meridian, only all could see there was one great difference, the outline of the edge of the sand they had drawn had used to be the outline of the sea.

The lieutenants could see that Ashton was sad, that something was bothering him, and who wouldn't be bothered about such a thing happening to any island? That everything but sand had disappeared from it.

Ashton thought, and then he said, 'We will go and explore tomorrow. Get some rest lieutenants, and order your men to do so as well.'

Willing they were to do as he said, for this heat had quite fatigued them, and they were sure it would also be a welcome order for their men, but Jennings wondered. 'Captain,' he said, and voiced what they had all been wondering, 'how will we sail into the beach where there is no water?'

A little smile grew above Ashton's chin, and he laughed within his eyes as he looked up, 'Why men, we'll just have to do a dry landing.' And seeing their startled faces he added, 'but get some sleep, we'll worry about that in the morning.'

So the sun went down and the moon came up, and all the stars along with it, and the night cooled so all were soothed and rested from the wicked heat. Ashton stood alone on the deck, with only a few spare sailors and Morris, and in the silence as he stood at the wheel, young Ashton thought of his father, of the hand that had pulled him out, out of the steaming ashes, the heat today had reminded him so, and so would the heat tomorrow; it would pull back the fear of those days, those dreadful days of ash and fire, and make him hold on more to the thoughts of his very dear, but dying, father.

Mathis St Amalric, he had first heard the name, as he lay without voice, recovering, as the men of the king, and the king himself, came and went watching over and caring for him. He had learnt later that the room he was in was indeed the king's very own cabin, and the ship he was on, which bore him back to Aeloran, was the king's best, the Aeolian.

When Ashton felt he could barely stand up anymore, and didn't have the heart to wake one of his lieutenants, not when they had so suffered in this temperature, and when even Morris had fallen into slumber, Ashton remembered those arms, those father's arms that had held him close to his heart as though he were his own son, and remembering the king, his father now, he was able to stand up for longer. Then he would search the stars, and confirm their path, yes, they were on the right course, but these stars made him sad too, for they seemed nothing like the bright jewels that had shone down on Novania.

In the early morning, even before light, Morris returned, and with thanks Ashton left him the wheel, and went to catch one or two hours sleep before they would attempt to go nearer. Morris whistled as the sun came up and all grew hot again, and the deck soon filled with many a man, back only by order of the lieutenants, for not out of choice would they have left the relative cool in the ship below deck.

And when the captain had breakfasted, the tray was brought up by Tom Needle, by order of Morris, he went out and addressed them all on just what was to happen.

For a dry landing to be a success, they must not touch the ground at all, no, they must stay above the ground as they went in and keep the ship in tight control. Indeed, he told them, he, Morris and Dew had done it alone when they had need, but the difference here was that this was sand, it was not firm rock or soil. So Ashton told them it would be helpful if there were lookouts at every post and men ready with poles and rope so that as soon as the Avaeste stopped they could be off and securing her, 'Oh,' Ashton added, 'and Tom run down and tell Dew, he must not let the engine falter, and once we're stopped, he must keep it going until I tell him he can rest her.'

'Aye Captain,' the men replied and all went about their duty, but they definitely weren't as keen for stopping here now, as they had been yesterday morning. For a barren waste this island looked, just a desert of sweeping sands, with neither tree nor river interrupting. It would have been better by the sight of things just to keep on going, but seeing it Ashton could not but feel it his duty to see if he could find any clue of what had happened, for a fair isle to lose all sign of life, to lose everything, well, it just shouldn't happen, it was like on Novania, only not ash was left, but sand.

They came down smoothly, just as Captain Ashton directed, and everything was going well, until a gust came up shuddering the Avaeste and sending a cloud of sand all over and through her. They held her well, and when the sand blew on they could see they were still on course, but then the engine spat and the engine sputtered,

'No!' Ashton yelled, 'take the wheel Morris!' then he jumped down the hatch and ran down to the room where the engine had now completely stopped, and Dew came out, all covered in black, began to speak, but then faltered and fell back. Ashton caught him, lay him down then turned the engine, but the engine was truly stopped, then the young captain grimaced as he felt the ship touch sand, as she heaved then came to a halt, throwing the men forward. He ran back up top, and gave orders all round, there was no choice they would have to quickly prop the ship where she was or she'd topple, with no engine and no propulsion, to the ground. So men swung down to the sand and with poles and with ropes, like a tent, they secured her. They hoped she'd hold and they did their work doubly well, for they did not want to be stuck here.

Ashton was proud of their quick and neat effort, and so he even told them, so they were pleased for he was not a boy who often told of his thoughts or praised them. Then Ashton found Morris, slapping the smoke out of Dew's back, and together they all went and studied the engine, yes, just as they thought, too much sand had managed to get in, and it would take a little oiling and cleaning. So Dew set about, with Morris's help, to clean and fix the engine.

Ashton called together his men and told them what was going to happen, that he, along with Phillips and his men, would go and explore, while the others stayed here, kept cool and kept their eyes open for anything that looked out of the picture. The team going out, out into that heat that rippled before their eyes, took with them water, put on their hats, and tied handkerchiefs round their necks. Then they followed Ashton down the ropes, and out across the dunes, up and down the weary hills, until all the world was spun. Any way they turned looked like the way they had come, any way looked like where they were heading, but the captain just looked at his compass and said, 'This way,' and they would keep going.

Just when they were about to turn back, for fear of being out here in the night, and being lost in this place where the dunes seemed to change shape even between blinks of the eye, and when they were weary and falling over the sand, when it had found every pore in their skin, Phillips, on behalf of his men, begged the captain to return. But Ashton said, 'One more hill,' and they climbed, and there, they found it: a pool with folk sitting idly in the shade of the trees surrounding, that is, it seemed an oasis.

Ashton had seen on the map of Baroco, a vast and endless lake in the middle of the isle, with hills all surrounding, surely it could not just disappear. Here at last Ashton had found it, a small pool at the base of this hill, and as they looked down on it, others looked up and hesitantly they were greeted.

Ashton told his men to keep their weapons away, even if they were challenged; these people where afraid, as they were entitled to be, and why, Ashton hoped to find out. They went down the slope cautiously, and greeted these few residents, Ashton bowed low to the chieftain there and spoke of Aeloran and Meridian. The chieftain at once invited them in, sat them down and ordered their beakers be filled, he was a man who had seen better days, though his eyes were still bright and cunning, and he opened now to Ashton.

'My name is Sabah Sabin, Captain Ashton, you ask how this tragedy has come to pass? Well, it was fifty-nine moons ago now, about five years by the low calendar,' he said to the men of Althorn, for it was obvious to him they were not of this place, as were he and Ashton, it was not their look so much as their way, or perhaps their simple manner. 'Yes, about five years now, when we took the advice of a foreign scholar and began some alterations to our capital and our harbour. They extended high and low and wide, magnificent they were, everyone thought it, and when we saw the beauty we had created we wanted more, and for the whole island. We extended our development even higher and deeper, and ever so terribly broad, until our constructions reached beyond the seas of this island, and into the cloud above and below us.'

'What happened?'

'Some dreamt, I believe, that we could broaden ourselves till our grandeur extended to the six corners of the compass, such was our pride. With everything we built, we did not notice, we had cut down nearly all our trees, we had mined our mountains till all was dust, and sand, all out of greed. When it was too late we realised our island could not sustain the monstrosities we'd created, no, and they all fell away. It is easy to see looking back, but at the time it was not so easy, indeed, none did see, until the end was full in its happening.'

'So it was not Calegra?' Ashton asked, almost surprised.

'Descada?' Sabin laughed, 'no, do not give him the credit, there is enough bad in us to do this to ourselves, without him coming into it, although, sometimes I hear the rumour that it was he sent that travelling scholar.'

Ashton thought, then shared what he was thinking, 'Yes, that would have been about the time Meridian and Aeloran called for your aid, but received no reply.'

'Yes, a pity,' Sabin replied.

'A pity?!' Ashton said, 'don't you realise what happened! Haven't you heard of all that befell?! It was a horror, not a pity.'

'My boy, what happened happened, look around you now, this is horror,' was Sabin's reply, 'no one stops here anymore, and all that could left us.'

'But back then you could have helped!' was Ashton's. There was a pause, a thick hot pause, it was so hot after all, they should have been relaxing and conserving their energy, especially Ashton, who was getting so tired. 'I'm sorry,' he said, 'I apologise. I do not mean to criticise, after all I was not here, what can I say of it? But I am here now, our last port was Meridian, we were told here lived friendly folk and we were passing and were going to stop here for a little respite, but we saw the way things were and thought we should see what had happened. To be honest I thought to find nothing here alive. Is there anything we can do?'

'My boy,' said Sabin, 'not unless you can take us with you.'

Ashton was silent.

'There are only fifteen of us, and a little livestock,' Sabin said, hopefully, 'our food is all you see here, and our water is trickling away like sand in a glass timer.'

'Fifteen,' Ashton repeated, thinking.

'And livestock,' added Phillips, not liking the sound of this. Not that he wanted to see these people waste here and die, but Phillips had been around a while, and he did not like the look in this Sabin's eye. They knew nothing of these people really, nothing but what they were told, and they hadn't been around long enough to really find out for themselves, and Phillips knew that young Ashton's heart was kinder than was good, but the other part of Phillips reminded him that, yes, the boy could be stern and proud too, not to mention possessed of an unusually clear forethought. So it was that Phillips had already resolved to accept the captain's command, when Ashton said, 'Alright. Phillips, have your men help these people pack up, cross the hills and come aboard. I think we can make room on the Avaeste.'

Sabin grinned, and Phillips saw it, though it appears Ashton did not, or perhaps he chose not to, he just said to Sabin, 'Tell your people to only bring what they need, I have not a large ship, but we will convey them to the next port.'

What a surprise the crew of the Avaeste received when in the last glow of the evening a group of strange people led by the captain, came towards them over the sand. They were helped onto the ship, along with all of their hoard, their goats, their dogs and their chickens and other birds, and barrels of this and boxes of that, and this and that other thing just in case, ignoring Ashton's kind request not to burden his small ship, and they promptly set up tents for themselves on deck, nailing the ropes into the wood, every hammer blow causing Ashton to grimace, but it wasn't for long, he told himself, indeed, it would soon be over, and he could fill the holes they had made in his Avaeste's precious timbers.

169

When he saw they were settled in he went down and asked Dew how he progressed, he had every faith the goblin was clever and they would soon be on their way, but when he asked the goblin, Dew shook his head and said, 'No, no I'm afraid we won't have her fixed by morning.'

Ashton was sad, Dew and Morris could see it, though he did not say a word, but that which was encouragement, and the monster and goblin looked to each other then laughed, 'But cap-tin we could leave now if you wanted.'

'She's fixed already?!' Ashton exclaimed.

'Aye cap-tin, she is.'

'Oh you clever goblin! I knew you could do it!' and with that Ashton picked up Dew and spun around as he hugged him. Dew blinked, utterly stunned, for goblins are not in the practice of hugging, and it was generally assumed no human would hug him for he was rather too ugly, not that that was a bad thing, for goblins don't aspire to be well looking, but now, what could Dew say, how did it feel, well, after Ashton put him down and he recovered from his spinning, yes, Dew thought, yes, oh, hugging was something, it expressed what a handshake or a head nod could not quite express, an exuberant thanks, and a close friendship.

'Start her up!' Ashton laughed, as Dew wobbled as his head spun, 'I'll get the men in their places,' and with that he ran back upstairs and was soon giving orders every which way.

The engine began with a sputtery cough, but then it breezed with a purr, Dew and Morris hadn't just fixed her, they'd cleaned and oiled her till she was so happy she was almost perfect, even despite the extra weight. Then the poles were hauled in, the Avaeste stood on her own, and the cords were all unfastened, then with careful manoeuvring and quick communicating they made their way out of the sand.

When they reached the open Ether Marine and Ashton had set the course, he retired to his cabin, pulled off his boots, and then he put his tired head to his pillow and slept as though he had never slept before.

Santee looked out at the new refugees but didn't dare go out, like

Phillips she had a bad feeling about this, but hesitated to shake her boy's kind heart. She knew Ashton was always very careful in whom he trusted, and would only be doing what he thought was right. It might just be a feeling, but nevertheless, she would keep her eyes open. Morris and Dew also did not make themselves known but stayed in the dark and the cool below.

Ashton had a pleasant sleep, a good, long and reviving rest, one of the best he had had in many a day, and he yawned and he stretched with a satisfied feeling, until he opened his eyes and found the point of a sword at his neck.

Even with the guard Phillips had posted outside, the leader of these refugees had managed to secretly gain access, perhaps with a little trick, a little distraction, then silently slipping in to the captain's cabin, and silently it must have been for even Santee didn't hear him creeping across then drawing his sword as the captain awakened.

'Sabin – what are you doing?' Ashton calmly answered.

Sabin frowned, looked Ashton over, then said, 'My friend, you must understand, I have the interests of my people at heart, otherwise I would never do this.'

'And what is it you are doing?'

'Why boy, acquiring your ship,' and with that Sabin took out a little gold tin which sat small in the palm of his hand, and as Santee now watched unbeknownst to him from up in the lantern, he whispered to the tin a chant of some kind then he flipped open the lid and let out a thing Ashton had never before seen. It was a beetle kind of creature, though what kind of creature Ashton couldn't quite say, and it flew onto his arm, then crept up to his neck, then burrowed its head into his flesh. The captain felt a pain, a sharp little stab further in, but soon fell back to the pillow, unconscious. Santee gasped, but stayed hid in the lantern.

Sabin put the beetle back in the tin and put his sword away, then he sat casually at Ashton's desk and studied the many maps and scrawlings. Yes, he knew where they were going. They would not be getting off at the port Ashton had made for, no they would go to a place of their own choosing.

Now outside, at the same time as Sabin had dealt with Ashton, his people had taken control of the ship. They sent Ashton's crew below, but they could not get to Tom or Harrick, who sat in the crow's nest above and bravely withstood them, hitting their heads with shoes as they tried to climb up, with Tom shouting and Harrick madly waving his pistol at them. And of course the refugees had not yet discovered the presence of Santee, Dew, or Swamp Morris.

Phillips shook his head and sighed, 'I knew something bad would happen, I did,' he said to the rest of the men, 'I could see it in that man's eyes. I should have done something, should have spoken up, should have warned the captain.'

'He and all of us were just trying to do the right thing,' said another, 'how could we have known that these folk from Baroco would become hostile like this?'

'How will the captain get to Wye, how will he find that sedge if we cannot take back the Avaeste?'

'And how will we get back? I don't know about you, but you must have wondered what our families think, for we just disappeared, you know, to thin air; I just hope they don't think we're dead.'

'They wouldn't think it!'

'Wouldn't they?'

'Well, I suppose, now I think on it maybe they would. Perhaps if we get through this I'll have to bring it up with the captain. Yes, of course, they must be quite worried, oh and how would they be surviving, for if they think us dead then they'll have to be living on the small widow's pension. Not to mention Tom's mum, she'll have thought her only son lost and never to return. Yes, oh, we have to get the Avaeste back in our control, for our families, our lives, and the captain.'

So the men sat together to plot and to plan just the best way to break out and take back the ship, while Ashton slept, and Morris and Dew crept and silently watched these ungrateful migrants. Santee gathered her courage and snuck down too, found her friends, and whispered in Morris's ear, of just what Sabin had done to their captain, and how other things above deck faired. She was all a-quake, this dear little sprite, she shivered out of her fear, and she talked with the monsters and they talked with the men, about what they thought they should do next.

Many a suggestion was counteracted for the plan was too uncertain, or perhaps it was more possible that the outcome would not be desired, and some plans they rejected because, well, they were just too violent, and if the captain was awake, they knew, if it could be helped, he'd achieve victory without causing anyone hurt. Morris asked Santee once and twice, if there was anything she could do, but she just replied that at the moment she was too shook up to think to do anything properly, and the poor sprite cried a shivering apology, hoping with all herself that she could calm soon and think of something.

They thought and they thought, to think of a way they could possibly overcome these occupiers, and surely, they thought, it wouldn't be hard for they were slightly more in number and they knew the ship better. But these people of Baroco, they were so bold and fierce, the men, the women and even the children. And while Ashton's crew sat down below wearing their minds out wondering, the leader Sabin altered course and caught the wind, and soon had left Ashton's path altogether. Little did anyone realise it yet, for none but Ashton would have noticed, for only he would have known, that the way they were going now was in the opposite direction to the direction that they wanted, and not only that, but very soon, as the breeze took them swiftly, they would soon leave the area for which Ashton had charts, and indeed, as this was a place Ashton had never been and where he knew no-one, well, it could be said, they were passing out of all knowledge.

Many hours later, perhaps even two days, as it did seem a very long time, 'Land-ho,' was called up above, and though they had tried many times before this call made Ashton's men brave once again. This time they went with Morris's new plan, they would follow his lead; he would go out and attract the crowd, and cause them to trip over themselves, even as he had the men of Althorn when they had first come aboard. Knowing his skill they all went with that, it was their job to come up next and take back their weapons and surround the Barocans, tie them up and then rescue the captain, then hopefully he would wake and know what to do with these terrible folk.

So the hatch went up and Morris ran out to surprised cries, 'Look, it's a Marsh Walump!' and the men down below chuckled and thought, 'Oh, they shouldn't have said that!'

Yes, Morris was at his best today, and the laughter of the refugees and their mocking further spurred him, they would soon wonder just what had hit them, and how did their plans come asunder. For Morris put his hands together as they approached him, he cricked his fingers, cracked his knuckles and grinned, yes, he was going to enjoy this.

The plan went just as the plan was and soon the tables were turned, the men of the Avaeste put the people of Baroco back in their places, they took away their weapons and they tied them up, and allowed them no further privilege, and Tom came down and Harrick too, 'Oh, what took you lads, come on, we're parched, get us a drink.'

And so all was good, but they looked around – where was the leader Sabin? They ran to the captain's cabin and found him; there he stood, sword once more at the throat of young Ashton.

Ashton still slept, well under the effects of the poison the strange creature carried, but even as this stand-off continued red drops appeared on his neck from Sabin's wavering cutlass.

'You will let my people free once more,' said he, 'you will give me control of this vessel, or I will run your captain through, and I am no fool, I can see that you all esteem him and there is no way you would let that happen.'

The lieutenants were speechless, and Morris as well, but then Morris winked at Santee and Santee back too, as though they had a plan, a plot, a way through.

'Go ahead,' Morris said to the leader Sabin, 'I'd very much like to see if you can.'

The lieutenants gasped, 'No, Morris, what are you saying?' said they.

'It's all of us and the Avaeste, or the captain,' the swamp monster explained, 'and what do you think they'll do to us once we set them free again? Hm? Trust me,' he turned to them and winked again, 'it will be better for us and the Avaeste; I can assure you, even the captain would choose this way.'

So although the lieutenants would never have thought they would ever trust the wink of a marsh walump, they had learnt swamp monsters weren't so bad, well at least this one wasn't, so with a heave of their chests they accepted his wink and played along with his game.

'Yeah,' said Banks,

'Yeah,' said Carter,

'Yeah,' said Phillips and Jennings, 'do him in if you're keen, we'd rather keep our lives and our ship.'

'But,' Sabin protested, surprised, 'you can't really mean that, in fact, I know that you're lying, you, none of you would want your captain to die.'

'Go on, try us, run him through, if you don't mind, then we can get on with it.'

'Yeah,' added Banks, 'if you haven't the stomach, give me the sword and I'll do it!'

Morris grimaced, they were a little overdoing it, but it seems it worked, for with a fit of rage this Sabin gave in and ran his sword into the captain's chest.

The lieutenants gasped, only, you see, then Sabin looked at his blade, and stabbed the captain again, but no matter how he did it the blade couldn't do it. Santee giggled; with a trick of hers the blade had become weak as paper and it wobbled now and crumpled! So the men grabbed Sabin, who was madder than mad, and took him away and put him out with the others, but they double bound his hands and double gagged his mouth, just as extra precaution, but then they had to un-gag him for they couldn't wake the captain, for though they tried many things the poison meant that Ashton slept on, oblivious and lifeless.

'Tell us what you did!' they urged Sabin, quite violently, with concern over Ashton. 'How do we wake him? How do we bring him round? Tell us!' they asked again but to no avail. But then Sabin smiled, enjoying their dilemma, their terrible trial as they paced and

175

cursed and worried as they could do nothing for the captain, not even give him water as he lay there, unconscious. Then when Sabin had had enough of that enjoyment he opened his mouth and spoke.

'Oh the beauty of this,' Sabin said, 'the beauty of this poison, is that Ashton believes he is awake, and your trying to wake him isn't real. What is in his mind now who knows but he will be living it. Usually those who are exposed to this poison don't live long if they don't come out of it. Though I haven't felt the effects myself, they say it is quite dramatic, for the sleeper re-lives the worst days they've had, although, with some alterations; they say any good thing that occurred in reality the mind forgets under the poison's influence, so, for some it can be quite tragic.'

'But how do we bring him out, how do we stop it?'

'I don't know, there is no cure, only the dreamer can get themselves out, although there was a rumour the old fablers spoke, that you could escape if you were kissed by a princess. But some story that, just a rare tale is all, many don't credit it, although, I do, yes I reserve that hope.'

'Like sleeping beauty,' Tom said, 'only in reverse.'

'Who?'

'Don't you remember your nursery rhymes sillies,' Tom laughed, 'but where can we find a princess?'

'It would be no issue if you'd give me the ship,' Sabin said, 'for in the land to which we were heading there are many a princess. One reason I had no apprehension in using the poison I used was because a boy this young can have no great thing to fear in his past; he sleeps a while, I take the ship, I take my people to where we want to go, I find a princess to wake him up, I return the ship and all is good. Let me do it, I can do it still.'

'But we can't trust you,' said Banks.

'Yes you can!' Sabin hopelessly argued.

'You could have arranged travel from where our captain planned to take you,' said Phillips.

'Not without considerable wait and expense,' Sabin explained, a frown on his face.

'But our voyage is of the utmost importance,' said Jennings.

'Aye,' Carter put in, 'the life or death of Mathis St Amalric, King of Aeloran and the surrounding Aethermarinus.'

Sabin repeated, unimpressed, 'The life or death of Mathis St Amalric, King of Aeloran and the surrounding Aethermarinus.'

'Aye,' they said.

'The wisest king that ever lived,' Sabin parroted, raising his eyebrows in contempt. 'Have you seen him?' Sabin asked.

'No,' they answered, even Morris and Santee had to admit they never had.

'And yet you come more than half way across the world for him? You foolish, foolish crew; following a boy, on a boy's fantastical adventure, for a king you've never met, not even seen.'

'But many speak greatly of him,' the lieutenants replied.

'And many speak greatly of his enemy,' scoffed Sabin. 'Trust me, set us free and we'll spare you, and give you back the ship when we're done. This situation is not as dramatic as you're making it, we'll even try and help you wake the captain.'

But just then they all turned back to Ashton, as Morris had gasped, for you see swamp monsters have large ears, and their hearing is rather sharp, and Morris, though they talked, now noticed something rather worrying – no longer could he hear the beat of Ashton's heart.

'Wake up, captain!' they shook him, they hit his chest and they cried out, they splashed him with water, they rubbed his hands, they sent for the surgeon's apprentice, but Morris turned to Sabin, 'What was it you said?' He took Sabin by his sleeves and shook him, 'What was that you said? That those poisoned re-live their worst days!' Morris growled angrily and glared at Sabin, 'You men! You don't know anything! I don't know much but I know this, no man here has lived worse days than my captain!'

And so the surgeon's apprentice was called in again, he went straight through the crowd to the captain and checked over him, shaking his head and was about to pronounce him dead, but, 'Wait, wait!' he said, as he listened through his wooden stethoscope, and lifted up his hand for silence as he did. They all held their breaths, then the surgeon's apprentice smiled, 'Ah, yes, there it is.'

A faint, faint beating, he told them, and then Morris heard it too.

There was some jubilation then, but the surgeon looked grim, and said it wasn't over yet and they should all give the captain some room.

While the men were being ushered out of the cabin by the surgeon Santee fluttered down and stood by Ashton, plucking up her courage to do as she must. She touched Ashton's cold forehead, and then she placed on it a hesitant kiss.

She did not know what to expect, or if it would work, she just had hoped he would wake up, but instead of him coming back to her world poor Santee found herself pulled into his. Oh that desolate dream place to which Sabin's poison had made him go. There she found herself, suddenly drowning in the tar of the dark mire and smothered by ash.

The world was black and empty, fires burned near and far, everything around her so ruined it seemed nothing could ever have been there. Surely this was not a place that had ever been? The blackest day for Ashton, surely this must only ever have been a nightmare, never real, no, how could such horror be?

'Where am I?' she gasped, 'where's the boy?' she said, and then she saw a finger lift hesitantly from the tar, but the rest of him was stuck in it and could hardly lift out; the hot gooey strings of the bubbling blackness holding him tight as he writhed on the ground.

'Boy!' she gasped and slowly made her way to him, through burnt and thorny briar, that seemed to grow up from nowhere, past dark serpents and terrifying insects that came at her then seemed to disappear back into the tar, or into ash, burning and falling around her. All the while she would lose sight of the boy, only to see another glimpse of him and keep on, until she thought she had lost him altogether, no sign of him in the waste could she see, but then a blue bird fluttered there where he had been, stuck there in the tar and being singed by the falling embers, but still the only living and beautiful thing that Santee could see anywhere here.

For some reason Santee made her way to it, finally reaching it, but as she did it seemed to lose all strength from all its fighting, lose all its will to fight and it sunk to the tar and stopped shaking off the ash that was falling. But then Santee gasped, she reached the bird and behind its wing, was Ashton's face, lifeless.

He looked so young and perfect, light blond hair, long and flowing, streaked with blue- it seemed the blue bird was a part of him, but he also looked dead, skin pale and his ice-blue eyes staring up at nothing, his body covered by fallen debris and ash, and burnt by embers. He had many severe wounds, some were bleeding, but from others the briars grew, and the petals of the red briar roses dropped into the tar like blood from his scars.

'Boy!' she gasped and stood upon his cheek, looked into his eyes and cried, 'wake up! You're not dead! wake up!' but his eyes still stared blank at the ashen distance.

Then Santee herself was caught as more embers were swept upon them, burning remnants of things no longer remembered and she screamed out as some fell upon her wings, singing them, burning through them, rendering her flightless.

She sunk to her knees in pain and tears, 'Wake up boy,' she wept. It seemed to her this place was the world at its very end, but she hung on to the memory of the men, of Morris, of Dew, the fair Avaeste, and of the boy's noble quest. 'Wake up,' she begged, as her tears fell into his.

And though all else remained unmoved, the boy's lips said, 'but I am dead.'

'No, you're not dead, you're alive and living.'

'How can that be? You can see I am dead.'

'This is a dream.'

'No, this is reality.'

'Boy wake up! You were poisoned by Sabin, this is the poison's doing. Ashton please!'

'Who is Sabin, who is Ashton?'

'Sabin is a bad man, you are Ashton.'

'No,' the dead boy almost laughed, 'Ashton is a name of common men, I am Novanian.' Then he despaired, 'Novania is ruined, all is lost, all have perished, I saw it all as I lay dying, and then I died, even I.'

'No, you are not here under Calegra's defeat anymore, you are a prince of Aeloran, King Mathis has already saved you from this, poisoned or not you dishonour him by your forgetfulness! Boy, wake up!'

'St Amalric?' he thought, 'the wise king?'

179

'Yes.'

And just then the Aeolian, St Amalric's ship, went by in the distance, then Ashton slipped away and Santee could not bring him back.

Santee hung her head and cried, but the blue bird raised its own and looked up at the sprite, watched her as she cried and it flapped again to be free, tried with all its might. Santee slid down to it, and managed to free its little claw, and it took her up upon its back and with tattered wings took to the sky, dodging the smoke and the raining fire.

Santee sunk her face into its feathers, all soft and shimmery, and when she looked up she was back in the captain's cabin, sailing along where they had been in the outer and unknown Aethermarinus. Santee found that instead of feathers she was holding onto Ashton's hair, she was thankful it was on the side where the men would not see her, because they all turned back at that moment, as Ashton gasped for air.

'I'm alright,' he said to their numerous faces and questions, 'I'm alright. Go, all of you go, I will come out to you soon.'

They went as he said.

Ashton breathed in, and to the little sprite he said, 'I owe you a great thanks my friend.'

'Nothing you would not have done for me.'

'But I have a question; how did you know those things? How did you know what so few know; what the king did for me?'

Santee sunk her head, 'Annabella Bien. She told me, only a little, that I might understand and help to keep you safe on this dangerous mission.'

'What did she tell you?'

'She said you were a prince by adoption, saved by Mathis after a battle with Calegra, and that you were Novanian, although, I know she knows that is something I shouldn't know, it was a slip she never meant, but that was alright because I don't know anything about Novania in any case.'

'I thank her for her forethought in telling you, and I thank you Santee,' Ashton said gently, 'but you must not say that name.'

'Calegra?'

'No,' a tear almost left his eye, and his voice trembled as he replied, 'Novania.'

Santee wanted to ask why, and what was so wrong about mentioning that name, but she refrained. For the Ashton here looked like the Ashton in the dream; deathly pale and shaken, and with a look about him – the traits of the Novanian more prominent than before, the thin physique, the narrow face, the piercing pale eyes, the hair growing back blonde and blue, and he so sorrowfully beautiful, with a vague, melancholic attitude. Santee had never seen anyone look quite like that, except maybe the elves in her home territory that kept mostly to themselves on a nearby island.

'It was real, wasn't it?' Santee asked, 'it happened, just as I saw?'

'Yes,' Ashton said, 'only, in reality, King Mathis did not just sail past.'

The boy sat wearily and finally stood up, asked Santee for the mirror, and as he stood before it he became the Ashton she knew once again, the Ashton none could mistake was a son of Aeloran.

The boy stood up straight, breathed in some courage, neatened his attire, and then marched out the door to face whatever new trouble had come while he had slept poisoned.

Chapter 15:
INTO THE UNCHARTERED LANDS

Ashton looked to neither Sabin nor his crowd only stepped up to the upper deck and studied the sky and cloud. And when Sabin shouted out that he could help Ashton find his way, the young captain only told his men, quietly, to keep that man silent. He may know this part of the world, but he could not be trusted so Ashton did not even entertain the thought of heading to the land Sabin had intended on going, nor using any information from him, and he told his men to wash their ears of all they'd heard that man speak.

Ashton sailed on and on, hoping to find some familiar feature that he could relate back to the maps he had gained on Meridian, but nothing they saw was of any worth for navigation, even the stars here seemed so unfamiliar to Ashton, and even his six-pointed compass was of no use without a known destination. Where could they take these people from Baroco? They and their livestock were using up the captain's precious supplies with every day that passed.

The captain kept on a steady course, hoping that sooner or later he would come to something familiar, but now and again his compass would waver from some unknown magnetic force so he couldn't even be sure of his true heading anymore. The captain grieved; their water was low, so was their food and blackcurrant juice. With no sight of land in so many days he was wondering what to do, and his men were worried too. Many began to suggest he talk to the man who had got them into this mess, but Ashton would not relent; he knew only poison came from Sabin however good his words might seem, and he surmised from things overheard, that Sabin had not always been a chieftain on Baroco, oh no, he was once a travelling scholar, it was he, it could be presumed, who had poisoned the heads of the Barocans with greed and pride till it destroyed them, and then squeezed himself to his current position, for there was no one left to oppose him. So, 'NO!' Ashton said to the entreaties from his men, he would not listen to Sabin.

Ashton retreated to his cabin one morning, weary from a night battling thunder and strong winds, and he sat at his desk and put down his head.

'Oh father!' he wept, 'I have failed you. Here we sail through the outer limits of the Aethermarinus with not a clue of direction! I have not yet learnt the charts of this place, if indeed they exist, perhaps not even you have been this way, but they say you know every place, for you've knowledge and wisdom beyond all others. Oh that I had your wisdom now! I have so many under my care, and soon we will run out of all sustenance. I don't know what to do. Father I'm sorry, sorry I am not with you now, that I have not found the cure. I can only beg your forgiveness.' For a moment young Ashton cried, but quickly dried his eyes, deciding to write a letter to his father the king, a letter explaining everything, of this adventure, why he had left, why he so desperately sought out the cure to cure all things, for him, what had happened, briefly all the twists of the journey, but Ashton had not even really began when he put down his quill, and looked at the window.

A butterfly came and sat upon the sill, and if a butterfly was here land must be close mustn't it? Ashton thought, becoming excited and running over to it. It was an unusual colouring - with wings of yellow, like parchment. Ashton smiled at its beauty, but then looked at it more, thinking the markings upon it curious he took it gently to his finger and lifted it up to study it closer. Then the boy let out a joyful, 'Ha!' as his heart leapt, for the parchment yellow butterfly carried on its wings, a small portion of map!

Ashton quickly sketched the markings, then another butterfly fluttered in, it danced with the other one and then sat down and waited while Ashton copied its map. Then together they danced and flew happily away, Ashton running out and giving orders with such refreshed command they were obeyed straight-away. 'Follow the butterflies!' he yelled. Tom was the first of the crew to see them, no one else had seen them but briefly just now, but his eyes were young and keen and Ashton soon appointed him chief butterfly watcher so they wouldn't lose them. Santee smiled as she sat in Ashton's collar and together they watched the little butterflies in the distance. Ashton took out his compass, it seems, still not steady, so he followed those yellow butterflies boldly.

When he looked at the map, thinking more on it, he realised something that might be rather important, you see the names upon their wings were written in an ancient goblin hand, so Ashton called Dew up and showed to him his quick sketch of the simple map.

'Ah!' said Dew, 'Aha!' he cried, 'so it does exist. This word is Sucitabek, indeed, the first goblin island. But Cap-tin, how did you get this map?'

'Butterflies,' said Ashton, with a look of mild surprise.

'Butterflies?!' spluttered Dew, bewilderment in his eyes.

'Aye. Do you think they will be friendly Dew, or do you think we should avoid the isle? Not that we have much choice, we must go in but – what do you think?'

'Well, if they sent you butterflies, friendly or not, they must mean you to go in.'

'In we go then,' the captain grinned, 'ready for anything. I'll need you up here with me Dew, you might find another to watch the engine.'

'Aye Cap-tin. I'll be back at the call of land.'

And so across the clouded sky the fair Avaeste kept on, and then all at once the haze did part and gave view to a dark and green island. The sea was charcoal green in the deep, then rose to an aqua-grey, and in the shallows mangroves came down and reached out across the cay. There was barely a beach anywhere to be seen, only mud-pocked inlets divided by rocks, where crabs and crocodiles and mosquitoes hid to catch anything that passed by them, where rivers spilled out and swept more and more silt into the calm sea with turbid discolouration. The forest was dense and the air was thick, the land all ridges and gullies, and in every gully a swamp was found, in every ridge a vast network of rocky cavities.

Morris hid as best he could, while still giving one of his eyes a view, though Dew tried to assure him, Morris replied, 'But Dew, other goblins are not like you, and I do not think that I should jeopardise all of us by putting myself in plain view, when you know what has existed between goblins and swamp monsters, that is, you know of the feud.'

Dew relented, 'Aye, I do.'

So they sailed down to the dark sea and into the mangrove cove. The butterflies joined their friends here and fluttered back to their flowers deep in the forest. Ashton whispered a thanks to them, and they danced a little as they went.

There was no sign of goblins here, no sign of life at all, but the buzzing of insects, the popping of mud and the crick of the crabs on the shore.

'Right,' said Ashton, 'right then Dew, where do you think I would find your distant relatives? For I would rather ask permission before refilling our water, but it does not seem anyone's here.'

'I don't know,' Dew replied, 'perhaps Sucitabek is deserted. After all it would have been long ago that anything from here was heard of, although that is the goblin way, you know, to withdraw, be unseen and unheard and so remain. Yes, if I were to take a guess, I'd say they're out there now, watching us.'

'I'd say that too,' said Ashton, 'so how do we proceed?'

'Just as you would if they were not watching, I think they would stop us if we went too far for them.'

'Do you think they'd mind if I tried to find them?'

'Well, that depends. Cap-tin I do not know these goblins, and goblins are just like men, they can be good and bad or both. Just what, I cannot say if I don't know them.'

'I'm sorry Dew, I know. But I have a request, you can say no if you desire, but I know you're a brave goblin. Do you think that you might find them and tell them of our predicament?'

'Me?'

'Yes, well, you're a goblin. I'd come with you if you like, or you can take some of the men, though I'd rather not send too many from the ship, what with these disruptive Barocans, but whatever you think best.'

Dew thought it through. The captain was right, it was a task best for him to do. He puffed up his chest and set his shoulders straight.

'To serve you captain, I am proud. Do not mourn me if I do not return in two hours, just get out of here and don't look back.'

'Dew, surely it won't be as bad as that!'

'You never know with goblins' he said.

'Then I'll come too,' said Ashton.

'No, no, it's best I go alone, you stay with the ship.' Dew turned and marched to the side, slid down the ladder and swam into shore, unlike Morris, he was not so keen on the mud, but being a goblin he didn't mind it too much, and to stop the mosquitoes biting him he smeared the mud all over, and so seemed like a walking mud-sculpture as he disappeared into the mangroves.

Now being goblins and not swamp monsters, Dew knew where to look; they would not be down here in the festering mud, no they would be up in the mountains, eating lichen in the higher forests and gnawing on stalactites in the dark caverns. And some, if he guessed right, would be hiding along the path that led from the sea to the mountain, it was not obvious to the men but it was to Dew as he was a goblin. So up and up he went through the thickly treed way until, well, until he was caught up in a trap suddenly.

Hanging in mid air from a vine in a tree Dew looked down as the native goblins surrounded.

'Hullo,' Dew tried to smile and wave as he spun, quite dizzy, 'greetings from Kebaticus.'

At once they let him down, and as he sat on the ground recovering there was much discussion.

And as goblins chatter they chattered, so it was more like grumbling and rumbling. Dew was rather frightened, but that was nothing new, for every goblin is scared of even his own parents, not to say these Sucitabekian.

Their big stomachs were bulging, their big teeth long and fearsome, their warts huge and hairy, their skin rough and spotty. And in their claws they'd spears long and terrifying, so Dew sat still and waited for the opportune time to reply.

But it wasn't long before they threw him questions,

'Who are you?'

'Dew.'

'You're a funny colour?'

'Yes, I'm an albino but I'm a bit muddy.'

'From Kebaticus?'

'Yes.'

'Do you know uncle Max?'

'Uncle Max?'

'Yes, you know, big hair, but balding, with a big wart on his head – so big he gives it a name?'

'Oh, oh yes!' laughed Dew, 'yes, he calls it Guedo.'

There was laughter all around and they helped Dew to his feet.

'So,' they asked, 'what brings you to our territory?'

'We are lost, that is all,'

'Well, you picked a good spot to get lost in. Come, take us to your ship, introduce us to the captain. Tell us, what brings you sailing? It's not an occupation renowned for attracting goblins.'

'Oh, I am the only one, and mostly I am fixed in the engine, the rest are, well, men.' Dew stopped, perhaps that was not something he should have said, and the look on the faces of these natives petrified him. 'But they are good men,' he quickly added, 'the captain is the best, his name is Ashton, a boy from the west.'

'A boy captain?'

'Aye, he says it were the butterflies brought him in.'

'Butterflies?'

'Aye, butterflies.'

'But we never sent them.'

'Oh.'

'Perhaps they sent themselves, but that only ever happened when we were visited by the king.'

'The king?'

'St Amalric.'

'Well, this boy is his son, yes, on Meridian we discovered he was indeed a prince.'

'Well that explains it.'

'Yes, it does.'

'We saw the flag of Aeloran and wondered, but none have come for so long. We will organise a feast at once in his honour. How many men are with you? They must come too.'

'Four lieutenants, five men each, plus old Gragan, young Tom, the captain, then there is Santee the sprite, and Morris of Swamp. I think twenty-nine all up'

'Of Swamp?' they turned towards angry, 'You mean to say, a *monster* travels in your company?!'

'We are good friends,' Dew tried to explain, 'you see the cap-tin is as proud and as strict as they come and he allows no prejudices to stand between his men. Old or young, skilled with muscle or skilled with mind, man or sprite, swamp monster or goblin.'

'A wise captain,' they concluded, 'I don't much like it, but alright, your friend Morris of Swamp will be welcome.'

'I thank you,' Dew sighed relieved, but continued nervously, 'friends, there is one other little thing,'

'Go on.'

'The reason we are lost, you see, still remains our problem. Have you heard of the isle Baroco?'

'A fair place, some distance away, neither good nor evil. It holds no charm, but neither is it loathsome.'

'Well, that was our information too, but we found the place changed.'

'Oh, how so?' they enquired, sensing some story coming, and goblins do like stories as you may have heard about them.

'Well,' Dew began, and he opened all with them, telling them of Sabin and all of what had happened, down to the captain being poisoned and the ship overtaken, and them taking it back but then finding themselves in a place beyond the use of chart and compass or any navigational instrumentation.

'And so,' Dew sighed, 'that is where they all remain, tied up on the Avaeste, distressing the captain, for what are we to do with them? and how will we find our direction?'

'We will think on that,' the goblins stated.

'Thank you. I think the captain would be loath to attend your feast as long as they remain. For they are cunning as you have heard and he would not want to lose control of the Avaeste again.'

'We understand. Go and tell him he is welcome to remain, and take on supplies from our rivers and streams. We will come and make our greetings when we have a solution to your problem.'

Dew bowed to them, tipsy like goblins bow, then skipped back down the mountain path to the mangroves, and swam back out to the ship, handing a wriggling fish to Morris, who delightfully licked his lips.

'Good news,' he said. Ashton didn't need to say the words, his face said it all, so relieved he was. Dew explained all that had passed, so Ashton sent some men to fetch fresh water and waited nervously, but with hope, for the arrival of the Sucitabek goblins. Now and then he turned to Dew and went over goblin customs, for of all the things Ashton had learnt, he knew one thing about goblins, that is, it is easy to offend them.

'How do I bow again?' he would ask and Dew would show him how, 'and how should I address them? When should I sit? When should I stand? When should I speak and when should I clap my hands?'

'You worry too much,' Dew laughed, 'they will not expect you to know our ways.'

'And Dew, did you thank them for sending the butterflies?'

'No, but I asked them about it and they said it wasn't they.'

'Oh, but how come they came?'

'It is my belief, my young cap-tin, that they were sent by the king.'

'But he is not here.'

'No, but he has been in years past, and they know him.'

Ashton smiled, what a wonderful thing, his father had been here before; he had seen these wild mountains, walked on this grey shore, got mud in his boots like Ashton would. Ashton sighed. Oh, his father! He must not waste time, and he eagerly searched the shore for the goblins or some sign, but to his surprise Tom Needle shouted,

'Ahoy look, it's a funny boat, coming 'round the island!'

They did look and they did see that indeed it was quite unusual, its stained sails looked like leathern hides, its timbers like rough hewn trees, but nevertheless it came up fast with a fearsome goblin crew. They came alongside and to the crew's surprise Ashton hailed them kindly and along with Dew they talked things through, and soon the captain ordered a walkway be erected between the Avaeste and this vessel.

The men were wide eyed, but Ashton explained that they had no reason to be frightened, their friends the goblins had only come to take away Sabin and the people of Baroco Isle.

So the plank was put up, the goblins boarded, and the refugees taken across. They were terrified, they screamed and they cried, and Sabin pleaded to Ashton, but Ashton just said, 'This is the best thing, they are taking you to another island, the people will be safe there and can make a new start, but you and your tongue, I'm afraid, will be imprisoned.'

And so that's how it was the Avaeste was cleared, the nail holes in her timbers were mended, the crew were all at last relieved that they didn't have that rowdy bunch any more to contend with. Yes, on that day they were all amazed, and how their respect grew for their captain, when they saw how the boy could hold his own when speaking and dealing with great big goblins that were three times his size and more, and not only that, but he could laugh with them, and the whole goblin company too soon fell into friendship and respect for him, he the eighth son of St Amalric.

They took Ashton and all the crew up to their village; a group of little mud huts under broad trees, and though they were ordinarily unsocial folk, they liked to come out on occasions such as this. They lit a great fire and spread out a feast – at first the men thought they would not like it, for they had seen what Dew liked to eat and they were not sure they'd like to try it, but the goblins were obliging and soon they saw that just about everything here was to their liking. So they ate and talked and danced and laughed all night with these friendly goblins. It seemed somehow they were caught in a dream, for how could such a thing ever be? That men and goblins could be friends, well, it was simply amazing, and in the early morning when the men grew tired in all wonderment, falling gently to the ground with much yawning. Ashton too fell asleep here, under the soft canopy, where the stars filtered down, on the soft, soft ground, with these kindly folk and full stomach, what else would anyone have done?

Now here we might say that again the crew were fooled, but it was not the case. No terrible thing happened this night, they were not murdered in their sleep by the goblins, no, of course not, for these were the friendliest, kindest goblins you will ever know. Yes, the kind goblins of Sucitabek lifted Ashton up and placed him on a bed mossy and soft; comfortably he slept, then they all went about and did what none would expect. In the dark of the night, to the Avaeste they went, carrying barrels of food and drink, filling the hold till she could take no more, then running back up the hill. Then they quietly lifted their houses up and moved them to another locale, then removed from that place every trace that they had ever been there at all.

So although the crew woke smiling as they remembered the night before, they soon scratched their heads as they looked around them, wondering where the village had gone. Were they all mistaken? Had the events of last night been only a dream and not real? Where were the huts, the fires, the animals, where were the goblin families? Then as they looked around wondering where the village that had been there could be, they saw their captain casually standing there, but looking down to the sea.

'Captain?' they asked, 'where did they go? Where are all the goblins?'

'What goblins?' answered the captain plainly, but they saw on his face a grin.

'The goblins! The village! It was here, surely it can't just disappear!'

'Was it here?' Ashton asked them, with a twinkle in his eye, 'but, men of Althorn you speak of goblins as though they were real and were alive.'

'Captain?' they said surprised, as Dew was in plain view.

'To be secretive is their way,' Ashton explained, 'don't be offended but they'd prefer it if Kebaticus and Sucitabek remain unknown to the realms of men. You have had a rare privilege, you must remember it only as it seems, that is, as a dream.'

'Aye, a dream it seemed!' Berens said laughing, 'that will be easy, along with everything that's happened to us since we left the fair harbour back on Althorn and were pulled into this mad adventure!'

'Good. Now let's get back to the ship. I have discussed these parts with the goblin chief, he has given me some direction, left me some charts and a compass of a different stone that does not shift uneasily as mine does in these strange parts. So, hopefully, we will soon be back on course and on to the isle of Wye, and hopefully, with your help my friends, we will make up the lost time.'

'Aye Cap'n,' they cheered, 'and gladly.'

But then Phillips spoke up. 'I don't want to ruin the celebrations,' he said, 'but on behalf of the men I need to ask, Captain, when will we return to Althorn? We've families to think of.'

'Well,' said Ashton, patting Phillips shoulder, 'a fair question. I would hope within a month. I hoped sooner, of course, I thought you would be back by now when I set out, but things have happened haven't they, and if they keep happening as they have been who can say, it might be two months or three.'

'Well you won't have any trouble from us now Captain, like you did in the beginning.'

'No, we're with you indeed. We can go a month more without worrying, can't we boys?'

'Aye, but the sooner we return the better in my opinion. For they've had no news of us for so long, who knows what our friends and families will be thinking.'

'Oh,' Ashton said, with surprise, 'but you see, you needn't worry about your family, no, did I never explain? Althorn is of the Terra Marine, that is, the low earth, where seas meet seas with no gaps in between, and down there time passes somewhat differently, for the Terra and the Ether move at different speeds. Let me see, there's an old rhyme they teach to calculate the time,' Ashton went through it under his breath, and counted on his fingers, 'Ah, yes,' he said, 'on Althorn it's still only a few minutes after we left.'

The crew all laughed, 'Well, they won't have missed us yet! Truth be told, when we're gone but an hour they'll probably say good riddance!'

So they all climbed back aboard with cheered hearts and good spirits, and the captain once again set the course and surveyed the outlook. The skies were clearing, the sun, moon and stars all in place, the wind gentle but kindly prevailing their way. The ship was alive with new hope, the young captain smiling, and the goblins up on the hill even popped out to wave them goodbye. Swamp Morris waved back with a tear in his eye, so touched was he that he had entered a goblin village and was still alive.

Then once they had lifted up from the dark green sea, and were out smoothly across the Ether Marine, the day wore on and the day wore out, Ashton sunk down on his weary legs and sat on the steps. So many days of constant worry, so many days of stress, so many days of constant doing and planning, when would be the end of it?

Santee was on his shoulder, Morris at his knee, Dew leaning on a railing by him and his men all congregating, for it seemed without words the captain had called them, or perhaps it was his manner. Whatever it was, Carter saw this first, their captain was just a tired lad in need of a good sleep, in need of a father's hand.

Ashton sighed, 'I don't know about you men, but I think maybe we'll make straight for Wye,' he laughed, 'no stopping anymore, I want no more Diamantines, no more Atolls, and indeed no Barocos with men like Sabin.'

'Aye!' they all laughed, and heartily agreed with him.

'Come on Captain,' lieutenant Carter said, 'let's get you to your bed.'

'But the course, I have to … well I …'

'We've got the tools and the map, Captain. You taught us how to do it and we can. It's alright to have a rest.'

Ashton nodded, and let Carter help him up with his big strong arms, and let him support him on his weary legs, back to the cabin, without further protest.

Jennings took the wheel, and Banks commanded the men, while Carter and Phillips too took their turn to rest, but down in the bunk room the men lay about discussing all the things that had happened so far and all the things that lay ahead.

They laughed at the thought of how it had begun with the crates of blackcurrant. Marvelled again at Diamantine, shook their heads in disgrace as they thought of the Atoll of Arinn. With wonder they recounted the sights, and with energy all the stories, until they came to talk of it, the place to which they were now going.

'The Isle of Wye,' one said, 'what a name, why is it not called Ex or Zed?'

'Or called If, or How or When,' they laughed. Indeed it was a funny name.

They relaxed as they talked, they played cards, they played cribs, they played songs of Althorn on homemade instruments. They changed shift and shifted again, sometimes seeing the captain, but other times he was away. And so far, to all surprise, no more incidents had occurred to cause new compromise, and so they grew closer to the Isle of Wye with every day, yes, they made good time.

Chapter 16

INTO THE WINTER OF WOLVES & WOE

Then the air grew cooler, and then it grew colder, till wintry gusts blew often and made their way harder, till they doubled their jackets, wore long singlets and scarves, socks on their heads and gloves on their hands, till their breath came out in chilled cloudy puffs. They kept on and they kept on and on day and night. The rain was like ice when it rained, and then came the snow, it piled up on the railings and across the sail tops, they swept it from the deck as they rubbed their red noses, shook the icicles from the ropes, and to keep from going numb they wiggled their toes and their fingers non-stop.

'We must be getting close,' they would say and would hope, but on they went still, and never did they slow, for in truth Dew was worried if they slowed even a little the engine would freeze and so stop, and who knows how far they would fall before he'd be able to get the engine to thaw, and besides which, full speed was just what the captain decreed.

Then one day, after three weeks or so, give or take a few days for there were some patches when it could not be said if it were day or night, night or day, and it had got so cold at one point the ship's clock missed time, but today, the captain jubilantly informed them, as he shivered hair-strand to toe-nail, that his six-pointed compass had started working again! And they had reached a point where his charts from Meridian met up with his charts from the goblins, so now they were close, oh yes, they were ever so near, and between here and there there was nothing to fear, save the weather, but they had been battling it well, so they cheered and danced all around, except Morris of Swamp, who despised the cold and stayed in his box sniffing, with a blanket and a steaming hot mug of a strange concoction that smelled of mud and salt, while Santee sat warming her hands by the candle light in the lantern above, swaying with the Avaeste as they battled through the next blizzard with such courage and heart.

With an awed silence they continued as out of the frozen sky they passed one after another, icy mountain by. So slow they seemed to sail, though they hadn't changed their speed, but their surroundings took them by surprise, it was so immense. It took their breath away as low and high the mountains were; apparently upon no island, as though they were just floating in mid air, but then they saw that below them there was a frozen and icy sea, so clear and crisp and perfect set it mirrored the cold and white speckled skies, and then they saw it, up ahead, these were no nameless drifting mountains, these were the outlying ranges of the white frosted island.

From out here the Isle of Wye appeared deserted, even desolate, as Ashton and his lieutenants looked at it through telescope and spyglass. The trees were under snow, the hills were covered too, there was no sign of people or animals, or houses, no, it was a white landscape of snow upon snow.

'What does your book say about this place Captain?' asked Phillips, as the rest of the crew present waited and listened.

'In my book the last pages are missing,' Ashton chuckled, 'I guess that's what I get for buying it second-hand from the markets. But the information I was given on Meridian by Highbury and Old Bartle suggested there was more life here than this. In fact I was told to expect a cautious welcome.'

'So people do live here?'

'That's what I've been told.'

'No goblins? No monsters no, well, who knows?'

'Oh no, no, Morris and Dew generally prefer places less cold, and if they did have relatives here they'd most likely be somewhere hibernating. No, I believe the people of this isle are somewhat like your own.'

'Like Althorn?'

'Aye, but a few decades behind.'

'So they don't have steam power yet? Nor mechanical weaving?' said Jennings.

'Nor coal mines,' said Carter, thinking of his late uncle's occupation.

'Well, this should be interesting,' worried Phillips.

'If anyone's here,' added Banks, so often the pessimist.

'Shall we go in and see then? It could be they are there and we just can't see them from here.'

'Aye cap'n, we're ready, and freezing, let's go in.'

The crew knew the ropes and the captain steered them in. Around the island they went, icy wind in their faces, purple lips, battling the wind. They made it to a place which seemed the most likely port, then across the frozen harbour, Ashton nodding to Phillips as he surveyed the approach, nodding, 'aye, a dry landing.' And down they came gently and anchored.

They could see other boats here now, covered in snow, all iced in, bound by the frozen ocean, it would be impossible for those here to sail out at all. A lighthouse was behind them, near invisible, the white upon the white, and with no ships expected it was desolate too.

The young captain looked out before them, it seemed so surreal, so silent and empty. Ashton studied the land ahead, the low fields, the ranges and further to the mountains that could be seen now and again when the snow fall weakened. All the men came out to see, searching the vast white openness for anything, any sign of life, but there was nothing.

With the captain's agreement, Phillips took a crew out to search the lighthouse and Jennings took another group to inspect the other vessels in the harbour, perhaps there would be some clue, as to where the folk were that were said to live on this isle. The men were uptight at finding such an empty place, as you can imagine after their experience with the Barocans, so maybe there were some here that would be just as glad to find no one and turn back. Although, turning back was not an option for the captain, and they knew that.

Ashton tapped the lid of Morris's bed, and when that good monster, from the warm bubbling swamp, lifted his head with a quizzical, if not annoyed eyebrow, the young captain made his request.

'Morris, my dear friend, and most capable first mate,' Ashton began, worry sitting on his face, 'I am going to go forward, into the snowed field, could I ask you to brave the cold, and accompany me?'

Morris shivered as he peered out from his warm little box and wasn't feeling inclined to say yes, but he saw that worry and he knew Ashton, 'You've some concern?' he asked.

197

'Yes, there is a grave fear sitting upon me, perhaps unwarranted, but I cannot shake it. I must go in, and I trust no one more than you to come with me.'

Morris thought about it, then relented, saying, 'Alright, I'll come.' And with that he jumped out of his box and wrapped himself in the warmest woollens, and over them, furred jacket and hat, and, thanks to Santee, a scarf to match, so all you could see of the dear little monster were his two little eyes and a few stray whiskers poking out.

Phillips and Jennings returned with their men, the place was empty, even the ships, said Jennings, seemed to be rotting where they lay, as if it were not just this winter, but longer, perhaps even years, that they had sat idle here in the bay. It worried the captain further, and gave more foundation to his grave fear, but he looked at Morris and together they nodded, they would still go on.

When they were about to make their way young Tom yelled from up front, 'Wait, I can see something,' they all waited as he focussed the large telescope, and the blurs in the snow became shapes, and then known, 'Wolves!' he yelled, and they gasped, and then they too could see, there racing down to the frozen beach were wolves, and not just two or three but a whole pack, and they didn't look friendly.

Lieutenant Banks grabbed his gun and fired it, straight into the white icy sky, and the noise echoed around them, running across the silence, but it did the trick, the wolf pack stopped in their tracks, then turned and skittered into the distance. Not until they reached the hills did they turn back to watch the men and their ship.

Ashton produced a telescope and studied them – they seemed to be ordinary wolves, hungry, and curious. Ashton told the men to stay on board with several posted lookouts, and on no account were they to let anyone get on board, if anyone came that is, which seemed very doubtful.

'Come on Morris,' he said and they left, despite wise words from his lieutenants against it, they were going to check out this harbour, just the two of them.

So the captain and first mate climbed down and proceeded across the ice and snow, Ashton being very wary of wolves, poor Morris just wary of the cold. They had gone so far forward it seemed as they trudged through the uncertain fall of snow and ice, but really it wasn't that far at all, when they saw a figure ahead, coming towards them out of the white, a person perhaps, they couldn't quite see yet but it was the right shape and size.

Ashton stopped, and Morris stopped too as the figure grew nearer and they saw their hypothesis was true, it was a woman, although she seemed more ethereal than human.

She was of an indeterminable age, wearing a simple grey woollen dress with a cloak and a hood over her head, behind her a finely-crafted bow and arrows were strapped and around her waist blades of many kinds were held, the largest was an elegant silver sword whose scabbard was engraved with a script, so beautiful, but unknown.

When she reached them they said not a thing, she and Ashton just studied each other, not quite like old friends, but like there was something between them that neither knew or could speak, but something they couldn't quite recall, like the echo of a dream. She had short, soft hair, piercing eyes and eyelashes which were long, catching the glittering snow in them, which slipped as she blinked, and then fell to the ground.

Ashton couldn't take his eyes from her face, she wasn't sweet like Annabella, nor forward as Yvette, nor gentle and funny and cutely gorgeous like Santee, no, she was something else, so magnetic.

'My name is Aolani, I am the guardian of Wye,' she said, 'and I must ask you to leave this isle.' She spoke with all seriousness and determination, as her graceful fingers touched the hilt of her sword.

'But I have come on an important errand,' Ashton replied, near overcome he explained, 'I have come so far, please, at least hear me.'

At the question she did not speak but touched Ashton's chin.

The minute she did she faded into the whiteness and to Morris and Ashton she and all she had spoken were at once forgotten as if she never had been there, the sun shone through and around them a village now appeared through the glare. Even as they saw them the doors and windows opened up, and many a curious head was poked out. What was this unexpected arrival? This foreign ship bearing a foreign crew, and what were they doing here in the winter, when none ever came as it was so terribly cold, and almost impossible to do so?

Ashton and Morris ran back to the ship, up to the deck, yelling to the crew that a village had been found, oh yes, there was life on Wye Island.

'Men,' said Ashton, 'be guarded in your talking, it's not that I don't trust the good folk of Wye, only that we don't know them in the slightest. And of all things, now that you have discovered the fact yourselves, please don't mention that I am a son of St Amalric,' he said, thinking that this isle was so far out they might not even know of St Amalric, if indeed they knew of Aeloran itself, but Aeloran and the wise king Mathis were known to most isles in the Aethermarinus so that was unlikely to be a danger, but Ashton wasn't certain. 'If anyone asks,' he said, 'we're sailing the Aethermarinus with an eccentric botanist.' Ashton continued, 'In fact while we're here I'd like you to act as captain, Phillips. I'll pretend to be an ordinary cabin boy, if you don't mind.'

'It'll be a nice change Captain,' Phillips grinned, 'if you think I'm up to the task.'

'I do think it. I'll let you know when I want my captaincy back. Until then, you're the captain, men do you hear that, Phillips is your captain.'

They gave Phillips a cheer and a pat on the back.

'Alright, what's the first thing you want me to do then Captain,' Phillips questioned Ashton.

'Who's Captain?' Ashton queried.

'Oh, I do apologise,' said Phillips, with the crew laughing, 'what would you do, Ashton, lad, in this situation?'

'Well, Cap'n,' Ashton took off his neat captain's coat, messed up his hair a little and put on the crew's accent, and you could tell they thought it a good joke as more laughter ensued. 'You might come to the captain's cabin and I'll help you into your official hat and jacket.'

Which Phillips did, and returned looking rather magnificent, and much more a proper captain than Ashton ever had, with a cloak bearing gilded stripes and a big tricorn hat. That's not to say the young captain didn't cut a fine figure, oh no, for certainly he did, and was everything a crew needed in a captain, so said the men, but it's just that Phillips was so much more impressive, the big chest, the broad shoulders, the strong arms and firm countenance. Well, what it was really, was that Phillips was not a boy, but a man. That is precisely what Ashton thought, and in this town, which seemed more like Althorn, where he was not known and where he was unsure of welcome, he was more certain that things would run smoother if this crew went in structured more like people everywhere were used to, a man for a captain, and boys only in crew.

As the crew of the Avaeste prepared to disembark the good people of Wye drew around, and they looked on and wondered what these foreign men were about. The crew thought these people looked alright; not fearsome or threatening, just ordinary folk. They were red-nosed and warm, and chatted calmly to each other as they wandered about, looking at the fine little ship and muttering at it as it sat there on top of the ice, between their own ships that were frozen tight.

'May we berth here a short while?' Phillips called down. No one said anything, just looked them up and down, but then at a nearby house an old man poked out his head, long bearded with white hair, and though he was definitely not very stout, Tom was sure he was St Nick, that is Father Christmas, or if you prefer, Santa Claus, and he said so to Berens, but the old man yelled up.

'That depends who you are and what you're about,' the old man studied them closely with a scrutinizing look.

'We are sailors of Althorn,' Captain Phillips yelled back, 'come to visit your fair isle.'

The old man chuckled, 'We haven't had visitors since the autumn and that feels like it was back a while now. Alright then, come down, we can talk it over inside, we'll all freeze our noses off if we stay out here too long. Come in, I'll put the kettle on.'

So the crew disembarked with no fuss at all, except Morris and Dew who protesting against the cold stayed on board in their respective holes. The men walked past staring children who'd managed to sneak out, and past the adults who appreciated this excuse to take a break away from their warm indoors and walk around. Some even went into the old man's house, it seems all were welcome and the house was large enough inside, though it did not seem so on the outer.

'Greetings travellers,' said the old man, as he handed them steaming mugs of tea, asking them as he did if they preferred it salted or sweet. He handed one to Ashton saying, 'and one for you good lad,' patting him upon the head, and it was all the crew could do to keep from cracking up as they knew their young captain's pride, especially then as the old man did the same thing to Tom, as he did not realise there was much difference between them, that one of these boys was more than a boy, oh yes, he was very much grown up, and of course, he was the real captain, and a prince, no less.

Then when they were all seated the old man took a mug for himself and at the end of the long wooden table, leaned back in his chair with pleasure and said,

'I'm the harbourmaster, the name is Muljone.'

'Captain Phillips,' the lieutenant introduced himself, 'of the Avaeste. I must thank you for your generosity sir.'

The harbourmaster nodded, 'Bah, it's just a little tea to warm you up while we discuss what we need to discuss. I haven't said you can stay yet,' he laughed, but added curiously, 'it's a fine little ship.'

'That she is,' agreed Phillips.

'So, what brings you here to the Isle of Wye?'

Phillips hadn't prepared himself with an answer and had to think a moment, which the keen eyes of the harbourmaster espied.

'We are on a botanical expedition sir,' Phillips finally answered.

'In this weather? In mid winter?'

'Yes sir, we understand there are certain plants which flower only briefly as winter becomes spring, it is these in particular that we came to see.' Phillips glanced at Ashton worriedly, but Ashton thought he was doing fine, and he himself relaxed and tried, however uncomfortable it was to him, to act like a normal boy and make mischief with Tom, like playing marbles on the table, for Tom often carried marbles with him.

Phillips went on explaining their search to old Muljone, knowing the sort of location they sought, and seeking the harbourmaster's wisdom. The old man mentioned many a place where such finds might be found, and together he and Phillips discussed the possibilities of location and modes of transport, for many of the places the old man told of were quite out of the way, on steep mountains, deep valleys or fields of rock, not the kind of places that it would be wise to try to take the Avaeste. She was a fine little ship but even she could not be asked to navigate to places like that, and also as Ashton had said at some time before, even though she could go just about anywhere, the place for ships was in the harbour and it was impolite to the residents to take a route across the top of an island.

By the time all had finished drinking their tea; which was rather a long time as little Tom Needle sipped his just like his Grandmother did – that is, one sip could last several minutes, longer still as between his sips he was trying to beat Ashton in marbles; anyway, it was after quite a while that the harbourmaster decided to let these men stay, and do their bit for the field of botany. He found for them a selection of more detailed maps and gave to them many words of advice, telling them of places that he would search out if he were they, and other people too joined in and conversed. Soon they had a good list of places to search, and the people were excited and asked that when they were finished they'd like to see their findings, some even offered to go with them and help them. Others offered details of what they might find, the different plants that grew in different climes, on this side of the island and on the other side, and even the kind of things that could be found growing down at the very, very end of the Y.

Phillips took in all that he could, he also had Banks and Jennings taking notes, Carter would have been too, but that he was not yet caught up to the literate skill of those other two, and they had much to note as Phillips had not said they only looked for a Silvertip Sedge, but just broadly any plant that grew out of the snow, so they learnt of sweet snow bells and spring stars, and winter aconites, the eranthis, the soft purple crocus that covers fields with colour all across the white, and so many more beautiful and glorious things, but of course, a grassy sedge was too lowly to mention.

Then most of the onlookers went home as the evening fell and with it brought clouds, high up they were and full of fine snow, which began to fall, the villagers going quickly for it would not do to be away if a blizzard came, said they.

'Blizzard?' said Phillips, 'are they a usual occurrence? We passed through some on our way here, are they an issue on the island also?'

'Aye,' said old Muljone, 'at this time of winter. It's a funny thing though, they've usually been coming in the afternoon, but today it seems they waited for you.'

'That was nice of them.'

'Indeed it was, for when they really get going the wind picks up, so rough it is lads I don't think you'd have made it in, not even in your fine little ship. It would have been a fool's errand, and you all might well have met your death.' The harbourmaster shook his head. 'I still can't understand why you risked your lives to come here to us at the far ends of the earth to document and sample a few rare plants.'

'Well, plants are important, in fact I recall in the museum in the city they have rare samples from as far away as Egypt which they used in the process to embalm; now I wouldn't like to have that done to myself, but it was curious, oh, and further, there are beautiful orchids there from Singapore, all different colours, which I don't know where it is but if you go there and come straight back I'm told it can take a twelvemonth, or more if there's unfavourable winds.'

The harbourmaster wondered at these men, for they did not look like men of the Ether Marine, that is, except for Ashton, and by and by Phillips had innocently let slip so the harbourmaster knew his wonderings were correct.

'Where do you hail from Captain Phillips?'

'I myself am a proud Althorn man, simple folk we are but not without redeeming qualities I hope.'

'Botanists, you say?'

'Well, no, not exactly, but-'

'No, you don't look to me like studied men, what I mean is, you don't look like botanists. Now Althorn, where is that? Oh yes, and where did you acquire this ship, The Avaeste?'

Now something had provoked old Muljone's suspicion for his questions were becoming more probing, not really prying, but more formally enquiring, so before the knot would be around Phillips' neck and tightening, Ashton felt it his duty to step in. The boy rubbed his head, he did not like this deception, and it was grating on him that he had done it. Wouldn't it be better if the truth was put clear whatever these people thought of it?

So Ashton stood up with certainty and with pride, and at once Muljone could see he was not as he'd thought him, not like any of the boys he knew from Wye Island.

Ashton said, 'Do forgive them, good sir, they do only as I asked, but I see now I should have been open from the start. My name is Ashton sir, and I am their captain.'

Muljone just stared at him with his eyes and mouth wide open, so Ashton continued,

'We seek not just any plant that grows from the snow, no, we seek a certain grass that's known to live in swamps and in marshes, or perhaps along reedy hollows or rocks near water flows. It's name is the Carex Argentius, commonly the Silvertip Sedge. We must find it, Mr Muljone, we must find it flowering, for it has curative properties and my father's life may come to an end if I don't get it to him, and as soon as I possibly can.'

Mr Muljone took a moment to take it all in, and though he thought it rather a rare and unlikely circumstance, he could believe by his speech that this boy was as he said, that is, that he captained these men. And of his relating their true endeavour the harbourmaster could now see the reasoning in what they did and what they risked to come here.

'Alright,' he said, 'I still have questions, but they can wait, I'll aid you as best I can. I've never heard of this plant myself but mayhap some other here has. I'll send for the doctor too, he may have some other thing that could help.'

'That is doubtful. Not that I doubt the skill of your doctor but nothing has been found in all the scattered realms; this sedge could well be our last hope, though I thank you most sincerely for your help.'

Mr Muljone stroked his beard then took up his trusty pipe and thought some more, in a way none spoke, as he looked as though he might soon speak something important, and he did.

'You'll need a way up them hills,' said he, 'you'll have to make the pass between Crag Dun and Crag Aroon, around Tórr Aganoth, then head for the Valley of Lore. It overlooks the southern coast, then yonder to the edge of the Aethermarinus. By my reckoning, if anywhere, that's where this sedge grass would grow. There's marshes there in summer, fed by the drips of the higher ice flows. It's a nothing sort of place where no one ever goes, in the shadow of the mountains, difficult to reach from the ocean, not much better over land but at least I think you might just be able.'

'What is the best way to get there?' asked Ashton, 'do you have any snow-dogs or such that could make the journey? I can pay for their hire if necessary.' Ashton offered, although he hoped much fee wouldn't be required. Yes, he was the son of the king, but this was his own undertaking and he did not have a limitless balance, and he was all the way out here, his store of coin was growing low and he did not fancy having to sell off his plane, though of course he would if he had to.

'Well, no, on that point I have been thinking. At first I thought one thing and then I thought another, and another thing again, but I have come to the conclusion that you should take the Wyotéa.'

'The Wyotéa? What is the Wyotéa?'

'The Wyotéa are the wolves,' said the harbourmaster delicately, knowing it was not the answer this crew would be wanting, nor indeed what they would assume.

'Wolves?' said Ashton, with surprise and, naturally, with a note of fear and hesitancy, for everyone knows that wolves are wild things with quick tempers and sharp teeth.

'Wolves?' muttered his men too, they didn't like the sound of this at all.

'Surely huskies would be better, snow dogs, horses, or even reindeer?' Ashton took courage and suggested.

'Nay,' old Muljone drew in from his pipe then puffed the smoke out in a peculiar cloud. 'The wolves will be best,' he said, 'we've no horses able to make the trek, no polar bears, and besides they're a touch too wild even if we had, and the snow dogs are all in use round town and upland at the moment, not that they would dare the journey anyway. Trust me, the wolves are the best way.'

'But, can they pull a sleigh?' Ashton asked, for he didn't know, could they?

'You won't be taking a sleigh.' Muljone drew from his pipe then puffed again.

'We won't?'

'No, you'll take the Dausle.'

'The what?'

'The Dausle,' Muljone explained, 'it's fast, lightweight and goes over more terrain with ease. Takes one man, seated, three wolves to pull. A neat piece of equipment I think, and light enough to carry if you have to. Watch though, the wolves won't take care for you, got to watch they don't pull you into low tree branches and what not.'

'Three wolves to one man,' Ashton thought with discomfort, 'and how many wolves are there?'

Old Muljone counted in his head, then answered, 'Nine, maybe ten.'

'That's only three men,' Ashton worried, he hadn't counted on a situation like this; three men, taken across the mountains by *nine wolves*? 'Wolves? Are you sure?' Ashton questioned again.

'These are no ordinary wolves Captain Ashton, they've thick coats and large feet, and an unequalled pace at need. They're tough beauties too, they do well on very little food comparatively, and they've a nose for danger and the fierceness to fight it.'

'That's what I'm afraid of,' Ashton worried.

'Oh, you need not fear they'll turn on you my boy, they're loyal enough, and wise. We call them the Wyotéa, it's a foreign name meaning, 'the protectors of Wye.' They are originally not of this island, no, the story is that the ancestors of these wolves were a gift to us from afar, if you believe the old stories they were originally from Arazin.'

'Arazin?' Ashton repeated, much shocked and not comforted at all by this news. He did not trust Muljone's words, indeed he began to think it all a lie, but he kept on for his father's sake, yes, it was the only thing that kept him going.

Old Muljone nodded with a smile, 'Aye, I know it's hard to believe, as Arazin is a mythical place none have ever seen, and Wye is too much in the ordinary way to have any association with such a name.'

'No, that's not what I was thinking; I have seen enough in my travels to believe nearly anything; but I was thinking, wasn't it, that is, isn't it told that the tyrant Calegra Descada comes from that land?'

'Aye, I suppose I had heard that at some point, but what of it?'

'Then let's not mention it, is there another way?' Ashton thought of his golden plane and of flying to this place, but too extreme was the weather and too rugged the terrain. 'Surely, there must be some other way.'

'I'm afraid not young Captain; if you want to get to the other side of Wye at this time of year, you'd best let the Wyotéa take you, there's none better to do it than they.'

'I suppose I will have to take your word.'

'Come, young captain, I know you are impatient to go and with all speed. I'll introduce you to them,' Muljone rose and went to the door.

'The Wyotéa? They're here? I didn't see any wolves when we came into town, only wild ones on the far side.'

'Of course you didn't see them,' Muljone laughed.

He opened the door that faced the street at the back, ushering Ashton and his men out. They shivered again in the face of the cold and Ashton wondered how he'd fare at so many days out in this bitter snow, but he wiped his fear of that aside for the moment as he watched the old harbourmaster.

Muljone nodded to another man waiting by; thin and gaunt looking like a man who regrets and has stopped caring for life and himself, and from the snow on his boots Ashton gathered he must have been standing there for quite some time, leaning idle, and perhaps listening to the conversation inside? He moved now, walked a few paces, straitening up, but they could see, though he did not seem that old at all he was a little hunched and there was a heaviness in his breath that rasped.

He nodded back at Muljone, then clicked his fingers and tapped his stick, then whispered hoarsely out to the empty snow, 'Wyotéa ey navre ca na.'

From out of the white covered street the wolves arose, shaking the snow fluff from their backs and stretching out, then coming casually across to the group at the harbourmaster's house. Most of them were white with flecked grey, but also patches of rust, but others were a blue, buttery white, or mottled smoky browns, and even black. So pure and so clean, they'd thick hair for the winter, long, full tails and an obvious strength in their limbs. They seemed friendly enough, but aloof and proud too, and of course, thought Ashton and the rest of his crew, wolves were wolves.

Ashton greeted them as all Novanian's would have, he knelt to their level, looked to each one, 'We seek passage to the other side of Wye, and return, we are told you can help us, and I would be most grateful if you would consent to -'

'What are you doing boy?' the harbourmaster criticised, pulling Ashton up, 'they're beasts, not men. Tell them not a word of emotion or what you think, only show them strength. Their respect for you is the thing you must maintain. Do you understand?'

Ashton was shaken but answered, 'Yes, I think.'

But the Wyotéa were already curious of Ashton, and watched him more intently, stepping closer to the group of men.

'Bey! Bey!' old Muljone shooed them back a bit. Even he did not like being crowded by the wolf pack.

'So what we'll do is give them a feed, while you get ready and I'll pull out the Dausles for you and make sure all the harnesses are sound.'

'Thank you.'

'And I'll tune the blades so you fly easy as music over the ground. Now what you have to do is decide who you're going to take with you.'

'Aye, not an easy thing to do, I feel as though whoever I ask, I'm asking them to face all things, even possible death, and for what, one other life?' Ashton said and thought to himself, 'for the king or not, I don't know that I can risk their lives like this.'

'Well, you can't go alone, so you have to choose someone.'

'Do I? Maybe I could go alone?' Ashton looked at the hungry wolves and gulped, 'or maybe not.'

'I volunteer,' said brave little Tom, 'I'll come.'

'No.' Ashton shook his head, it would no place for children out there, he well knew.

'But Cap'n I'm light, like a needle sir, remember, if you took me and someone else little maybe four of us could go.'

'No Tom, it's alright, although, actually, you might be on to something. Alright, I'll have you Tom, and Morris and Jennings.'

'Me cap'n!?' worried Jennings, wondering what help he could be, he wasn't one for slip sliding across the snow, nor strong as others he thought, nor as bold. It was true that most of the time he just went with the flow, 'But what help could I be? Morris too – he can't stand the snow.'

Morris would have agreed and thanked Jennings very muchly for his support, though he'd give his life for Ashton he really didn't like the cold, but as it so happened Morris was still on the Avaeste, having finished his hot muddy cocoa and fallen deeply asleep in his bed. Which is what they reported to Ashton when he sent men to look for him. Ashton sighed, what was he to do? He couldn't ask Morris to come when in all honesty the Swamp Monster was only following his body's seasonal rhythm. And Jennings was obviously fearful of going, with good reason, Ashton was too. Tom was still brave, but that may only be because Tom was still young and he had not yet really known what it was to fear, had not seen family nor friends find their end.

'Well, you really can only take one other man with you,' said old Muljone, 'as the keeper always has to go with the pack.' And he pointed to the other man who had said nothing, but in a foreign language and to the wolves as yet.

'I'll go with you,' stepped forward Berens. The sailor so admired his young captain and though he feared the journey that would lie ahead nothing would make him prouder than to say that he had been as brave a man as Ashton.

'No Berens,' Ashton said, 'I cannot ask it from any of you. Who knows what lies ahead.'

'Someone has to go with you Captain, please, let me come, let me represent the men of Althorn.'

Ashton thought. Berens was indeed a good choice for a brave and true man he was. He sighed, 'Alright then. Let's get ready.'

So while the wolves ate and the harbourmaster prepared the dausles which looked more like skis and less like sleds, Ashton and Berens went back to the ship to pack and prepare for the journey ahead. Warm clothes and a change, food, navigational aids, writing equipment; now, what else would they need?

'So you're going then?' Santee looked down at Ashton and said.

'Aye, as soon as we can,' Ashton answered as he continued to pack.

'Don't forget, if you find it, you'll need something to keep the sedge plant in,' Santee suggested, 'a jar, or maybe a box, perhaps.'

'Thank you Santee, yes, perhaps I'll use the canister in which I keep the extra maps, do you think?'

'Yes, it would do well. Do you want me to come?' she asked hesitantly.

'No.'

'Are you sure? I could come, I think I should, boy, I could help.'

'No Santee, it's too dangerous, stay with the men and the ship, you might be needed here. I did not expect this, I had thought to find this a simple place, like Althorn, where nice or not men are what they appear to be; yet I have a feeling there is more here than there seems, something I cannot yet see. It has not helped that Berens and I are going with a man I do not know, with a pack of wolves they call the Wyotéa.'

'Wolves?'

'Aye. I've nothing against them, but I don't know what to expect. It seems strange, even convenient that the wolves were about and not the dogs, but the harbourmaster does seem an ordinary and good sort of man, how I wish I could just stop worrying and trust him, after all, if I forget my fears, he has been very accommodating.'

Ashton was ready, he picked up his gear, taking one last look around the cabin. Santee said once again, 'Boy, I should come.'

'No Santee,' Ashton forced a smile, 'I'll be alright.'

'Goodbye then, take care, I'll see you in spring,' Santee said as happily as she could, but oh how her dear little heart trembled with fear for the best boy she had ever known, as he walked out the door, across the deck and down the platform. He took up with Berens and farewelled the crew, then they strapped their gear upon the dausles and took the seat, had a crash course in steering and wolf speak, then off they went, Ashton, Berens and the keeper, three wolves to each.

Chapter 17:
INTO THE VALLEY OF LORE,
THE FIND, AND THE FOES

The blizzard had abated and their aim was to make the high caves while the twilight lasted and so have made a good start, then sleep, and continue early in the morning. To Ashton's surprise the Wyotéa were indeed very fast, they were quiet in their work, alert and single-minded, and the dausles they rode were light, easy to manoeuvre and smooth across the snow and ice.

They reached the caves easily in time, and when Ashton bent to let go the harnessed wolves the keeper shouted at him and sent him away, bending down himself and setting them free, giving Ashton a warning look as if to say, 'No one meddles with the Wyotéa but me.'

Berens and Ashton set up a fire and after a while the man joined them, sitting afar and staring at Ashton on and off, so much Ashton found his spine crept with unease, until he could not sit still any longer but had to do something about it. So he stood up and stepped across to the man, and introduced himself politely. 'My name is Ashton,' he said, holding out his hand

'I know who you are,' the man replied, but said nothing more, not taking Ashton's hand but ignoring it. He only stared, with firelight in his eyes, piercing like the look of the lady on the ice, who had addressed herself as the guardian of Wye, but as you know she remained unremembered to Ashton at this time.

'Ah,' Ashton put his hand back in his warm glove but went on, he would not let this strange man or his own anxious heart get the better of him. 'I don't believe Muljone told me your name?'

'I doubt he did.'

'He said you were the keeper of the Wyotéa.'

'Yes,' the keeper said, then relented, 'my name is Samazan.'

'You're not from this Isle, are you?' Ashton questioned, for a name like that was certainly unusual, a name more likely to be found in the hidden realms, now the shattered lands of Oundin and the Gaardeveran, and of course, the forgotten land where old Muljone had told the Wyotéa came, the land of Arazin, which lay high in the realms of the Ciel Marine.

But Samazan changed the subject, 'Is it right you wish to make it to the Valley of Lore before the first melt?'

'Yes, that's right.'

'It does not seem far on the map but the way is hard. You must be prepared for many difficulties. Are you prepared?'

'As much as I can be.'

'Is it right you seek there a medicine?'

'Yes, a particular plant.'

'Mm. With curative properties. For whom is it you seek it?'

'My father.'

'Your father,' the keeper repeated in a way that made the poor boy uneasy, and he stared at Ashton disconcertingly again. The wolves were back now, after their free run and sat around behind their man, eyes also staring. 'You'd best get some sleep,' Samazan said to Ashton and Berens and although Ashton replied that he would try, he wasn't sure that he could, for he'd a feeling that if he closed his eyes that would be that end of him. But he curled in his sack by the warm fire and soon he could not help but let his eyelids slide, and the next thing he knew Berens was waking him, for it was morning and time to move on. Samazan had the wolves ready and harnessed, and he laughed at Ashton and Berens surprise that nothing untoward had happened in the night.

Days they went on as hard as they could, over mountain and frozen stream, through forests black and leafless, to fields empty and desolate. Nights they slept, for their bodies ached from all their efforts and concentration; even the wolves were tired and closer to the fire they crept. They had many a time nearly lost one or the other, when holes had been hidden or dangers buried and unseen, causing a dausle to flip or spin, or almost losing wolf or man to a chasm, and they spent two days circuiting a ravine for the narrowest place, then another half day chopping down trees and forming a bridge to cross it.

They went down into valleys and then up to high peaks, making the pass that Muljone had told of, between Dun and Aroon, where the cold was ever so frore and all were nearly frozen, even the wolves despite their thick coats. Now they were rounding a very large mountain, the Tórr Aganoth, renowned in the warmer seasons for being a black tower of rock upon rock, but now mostly white just like everything else.

At this moment they traversed its exposed western face, they had to go this way for there was no other path, for from here was the way to go on and down to the Valley of Lore and the Silvertip perhaps. But even as they reached the narrowest way on a very open stretch, even as they stood off of their dausles and let the wolves free to let them go safely ahead, even then the sky turned from clear to covered, and a full whiteout was unleashed, yes, the fiercest of blizzards fell upon them. They trudged through the snow, on and on through the white, barely moving, only inch by inch at a time. They couldn't see even a foot before them, nor behind, nor left or right. On they went slowly, until the keeper Samazan stopped, finding a cavity in the hillside. He pulled them into that snow hollow which the wise wolves had also discovered, and they sat there against the blizzard, all so closely huddled.

'We will wait it out,' Samazan gasped with heavy breath, 'it will be safer to wait here than go on in this.'

'Agreed,' said Ashton and Berens, leaning back and catching some air. It was a small space, and a little confined what with nine wolves and three men, but it was certainly better at present than bearing the direct force of the blizzard. Soon, though the storm continued only a few feet away, what with the group all together it grew warmer in the snow cave and their chilled bones and muscles relaxed. They sat there in silence for such a long time as the blizzard continued with fury outside.

'Do they have names?' Ashton asked of Samazan after a while, 'the Wyotéa?'

'Of course,' the keeper said, he did not smile but he gave Ashton a curious look, as though he was beginning to think that Ashton might be alright, but he hadn't yet made up his mind.

'The butter-cream one with the diamond is Kairu. The pure black is Azatar, the brown-russet is Ruvin, the white is Suma,' Samazan paused, 'they think you strange boy, you, your behaviour.'

'How so?'

'For one, they are not used to quite so much respect. The people of Wye fear them and accept them, but they have no other consideration.' Samazan let that sink in, then said the next thing. 'For two, they are not as blind as the men of Wye, they can see many things others might have missed.' Samazan paused, looking Ashton over, then asked with a grin, 'What are you really doing here? Where are you from? You are no ordinary captain.'

Ashton raised an eyebrow, 'It is as I have told you and Muljone, I seek a rare plant for my father's sake. As to my home, I come from Aeloran.'

'Aeloran? I might have guessed,' Samazan examined Ashton knowingly.

'But I'm from Althorn,' Berens added.

'Yes, so I overheard before we left,' Samazan said. 'I can't say I know where it is but I must assume it is in the Teramarinus? For most of the Aethermarinus is known to me, but Althorn is unfamiliar and sounds like it would belong in that place.'

Berens just looked at Ashton for help to answer.

'Yes,' said the young captain, 'Althorn is in the Terra Marine.'

'Where the land meets the sea, meets the sea, with no gaps in between,' Samazan said thoughtfully.

'Indeed.'

'But, Aeloran, this is a gift indeed, for no island in the Ether has a greater rapport with the Ceil Marine,' Samazan said excitedly, a prospect dawning. 'I will open with you Ashton,' began Samazan, 'it is as you guessed, I am not of this place. I and the Wyotéa came from Arazin long ago, we are not the descendents of those that came as the people of Wye proclaim, no, we *are* they that came.'

'Oh.'

Samazan grinned at Ashton's concerned countenance and Berens astounded one; he had no idea what any of this meant.

'What I would ask of you, as a Captain of Aeloran, is that when we have helped you do this, find this medicine, you can help us too. You can help absolve us of our crimes, help us get a pardon. You see, we have been hiding here all this time, for back in our homeland, a long age ago, there was an uprising against our king. The charge was led by Calegra Descada, yes he who you mentioned, a tyrant if ever there was one, and we were in his army.'

The colour left Ashton's face and there was a shaking in his fingers, Samazan just grinned regretfully and continued. 'We were misled and we joined him, and not till after did we realise our mistake, but too late; our king banished him and we heard he would do the same to all who had stood against him, so we banished ourselves to this place before he got the chance. They are not wolves, not Wyotéa, Captain, we are men of Arazin, hiding here from our king and from the tyrant all this time, for both want our blood. We fear to show ourselves, or return.'

'You are all men?' Ashton looked at the wolves, who had gathered close and were listening still. 'Gladly, if there was anything I could do,' Ashton answered, just as all knew he would, for in his kindness this young captain was all too dependable. He continued, 'But, how can I help you in this? How can I possibly gain your pardon? I have no sway with the king of Arazin, I do not even know him. And those that believe Arazin exists say the way is blocked in any case, blocked since the rebellion, which must be the war of which you speak.'

'Yes, it was long ago, and the Cielomarinus has been so long closed – you can come down to the Ether but cannot return. And Arazin is almost a myth as you say; but you are a captain from Aeloran, surely you must have high friends, friends who might know our king?' Samazan pleaded, 'and surely you must know a way through to the Ciel Marine if you could make the way to the Teramarinus and this Althorn?' He had a wild, desperate look in his eyes, the look of a man who is at the end, oh so tortured inside, and so tired.

Ashton shook his head.

'But, surely you must know someone who would? There must be a way back, there must be a way to plead mercy for us and for us to return home again.'

'I suppose my father might know,' Ashton relented.

'And who is your father, Captain Ashton? I feel he must be a great man.'

Ashton felt he could no longer avoid it, and answered, 'He is. He is the king, St Amalric.'

'The king?! St Amalric?!' Samazan repeated in surprise, and even the wolves shifted and seemed to refocus their eyes on this brave son of Mathis, who didn't feel so brave at the present but felt his spine quaver.

'Yes, I should have seen by your character,' Samazan said, 'I believe what you say, that you are the son of a king, but, forgive me, another question, what again is his name?'

'Mathis St Amalric.'

'And how long has he reigned?'

'Since the fields of the Thale Wold were shredded under his boots as he defeated the tempest there. And then, I have read, the people of Aeloran made him king. It seems long ago, but it cannot be that long for he is not an old man, but then it must be a while ago because it was long before I knew him, and he has a name of such renown, in most of the realms they call him the wisest king that has lived.'

'I fear that I must know him,' Samazan said.

'You do?'

'I believe so, and what you say makes it more possible – he is not old, but he has lived long, even as we who are from the Ciel Marine, he is so.'

'From the Cielomarinus?'

'Yes, it must be, and not only that, but amongst his many names the king of Arazin is also known as the wisest.'

'Surely they are not one and the same?' Ashton gasped.

'Or father and son,' Samazan said, and though he too was overwhelmed by this news he chuckled at Ashton's stunned expression, 'but if they are one and the same, tell me, do you think there is a law against being the king in two places at once?' Then seriously, 'But whatever the case, this must mean the king of Aeloran and of Arazin are somehow related, which means you can help us Prince Ashton, if you will.'

'I don't know the extent of your crimes, perhaps your punishment will still stand – perhaps I will make your plea and then you will receive not pardon from the king of Arazin, but death.'

'If he hears us, and that is the judgement, so be it, I am done hiding.'

'But by the time I return,' Ashton explained, with a glistening tear rolling down his face, 'it may be too late.'

'Oh,' said Samazan, realizing, 'oh, you seek the medicine for your father who is dying – your father, the king!?'

'Yes.'

'Oh, so is it that you say the king of Aeloran is dying?' Samazan asked again, finding it hard to believe. 'The king who may be able to affirm our pardon?'

'Yes. He was gravely ill even when I left, so ill I fear he may have passed long before I get back.'

'This is a terrible thing,' Samazan said, deeply saddened at the news, but also deeply thinking. 'Who would have thought the wise king, he of Aeloran and Arazin if it is him, could be unwell like this, when he has every help at his fingertips, and all of the Aether and Cielomarinus to help.' Samazan looked at the Wyotéa and they looked to each other and at him as though they could understand all that was spoken.

'But, it is perfect!' Samazan exclaimed, 'don't you see? If you are a son of our king, which it is almost certain, if we help you find this sedge thing and get it back to him – and if he lives, do you think then we would have a chance? Do you think then we would gain our pardon? Tell us yes. We know our mistakes, and every day we regret.'

Ashton certainly had known something was strange about the Wyotéa, but he had not expected this, but he answered, 'I know my father, the king; he is renowned for his justice, but also for his mercy, and if your hearts really mirror the regret of your words you can count yourselves already pardoned.'

Samazan sighed, leaning back and closing his eyes, a trace of a smile, of relief across his face, indeed his whole being seemed to relax.

'The blizzard is weakening,' he said at last, 'but Ashton, before we go, tell me, how are things going in the world out there? We don't hear much all the way out here.'

'What can I tell you?'

'Anything, any news, but weighing on my mind is the outcome; by your expression I might guess Calegra has not been idle in his exile?'

'Yes, you are correct.'

'What of him?'

'It would seem his rage and intent grew when he was banished. He raised many armies throughout the Aethermarinus.'

'No!'

'Yes. The worst is over, he was defeated by a vanguard of able allies, though that was some time ago now, but Descada himself denied this defeat and said he'd only ceded for the time being, and he keeps trying to regain what he lost then.'

'I did not realise he could gain such sway in the Ether Marine.'

'Well, he has many fine words to mislead the unwary mind. Much has happened since, it took some time but by and by the peoples are recovering. Aeloran flourishes and it could want no more, but that my father grow well again. Without him, what will become of Aeloran and the rest of the Aethermarinus, I don't like to think,' Ashton worried.

'And Arazin,' Samazan put in, he too with worry lines on his forehead.

'I have heard it said that he is the greatest man that ever lived.'

'Yes, in Arazin they believed nothing could bring him down, though Descada tried his best.'

'How Edward and the others will go on when he is gone I do not know,' Ashton pondered, 'I know they will do all they can, but none can fill his shoes.'

'No.'

Poor Ashton, his heavy heart, if anyone knew the truth! It was he brought down the great king, he, as he died. If only the king had left him! But what had Annabella Bien told him not to forget? The king knew what he was doing, he would have known what lay ahead. Even the poison that Ashton somehow passed to him, even this sickness, even his death if it came to that.

'What other news?' Samazan continued, 'what is the state of things at present?'

'The other allies prosper again,' Ashton told, 'though much of what was lost in the wars remains lost; some isles which Calegra met before Mathis stopped him are still naught but scorched earth, still ashes and smoke. On our way here we passed through Meridian too, and while we were there he attacked again, but was beaten. It seems he still has his spies everywhere, still has his eyes open for weaknesses, for ways to attack.'

220

'Yes, Descada isn't one to give up easily; he will try one way and if that doesn't succeed, he's a thousand other plans to try, and he's not one that minds biding his time.'

'I'd like to thank you Samazan, and all of you, for bringing us across the snow. I don't know what I would have done without your help.'

'I do. You, my young captain, would have trudged over these mountains till your feet were black and blue.'

Ashton laughed, so did Berens, agreeing, 'That's exactly what he would have done.'

'Yes,' Samazan said, 'I see more than a streak of determined stubbornness in you.'

'Shall we head on again? It looks like the worst of it is over.'

'Yes. We can't be far now. Two or three days more perhaps, and as the lengthening sun suggests, we'll be in good time for the first of the melt. But we'll have to take more care, it will be more dangerous, especially coming back as all thaws around us. We may find we have to back track a lot more.'

And so they continued on, but as soon as Berens could catch a word alone with Ashton he voiced his concern, 'Captain, I still don't trust them. I know more was said between you and the keeper than I could comprehend, but the wolves themselves, or at least some of them, well, I've a feeling in my gut Captain.'

'I know, I too feel I can't yet fully trust them. We will be wary Berens, and stay on our guard, but I hope we are mistaken. I know myself I have an involuntary prejudice against anyone with even remote association with the tyrant Calegra, but I am glad it is not me alone, but you also feel uneasy. It is a shame, I wanted to believe Samazan, and trust him.'

'Maybe you can, I certainly hope my gut is wrong this time. Although, it hasn't been wrong for a very long while.'

And while Berens talked with Ashton, the Wyotéa talked too.

'What do you think you're doing Samazan?' they asked the one that represented them as a man, 'making deals with the son of the one who would banish us, or so it would seem, the one who exiled our leader and stripped him of his powers and ours, leaving us as nothing, as the lowliest of minions in the kingdom. When we served Calegra we had all the power he had, we were great!'

'Calegra's time is over, we knew that at the first victory of the king. Calegra can cause trouble, but he cannot win.'

'But, if St Amalric dies, as it seems he might, then Calegra *has* won, and then what do any of us need of a pardon?'

'I know what you're saying but that's not the way.'

'Yes it is,' they pressed, 'Calegra will soon take us back for he knows us and knows what an asset we would be to have back in his company, especially when we bring good news to him – that we prevented this Prince taking the cure to save the king, indeed, we destroyed it. Then it will be as we dreamed, we will have wealth, riches, and the very souls of men tied to our fingers, we, with Calegra would own the Ciel, the Ether, and the Terra Marine. From the lowliest of towns, like this Althorn, to the blessed Aeloran, to the king's own city in Arazin. Then we would all agree that our little sojourn here had been worth it.'

'But,' Samazan argued back, 'if we help this Prince of Aeloran and so aid the king, if we are pardoned, don't you think, well, it is my wish, to go back to being ordinary, to see Arazin again, as I was before all of this, to go back to the glorious Cielomarinus, not as a persecutor or a conqueror, just as one of them, as who I was.'

A few of the wolves nodded, they understood Samazan and agreed, but the others kept on, they laughed at them, saying, 'Is that what you think? You think you can go back like that? Impossible! Ha! Don't you remember what we have done? Who we became when we followed Calegra? They would never take us back, and despite what this Prince says, the king would never forgive us!'

'I suppose you're right,' Samazan sighed, 'no one could ever forgive us our crimes.'

'No. We must go on as we began,' pressed Azatar, with his cunning tongue, 'foil this prince's plan. We will help him find this plant then destroy it and so destroy the king's last chance.'

'Then we'll crawl back to Calegra,' Samazan despaired, 'and beg to be his slaves, for that is what he requires, or don't you remember?'

'What would you prefer Samazan? Pay the penalty for your treachery, or be free to keep committing our deceit, for as long as we subvert more to Calegra's cause he won't pull us to account for running when we did.'

'I wish the boy had not come here. Then at least we would have just remained as we were.'

'This is no life. Or do you forget Samazan?'

'Don't begin to lecture me. I have oft enough joined you, and don't forget this man who I pretend to be is not who I am either.'

'So what is your choice Samazan? Action must be decided.'

'I suppose we will help the Prince find the Carex Argentius,' Samazan yielded, 'then we will destroy it. Then, if I'm not mistaken, we will need do nothing, for he seeks this thing so terribly, having it pulled from his grasp will utterly destroy him.'

'If indeed we find it.'

'Oh, we will, I am fairly sure, for the prince has talked to many well studied men, so he said to the harbourmaster. If the plant exists anywhere it will exist here, it is almost certain, and besides which, he has with him a description of it, and if I am not mistaken, I have seen it and know just where it is.'

'And,' Azatar continued evilly, 'after it is done and destroyed, our plan is easy, for this prince has brought us the perfect ship to make our way back across the marines, and even back to the Ciel and back to Arazin. Did you see his ship Samazan?'

Samazan sighed, 'Yes, the Avaeste.'

They all went on, just as they had been, neither group aware of what the other had spoken. They reached the north face and then proceeded the difficult way down.

'Do you know why they call it the Valley of Lore?' Samazan asked Ashton as they stepped carefully down a particularly steep corner.

'No, I can't say I do.'

'Before the clans of Wye united every clan had some knowledge about this valley, but only a fragment, usually a fable of some kind, a tale with a point. Put the fragments together and they had a very strange picture of the place. Hence, the valley of many wisdoms.'

'Muljone said you were the only ones that would venture here, why's that? Are there things to fear out here besides the elements and the environment?'

'There are wild things here that have been left to grow beyond their usual scale and untamed, for they wander into this valley, get lost and cannot escape, or they are seeds, finding root in the rich soil of this place and gorging on it, becoming overgrown. But you need not fear this place, we have been here many times before over the years, we know how to deal with the creatures here, and besides which, this time of year nothing much will be stirring, the only thing I fear here,' Samazan said thoughtfully as he studied their surroundings, 'is ourselves.'

Ashton asked, 'Why's that?' but didn't get an answer.

They covered much ground, going down and down, and just as Samazan said, it was two days only, then they were well and truly within the valley. The water was melting from the snow-laden branches and a trickle could be heard running under the ice. Old trees and young towered above, with wide, wide trunks, and the way was hard through thick vines and undergrowth, but apart from the plants and the odd very large pheasant there was hardly a sign of other life yet.

They camped the night with the firm intention of an early rise, and in Ashton's chest grew an uncontrollable fear and excitement, oh he could hardly sleep! To think they were here at last, and possibly, even tomorrow, they would find the sedge with the silvertip, its flowers boldly shooting out of the snow. To find it at last would be such an incredible and wonderful thing, oh, a balm to banish his sorrow, but he still held a worry about the wolves all around, he would just have to trust them, there was no other option.

Samazan couldn't sleep, if he could just get Ashton alone and warn him of the wolves malevolent intent! But Samazan was watched by the pack at all times. There were two at least he thought who would stand with him, who did not wish to go and rejoin with Calegra, but they would not make their decision on their own. Even if the three of them made a stand, even with Ashton and this sailor Berens, it would not be enough to go against the seven wolves of Arazin that would be left. They had been bad men in their time and being wolves for more than a generation had not softened them in the slightest, oh no, if anything, their hunger for blood and war had only been further ignited. Some had come to this valley for too long before as well, they were giants now and wild, though like dogs they still longed to return to their master, however cruel he had been when they had been his agents in that first disaster. Samazan despaired; there would be no stopping them now they had this plan in their heads. When it came down to it, it would be help them destroy this sedge and destroy Ashton, or face death.

When the first twinkling of light filtered through the dawn Ashton was up, and Berens too, they were so cheerful and much refreshed, and they could hardly breakfast fast enough, so excited they were at the day ahead, even though they wondered where Samazan had gone with half of the pack.

The remaining wolves lay around, relaxed as they waited. Ashton and Berens picked up their sacks to head off on the search, but even then Samazan came back.

'Come,' he said, he seemed somewhat sad, 'I think I have found your plant.'

So they hurried to follow him through the undergrowth of the overgrown old forest still all covered in snow, and they followed him across small clearings and more forest, over small flowing rivulets of melting ice. Then they came to a certain place, getting close now, Ashton could feel it, the air was warmer here and denser, and the other side of Wye could be seen now in the clear sky, the very bottom of the island, at the last point of the stroke of y. And this place had a similar aspect to the lake high up the hill on Ile de Merle back in Meridian. It had to be here, the Carex Argentius, it had to be!

Ashton held his heart as he saw it. He exclaimed and held onto Berens arm and laughed, shook Samazan's hand with his most sincere thanks and all the warmth of heart he possessed; it almost broke poor Samazan then.

Quickly Ashton went and knelt by the plant with all carefulness. It was fairly plain at first glance, just a common river grass: a thin, flat leaf, coloured a dull grey-green and soft as dust, with little white flowers clustered together on a tall shoot, leaning in the breeze and blown over by gusts, and seemingly unaffected by this valley's propensity to make everything giant. And upon a second and closer inspection, the Carex Argentius was a rather rare specimen: the leaves of the grass were cloaked in a fine silver suede, that shimmered as one turned it to the light in different ways, and the flowers themselves, if one could understand their voice to hear what Ashton could, he being Novanian, sang like silver bells as they shivered in the breeze.

Ashton took out the leather-bound cylinder in which he had used to keep maps, and took from within it a cloth, and this he wet, preparing it to wrap and place the precious plant in to convey it safely back to the ship. And then he drew out a spade and prepared to dig it out, carefully maintaining dirt around the roots, just as the botanist Henry Bartle had told him he should.

He dug it out so carefully and gently with the help of Berens, and they wrapped it in the wetted cloth and slid it into the container. They breathed a sigh of relief. They had done it!

Berens said, 'Captain, I think we should take another, or perhaps even three specimens in case this one fails us.'

'I will take one more Berens, but no more than that, I would not want to rob these shores of this rare plant.'

'I'm afraid it's too late for that,' Samazan said, taking the cylinder from Berens, as he and Ashton turned to find they were surrounded. Not wolves, oh no, but ten men were there, giants almost, fearsome and refined, like genies out of golden lamps, with precise moustaches and piercing eyes. Samazan took the cylinder and without an ounce of hesitation crushed it in his hands, Carex Argentius still inside.

Ashton gasped, 'What are you doing? What have you done?' he yelled and fought back with spirit but they took him and Berens and bound them up on opposite sides of a wide tree trunk.

'They have decided they would rather serve Calegra than face the king and his judgement. I tried, but I could not sway them, so I am with them Ashton, forgive me, now you have confirmed that this is the plant you seek we will destroy all traces of it.'

'No!'

'Ashton, at least I have convinced them to spare your life.'

'No, you can't do it, don't you understand, the king will surely die! As will I.'

'That is the point,' said Azatar, 'Calegra will be pleased and we will be re-hired.'

'No!' Ashton cried, 'Don't rob me of this, I must take it back to him.'

'You could never have saved him anyway,' mocked Ruvin, 'to most of the world this plant never did exist, and now it is true, it doesn't.'

The merchants of Calegra's fury covered the valley up and down, and pulled up every plant that looked remotely like it. Then they made a bonfire and burned up every last piece of the Silvertip as Ashton looked on with horrified despair, watching the leaves burn and blacken then turn to sooty nothings before his eyes, smoke rising and swirling about them, the pretty white flowers ceasing their song, and shrivelling and dying even before the flame reached them.

Ashton thought of his journeys - all the way from Aeloran, finding the Avaeste, plotting the path, so far! Then having to make for Althorn, finding the men; all that had happened since then – all for this! All that pain, all that way, for these plants, now they were gone! Gone! A tear left Ashton's eye as he stared at the waste that remained with a lost and desolate gaze. There was no hope left, no more to find, these wolves had taken Ashton's last hope; the king would die.

Samazan asked that they let the prince and his man free, but instead Ruvin took a knife and nicked their skin, whispering in their ears, 'We agreed not to kill thee, but now your blood is free there's plenty a creature here will do the job for us and finish you off. Goodbye then, young prince, enjoy spring in the valley,' the pack laughed cruelly as they left. At the last minute Azatar could not resist and thumped Ashton on the head with a powerful fist, knocking him out cold with that one hit.

Samazan went with the others, but turned back pleading to Berens, 'Say goodbye to the prince for me. Tell him I'm sorry. I had no choice in this.'

Chapter 18:
TO THE AVAESTE WITH ALL HASTE THEY RACE

It was already afternoon by the time the wolves left the pair alone, and as Berens struggled to get free the noon soon turned to evening. Berens wriggled and squirmed and tried to get free any which way he could think of, but he couldn't get out, and he tried to get Ashton to wake up but he found Ashton was still very much out of it.

The evening grew on and the night gathered around, but the stars and the moon still shone through enough to give Berens some outline of the landscape surrounding, then finally a little cough came from Ashton's direction, and a little moan and a groan, 'Oh my head!' he whispered with a dry tongue.

'You alright Captain?' Berens asked.

'Is that you Berens?'

'Aye Captain, right here.'

'How do we stand my good man? Please tell me what I am recalling did not happen today.'

'Well, that depends, if it's after midnight I could tell you it happened yesterday. I'm sorry Cap'n, I shouldn't make fun at a time like this. It happened alright, them wolves were men in disguise! And bad men they, ho aye, and no other like, 'cept maybe that Marax von chap we fought on The Everlast that time, oh an' that Sabin fellow, but thanks to the goblins we don't have to worry about him.'

'And they burnt up all the sedge grass.'

'Aye, that they did. But come Captain, now you're in the land of the living, let's keep it that way; are you up to making a go of breaking free?'

'Aye, we'll make a go,' Ashton said the words but he lacked the strength and the will to put to it. He had grown uncharacteristically despondent and his mind wasn't thinking quickly like normal. It was just as Samazan had predicted, that the loss of the Carex Argentius could be the end of Ashton; it was the reason he had sailed to Althorn and borrowed these men, the reason he had acquired the Avaeste, the reason he had sailed for so long and so far through every weather and so many dangers. At last he had found it, then so quickly gone, and the despair in his heart was as though he were dying once more, and what with that, his throbbing head and the loss of blood from the cut, it could be said that he was.

'Ashton, come on,' Berens urged, 'what's wrong? Is that cut very deep?'

Ashton looked at his arm, the welling blood that ran down past his wrist again as he struggled, down his fingers then dripped to the ground. 'I don't know. Perhaps it is, perhaps that's the cause of the lightness I feel in my head.'

'Do you think they were joking, or are there really creatures here that will come to eat us?'

'They weren't joking. The only question is the matter of when, will it be tonight? With the real wolves and wild cats? Or tomorrow? Or perhaps it won't be till we're half starved and dehydrated, perhaps even a week or two. I can't say I'm familiar with the wildlife here. The rats and carrion-fowl might come and pick at us, after the flies and the ants, then the bears, if we're still alive when they come out of hibernation, if indeed bears live in this place.'

'Ashton stop this, at least try to get free again, come on, help me!'

'And then we have to get out of this valley,' Ashton said, disconsolate. He was tired, pained and at his end. 'A little hard without our gear, Berens, it's a maze down here, and a steep climb out. I have failed. There's no point now. I can't do it. I'm ready to give in. It's not such a terrible place to finish.'

'I'll have no talk of dying Captain,' Berens urged strongly, 'nor of giving up. If I have learnt one thing while I have been in your crew, it is that there is always hope, Ashton, and never long to dwell on sorrow.'

'You don't understand.'

'Maybe I don't, but don't lose hope; surely there is some other place the sedge might exist?'

'Oh but too late!' Ashton despaired. 'Even if it does, as soon as Calegra finds out about it it will all be destroyed.'

Berens changed his tack, he could see this line of talk wasn't working, and he was getting nervous as the moon came through the canopy again and showed several pairs of eyes roaming around them, and there were noises, Berens wasn't sure what made them but he was certain that whatever it was he didn't want to meet it.

So he began a different track to spur his young captain to action. 'What about me Captain?' Berens charged him, 'and the men. I don't want to die here, and I'm sure the crew don't want to be stuck here on Wye forever, no, they want to get back to their families on Althorn; it was you brought us here and you have to get us back, think about that.'

The eyes drew closer round them, so Berens continued with more haste. 'Lad, come on, only you can really sail the Avaeste with any expertise, and though you've taught us many things and how to go along and navigate in the Ether Marine, Captain, you've never told us anything about how to get back to Althorn, only that it's mighty hard and nary but few a ships can do it, you know, because we're down in the Terra Marine'

'Where the land meets the sea, meets the sea.'

'That's right, with no gaps in between.'

'I suppose you're right.'

Then the light finally filtered down into the mire of Ashton's dim thoughts and through his pain and his hazy head – and it dawned on the young captain; how would the wolves of Arazin make their escape from the Isle of Wye? Last time he was in the harbour there was only one ship that was not frozen into the ice, and even if the others were no longer frozen in there was only one ship that could make a long flight, and those men would certainly have such a journey in mind!

'No! The Avaeste!' Ashton gasped.

'Yes!' cheered Berens, 'Quick Ashton, we've got to do something! There's something watching us!'

'Wild cats.'

'What?'

'Stay still Berens, I don't think they'll attack,' Ashton said, he wriggled about again to try and get free, but it was hopeless; those wolves of Arazin certainly knew how to bind a prisoner and tie their knots tight in a way the ropes tightened with every move that was made. There would be no helping it, Ashton concluded, there was no other option but to be the Novanian he was to escape, and though he would rather not, and though he was afraid to show his identity in this strange place, Ashton sucked up all his courage and Berens at once felt the rope around him relax and he was able to get free.

'Well done lad, you did it!' Berens exclaimed as he hurried to get the ropes off his shoulders, he turned to face Ashton around the tree trunk, but the young captain was gone, nothing but a host of blackbirds startled him as they darted off past, then disappeared into the shadows about.

'Ashton?' Berens whispered, and whispered again, where did he go? Berens walked around the tree trunk, then the little moonlight there was faded even more and it renewed Berens' fears of being eaten alive. 'Ashton?' Berens desperately whispered again.

It was a dangerous thing for Ashton to do, to separate like that when he was so injured, but of these things the young Novanian had little been taught, but at last the final part of him, the last blackbird, which carried the worst of his injuries, made it back, and the birds pieced together and Ashton was a man once more.

'Right here,' Ashton stumbled into Berens, 'come on, let's hurry, let's get out of here.'

'I'm with you. Let's go,' Berens said gladly, 'but here, lad you're bleeding quite badly, let me bandage you up.' For once in his life Ashton didn't protest, so Berens tore out a piece of his jacket lining and tied Ashton's arm tightly about the slash, then he saw to his own cut, which wasn't so bad. 'Right then, let's go,' he said, and together they ran.

The Valley of Lore was a maze indeed, even as was told them by Samazan previously. They dodged through the undergrowth and around suddenly visible trees, that loomed out of the darkness so quickly, as though they had grown out of the ground that second to hem them in. Indeed it seemed a veritable cage, it was easy to believe that creatures would go in and get lost here and never ever come out again. You could find your way in but not make it out despite how you tried, no matter which way you took to get out, especially at night, in the dark with nary a light, and chased by who knows what creatures that stalked one, that waited ready to pounce should you trip or make a slip up.

But to Ashton's surprise he found he could get his bearings and hope grew within him of finding the way out of here, for through the cracks in the canopy the stars were the same, and he was used to navigating and back-tracking at need, even when the terrain seemed to have changed, so at every point where they were held in another way was tried, until the way which they came was come to again and they could continue on, but it was a terrifying maze of vines and trees nonetheless, of unknown growls and howls, of peering eyes, of screeching owls, of such unseen and untold violence.

Wall after wall of forest hindered them, but gradually they got through it, and by and by Berens recognised the steep path back up the mountainside.

'You did it Cap'n, you did it, look, we made it!'

'Aye,' Ashton smiled, it was a small victory, on what could prove to be a very long journey back, but it gave them hope again, though Ashton swayed from his light head and Berens steadied him. Berens had lost blood too, but he had not been concussed as well, and nor, thought Berens, did he have such a weight on his shoulders as did the captain, although he was growing concerned that at this rate the wolves of Arazin would reach the town and the harbour well before he and Ashton would, and by the time they got back, he worried, the Avaeste may already be captured and sailing on without them.

Once out of the valley the morning was clear, 'We made it!' Berens sighed, so relieved, but then it hit him, it was still so much colder up here than it was down there, and how many days was it back to the town? Through how much snow would they have to trudge without dausles or wolves to assist, and face how many blizzards? The crisp fresh breeze that caught them as they reached the exposed trail chilled them through as it ran and whipped towards them from across the snow.

They collapsed into a little sheltered spot and had to catch their breath before they could go on. But go on they did, they pushed through and pushed on, trudging up the path and in parts climbing, at times slipping back and having to try another way, having to wait to gather the necessary strength and energy to try again.

They made it to the place that they had camped halfway along the descent, this had been Ashton's goal and so here he stopped, sat down wearily and leaned back. It was a small hollow in the rocks, it still smelt of wolves and also of smoke from the fire Berens had previously set up. Berens went now to light it again to give them a little warmth for a while but Ashton admonished the sailor.

'Of course,' Berens realised, 'we don't know how far those men have gone. They could be nearby couldn't they? I hadn't thought.'

'Even if they are far, they may see the smoke and return if they think us alive.'

Berens nodded, they would be cold, but wise.

As soon as he had fallen asleep it seemed, Berens woke to a nudge and up he got again, and they were off. It was hard going up the slope, many a time Berens had helped Ashton up and the other way around, but they carried on and they made it up to the very top. By the end of that day they had reached the narrow place where they had encountered that last extreme blizzard, but it was easy now, the snow had thinned out and the only hindrance was a frosted wind. What a way they had achieved! They were both amazed and heartened by their effort.

The evening fell, and all light went out, apart from a few flickering stars, and Berens said, 'What, we're not stopping?' Ashton did not falter now but pressed on. Surely he was at the end of his strength, Berens felt sure the young captain was about to tumble, as he was himself, 'Come, come, Ashton, we should stop, we should rest.' But the young captain wouldn't listen. In truth, now that Ashton had put aside his own despair, he was gravely afraid for the people of Wye, not just for his crew and the fair Avaeste. For what would they want? Those wolves would want their revenge, revenge on the people of Wye for the years they had spent here and been treated so poorly with so little respect, they would take all the plunder they could. They would need supplies for their journey, they would want treasure and gold, and being as they were, full of rage and regret, they would cause all ruin that was possible, set alight the homes and boats, and the little food and stock feed the people of Wye had left, out of spite, and they might even take the young men, to train them up, yes, apprentice them as Calegra's agents, and they would steal that fine little ship, built by the famous Phineas Tuck, the only ship like it, sailed by the explorer Trevallian Valentin until its demise in ten-thirteen, reclaimed by Ashton not that long ago and restored to her former beauty. He would not let them tear up on the men of his crew, nor get their hands the Avaeste, oh no!

So just when he thought they couldn't possibly go faster, Berens noticed a quickening of Ashton's step, head down to the wind and that determined stride as the young captain charged forward harder. Through fields of snow they went, returned over the mountains and valleys they had traversed before, the crevasses were crossed carefully on the log bridges. They had to keep their heads steady and mind their step for the slip of snow melting, and over the breaking ice in the streams they stepped quickly, breaking it up as they went but making it across barely wet.

And so they went on till they had to stop absolutely, for the dark of this night and the incredible weariness of body, and they slept and slept well, and well into the next morning.

Ashton woke hazily, his whole body aching, and when he realised how long they had slept he put his hands in his head. He was also so hungry.

'Berens,' Ashton shook him, and as he woke groggily, and before he could say anything coherent in protest Ashton told him, 'come on, we've got to keep going.'

So the two stood but found they could hardly move, their muscles were as stiff as the frozen tree trunks and as sore as they could ever remember.

'I can't go on, I can't hurry,' said Berens, 'I'm sorry.'

'No, neither can I,' puffed Ashton, 'we won't make it.'

'You've got to, Captain, if you can go on, if there's anything you can do, go ahead, I will follow as I can.'

They had made it out to an open field, the steep side of a hill, bare and treeless. They could see the long way they had yet to go, over the ravine and on through the forests, across the low hills and then back to the village. So far, and somewhere along the way the wolves were, too far ahead to catch them now. The wolves of Arazin would reach the town, cause mayhem, then seize the Avaeste. Unless, Ashton thought, he could warn the crew and the townsfolk, which he could do if he flew as swifts to the village, for he knew swifts flew at a rapid pace, indeed up to 77 miles per hour, whereas wolves could only reach 40 at best, but that would mean letting Berens know his untellable secret.

Ashton looked at his faithful crewman, did he have the courage to admit what he kept so well hidden?

'Berens,'

'Aye Captain,'

'I um,' Ashton swallowed, there was no time to lose, 'well, I'll explain when I get back,' Ashton said, then turned and jumped, breaking up at once into a flight of swifts that darted straight forward and over the cliff, flying towards the village, leaving Berens speechless.

The swifts flew on, and crossed the ways with ease, Ashton knew he had to hurry for the wolves of Arazin were well in advance. But a hawk soaring above saw the swifts and thought he'd try them for prey and dived a couple of times, but thankfully Ashton saw it coming in time and the birds flew together and into the thick cover of the pines.

The swifts were about to dart ahead again, when they came to that long ravine and saw the tree-bridge they had made, and here Ashton could see the crowd of wolf prints and not just that, there was something else. Ashton came together and knelt down to study the prints. They were clear, the wolves couldn't be too far ahead, perhaps a day, though it could be more or less. But he looked around, smelt the air, what was that something? Went up ahead, there was blood on the snow here. Then from behind the snow capped heath he heard a whimper, and a plea for help. Ashton ran and then cautiously rounded the bushes, finding what he did not expect – the bodies of Kairu, Samazan and Siah, wounded and hiding.

Samazan sat slouched with the head of Kairu in his lap and his arm over Siah, all were torn at and bleeding, only just clinging to life. The keeper saw Ashton there and was surprised, but he had so little strength left to show it. Ashton's heart went out to the man, quickly he was by his side, trying to help, but Samazan stopped him.

'You,' Samazan said, amazed, 'you were the birds?!'

'What birds?' Ashton answered without blinking, kneeling by these wounded three and wondering how to help them. 'What happened to you Samazan?'

'The others, we had an argument. Kairu, Siah and I stood up to them, we thought Azaire and maybe Tehu would stand up too but they stood aside to let us die. I finally gathered the courage to stand up to them, what was death compared with serving Calegra again? Why,' Samazan concluded, 'I thought I would prefer it. Oh, but here it is now at my doorstep and I fear it. But how did you escape and make it this far?'

'With difficulty.'

'I wanted to come back and help you free but, as you can see.'

Ashton put his hand to Kairu's mouth, he could feel no breath, then he put his head down to the chest but could hear no heart beat.

'He's gone,' Ashton said.

Samazan nodded, 'Siah too, I know. Soon I will be as well,' Samazan answered with a shallow and hoarse voice. 'They know their methods boy, that's why they didn't hang about, they knew we would soon be dead. So you can tell me boy, you can tell me the truth, because I won't be long able to speak it; it was you, wasn't it?'

'What was?'

'Don't make a dying man repeat himself; the birds, the swifts.'

'Yes.'

'Then you can't be from Aeloran,' Samazan went on, 'you can't be the son of our king St Amalric, no, for he is of a different race,' he gasped, 'no, you're one of us, us Uthain!'

'No. I'm not. I am neither of your people or his.'

'I had not guessed. Who are you then, if not a son of the king?'

'I am a son of the king, by adoption, but I'm not like you, I'm not of the Ciel Marine, I am but a mortal of the Ether, I am Novanian.'

Samazan gasped, and had to take a moment to take it all in, in his dying moments he felt there was something important behind all this, something that could matter and matter to him, so he pressed on, and pressed Ashton to tell him more of these things.

But Ashton stilled him, Samazan was so close to dying, 'I don't want to die without the king's forgiveness Ashton,' Samazan almost cried, with his pain and regret, 'but I have done terrible things against him, I don't deserve his pardon.'

'I will tell you something Samazan, something I have only told one other in all the ether. It is because of me King Mathis dies. He knows it was I, and yet, even after that he took me into his family. I don't deserve his pardon either my friend, he should have left me to die on Novania and saved his own life, but such is the heart of the king, his mercy. There it is, take it Samazan, he would extend it to you I am certain.'

'You will tell him of all this, tell him I tried to stand up for you and I died.'

'Yes, if I make it back I will tell him.'

Samazan gasped painfully and grasped Ashton's hand, 'I should warn you, the others are ahead, they run for the harbour, they plan to burn the village, then take the Avaeste.'

'So I guessed.'

'Don't try to take them on Ashton, they are maddened,' Samazan warned as he saw that dangerous spark in the young captain's eyes, 'they wish to destroy this place as Calegra would have.'

'How can I stop them?'

'You cannot, only others from the Ceilomarinus can contend with we Uthain. You may be able to sail out, if you get there in time, but you can do nothing for the town. Besides, they must be almost there now, you won't make it in time.'

'Won't I?'

'Even if you run all the way, or fly, they are far in front,' Samazan was fading.

'But I am Novanian,' said Ashton.

'And they of Arazin! But go then Ashton!'

'But you're dying.'

'Aye, exactly, so go and save the Avaeste and your men!' Samazan's sight grew dim minute by minute, 'Your faith in your father has rested my heart, I go a contented man, so go now Ashton, do what you can. Don't forget your short sword, it will defend you well if there is need, for I see it too is from the Ciel Marine.'

'Yes, it is made of fallen debris from the Cielomarinus, forged by the smiths of St Amalric.'

'A fine weapon indeed,'

'But I find it hard to use, I feel too small to wield it – it is made for me, I know, but still, the power in its short blade astounds! And I am unused to it, though I have trained.'

'Don't be afraid to use it if there is need,' Samazan urged with the last of his breath, 'I'm glad that I met you Ashton, now go.'

'Goodbye Samazan,' Ashton backed away and left.

Again he disappeared into a host of brave swifts, flying ahead at a pace fast and fleet, but then at once he found himself standing out in the bare snow plain, out from the Avaeste with Morris and the gathering sleet, facing the lady who stood in grey, the guardian, who then took her hand away from Ashton's cheek. He looked around in surprise, how could he be here when he was just in the mountain? He remembered all that had happened, and still it felt real, although he began to realise it must have all been an illusion, or at least partially so.

'I hope you will forgive my deception,' she said, and explained, 'when I looked into your mind to find your need to remain I saw so many other things and realised who you were, and then I realised you could help me solve my dilemma. Indeed, I must thankyou, for your presence in the illusion allowed me to see the reality.'

Morris did not understand, for from his perspective no more had they been here but less than a minute, but he was becoming aware that when she had touched his captain's face something must have happened, and he drew together his great big eyebrows and studied them as the young captain studied her and she studied him.

'Can you use that?' she asked Ashton, as she looked at his sword.

'Yes, at need I can.'

'Good, for soon they come,' she breathed, her pulse quickening.

'Who?' Ashton asked, still recovering from the dream.

She looked at him with a face at once energized but grim, and said, 'The wolves of Arazin.'

Then they could see across the snow from the distant mountain, a line of shapes moving quickly towards them, then 'Look!' Ashton cried as his sharp eyes espied, more wolves were coming also from the left as well as the right.

The guardian saw the fear on young Ashton's face, the horror as he realised he was to face them again, these wolves, these men so full of hate and revenge that had festered within them as they had lived out their banishment.

'I should warn you,' the guardian said, 'some of what you saw was real.'

'What? I don't understand?'

'Some of the things that happened did happen.'

'So, what are you saying – are Samazan and the others dead?'

'No, but they will remember the Avaeste, their chance of escape.'

Ashton just stood still, staring fearfully ahead.

'But don't lose heart dear boy,' she continued, 'not now, not yet, if you'll allow me,' she touched his face again.

It seems at the touch time was paused, they remained were they were and the wolves did not grow nearer, it was just Aolani the guardian and Ashton in the silent white world, even the snowflakes sat still in the air.

'A blizzard is coming, and a terrible battle,' she said, not taking her eyes away from Ashton's. 'I have many things to say and ask you before you go, before the wolves come and do what they will and before the blizzard comes.'

'But who are you?' asked Ashton, 'where are the people we were told lived here? Nothing here is as I was told it would be, apart from this frozen winter.'

'As I said, I am Aolani, the guardian of Wye.'

'I still don't understand, the illusion - why did you do it?'

'All who come are tested, you passed the test, and as well as that you helped me to find which of the wolves I could trust. There are many things to fear out there in the Aethermarinus, and since the entrance of Celagra I have been here with my tests.' Aolani grew sad as she explained, 'Aeloran has soldiers and a strong government, Diamantine has the weather chest, everywhere has some defence, but here at the end of the ether where no one can come to their aid quickly, they have me, and all I can do is pause time momentarily and create illusions that seem like reality.'

'I have to say, you do it amazingly,' Ashton praised her, thinking of the illusion's potency, and watching the world around them as it hang strangely in its suspended state. Even Morris was paused in the act of itching the whiskers above his lip.

But the woman gasped as she cried, so strange on her firm, brave face, 'Everyone else, the villagers here whom I was supposed to protect, they are gone, winters ago. If only I had realised in time.'

'But what happened?'

'The wolves were already here when I came. I didn't look to the town, I was watching the ways of approach. For some time the wolves lived in relative harmony with the people but after a time their patience wore thin. As you were about to see in the illusion, they made for the village and the harbour with terrible intent – they plundered and burned and lay all to ruin, and as you know the people of Wye had little chance at defending themselves for they have contrived no weapons that can harm those of the higher sky, there is nothing here can really stop them, at least, not to any great degree; why do you think Calegra comes out of every fight still living? Although, weapons such as your short sword will do well at defending, it is a pity there are so few blades like it, and so few who know how to well wield them. But to the story, some wise resident discovered the wolves deception, and the wolves went mad, the people that survived the wolves attack have fled to other parts of the isle, all the ships are ruined and unsailable, all the equipment to mend them or make new ones destroyed as well,' Aolani looked down, 'I did that. It's not that I wanted to trap the people here, but that I did not want the wolves to escape. I can't understand how I missed it, the wolves of Arazin were here before the people knew of Calegra, of course no one knew that they were what they were, and I didn't guess it, so all of my tests were useless – the enemy was already here! So suddenly they changed and attacked, in fear I doubted, I was slow to act, and I failed the people.'

'I'm sure you did all you could,' Ashton tried to encourage.

She shook her head. 'No, but Ashton, may I ask, are you really Novanian?'

With hesitance Ashton admitted, 'Yes.'

'You have no need to fear, I will keep your secret, but my question is, from what you said in the illusion am I to believe your home no longer exists?'

'Yes, Novania is gone.'

'How my heart falls to hear it,' she said, so sincerely. 'But perhaps it is that not only I failed – did no one receive a warning? It was thought Novania would be one of the first where Calegra's full arsenal would have been employed, for Novania's beauty and innocence was a detestable thing to him, and your particular skills would have made you most terrible enemies. I and my brethren were sent out across the Aethermarinus, to be there as a warning and help after Calegra was expelled, for his ire was known, and his terrible plans. My brother was sent to Novania I'm sure, did he not give fair warning?'

Ashton looked down, 'I believe a warning was given, but I am told it was not heeded.'

'Oh,'

'Too late the realisation that with that choice our utopia would vanish. I was young, but still I have to live with that decision as if it were mine, and to be honest, bluntly, it probably would have been, I know I was curious, I wanted to see what the whispers were about, I wanted to know, for the innocent do not have the knowledge of how terrible things can be, they cannot imagine it. Now Novania is nothing but ash and I am all that remains, only as the king chose to save me.'

'I'm sorry for what you have lost,'

'So am I.'

'But I am glad he saved you, Ashton, it has been so long since I have talked with anyone. There was none with whom I could speak – all average folk of Wye to whom I am to remain anonymous, the wolves of course, and apart from them, rare ships who turned back long before they grew close, even with the illusion of storms ahead, but you, you continued. You are braver than even you know, you have such trust in your men, and they such respect of you. You question why it is that our beloved king risks his life for yours?'

'Yes. And then sometimes I question why he didn't come sooner and stop Calegra, when surely he could have, surely he could have saved everyone! Why didn't he come and tell them how bad it would be if they made the choice they did? If they didn't just trust him and heed the warning? Surely those that made the choice did not know that they were choosing such evil and such suffering? And then I hate myself, for how can I ask these questions of my father? How can I have these doubts? He is all I have, the very reason I exist, why I have what I have, and am who I am. I just don't understand.'

'Ashton, the answers will come. But know this, whatever the reasons, the character of the king does not change, and you know him – you know him as the father who even now dies to save your life, this same king is the king you say you sometimes doubt. Ashton, it is alright to have questions, and as I said the answers will come.'

They were silent for a time, watching the wolves far away, paused in their run.

'I suppose I better get on with this,' Aolani said at last. 'Go Ashton. Go back to your father, the king.'

'But what of the Argentius?'

'Here, I saved two of your silver grasses,' she placed them in his hands. 'I know they are not the finest specimens, but all the others are burnt up.'

'How?'

'I did it, I could not have them getting into the hands of the wolves, they are more potent than you realise.'

'This is not a dream?' he asked, overwhelmed, looking at the small plants, their flower stems only near-invisible shoots.

'No, it's not a dream,'

Ashton didn't know what to say but just looked at the cure in his hands.

'This is what you came for isn't it?'

'Yes, yes with all I possess I thank you for these.'

Aolani nodded, but said, 'I don't think your father will need them, but take them and go, and whatever you do don't let Calegra get his hands on them.'

'Come with us,' Ashton invited, 'you don't have to stay and fight them.'

'What?'

'Come with us.'

'No,' Aolani said firmly.

'Well, you can't stay here alone. Come with us, come back to Aeloran, you'll be safe and welcome in St Amalric's house.'

'No Ashton, don't you understand – I have to stay here and warn anyone that comes and protect those that are left. I can't let any travellers stay for long or the wolves will come in and either take them or worse, their ship, and then get back out to the Aethermarinus. No, I have to keep them here. This is my place, I will stay.'

'But you – how can you fight them all, and alone?'

Aolani showed just a hesitant smile, and looked down at Ashton, 'I too am from the Ciel Marine, with bow, sword and spear made in Aeranimh and blessed by our king.'

'You are of Aeranimh?'

'Yes. I am here by the king's command as I said. As you saw in the illusion they fear him and what he might do to them, that alone has been on my side, but now thanks to you I am sure I have allies in Samazan, Kairu and Siah.'

'Surely there's some other way.'

'This will not be forever, but while things remain as they are this is my place. Now go Ashton, hurry back to the king.'

'I'm worried for you. I can stay and fight too.'

She smiled, though there were tears in her eyes, 'It is my duty and not yours. Ashton run back to your ship now, take it straight up and don't return whatever the outcome, now go – GO!'

Aolani and Ashton nodded in farewell, she readied her bow and stood firm, ready for the wolves as she stopped holding the pause. Ashton clasped the plants as Morris cried in surprised monster voice, 'Cap'n, you've got the Argentius!'

'Yes,' Ashton said, 'Morris, come on, we've got to run!' Ashton and Morris saw the wolves now, bolting forth out of the white distance, and they turned and ran back to the Avaeste with all haste, climbing back on board and issuing orders for a speedy exit.

'Take up the anchor and the stabilising poles! Set sails to windward and get ready to go!'

Soon they were up and sailing out of the harbour through the thickening sleet, as behind they could just make her out, Ashton handed the plants to Morris and breathlessly asked for his spyglass, the last thing he saw was that brave figure swinging her sword in defiance, then all was lost in the midst of a blizzard.

When they were out and far into the flight Ashton sat down, his head swimming, and when he looked up he was surrounded by crew, all astounded and wondering, and all of them thinking, the lieutenants and their men, that their young captain was strangely amazing. For what does he do? He goes and talks to one girl, in the middle of an empty snowfield, gets the Silvertip Sedge and returns, simple as anything.

'It wasn't simple,' Ashton answered them, 'that was one of the hardest things I've ever had to do, and hope I never have to again.'

They laughed at his joke, and he refrained from telling them that it was indeed not meant to have been funny, of how he had nearly died, how he had had to show his identity to survive, and though all that had turned out not to be so real, it had felt so and felt so terrible now to leave Aolani behind.

Everyone watched as Morris planted the Carex, and Ashton could hardly breathe as he worried it could be killed, but Morris was the greenest thumb they had, quite literally, and he knew swamps and he knew how to deal with plants. He wrapped extra cloth around their soil and put them in beakers with a little snow on top – for they were not flowering yet, but he said they soon would. And then they were put on the window sill where the captain could watch them, in his cabin, right near his bunk.

Ashton couldn't stop watching them for quite some time – the silver leaves, the shimmering, the otherwise ordinary little plants. Then he turned and sat at his desk, and began to right up his notes. He supposed he should inform the shipping authorities all over about the state of Baroco and Wye Island, but his forehead furrowed as he tried to say what he knew without giving too much away and without sounding too far fetched, for who was he to say anything that would be believed, he was just a boy with a nose much smaller than any one of the men in the admiralty. Then again, he was a prince wasn't he, though most would say young, and lacking experience.

'Something happened out there didn't it?' Santee asked.

'Did it?' said Ashton, not really taking notice as he kept writing.

'You can't pretend nothing happened, I've never seen your face like you looked when you came back, except when you were caught in the dream,' Santee worried,

'Like what?'

'Well, oh, it doesn't matter. Who was that person on the beach?'

'I'm not exactly sure, her name was Aolani. She said she was from the Ciel Marine, from Aeranimh.'

'An Elf?'

'Maybe. But I think not.'

'She was very much like you, you know. Well, from here she looked it, at least.'

'Like me?'

'Yes. Are you from the Ciel Marine?'

'No, you know where I'm from Santee.'

'Well, I know a name, but I don't know anything about the place, it could be in the north or the west, up or down, I don't know. I'd never heard of it before Annabella Bien mentioned it by accident. Are you an elf?'

Ashton laughed, 'What? Me? What makes you think that?'

She didn't answer but shrugged her shoulders, and went on to other questions.

So while Santee annoyed Ashton with many and varied curious question, the crew went about as usual, and they looked down on the snow covered isle as they went up higher, and then it all made sense to them.

'Ah, now I see,' they said, 'why it's called what it is, why Wye is called Wye and not If or How, and indeed not Ex or Zee.'

'Zed,' corrected Jennings

'Zee,' insisted Banks

'Zed,' said Phillips and Carter.

'Knock it off guys,' said Tom, 'come on, you're grown men, act like it!'

For as the left they went higher faster and so their vantage was better for seeing the island as the explorers had seen it the very first time they'd arrived. Yes, rising out of the glassen ice the Isle of Wye arose, and they could see it was shaped like the letter itself, like the letter Y in capital style, or indeed, as Tom thought, the shape of a twig that would be good to use as a slingshot. Ah, now that was an idea, Tom thought, and went to construct it.

The lieutenants stuck their heads in and asked Ashton's plan. What were they to do now, where would they be heading? Had they set sail in the right direction? Ashton stood and broadly smiled, saying, 'We're going home, as quick as we can.'

You can only imagine that cheers that shook the Avaeste as news of this plan reached the men.

Chapter 19:
THEY MEET HAIM CLOGH, THE CEANN OF HARNOGH

Of course there needs must be stops along the way on a trip as long as from Wye to Althorn, where he would of course be taking the men. And Ashton had in his head a good plan, and he went over it just one more time, and one more time again. There had been so many incidences, so many irregular happenings, that Ashton was beginning to become quite concerned that there was some universal plot to obstruct him.

But the sun was shining, the cold behind them, the weather perfect with an almost autumnal feel, so clear and crisp. And he had his maps, he had his compass, all was working and all sound. He'd even got around to oiling the hinges on his door so they didn't creak anymore, and that was a small but satisfying accomplishment. The men were cheerful, and content, there hadn't been a brawl or bad word for so many days now. To be the captain of the Avaeste was indeed something of which to be very proud, as she sailed through the wide open skies and the cloud.

And, Santee was happy, and that mattered a lot, for if Santee wasn't happy then Ashton couldn't possibly be, no he could not. All the men knew of her now and it was no surprise to see her here and there fluttering about, often sitting on someone's collar and telling them a joke while they worked to keep the ship aflight, or perched high upon some part of the rigging looking about them and humming or singing. And while Ashton was glad that she was so happy to be free now with this big extended family, he missed her when she was not with him, when she was not annoying his ear or catching a minute's sleep in his pocket. And he wondered at it, this strange, wistful, involuntary feeling, that worry and lump in his throat that rose up when he did not know where she was or what she was doing. But Ashton dismissed it, well, didn't he feel concern for all of

247

his friends? For all of his men? Yes, he did, it was his job, he was the captain, and Santee so much more fragile than the rest.

They sailed on for many more weeks, with nothing much occurring, just the odd albatross landing on the rail having lost its bearings, but it would go just as soon as it had sat a while and rested. They made a stop at an equatorial port but didn't see much as the monsoon had begun, so all that they saw as they loaded supplies was rain, rain and more rain. It had been several weeks since then, on a different course, away from Meridian, Arinn, and Diamantine, and the young captain checked the date and time again, and calculated their point on the map, well pleased. He couldn't be happier really, they were making good time, and there was nothing in the immediate future that he could see to bring any compromise to their journey.

He sighed a relieved breath and leaned back, as he listened to the sound, coming nearer and nearer now, it sounded like a rustic fiddling and singing. Wait. Fiddles? What in the ether was going on here? Ashton sat up, he knew the sound of his crew's musical talent and this, well, this was similar, but very much different.

The sound grew closer and closer still, then even the crew could hear something and wondered themselves, where was it coming from? What an unexpected and strange thing to hear when sailing alone in the wide empty sky.

Then out of the clouds and the blue heavens above them, even as Ashton came out of his cabin, floated down balloons of many bright colours, well, not balloons, but numerous parachutes. Only, no one could be seen floating down with them, it seems, only suitcases weighted them down, but then the crew saw, as the chutes fell some more and drifted lightly by them, the passengers of the parachutes weren't strapped to the straps, no, they were sitting atop them! And, it seems the passengers weren't at all afraid or worried, for they sat and stood as if they did this every day, and jovially sang and danced and played – the crew looked up, a whole little band of them was falling.

'Ahoy laddies!' yelled one, with a laugh, as he was wafted past; he looked to be some kind of dwarf, complete with a ginger beard and tartan braces holding his breeches up.

'Come on then, throw out a rope, well, what are you waiting for, you're not going to let me fall any further are you?'

'Cap'n?' they questioned, 'do we reel 'em in?' Ashton nodded, and just as well, for a few of the parachutes practically landed on the deck even then, with a thud from the suitcases and much laughter from the dwarf folk as they landed and tripped up in the metres of silk, crying, 'oh fiddlesticks!', 'ha-he-har', and 'ah, made it.'

Oh the commotion the dwarf band made as they came down upon the deck with laughter and a profusion of thanks, and they got straight into talking with the crew of the Avaeste and exclaiming with wonder at the timing of it, and what a blessed wonder it was to have happened just so, that the moment they fell was the moment they had happened to come along, and not just any ship, but one with a kind crew, and where must reside a good captain too.

'Where is the man?' their chief asked, and jovially yet warmly said, 'request us an audience would you lieutenant, we must thank him, we must, and inform him of our circumstance.'

Now Ashton had been on the deck just a moment ago, he waited until he knew these falling dwarves were all in and all safe, but then had withdrawn to his cabin once again before any knew or realised he had gone away. So the lieutenants and the crew looked around them bewildered, but then Morris said to Phillips, 'The captain withdrew.'

'Oh,' said Phillips, 'the dwarves wish to meet him. Let me just ask if he will receive them.'

Phillips knocked and then stuck in his head, seeing the captain at his table, which was as usual all covered with instruments and maps, and before Phillips could even say a word, Ashton answered him, 'I will come out to meet them in good time, but for now Phillips, they are good folk, what I know of them, do make them at home.'

Phillips nodded, then went out, conveying the captain's wishes to the men and making the dwarves as comfortable as they could, and soon the little band had eaten and supped, and were much satisfied and sat down and formed a round and picked up their instruments to begin their playing as the night drew in.

In all truth the young captain didn't want to meet them, at least not yet, as he was feeling rather shaken. He knew these dwarves, by reputation, they were good folk, and friends of Aeloran, travelling musicians it was said, though also good craftsmen and skilled chefs, and Ashton was concerned, for he feared what could have happened, he had read and had been told of a wonderful little village called Harnogh, a floating village built around a ship, wonderful and simple, with gardens and houses and industry all linked by wooden bridges, floating up here in the Ether Marine despite the supposed impossibility of it. But if the dwarves who lived there, were down here, on his ship, carrying with them their suitcases, travelling coat and cap, what had become of their village ship? What had become of that peaceful home of these dwarves who liked nothing better but to sit and sing and make music? Ashton didn't think he could face another tragedy just yet, but soon the music of the dwarves drifted in and he could not but listen.

The fiddles played, the pipes sang, the piccolo twittered along the high notes and the rough voice of the leader, Haim Clogh, rose over the drums as they rumbled. It was a sad song, but they sang it almost merrily.

'Twas a morn o' bright sun shining, tru them silver clouds across the air, it was a morn like any other morning, as any other day so bright and clear, oh but how it were quick to change, oh, the trouble brought by the wind, what sees our eyes coming, fast from the horizon? but a grand old ship.

'Twas a day we planned to carry on just as we had before, and yet, how changed the day as it wore on, as the proud ship came along. Of course we didn't recognise it, until it were too late for us. The sight, the grand old frigate were nought but ol Calegra's ship. Oh, ho, if we had only had listened to the dispatches from the king, then we would not have fallen at Calegra's simple plan to sink our ship!

'Oh this war that started long ago, that continues now across the ether, toppling those who least expect it! Though he's been defeated, Calegra keeps on eager, thinking he will win and have back his power when the good king Mathis meets his end! Oh, ho, if we had made ourselves familiar with the words from the king, then we would not have fallen like Novania at Calegra's scheming hand!

'Now if we'd ha remembered the last dispatch we would ha known the ship was Calegra's before it were too close, and we would have had time to steer away to safety before the tyrant let the cannons go. Oh, ho, if we had only had listened to the dispatches from the king, then we would not have fallen at Calegra's simple plan to sink our ship!

'But don't be afooled boys, and don't be sad, don't be thinking we're a sorry lot, no we're still glad, for one day the king will have had enough, as we know, and end the writhing of the defeated tyrant! Oh, ho, and then we'll make the journey, all the way to the house of the king, and then the celebration, yes we'll play our fiddles, if he'll have us, that is!'

The dwarves all broke up laughing then regrouping to play another tune. Some musicians from Althorn also joined in and the sailors shared some songs too.

Finally the tunes ended and the talking began, the tales and the stories, told by sailor and dwarf in turn. The folk from Harnogh were keen to hear the story of Calegra on Meridian, supposing that his humiliation there must have caused him to go off on this senseless spree attacking the harmless little folk that occupied this open region of the Ether Marine.

'Tell us the story of Calegra,' said Jennings, 'we know very little, for we come from what I believe you call the Terra Marine,'

'The Terra Marine?' wowed Haim Clogh.

'Aye,'

'But how in high heaven did you get here then?'

'The captain of this ship is of this world, he brought us.'

'I see, and a fine little ship it be.' Haim nodded. 'So you want to hear of Calegra do ye?'

'Aye, how did it all start?'

Haim gathered his thoughts. 'Well, that all depends who you believe, and how much time you have to hear the tale. I will try not to go on too long. The common tale is that Calegra was banished from the Ciel Marine with his cronies after trying to overthrow the king of Arazin, for whom he was a messenger. But there are those here that don't even concede the existence of the Ciel Marine, much like you would not have believed in the Ether would you, if you had never come here, so that point is hotly debated whenever the subject arises. But, any which way you take it, Calegra came into force and formed alliances with whoever he could, gathering around himself a ready and willing band of miscreants and misguided men, even some well meaning folk whom he deceived, and he gathered knowledge of this place, one must assume, for he knew the weak points, where it would hurt the most, and where he could do the most damage before he would face great opposition or be stopped. Several small island countries he conquered and set up governors there under his rule, and then proceeded out to the ends of the Aethermarinus and began to conquer the small nations there, so quickly and brutally, hoping to escape notice, and to quell them so entirely that none would be left from these strong peoples to oppose him and come to the aid of the larger isles when he wished to set about conquering them.

'Of most distress to us all was that he found and near destroyed the hidden realms, there were three islands high in the Aethermarinus, so high and so far out they could almost be mistaken for belonging to the Ciel Marine, they were Cierrecay, Oundin and Gaardevaran; the people there kept to themselves but even so were known across the Aethermarinus for their particular prowess. The peoples of each country possessed such unique talents, Cierrecay was known for its skilled shipwrights, Oundin for its detailed and strong craftsmanship, and the Gaardevaran for its drigans and sages, and all three for their warriors.

'The tyrant did not want these peoples for enemies, and destroyed them to the point very few lives were left, and there was a fourth isle, Novania, called Utopia by many who knew it, but few did except as myth. The rumour was that the folk there were not folk like you or me, but possessed of a talent for disguising themselves as any other living thing they wished to be, and it was as close to the Ciel Marine as anything in the ether could ever be, so close they say it was practically in it, and this is why those who lived there were so unique, it was an anomaly of heaven and earth where anything was possible, but Calegra destroyed it utterly.

'So the hidden realms are now nothing more than a few desperate colonies and Novania a complete wasteland, all ash and tar, they say it still burns, all these years later. But Calegra, so much for his grand plan, Mathis St Amalric, king of Aeloran, took a fleet and together with a force from Meridian and other allies including ships from West Fall, Hylethar, and Diamantine, confronted Calegra and his fleet over Novania and dispersed them then and there, destroying all tools he had brought with him from the Ciel Marine, with which he had been causing such unheard destruction, but Calegra himself fled. And now he wanders the ether like a dead serpent, still writhing, still able to deceive or kill a man, if man is silly enough to let him, but dead nonetheless.'

'He still seemed much alive on Meridian, we were worried he would succeed and take it.'

'Did you see Celagra or just men following him? Men whose hearts are bad enough without any prompting.'

'No,' answered the men of Althorn, 'you're right, we did not see Calegra.'

'Ah, so there you are lads, the story of how it is.'

But a voice echoed out the darkness then, 'You don't give him enough credit.' And they looked to see who had spoken and the young captain came forward.

'You say he was defeated, and yes, he was, but still he has the power to make bad men wicked and cause good men to lose heart. Until the day St Amalric deals with him and those who act for him, once and for all, we must still be on our guard men, unless like Baroco, and Wye, we fall.'

Haim looked over Ashton, and hung his head, 'Aye, and like Harnogh.'

'I believe you are the chieftain, the Ceann of Harnogh?' Ashton put out his hand, 'I'm Ashton, the Avaeste's captain.' The dwarf took it and firmly shook it, saying, 'Aye, I am Haim Clogh.'

'It is my honour to have you on board the Avaeste, friends, I hope my men have made you welcome.'

'Much welcome, we thank ye Captain.'

'Good. I would have words with you in my cabin, if you'd be so kind, Ceann Clogh.'

The chieftain nodded, and followed on.

253

Once behind the cabin door and seated the dwarf and the boy surveyed each other for a minute. Then both spoke up at once, and then again at the same time,

'Do go on,' Ashton begged.

'No, I insist,' Haim said, 'you're the Captain.'

'Alright,' Ashton said, 'tell me, simply, what happened?'

Haim shifted in his seat, rubbed the top of his beard and winced, then he leaned forward, 'Captain Ashton,' Haim was hesitant, ''tis such a thing, a terrible thing, I don't want to burden you with it.'

'But I must hear it.'

'Aye, seems you must. Twas such a blessing you came along, and flying Aeloran's colours, oh my heart jumped. I knew we'd be alright.'

'Haim, what happened?'

'Oh but you're such a young captain,' Haim evaded, but seeing the seriousness across Ashton's brow daren't hesitate any longer and indeed he did feel this young captain should know. 'Well. We weren't on our guard. We saw the frigate in the distance but didn't think anything of it. If we'd ha watched it, if we'd ha taken notice and noticed its make, we'd a seen in the posts it were a ship of Calegra's. But we ne'er expected we were worth anything, just drifting out here in the open Ether Marine.'

'But you know his character, you know he goes after the vulnerable and the least expecting!'

'Aye, we know, we were complacent, it's our fault, we don't deny we made ourselves easy targets. They didn't even have the courtesy to fight us hand to hand, but they just blasted us with cannon and burning shot.' Haim shook his head. 'Thankfully you came along, else mayhap we'd a floated all the way down to the Terra Marine, where the land meets the sea, meets the sea, with no gaps in between, and mayhap we'd be meeting these men of Althorn in their own land, a thought too terrible to think more on, mayhap we'd never be able to return, although they say dwarves are thought to be almost magical down there, so it could have been fun.'

'So, he would still be close then, would he, Calegra and his men?'

'Ah, well, aye, must be near at hand somewhere, but they did take off once they knew we were done for so I doubt they'd be too near.'

'Too near for me,' Ashton said, quickly stepping out and

commanding his lieutenants to set a double watch on every side, and getting all aboard to lower their voices and hide their lights.

The Ceann of Harnogh was still sitting there when the captain returned to his cabin, still sitting with a air like he had been thinking, and he looked at Ashton, then said with great meaning, 'We may not give him enough credit, but you give him too much, my young captain.'

Ashton considered these words for a time, 'How can you say that, when he has just destroyed you?'

'Not us, our home yes, our ship, to be sure, but dear Ashton, he did not take what lies in our hearts, and that's what he wants, our loyalties, and our care for each and other, our friendships; he wants to destroy what's in here and make us despair.'

'He wants to sit where the king sits.'

'Aye, both in reality, and in here,' he tapped his heart. 'And that will never happen now, will it my young captain, not while we are strong and St Amalric is king.'

Ashton nodded in agreement, then ushered Haim out, locking the door. Our poor young captain could hardly keep upright upon his legs, indeed he shuddered, then sank to his knees, falling to the boards at his bunk and putting his head in his hands, then filling them with tears. He tried not to sob, no one must hear! He was the captain, he must be strong! Oh but it was for him! For him the king lay dying, and the king must not die! Just as Haim said, that wise dwarf Ceann, Calegra could not win so long as St Amalric was king. But Ashton was afraid that his father was still dying, if not already dead.

Finally he lifted his head and looked at the Silvertip Sedge, which still sat flowering now upon Ashton's window ledge. He must get it to his father, as quickly as he could. There was no ifs or buts, it had to be done, could he do it? He didn't know, but he was determined he would. And beyond the window, beyond the clouds, the moon shone still, bright and glittering in Ashton's eyes, and in his tears as they dried.

Chapter 20:
SHIP AHOY! WHAT'S THIS IN THE MIST?

They came and went from another port, dropping off the dwarves, and though the men were still amazed by the new sights, however brief a time they had to view them, Ashton wore a blank face on deck, his smile had left him, along with his self-assurance and pride. He had set Dew working the engine as hard as was safely possible and had the lieutenants making the most of every breath of wind, but he himself stayed more in his cabin, sitting on his chair, often found by his men with his head in his hands, or staring at the plant, the carex argentius, as if staring at it would speed them home faster.

Santee worried about him, as did the men, especially when he started turning food away, saying he wasn't hungry. In truth he wasn't, guilt had crept upon him and set in, and who could be hungry with a thousand grey thoughts creeping up their neck?

It was his fault the king lay in his bed, dying still, if not already dead, and if his father, the king St Amalric died, then Calegra would win, he would come and take over and ruin every good thing and that would all come back to Ashton. He couldn't bear it, he couldn't.

Then one day, when a broken haze stretched before them as far as any could see, a big yell, a 'Ship ahoy' came down in the voice of young Tom Needle.

The lieutenants all picked up their scopes, and scanned the far horizon, and yes indeed a ship could be seen coming fast towards them.

Carter ran down, and with a knock and a bow, dutifully informed the captain, and said with the grin of a happy man, 'Cap'n she's flying the colours of Aeloran!'

'Aeloran?' Ashton looked up with a hesitant hope in his eyes.

'Aye Cap'n, no mistake,' Carter told him, 'we checked, and double checked, and then again twice.'

'I must see it, which direction does she lie?'

'Ahead Cap'n, along our path but a little to the starboard side.'

So the captain went up and sure enough there ahead of them was a ship of St Amalric's fleet, flying the colours so brave and so proud, it lifted Ashton's heart a great deal, and Santee was pleased for the boy smiled, and if he wasn't smiling then nothing else meant anything.

He turned to his men, 'It's my brother!' he said, almost laughing.

'Prince Edward?'

'No, the third eldest, Simon!' Ashton exclaimed. 'Come now men, we must get prepared, look at this place! Look at me, all a shambles! Morris, with me, help me get dressed, lieutenants attire yourselves in full uniform and see to your men, and the ship my good fellows, she's to be sparkling within five minutes!'

'Aye Cap'n,' they said and set to it hurrying, all abuzz was the ship with excitement, and all were relieved to see their beloved young captain stir from out of his wallowing listlessness and to see his face brighten, and they all of them hoped that this Simon, Prince Simon that is, would bring news that was good and not the opposite.

Ashton ran into his cabin, 'Santee, the mirror!' he called, and at once she did her trick with the door. He looked at himself, for the first time in days, and his chin hung down, and his eyebrows went up in dismay. 'Is that me! Surely not!' he scoffed, 'are you playing tricks Santee?' he looked up, but she shook her head most adamantly.

'Why, but I'm so old looking, so sad, and my hair, look, lifeless! Oh and the blonde is growing back under the black. And my face!' He scrutinized it, horrified at the thin, hollow cheeks and the grey under-eyes.

'And you haven't had a bath in days.' Santee pulled a face and held her nose.

'Days? Haven't I?' Ashton said, surprised, 'but I'm not that bad am I?'

Santee nodded, 'Unfortunately, yes.'

'Oh!' Ashton agreed, smelling his clothes, 'Oh, we can't have that, no, Morris, fetch me a bucket of water quick, I certainly cannot meet my brother like this.'

So Morris ran off to fetch the pail as Ashton undressed down to his breeches, and worried with Santee what to do about the state of his hair, blonde and black! That would never do!

'You could make it blue?' she suggested.

'Blue?' Ashton mocked, 'I'd be the laughing stock of the crew.'

'It was blue in the dream you dreamed, the one Sabin's poison made you dream, the one where I saved you.'

'Was it? Aye I suppose it was, but that was a dream.'

'Sabin said it was more like a remembrance,'

'Aye, so, once my hair was a blue tone of white, to be sure that is the colour it is when it's natural like, but out here that would never suit.'

'It bothers you doesn't it?'

'What?'

'That your hair is naturally blue.'

'What? No, it bothers me that it is now black and blonde, surely there is something else you can suggest that I do?'

'I do red hair quite well,' Santee chuckled, then burst into laughter as she saw Ashton's face, as he glared at her a little irate, then he too chuckled and couldn't help but laugh all the more at the thought of himself with red hair and a ginger beard, like the dwarves.

'No,' he sighed, 'no, I couldn't.'

Then Morris came back with a bucket of water and scrubber. He stood Ashton in it and would not let the young captain do anything, despite all his protestations, but scrubbed and scrubbed, until Ashton exclaimed he was hurting all over. Then Morris, oh what a loyal first mate, sat the boy down and rubbed soap all through his hair, and rubbed and kneaded until bubbles and lather went everywhere.

'What do you think, Morris,' Ashton asked, 'what should I do with this hair, I can't have Simon seeing it as it is, I'll have so much explaining to do, so much more explaining than I think I can bear.'

'Well,' said Morris, still washing Ashton's head, and very roughly at that, 'if you're that concerned about it, just wear a hat.'

'What an idea!' Ashton said, 'but it would be impolite if I don't take it off when we come inside.' The young captain sighed, and he did not see that Morris winked at Santee and Santee back at he, as she sent a few glittering stars down from where she sat, and they fell upon the boy's head and made the soapy lather very bright. She knew Ashton did not like her to use her skills on him, but surely it would be alright to do this one little thing, and what was that the men did say? What he didn't know wouldn't hurt him.

So Ashton got out and dry, and Morris helped him into his neatest attire, all clean and pressed, and then set his hat upon his head, breathed in and dared to looked back into the mirror again.

'Alright, now let's see, how bad is it?'

'Well, better than before, much better.' Morris observed, but added, 'by your standards that is, I myself don't mind the smell of worn clothes, in fact if I stuff these in my pillow they might help me sleep.'

'But how did you do it Morris!' Ashton's smile was wide as it ever was, 'oh, Morris how? All the black is back to blonde!'

'Oh, a good scrub it was Cap'n, with some help from above.'

'Santee you didn't?!'

Santee grinned guiltily.

'You did! Well, it worked! Look! Me, Santee, and it worked!'

'Well, I know you better than when I tried last time,'

'And no side effects, no strange happenings, you're brilliant, you did it!'

'Well,' Santee cleared her throat, 'there is one thing.'

'What?' Ashton studied himself, and could see nothing amiss.

The little sprite couldn't help but chuckle as she answered, 'Morris!'

Ashton looked behind him, to his loyal first mate, who having scrubbed and washed Ashton's hair had also got covered in bubbles with Santee's stars inside, and though it had not happened at once, where the bubbles had burst on him where now big white spots.

'Oh, Morris!' cried Ashton, as Santee laughed till she wept. 'Morris, I'm sorry, you didn't have to do it.'

Morris just screwed his mouth in a funny sort of way, as if he did not know whether to laugh or cry or just what to say. He put up his finger and then put it down, then rubbed the wrinkles around his mouth, then said, 'I'm going to find Dew to commiserate, he'll have more sympathy at my predicament than you two.'

'Morris wait,' Ashton called as the swamp monster walked out the door. 'Santee can fix it, can't you Santee, Morris-' but Morris was gone.

'Did you know that would happen?' Ashton asked the sprite, 'you didn't have to do it, I could've lived with two-tone hair, really I could have, poor Morris,'

'Don't worry about him, he'll be alright.'

'I trust that you will make sure that he is, Santee, I can't have my first mate in low spirits now can I?'

'He knew what the plan was, don't worry about Morris, he was willing to have a few white spots just so long as you got back your self-respect. We've been worried about you all these days and nights. But here you are, look at you, back to your old self again now, or at least close.'

'I was low wasn't I.'

'Yes, Boy, you're too hard on yourself,'

'You wouldn't say that if you knew why, but enough Santee, I have to go out and meet Simon.'

'Is he a good man, your brother Prince Simon?'

'Yes, indeed, all St Amalric's sons are far better men than I.'

Santee shook her head as Ashton left, and said to herself, 'Only because you're not yet a man, best boy I know.'

The crew of the Avaeste lined up and the whistles were blown, and the riflemen let off a shot in salute to greet this prince of Aeloran as he pulled alongside in his fine old ship. A lateen-rigged caravel she was, larger and sturdier than Edward's schooner, with a hale crew and a tall and proud captain, Prince Simon. He stood on deck and to their kind welcome raised his feathered hat in return.

'Simon!' Ashton called, 'Simon, do come on board.'

'Ahoy little brother, I shall, I shall, just as soon as we've turned the ship about and gathered our pace to go on alongside with you.'

So the Eventide, as the old ship was called, soon turned around and came alongside, and with the Avaeste kept perfect time.

The board was put across and Prince Simon and a few of his men were soon on the deck of the little Avaeste, greeting the stunned faces of the men of Althorn. Now they had thought that Prince Edward embodied all the traits that a son of the king should have, he was tall and proud and kindly yet with a bearing that he could lead men and sway them, but this Simon, this prince, he was all that and more yet, he and his men, and so tall and well built. And yet, who was this, that came along with them? A tall man yes, but a little bent and withdrawn, and quite incongruous and out of place, with a shake in his hand and large spectacles sliding down the nose on his face.

'Lucas!' Ashton yelled, his smile further brimming, as he embraced the odd fellow with a brother's embrace, and then Simon along with him. 'I had no idea I'd see the both of you out here! Come into my cabin, we've much to discuss,'

'Indeed brother, much,' Simon said laughing, with Lucas hobbling along behind him, smiling, for it was so good to see little Ashton again.

'These are my lieutenants,' Ashton introduced as they passed, 'Carter, Jennings, Phillips and Banks, men, these are my brothers, Prince Simon, and Prince Lucas, the eldest after Prince Edward.'

'Only, you can drop the 'prince', Simon grinned as he shook the men's hands, 'we're both quite happy with just plain Lucas and Simon.'

When the three brothers were inside Ashton's cabin, finally silent and with the door shut behind them, and when Simon's joking about the tiny size of the room stopped, and when Ashton had gathered they didn't want for anything, not drink nor food, well, then the atmosphere changed, yes, more serious it grew.

Ashton hesitated, but gathered the courage to ask, 'How, how is our father? Tell me all, does he live still?'

'Aye brother, he lives,'

'How it gladdens my heart to hear it!'

'But Ashton, if you saw how he suffers you would not be so glad,' Simon said, 'there are some who say he only lives because he waits,'

Ashton was visibly upset and confused, so Lucas explained, 'He waits for you, dear Ashton, to come back.'

'But I am, I come with all speed now, as you can see,'

'But why did you leave in the first place? All he wants is for you and all of us to be by his side, Edward returned to us and told us of your exploits in Meridian, we could hardly believe all he said of you but the dispatches from the queen's secretary and her general seemed to indicate all was just as Edward had said. He told us too of your crazy search for some rare cure, when you should never have left Ashton, you should have then come home-'

'But I have it,' Ashton pointed to the window sill, 'it's there.'

Simon and Lucas studied the plant, the shimmering silver leaves, the stem sprouting up, not flowering yet but growing well thanks to Morris.

'This is it?' Simon laughed at the tiny leaves, 'looks more to me like a common bog weed.'

'It grows in the swamp, you're right there,' Ashton said.

'What's it called?' asked Lucas.

'The Carex Argentius, or Silvertip Sedge. I read it was a cure for all ills in an old book of medicine, so I set out to find it, and there it is.'

'And where did you get it?'

'The Isle of Wye.'

'What?'

'The Isle of Wye.'

'No, I heard what you said, and we discovered that you planned to go there, but how could you have got there and back again in the time that you had? I can see you're not bluffing and you've no reason to, but it's phenomenal, it's astounding, wow, what a voyage! And made by a brother of mine.' Simon patted young Ashton on the back, 'you know, I think I'll boast about you.'

'Do you think it will work Ashton?' Lucas asked, 'Do you know how to prepare it?'

'I don't know if it will work, I can only hope. I think that the flower is used in an infusion somehow.'

'You are very brave Ashton,' Lucas said, holding his chest as he breathed painfully in, Lucas had been like this all the years Ashton had known him, from injuries they say, from a battle long over. He was usually found pondering over books in his study, so it was unusual to see him out here on the Eventide. Lucas saw Ashton wondering and explained, 'They thought you might need a second brother to sway you, but I see you are really returning, so I was not needed after all, was I.'

'No, but I'm glad you came, it's good to see you Lucas, and you Simon. But, there is one thing I must do before I make straight for

Aeloran,' Ashton explained, 'I promised the men I would get them home, and I will.'

'Well, we can do that, and gladly; just go and grant father's wish to see you again before he passes on, and with this plant maybe, just maybe, stop that from happening.'

'You cannot take the men home brothers, they are from Althorn.'

'Althorn? That's right – I remember the name in the report from Meridian, but before then I'd never heard of such a place.'

'That's because it's of the Teramarinus.'

Simon and Lucas St Amalric sat in stunned silence for quite some time, 'Now, that is something Edward did not tell us, the Teramarinus!? Did he know? Did you tell him?'

'To be honest I can't recall, but I must thank him when I see him for not telling me off, and for not telling you, if he did.'

'But what were you thinking?!'

'My only thought was save our father, the king.'

'But you cannot take them back, surely it's far too dangerous!'

'Well, I have promised them.'

'Even despite that,' Lucas considered, 'how do you propose to return? It is a perilous flight don't they say, not one I would like to make, seeing the condition of your hull as we came.'

'The Avaeste has made it before, she will make it again.'

'And return?'

Ashton had worried about that aspect.

'Let us take them Ashton.'

'No, the Eventide has less chance of making it than the Avaeste, you might not even make it down, let alone make it back!'

'And that's a chance we're willing to take,'

'No. You take this,' Ashton handed them one of his precious plants. 'Take it and head back to Aeloran as fast as you can. Take it, you and I one each, the plan is perfect, then if anything happens to me the cure can still be tried for the king, and if all goes well, the Avaeste is faster, it might just be that I will arrive even as you do or not long after.'

Simon nodded, 'A sound plan, as far as can be seen, but I still have my concerns about you heading back to the Terra Marine.'

'I have a good crew.'

'But when the men are gone, what will you do?'

'I will still have a good crew,' Ashton grinned, 'I've Santee, a sprite, Morris a swamp monster, and a goblin, called Dew.'

The brothers shook their heads, 'You continue to amaze me little brother, I never knew you had it in you. You were always so shy and reserved, and don't take it badly but I never thought you'd do anything the least bit daring.'

'Well, you don't know if you can fly till you're thrust into the sky. That's what my father used to say.'

'Father? Did he?'

'I mean, *my* father. I'm sorry, I meant my father by lineage, I meant no disrespect to St Amalric, none at all, it just came out,'

'It's alright Ashton,' Lucas smiled, 'we know what you meant.'

'There's something you should know,' Simon said earnestly, 'something St Amalric told us all to tell you when you'd settled in a bit at home, but none of us ever did. I don't know why, perhaps it made us feel bigger that you did not know, but we are not that young now, we grew up and forgot, but you are still young and should know.'

'Know what?'

Simon smiled, 'We are all of us adopted in St Amalric's house.'

'What?'

'All of us were orphaned, just like you.'

'But you are all so alike, everyone says so, you are all so easily recognised as sons of St Amalric, how can that be true?'

'But Ashton, isn't that what they say about you?'

Ashton considered, and recalled it was so.

'His character, Ashton, is what they see in us, what they see in you. Now, the thing we haven't been able to discover is where *you* hail from, and he told us never to ask you. All of us hide secrets and all of us bear names that were not ours at birth, and we know you're no different. So, when you're ready little brother, we're eager to know.' Lucas said, 'Edward's father was a soldier of St Amalric, killed in a battle at Yore and his mother in an ensuing raid; Simon's father was a shipwright in Cierrecay, his mother a net-maker,'

'And you don't want to know how they died,' Simon put in.

'I myself hail from the Gaardevaran, from the range of Narr Arceonath itself, my father was a sage, murdered there. The rest all have their stories Ashton, the reason I tell you this is that whatever happens, know you are not alone, we are brothers, all of us, and what binds us binds us tighter than if we were kin by blood, do you understand little brother?'

'Yes, I think I do,' Ashton nodded. Lucas gave Ashton's shoulder a meaningful grasp and a pat, as Ashton stared ahead, 'I had no idea that all of you were just like me,' he said.

'Well, now you know.'

'I would never have guessed it. I suppose Sebastian is from West Fall?'

'Yes, see, now we've told you it's easy to see isn't it. Only we can't pick you, your origin remains a mystery.'

'Thankyou for telling me, I, I am,' Ashton tried to gather the courage to tell them that he was Novanian, but try as he would he couldn't get past the N.

'It's alright Ashton, father said that for you it would be extraordinarily hard. When you ready to tell us, we'll be there to listen,' Simon smiled as he stood, taking care of the plant in his hand. 'I really am proud of you, you know, though you should be home, most of us only returned a few weeks ago ourselves, but we had nothing to show for it, whereas you've achieved so much. I want to hear of all of your adventures, alright, but later, as I suppose we better be going, and let you continue on to this Althorn.'

'But Simon, how did you find me?'

'With difficulty,' he laughed, 'we went straight to Meridian and the wise cartographer there, what's his name?'

'Highbury?'

'Yes, Highbury, such a good man. He told us your most likely direction, but we kind of came round about, thinking we might catch you on the your way back but this wasn't even the track we were going to take because we didn't think you'd be this far on your way back yet, so a fluke I suppose, a chance most fortunate!'

'Yes, on the return we have had fair winds and very little incident. Oh, Simon, Lucas, I have missed you,' Ashton gave them a parting embrace as little brothers do, 'and father too, oh, all of you! I will go with all speed and all haste and see you back in Aeloran as soon as soon can be.'

They walked out to the main deck, and with brave hearts farewelled, Lucas held Ashton's shoulders, and blessed him, saying, 'May the father of our father guide you.'

Then Simon messed up Ashton's hair, 'Goodbye little bro, take care. We'll see you when you get home.'

Then the princes boarded their caravel again, with Simon turning back, 'You know, I would be glad to lend you some of my men for your journey home.'

'No, we'll be fine, you keep them.'

'We have heard news of Calegra's ship in these parts, Ashton, are you certain you won't take them?'

'Yes, I am certain. My men have good eyes and the Avaeste is fast, I am sure if we spot the Descalabro we can easily outrun it, and even with a few of your men we would be overcome in a hand to hand fight, so that is something I will be sure to avoid.'

'Yes, that would be wise,' Lucas said, 'fare thee well then, and goodbye.'

The Eventide drew out and sailed off, and soon was no more than a distant spot in the mist, then the night drew in and darkness engulfed them, and Ashton wondered if that would be the last thing he saw of Lucas and Simon, for he feared what lay ahead, though he would never admit it. At least, he thought, somewhat comforted, that now even if he could not make it, they would be able to reach Aeloran with the Carex Argentius, and give the plant to his father, the wise king, Mathis St Amalric.

Chapter 21:
FEAR, AND THE DARKEST OF DIM, SHADOWY THINGS

His crew still stood overawed at the royal company that had been on board, as they sailed on and on through the growing night and cloud. Tom ran up with an excited step, 'Look Cap'n, look, one of those sailors gave me this!' he showed off an etched silver compass, whose bearings and markers lit up like stars in the darkness. And wide-eyed, Tom Needled surmised, 'Now that'd be worth a pretty penny I bet.'

'Much more,' Ashton said, 'but don't ever sell it Tom, my friend, it is worth so much more than what you would get for it in the Terra Marine, where you live.'

'Oh, don't worry Cap'n I wouldn't think of selling it, no sir, I'll treasure it. Is it made in your country, Aeloran, do you think?'

'Let me see?' Ashton studied it, turning it over in his hand, 'no, I think this craftsmanship could only be from Oundin.'

'Oundin?'

'Which means it's far more valuable than I first imagined. Keep it close Tom, it will guide you well.' Ashton handed it back but then said, 'Hold on, show it to me again.' And he took another look at the valuable thing, 'Why would the sailor give you something so priceless?'

Tom replied, 'I don't know Cap'n, I didn't do anything.'

'Actually,' Ashton changed his mind as he studied the compass more closely, 'I don't think this design is in the style of Oundin, I think-' Ashton paused as he thought, as the creases grew more pronounced upon his brow, and worry could be seen growing in the curve of his lips.

'And it's funny, you know,' Tom went on, 'he didn't come on board when the others came on. I was the only one that saw him, he kind of appeared out of nowhere. Maybe I just didn't see him step across, or maybe he came down in a parachute,'

'I think it's more likely this comes from, from Arazin!' Ashton concluded, but that so gravely troubled and puzzled him.

'Like the dwarves,' said Tom.

'What?' Ashton was confused as he had not heard Tom's chatter before, 'Dwarves don't come from Arazin; Arazin is in the Ciel Marine.'

'No, in a parachute. Weren't you listening?' Tom shook his head. 'I think the man that gave me that came down in a parachute like the dwarves.'

'What?! No!' Ashton looked up to see if he could see any lights that might disclose a ship travelling up there close by. He couldn't see anything, but it was very dark and the fog crept close around, and between them and the stars.

'It's alright,' Tom assured, 'he was nice, and he gave me the compass didn't he?'

'What was he like?' Ashton pressed, 'Did you see him leave?'

'No, he gave me the compass and I was admiring it; I think he was heading towards your cabin, he said he was just keeping watch on the princes, but that was ages ago, I just assumed he would be heading off with the others, I didn't even look.'

'And you didn't think to tell me!' Ashton asked Tom, much distressed, 'you didn't think there was anything strange about that?'

'Well,' Tom defended, 'everything that happens up here's a bit strange now isn't it, how's I supposed to know from one minute to the next who's good and who's bad? One minute a man's a pirate wanting to sell Banks as a slave, and the next you're on talking terms with him, saving Meridian! One minute the governor's welcoming us to Diamantine, the next we're being chased out! It's insane!' Tom complained. 'It was fun for a while sir, to be sure it was, and still is, but there are some things about home that I miss.'

'I'm sorry Tom, all going well, you'll be home very soon. I shouldn't scold, but what did he look like? Was there anything else unusual about him?'

'No, he was just like the other men from the Eventide, aye, but I guess it surprised me he had a nasty looking blade at his side.'

'And you didn't see him leave?'

'No, no I didn't, but that doesn't mean anything.'

'Alright men, listen up, it may be nothing but I fear that we have on our ship a very dangerous figure. From what I can gather a scout from Calegra's ship is on the Avaeste. He'll be cunning and clever men, don't let down your defence. Now, three things we must do and do at once, arm yourselves and prepare for a fight, search for the scout, if he's still here, secure him, then meet back here and wait for the fray to fall on us from out the night. For if I was ever sure about anything I'm sure about this, if we see no sign of them these dark hours and morning comes, Calegra and his men will creep up on us from out of the mists on the dawn. Now to it!'

The men set about to do as he said, arming themselves then searching the ship, while Ashton himself called out to Santee to send off a few flares in case someone, somewhere, was watching, perhaps the Eventide would see their distress and return to their aid before all was lost, but Ashton did not hold out too much hope of that, their paths had separated so much, and besides which, Ashton hoped they would not see, for they must ahead with all and more speed to get the Silvertip Sedge to the king.

So the young captain buckled the sword to his waist, the knife to his belt and set the pistol in place. He didn't like to think that he would ever use it, but to save a man's life, he wouldn't think twice about doing it. Then he ran down to the engine room, and was surprised to find the monsters laughing there as so often was usual.

Morris's white spots were covered in engine soot, so he was happy as if he was back in his swamp, and said, 'My dear Captain, have you heard the one about the sailor who discovered a fly in his pie?'

'Morris, this is no time for joking,'

'He wriggled and giggled and-'

'The situation is dire, my friends, this may be the end.'

Morris and Dew grew serious at once.

'And now more than ever I need you by my side.'

'Ashton, what is it? Aren't your brothers here?'

'No, the Eventide has left long since. I fear we will soon have company from the Descalabro on this ship.'

'Calegra's frigate?'

'Yes, there is reason to believe one of his men is already here and has scouted ahead. Be ready for anything, I'll meet you back up on deck.'

Ashton arrived back up top as the last of Santee's flares were sent off, shooting up through the cloud and the fog then lighting the darkness with a glowing haze after a short fizzle and pop. The young captain searched the horizons all around them, not a sign of a ship, nor a light anywhere by them.

The men returned to the deck and reported.

'Anything?' Ashton asked.

They shook their heads, 'Nothing.'

'Are you sure there's something amiss Captain?' asked Banks. 'What made you think that your enemy would soon set upon us?'

'The compass, from Arazin, and Tom's report of the man,' Ashton said, going over it once again in his ahead, 'perhaps I was wrong.'

'I hope that you were,' said Jennings, a crease on his forehead. 'I don't particularly relish the thought of going up against any like that Von Marax or his men.'

'Yes,' agreed Ashton, but then Morris ran up to him, puffing, and with a look in his face Ashton did not like to see, a frown around his mouth and his big ears dipping.

'Captain!' the swamp monster whispered, 'the sedge!'

'What?'

'It's disappeared!'

All who heard gasped, then Santee flew to his ear and cried, 'Boy, look up!' and she sent out more flares, so all could see what she had just then espied.

A fleet of dark ships had now gathered beside and below and above, led by Calegra's Descalabro for certain. And from the dark ships, many upon many dark shapes could be seen floating down, and though the crew drew their swords it was a hopeless situation, the men of the Avaeste were soon surrounded. The soldiers of Calegra, dark shadows that they were, took the men and held them, sword ready at the neck of each one, then waited as Calegra himself, the giant-size leader, pounded down, boots and all, to the shuddering deck of the poor Avaeste. Ashton himself had not been seized, but stood opposite this despot, who had been banished from Arazin and the Ciel Marine, and Ashton could do nothing but stand where he stood and wait to hear this tyrant's speech.

Calegra studied him, and he laughed, 'So, you are the eighth son of St Amalric?'

Ashton did not deign to reply, but the two stared at each other until Ashton blinked aside.

'There's not much to you is there boy? How is it then that you confounded my general in the assault on Meridian as they say you did? And how is it that you, so young and so unschooled, could sail to the ends of the ether and return in one piece? Tell me that?'

Ashton remained silent, wondering how in the ether Calegra knew that!

'It's a question I asked myself,' Calegra said, and thought further as he paced side to side on the deck, 'and I have come up with an answer.'

Ashton gulped, but Calegra just said, 'You must have had help. But, that is hardly why I am here, you must know I came for the plant you so carefully and skilfully found. But also, I wanted to meet you, my lad, are you sure you won't join us? I could use your skills well.'

'Never!' Ashton said as he gritted his teeth.

Calegra then took the sedge plant from his man, and studied it, before burying it in one of his inner cloak pockets right then.

'If it's any comfort,' Calegra went on, 'I don't think the king would be strong enough to take the cure anyway, but someone like me has what it takes'

'What do you mean?' Ashton asked.

'I could make good use of this; you don't know its full potential do you my lad?'

'I know of its great healing powers, of that I have read.'

Calegra laughed, 'Oh it's much more than that, but of course you would not know, for I have the other page,'

'The other page?'

'From the *Encyclopaedeae de Floradae cum Medicus in Orbis Terra Antiquituus*. Yes, the other page, if you follow the numbers you will see it does not follow in sequence, a page is missing, I have it, and have poured over the information it contains, dreaming one day of getting my hands on it. For me this little plant is the gem of all gems, but if you had read what it says I don't think you would have tried to procure it for St Amalric.'

271

'Why wouldn't I?'

'I think you might have wanted it for yourself, even as I desire it.'

'But you're not sick are you, nor am I? What good is a cure for those who are well with life?'

'No, this plant is not just a curative lad, it's far more, as I said.'

'How so?'

'Well, that's my secret, and besides it will matter little to you when you're dead,' Calegra said, pulling out his gun right then, saying, 'Are you sure you won't join me, eighth son of the king? I could teach you of things otherwise out of your reach.'

'Never,'

'I could give you such power, and more than you've ever dreamed.'

'I've no wish for power.'

'Riches that would surpass that of Diamantine.'

'If you think that tempts me you do not know me!'

'I could make you a king.'

'I am pleased with St Amalric and have no wish for a throne of my own.'

'What then? Join me and I will ease your suffering.'

'What? I don't suffer much.'

'You will if you don't accept my offer to you.'

'I'll suffer even more if I do!'

'You're a brave one, I'll give you that,' Calegra said, 'but I've got what I want now, this magnificent plant, so I'm afraid that's that, goodbye Captain, goodbye Avaeste and goodbye St Amalric!'

'No! How did you know where I was, what I had, and why I had it?' Ashton demanded as the soldiers of Calegra held him back by his shoulders.

Calegra laughed, 'My, my, foolish lad, I know just about everything. What? I could have made spies of Morris or Jennings.' He chuckled at their stunned faces, 'Oh yes, I know all of your names. But don't fear young captain, you've no traitors here, but I've my spies everywhere nonetheless. You might remember the name of Sabin, and the ravens he brought with him onto your ship? He's a clever one he is, he notices things, and he does a lot of reading. Messages travel faster than men my friend, I know everything.'

'Then you know you'll never get away with this!'

'Oh, but I have.'

'No!' Ashton yelled as Calegra lifted his gun, as the trigger was pulled and the shot rang.

Out across the deep silence the echo reverbed as the bullet flew across the long deck heading straight for the captain's heart. As half the men held their breath and the other half gasped.

It was like all the world was suddenly slowed down, and all the crew watched as the bullet sped forward, no one could do anything for all were held back, even Morris and Dew had a sword to their neck or a gun to their head, and Santee was so upset she was all fuddled and couldn't think how to stop this, and there was that other fact too, that by a deft move of one of Calegra's soldiers, she had been trapped in a jar, like a common insect.

For a second some thought that Ashton had disappeared, but only a second, blink and you'd miss it, and besides it couldn't really be clear in the strange light in this night, it could have just been a shadow of cloud, a flicker of distant lightning or some other such thing. But then they all saw that Ashton appeared to feel the impact, grab his chest where the bullet was sure to have hit, and fall back, flat to the deck, unconscious, in shock, no, Calegra's man shook his head, and said, 'almost dead.'

'Are you certain?' Calegra asked, for this brave young captain was one he didn't want returning.

'Your shot was true sir, I'd give him another ten minutes maximum,' said the man. He happened to be the one Tom had seen much earlier on the ship, the one dressed in black that had given him the compass, and he saw Tom there, with his little heart all distressed to see his captain gasping on the Avaeste's deck, and the man in black stepped to him and rubbed his head, 'Here boy,' he grabbed the compass in his hands, 'I'll take that. Unless that is, you want to come with us, we can always use new hands like you.'

'Never,' Tom said, half crying, half shouting.

'But if you stay on this ship, you'll soon be dead,' the tyrant's man explained.

'Never!' Tom shouted again, 'never ever will I join you and that man!'

A few of the crew nodded to Tom with brave encouragement,

but the man just said, 'Foolish lad,' and walked away.

'So he's dead?' asked Calegra again.

'Aye sir, just about,' said the man, 'but I don't know why you're waiting, you have the Argentius now, so what are you still doing here? You can use it to do just about anything you want to.'

'That's right,' Calegra recalled, and his teeth could be seen as he grinned wide with devious schemes, 'that's right I do. Alright men, tie this lot up and then let's go, soon there won't even be so much as a memory left of this captain or crew.' And he laughed, how he laughed with such haunting delight. 'Let them rot here,' he said, 'sailing aimless in the empty ether till then.'

So the feared tyrant went back to his own ship, carrying with him the Argentius plant. He sent signals out to the rest of his fleet and soon they had sailed off into the distance.

Now the crew were tied all secure and tightly, along the rails, to the masts and even to the rigging, singly and doubly and triply, but with no chance of escape, neither by cutting or wriggling, and the Avaeste sailed with no real direction just pushed by the drafts that came and went, and carried along by the lone trusty engine. Morris couldn't even get his teeth to the ropes, no, being a monster he was bound and tied doubly tight, and Dew had his mouth tied shut and could not even talk had he wanted.

They all looked to the captain, still lying on deck, with a look on his face like it was just as they said, like the life that he had was running right out of him, in the blood they could see spreading from that point on his chest.

But then as the ships of the Tyrant sailed out of sight, Ashton sat up, then stood up, then ran out to his crew with a knife. One by one he cut them all loose, Berens, Old Gragan, Jennings and Banks, Carter, Tom Needle, Dew, Morris and Phillips, oh all of them, yes. They were surprised to see that he was standing up and alive, and they were full of questions, for indeed they none of them could understand how Ashton survived, but Ashton just stopped them as he looked around, worried, and asked, 'Where is Santee, my friends?'

They pointed up to the front of the ship, to the long arm of the Avaeste's bowsprit, where a dim little light was hung there in a glass jar, swaying in the wind that came up with the morning.

'Santee!' Ashton cried and ran to the bow, then stepped up and edged along the arm forwards, he held to the ropes as long as he could but he would need to let go and balance now to bend down and to her rescue.

The dear little sprite was sitting forlorn, some cruel soldier had hung her here as they left, oh, such a malicious prank, and she hung precariously over a great deal of nothing. Now she stood up as Ashton came nearer, as the crew held their breaths and said, 'Be careful now Captain!'

The wind was certainly blowing strong across, making this rescue a most difficult task, but Ashton held on, he was almost there, and that's when he noticed Santee gasping for air. The little glass jar didn't hold much of the stuff and what with breathing and worrying Santee had just about used it all up. She banged on the glass and to Ashton's dismay, collapsed right then. 'No! Santee stay with me!' yelled Ashton.

He quickly lunged down and caught the cord, pulling up the jar then clutching it tightly, then he slid back along the bowsprit with caution, until he felt the hands of the crew drawing him back.

Ashton fell to the deck, handing the little glass jar to his men, 'Quickly! Quickly, get it open!' he yelled.

The lid was on tight, it certainly was, no wonder the little sprite could not get out herself. One tried, then another tried, then another tried too, until they handed it to Phillips saying, 'Lieutenant, this is a job for you.'

Big Phillips, with his grit and broad shoulders, took the little jar in his hands, still with Santee unconscious, and carefully, with all his strength, unscrewed the lid.

They tipped the sprite out into Ashton's careful hands, but she wasn't moving, wasn't breathing, she was so small it was impossible for them to do anything for her. Unless, Ashton wondered, unless, that is, he stood up and quickly made for his cabin, 'Morris, come with me I may need you, the rest of you – man your stations we need to keep moving!'

'Will she be alright?' they all yelled after.

'I will save her,' Ashton said, 'I will try my hardest.'

Ashton closed the door and he locked it, and put Santee carefully on the maps, by his compass.

'Well, Captain, what do you propose? I can't think of anything I could possibly do to help her now.'

'No, she needs someone her own size Morris,' Ashton said, giving Morris his hat, 'if anything happens to me, you're in charge of the ship.'

'I don't understand?'

'I'm just afraid,' the young captain admitted, 'you see, I've never done anything like this.'

'Like what?' Morris asked but even as he did, Ashton disappeared into a sparkling of lights.

Well that's what it seemed until Morris looked closely – as the light that was Ashton floated like seeds down to the map by the compass, and in amongst the lights Morris could see, there flew Ashton, very small, indeed, as small as a sprite.

He ran and knelt down by Santee's side as she lay there on top of the Meridian Isle, her glow was so faded, she was hardly alive, and he worried and wondered what to do, oh she had to survive! He fanned her face, he hit her back, he rubbed her arms, but to no effect, all the time Morris peered over the desk and asked if there was anything he could do to help. Ashton just yelled up to him, 'I don't know what to do, it seems as if she cannot take the air in, and I fear that if she does not soon she'll die from lack of oxygen! So unless you know a way Morris, to get air into her, than I think she's gone!'

'Perhaps you could use a pump?' said the monster of swamp, 'something to force the air back in, I know that's what we used to get water in when our home was drying up, maybe air moves the same?'

'A pump? This small? There's no time for that, unless...' Ashton thought, 'my lungs! My chest!' and he didn't stop to explain to Morris just what he meant, but bent over Santee and gave her his breath. In he blew and out he pushed, he did this more than three times, more than five times, more than ten, but still no life could be seen coming back to his very, very dear friend.

'Breathe Santee, come on, breathe!' Ashton cried, for he loved her so, so sure, and he didn't know if he could ever love another someone more. He lifted her and embraced her there, upon the well marked map, upon the Isle of Meridian and the lines of the

Aethermarinus, and he cried, for sure he cried, with her head upon his shoulder and his tears running down her back.

Then, 'Am I in Aeranimh?' a little voice said, so broken and so sweet, she didn't move but Ashton knew that he had done it, he had saved Santee! And he tried to stop the tears that kept falling from his eyes, but so happy as he was now it was impossible to try. She hadn't moved yet, but he could feel her heartbeat close to his, and her breath across his neck.

'But if I'm with the sprites on Aeranimh,' the little voice said again, 'how is it I'm still in Ashton's cabin, on the Avaeste, sitting on a map?'

Ashton laughed, so happy, 'Santee it's me. You're not dead, you're not gone to the Cielomarinus yet.'

She sat back and looked at him, and poked his face to see. Then she looked around the room and at his instruments, so big, around them. It was the captain's cabin, yes, 'But, you're so small boy, and you've got wings and light, like me. What happened?'

'Well I had to save you Santee, you couldn't breathe,' he told her, conveying his previous distress. 'Are you alright now? Can I get you anything? Water? Tea? Lemon-Ice?'

'No, no, thankyou, I'll be alright,' she smiled, then held onto him again, head on his shoulder, tired. 'I like you being my size, can you stay like this for a little while?'

Ashton smiled and held her in return, saying, 'Alright.'

'Oh, there's something I should tell you,' Santee remembered.

'What's that?'

'The plant Calegra has is not the Sedge.'

'Oh, what is it?'

'Your mug, the one with your half finished hot-chocolate. I changed it to look like the sedge, so now Calegra has it.'

'Oh! My mug!' Ashton laughed, 'you're cleverer than me, I never would have thought of that with all that was happening, but the real sedge Santee?'

'It's safe, don't worry, I hid it. I'll show you where later, for now,' Santee yawned, 'I think I might sleep. Can you get big again boy? Do you think you could put me up in my room please?'

'I think I could do that,' Ashton said, 'but why don't I fly you up and tuck you in myself,' Ashton suggested.

'Even better,' Santee grinned. 'Can you be anything, anything at all?' Santee asked as he flew her in his arms up to the hanging lantern.

'Anything alive that once lived on my isle,' Ashton replied, at once proud and sad, but he smiled, 'even sprites.'

Santee smiled back, 'Thankyou boy, for saving my life.'

Ashton shook his head, 'No need for thanks. Now, sleep well, I must go and speak with the crew, if Calegra does not have the true plant he will be back when he discovers it and be back with a thirst for revenge and I certainly don't want to be anywhere near here when he returns.'

'No, of course, go and do what you must, but wake me if you need me.'

'Thankyou, but don't let anything trouble you for now Santee, rest,' said Ashton, as he shut the door of her lantern, then left, stepping down with the lights converging, then flickering back together, once again Ashton.

He breathed. Oh that was the most difficult thing he had ever done! He held onto the desk and swayed over the maps. He had to gather himself before he stepped out to the men. The glow still hung about him and he wondered at it there along his arm, but slowly it faded and he was completely back to usual as the last of the light returned to him.

The young captain turned to go out but Morris stood in the door and gave him a look with a question.

'What is it Morris?'

The swamp monster looked at Ashton darkly and answered, 'You were just a sprite! And for a second when Calegra shot I thought I saw on board something I'd never expect to see but in the dark hours on Kebaticus,' Morris began, 'a dark and dangerous phantasm that feeds on the likes of me. Right where you were standing it was, for a second, as Calegra shot. It was you, wasn't it.'

Ashton sighed, 'Yes.'

'Oh, you ought not to go there Ashton, it's too dangerous.'

'Well, I'm alive aren't I?'

'Aye, you're alive,'

'And the shot all but went through me without harm, but it took a while to recover what of me was displaced.'

'But a troll eater Ashton!' Morris said afraid, 'a creature of fog, shadow and darkness that cannot be touched but by those it devours. Stay that way too long and you'll be wanting to eat *me*!'

'No Morris! It was only for a second – I didn't even think, it just happened! Call it instinct, or self preservation.'

'You can just be thankful what you were was so dark the men didn't see. Couldn't see. Not even Calegra saw, and that's saying something.'

'Morris, I'm sorry, I didn't mean to do it, believe me.'

'Is it what you are? Really? I know you are not just this Ashton we see, I've known since you saved my life that day, I've known you were possessed of an innate enchantment, but I never thought this. Dew said you became a host of birds to save Annabella Bien, and then just now you were a sprite! What being can do that!? Ashton, what are you? Tell me you are not this ghost that eats us monsters in the night?'

'No.'

'Really?

'Morris, well no, think, they cannot be birds or sprites. I'm, I'm N-.' Ashton slid to the floor and sat there staring at his hands.

'You're Novanian, aren't you?'

'Yes,'

'But that's impossible! Ile de Novo is gone, worse than my home, I heard it was utterly destroyed. Tell me how is it so?'

'Aye, it was destroyed. St Amalric pulled me from the fields of the dead. I'm the only Novanian left.'

'But what is your true guise? Is it this Ashton?'

'Almost. This is me,' Ashton looked up – just as Santee had seen him in the dream, the young man with the elf-like countenance, the blue-blonde hair, the long face and long fingers and thin limbs, the expressive eyes, so full of sadness, still like Ashton, but different, more of the realm of the higher Aethermarinus, and Morris could see at once that indeed he was Novanian, but he could hardly believe and put out his claw to touch him. But then Ashton ran his hand over his face and changed back.

'I am everything, and nothing,' he said. 'Morris believe me, it frightens me that for a second I became this thing I did not plan to be. I do not know much of my people because I was too young to have begun the deeper learning, but I do know the rule they always said, never become anything you would not wish to stay as. And also, it is my greatest fear that Calegra will know who I am, if he knew he would hunt me down slay me without mercy, for he hates Novanians so terribly, the last thing I would want would be for him to see my true identity, trust me, I would rather be lying there with a bullet in my chest, a common man, than have Calegra know who I really am, I would never have chosen to do that, it just happened.'

'But – were there those shadow ghosts on your island? I thought Novania was all peace and beauty.'

'They were there, but they were not as they are out here, they kept to themselves, ghostlike yes, but living only on vapour from the swamp and on the poisonous flowers there. But I don't want it to happen again. You've no idea how afraid I was in that second, indeed that's why I did get hurt a little, I became myself again even as the bullet was still passing through me.'

'Oh, I think I have some inkling of your fear. But now, if you want to master yourself you must practice, so the next time you meet with such imminent danger you will be prepared to be cleverer than that.'

'But I can't, the more I am who I am the more dangerous it is that someone will see.'

'And you will always have that fear. Look at me – I am a swamp monster, people see my face and run for the hills or their guns and I can't change it, I am stuck this way, it is who I am. You on the other hand, if you practice, could be so that people could see you and know you but it wouldn't matter, even if Calegra saw you and sent his whole army after you, it would not matter, because you'd be ready.'

'No Morris, he is of the Ciel Marine, and I of the Ether, it would not matter what I would do, he could defeat me, like he defeated all of us at Novania.'

'They were not ready, they did not know the real tyrant nor what he could do, but you do, and you will be ready.'

'You're very confident, but there is none but St Amalric can defeat him, and because of me the king is nearly dead.'

'Aye,' Morris said with a spark in his eye, 'but you're a son of his now, are you not? You bear your father's name, and besides which, I said nothing of defeating Calegra but holding your ground.'

Ashton did not look that certain. Morris went on, 'You need a tutor, that's what you need, someone to train you to sharpen your traits and your skill.'

'No. Besides, there is no one left to teach me.'

'There are books Ashton, and there are many wise men, and wise monsters for that matter, who could tell you a thing or two, even though they are not Novanian.'

'It will have to wait Morris, right now I have to evade Calegra, get these men back to Althorn, then with all haste back to Aeloran.'

'Of course, but take my advice and practice when you can. Then after we get the plant to the king perhaps then we can find some teachers for you and begin your learning.' Morris smiled, 'it's still so hard to believe.'

'What?'

'That a Novanian exists,' Morris said, 'and that you're him, and my friend. A Novanian exists, that's another reason not to hide captain, you are the embodiment of hope for the return of things lost! Novanian! It answers a lot of questions I had, tell me – is that how you rescued me?'

'Maybe it helped, but it was mostly ingenuity, coupled with a fair amount of timely opportunities. But come Morris, let's get back on course and tell the men Santee lives.'

So Ashton went out to see how things lay, and found the men had the ship nicely underway. He told them the good news of Santee's recovery, then began throwing orders to make further haste and formulate a more suitable course. But the crew was acting rather slow and unusual, so he stopped them all and said, 'What? What's wrong with you? Don't you understand the tyrant will be back, we have to make haste or be caught by him again?'

'We understand that Cap'n,' they replied, 'we just can't get this one question out of our minds.'

'What question?'

'How did you do it?' they asked him,

'Was it magic?' asked Jennings.

'A trick of the eye?' asked Phillips.

'Are you an illusionist?' asked Banks, while Carter just stared, waiting for the answer in utter bewilderment.

'Yeah Cap'n, how'd you do it?' asked Needle, with much excitement, 'how did you dodge the tyrant's bullet? How did you make it seem like you'd been shot, then get up, like nothing had happened?'

'I, ah,' Ashton was naturally hesitant to explain that as Calegra had shot he momentarily became a monster of a shadowy kind. 'I didn't, I was hit, but only a scrape my good men, and a momentary shock, you see.'

'But they said you were good as dead.'

'Well, for a moment there I thought I was too, but it was nothing, a bit of blood, a mere flesh wound. Well, what are you waiting for? All of you, come on! You men, let out the sails, the wind's fair, the air clearing, Dew, to the engine! Berens, and you men, get up the rigging! Tom, man the crow's nest with Harrick, we can't afford to be unprepared if any ship comes across us, keep a sharp eye out. Banks, tilt the lever to descent, make it a two degree course for the minute, till I think. Gragan, take the ledger and write the names of everyone, I haven't forgotten my promise, there shall be a reward for all when this is done. Now, those not needed up here, go and get you some rest while you can, Morris, with me.'

'What do you want me to do?'

'Come below deck, I'll explain.'

So the Avaeste was brought up to fine speed, shooting through the ether she was, like a cup winning steed.

'So Captain, what's your plan?'

'Well, I've been thinking, now that we're getting closer to Althorn, the easiest way to evade Calegra would be to take these men home.'

'An early descent to the Terra Marine?'

'Yes, that should keep the tyrant off our tail when he discovers the plant is not what it appears.'

Chapter 22

NOW WE MUST RETURN THE STOLEN CREW

Now you can imagine that Calegra was more than mad when he pulled out the plant and found it did not work just as he'd read. No, he sat the thing on his table and studied it, pulled out the page from the book of rare old medicines, did what it said to do, and did so again, but nothing happened. Yes he snipped off some leaves and made an infusion, a strange smelling tea, to which he also added some roots, and he drank the whole jug of it, the entire sum of it, and he thought it strange that it tasted subtly like chocolate, which was very odd for a plant from the bog.

Now we know Calegra did not want the plant for a curative, nor for a sedative, laxative or purgative, no, all that we do know, without seeing that second page, is that he wanted this plant for his own devious purposes, and whatever they were had something to do with the death of St Amalric and Calegra's desires for himself to rule over the islands and the Aethermarinus in its entirety. But Calegra just sat there after he had drunk the tea, and nothing happened, but for a boiling of his anger, and a burp, or two or three.

So he called in his sages, his practitioners and his specialists and had them all analyse the little Carex Argentius. They smelt it and pulled it and poked it and prodded it, boiled it again, bit it and pounded it, dissected, scrutinized, sliced and tore at it and looked at it under magnifying lenses.

'It appears to be a plant,' one nodded profoundly, 'a plant that reads here as the Carex Argentius.'

'Yes, well I know that!' spat Calegra, 'imbeciles!' he said.

'But you missed the point,' one sage answered back, 'the key word here, is *appears*.'

'Your meaning?' the Tyrant asked, rubbing his chin.

'I'm afraid this is not what it seems, not the Silvertip Sedge at all, my leader.'

'But what is it?' Calegra said, with his lip curling up, with a seething bitterness growing within him.

'You are the one with the power to reveal it,' they answered.

'Ah. It is the sedge by enchantment?' Calegra said, understanding.

'Yes, as you know there was a sprite on the ship.'

'But Sprites are foolish and simple beings that keep to themselves, I've never met one as clever as would do this, nor in league with men.'

'Well, that's my explanation, take it or leave it.'

'No, no, I'll believe you, let's see now,' Calegra drew all the pieces that were left together in a heap, touched it with his finger and whispered, 'Aperio!'

At once a little whirlwind spun on the table, the pieces of sedge all swept up in it, then there was a mug there, wobbling, then tipping over, spilling the chocolate Ashton had not finished everywhere.

'Aaaaarrrrgghhh!!!!' the Tyrant yelled, and his shout could be heard all through his ship and his fleet following. 'Fooled by a common trick! A child's prank! Duped by a boy with a crew of misfits! Well, no more fool me, I'll find them again, and when I do I'll have it out of them, I will. I'll have the plant, every piece of it they have, and I'll do it properly, and leave none of them alive this time! Who was it said in my ear we could take the thing and be off without a fight, without bloodshed, where is he? There he is, take him away and murder him. I will be what I will be, what is a battle without fighting!'

And so as the Descalabro and Calegra's fleet was turned around to go after the Avaeste once again, Ashton's men were excited for home was so close they could almost feel it! The air, the sky, it was all beginning to become more familiar. But below in the hold Ashton looked over his aeroplane, the golden contraption Gualtiero had made, he pulled the cover off and ran his hands along the well shaped frame, smiled sadly, then turned to Morris saying, 'Melt it down.'

'What?' Morris was startled, that was an order he least expected.

Ashton explained, 'Well, I must keep my promise. How else can I pay these good men for their services? How else can I give them a reward? After all they have helped me sail across the unknown and acquire the cure, without them I could not have done it.'

'The men would not want you to do this.'

'Wouldn't they?'

'No, not even Banks.'

'Even so, the decision has been made, they will have their due pay. We'll make the sheet into coins if we can, thirty pieces each man.'

'If you say so.'

'Also,' Ashton went on, 'thirty pieces each friend.' He knelt down on his knee, took Morris's hand and shook it, 'I don't thank you enough, Morris of Swamp, please accept it.'

Morris didn't know quite what to say, thirty pieces of gold and he'd be the richest monster in his family tree. 'Do you want the coins embossed?' he asked, 'perhaps with a picture of the Avaeste, or your face?'

'No, nothing that can be traced back to the Ether Marine, just plain, but if it must be marked with something, mark it with an A, like this,' Ashton sketched.

'For Ashton?'

'No,'

'Avaeste? Amalric? Althorn? Aethermarinus? Aeloran?'

'No, nothing so grand,' Ashton laughed, 'A for Aeroplane is what I had on my mind, but I suppose all those things are alright.'

'Then A it is. I'll carve the mould right away, it will be rough but it will do the job.' Morris patted the plane sadly.

'We'll still have the frame Morris,' Ashton encouraged, 'we'll still be able to fly. Perhaps I can procure some other cheap metal or something on Althorn, something we can shape to it and paint up a bit, even canvas and stiffening. It'll be alright.'

'It always is, isn't it?' Morris grinned.

From time to time Ashton went up on deck, checked the course, checked the wind and the speed, then ever so slightly altered the descent. As yet they had not been followed, had not been sighted by any other ship and that was a very comforting thing. Now all that remained was to hold her true and steady, and they might even reach Althorn in time for afternoon tea. And it wasn't likely that any would find them now, for they were quite well on their way down, and not many ships could follow the Avaeste from the Ether to the Terra Marine through the dividing mists, and no other ship could dive quite like this, and if they could follow in any case it would be very cat and mouse in and out through the cloud.

But nothing was seen and so they continued, Ashton and Morris working quickly to turn the gold out, filling small pouches with the coins as they cooled. Ashton commenting now and again about the intricacy of the embossed letter 'A' and marvelling at and praising the skill of his first mate, Swamp Morris, who'd carved it so quickly.

Morris just smiled and got on with it. But they got to talking as they went on, Morris still found it hard to believe his boy captain was Novanian.

'Have you been back?' Morris asked, 'have you returned home since you left?'

'No, in truth I'm afraid to go.'

'Why? It has been many years.'

'It's a sad picture now I've heard. Highbury, on Meridian, said it was still burning last time their people went past.'

'I'm sorry Ashton. It used to be said that Novania was the closest anything here in the Ether could get to the Cielomarinus, in splendour and peace and beauty.'

'Yes. It was beautiful.'

'You must go back there one day. I'll go with you.'

'No. Why. There's no point. There won't even be bones to bury, only ashes and tar.'

'But it's your home,' Morris went on.

'No,' Ashton said with all determination, 'no Morris, it's too hard.' Then the young captain softened, and sighed, with that same mix in his face of sadness and pride. 'I am Ashton, son of Mathis St Amalric, and my home is with him, on Aeloran.'

Then after a while of more silence and concentrating on coin making Ashton spoke up.

'Do you know,' Ashton began to ask, but stopped.

'Do I know what?'

'Well, I have learnt much in the last few years, but mostly rules of arithmetic, geography and science, and skills of a practical nature, sailing and navigating, for instance, but in many ways I am still as new to the fables and lore of this place as the men of Althorn, for I have not had the years of historical learning in my childhood, for Ile de Novo was much secluded and the freedom of a child to run and learn the ways of the island was considered more important than a formal education. And I know there is much in a monster's head worth knowing.'

'Aye, for we tell and retell our stories for generations. What is the question?'

'Forgive my ignorance, but is it really true that St Amalric is not originally of Aeloran,' Ashton lowered his voice, 'but of Arazin?'

'There are some that do not think so, mostly those that do not concede that there are other marines that move together but at different speeds, but I believe it to be true. I hear he has the bearing and voice of one from the Ciel Marine, but I haven't seen him, so I can't say. Although, I can say this, from all I've heard of him, it seems most likely; no ordinary man could do what he's done. It is said his father is the king of Arazin, Aeranimh, and all of the Ceil Marine.'

'Oh. And Calegra is from Arazin too?'

'Yes, that's why he's so powerful here.'

'Aolani said he was banished here.'

'The tyrant and his cronies were banished from the royal city and the entire of the Cielomarinus I believe it is told.'

'Why would the father of my father do that?'

'Punishment.'

'But here?'

'I cannot pretend to understand the ways of them, I cannot even understand ordinary men. Consider this, the governor in the closest town to ours banishes murderers to our marsh!'

Ashton laughed, 'They probably think you'll eat them.' Morris looked guiltily at Ashton, Ashton gasped, 'You don't! Do you?'

Morris laughed heartily, 'No, murderers taste like chicken, there's no way we'd touch them. No, swamp monsters like bugs, worms and other insects.'

'Then how do you know they taste like chicken?'

Morris rubbed the folds around his mouth and raised his eyebrows and rolled his eyes from left to right, well, he couldn't quite answer that one.

'Hang on,' Ashton said, looking strangely at the monster, 'Morris – why are your spots orange?'

'Orange?'

'Yes – the ones from when you and Santee dyed my hair, they're orange.'

'Are they?' Morris looked, 'so they are,' he said, and continued with the work unperturbed.

'But if those spots are orange and they used to be white,' Ashton worried, thinking of his hair.

Morris laughed, 'I can't believe you just noticed, you've had ginger hair since this morning.'

'Oh no! Have I?' Ashton pulled it around to see, his eyes widened and he sighed. 'Is it terrible?'

'No, no, it's fine. You'll just have to tell Santee to work on her potion next time.'

'Oh well,' Ashton said, resigned, 'at least it was fine when my brothers were here.'

Ashton and Morris worked quickly now, they had most of the gold done that they needed, Morris still heated, poured, and turned out, Ashton still counted and put them in little pouches. And when it was almost done and Morris could finish off, Ashton ran back up to take over from Banks and make the way to Althorn himself.

No one could see it, but Ashton knew where it was, the tricksy mist that hung between the lower world and the one above. It could not be seen, for it looked just like the sky, all blue and cloudy, but it was just a trick of the eye, it was like some sort of slightly reflective puffy stuff that hovered between the realms, making one think there was nothing beneath them and the one below think there was nothing above, yes, it was kind of like clouds, and they hit it and felt it, then could see nothing for a moment, but then the entire world of the Teramarinus was suddenly below them as they broke through it.

'Home!' said Banks

'Home!' said Carter

'Home!' said Jennings and Phillips, and indeed the rest of the crew sighed sweet home sweet, along with them.

'Yes,' admired Ashton, 'a sight isn't it. The Terra Marine, where the land meets the sea, meets the sea, with no gaps in between. It's beautiful, I can see why you like it.'

'Like it? Lad we love it!' said old Gragan. 'Don't know how you folk get around up here without living every moment in falling fear, fear of falling, I mean to say. I'll be glad to set my feet on homely ground again, I tell thee.'

And so it was that the Avaeste sailed down to the sea and then into Althorn like an ordinary ship, heaving to at the harbour, and setting down her plank, with the crew saluting their young captain, no they did not hesitate, not though all the folk on the street and on the port, and though all the rough men of the other ships stood by to see, surprised at the sight and laughing heartily.

The crew had said goodbye to Dew earlier, for the sight of a goblin in port would cause quite a stir, so he remained below deck, and they had found Santee out and presented her with a bouquet of flowers constructed with paper and wire, and had blown her kisses as they left, and then turned to Morris, and gave a salute to the Avaeste's first mate. It almost brought tears to Morris's warty, swampy face.

'Never again will I call you a Marsh Walump, unless it be in jest, my friend,' said Phillips to Morris, as he left.

The men took Ashton's reward with surprise and hesitance, but Ashton insisted it was well deserved, for they had been a loyal crew, most diligent, and of course, very forgiving considering the way Ashton had first enlisted them in his employment.

The only thing the men could not take was their uniforms, for they clearly were from the Aethermarinus to be sure, besides possibly being of Santee's conjuring, who knows what they were really, maybe sheets or old sails, or straw, could be anything. So just as they had come aboard the men left the dear little ship, repeating to Ashton their very best wishes for the rest of his journey, encouraging him that he would be able to outrun Calegra and reach the king with the Carex Argentius. Some even offered to continue on with him but he would not have it.

And as they walked back along the main street the men of the crew passed that fine establishment where they had first met the young captain. And the bartender's wife ran out as they walked by, saying, 'Well aren't you going to come back for your free drink then?

You've been over two hours loading that gear! Blessed if I know what took you so long.'

But they all shook their heads, wanting nothing more than to find their families, oh yes, to go home to them. Back to their wives, their children and back to their friends. And those people thought these fellows were new men, and wondered what had happened to them, they certainly must not have been doing their usual afternoon thing and drinking till they ran out of coins down at the inn, no, these men, they returned with an air about them, a confidence and assurance that could not be explained. When asked the men just smiled a satisfied smile, and answered, 'Oh, I've been away.' The response was surprise to that reply, as they had not been away for very long, what, only since noon, and it was not yet tea time. So the men found they could not really explain, without being thought a buffoon, that they had in fact been to another land, where very few men from this place had ever been, a place called the Ether Marine, where everything was amazing.

Now Ashton and Morris acquired materials with which to replace the gold sheet that they had taken from the aeroplane to reward the men. They decided on canvas to do the job, which they would wrap like a bandage over the frame with a sort of glue between each sheet. But they did not dwell in Althorn, just did what they had to do then sailed on, out to the ocean, then lifting up and to the skies ascending, and ever hastening to get back to Aeloran.

Chapter 23:
FIND FRIENDS AND ENEMIES AGAIN

'I've something to show you,' Ashton said to Morris one morning on deck when all was well, and they were in-between coats remodelling the aeroplane. 'I've been practising,' the young captain said proudly.

'Alright, let's see it,' encouraged his first mate.

Ashton put his arms up, horizontally, with his fists to his chest, then took a deep breath, exhaled then said, 'Are you ready?'

'Aye, go ahead.'

Ashton laughed, 'You're going to love this.' Then he spread his arms out, but no more was he there, only a flurry of black and orange butterflies fluttering everywhere, then as they twisted about all at once they were swallows darting here and there around the Avaeste, with the sunlight on their deep-blue feathers and swooping Swamp Morris in fun. Then they all flew out of sight, reappearing out to the front, together coming in fast then hitting the deck, but as Morris watched, his eyes wide with amazement, the swallows were no more, but a horde of field mice were running towards him, only they were not mice for long but in a blink they were moths, flying up and landing on Morris, who quickly closed his lips so scared he was that he'd breath one in, for indeed swamp monsters did eat moths, but then they fell away, just leaves, like in autumn, blowing back towards where the captain had been standing. Then there was Ashton.

Morris gave him a standing ovation, then Santee and Dew stepped out and clapped also. Ashton bowed.

'Were you watching too?' he asked his friends, slightly embarrassed.

'Aha,' said Dew, squinting in the sun, 'tell me, can you be a goblin?'

'I don't think so, I don't think goblins or swamp monsters ever lived on our isle, but you never know.'

'But he can be a sprite,' Santee gloated.

'You have been practising indeed,' Morris encouraged.

'Aye,' Ashton smiled, catching his breath, 'I've never tried moths before, nor mice, I tend to try and stay away from insects and rodents. Although, butterflies are good, I remember doing those as a child, difficult, but worthwhile. And the birds, I'm good at birds, mostly it's effortless. Every Novanian has their forte and that's mine, my father said.'

'From what I've seen, everything is your forte,' said Morris.

'Oh, but thirsty work, I need a glass of water,' Ashton said, then went below deck to fetch it.

'What are we going to do with him?' Morris sighed.

'What do you mean?' Santee asked.

'Don't mistake me, I am much impressed, but a Novanian can be so much more than that,'

'More?' she said, surprised by the statement for she found Ashton's tricks amazing.

'Yes, more. He is so lacking in strength and knowledge. He was very young when he lost everything I imagine, and even the memories he does have are probably discoloured. But a Novanian, well, I have heard stories, and I will keep them to myself for now at least. But he has such potential within him, and he doesn't even know it, for he is so unlearned in these things. I wish I had known his origin earlier.'

'How can we help him learn it when we know nothing?'

'We can encourage him to be himself to start with. He has been so afraid for so long it's hard for him to show it.'

'Not today it wasn't.'

'That's right, a little progress, but he's happy this morning, wait till he's down again and there'll be no coaxing him out.'

'And he's more often down than up.'

'That's right.'

'Who's down and up?' Ashton said, coming back on deck.

'Dew, see, he doesn't like the sunshine, he's so often in the dark of the engine room rather than in the light, see how he's squinting his eyes.'

'Like all good goblins,' Dew said, 'My eyes are more suited to the night.'

'Exactly so,' laughed Ashton,

'In fact I'll go check the engine now.'

'Man the wheel Morris, I'll scout around. I don't want to come too near any unknown or unfriendly craft.'

'Can I come?' asked Santee.

'I suppose so, if you don't mind a swift flight?'

'I'd love it.'

'Hold on then,' Ashton said, then as Santee grabbed his hair he ran up the stairs to the upper deck then jumped out, disappearing once again as the flight of swifts, flying every which way from the Avaeste to scout.

Morris shook his head and sat down for a minute. Despite what he said, he still thought what Ashton did was astounding, indeed it took away his breath, and pulled the blood from his limbs making him weak at the knees, that here was the only, the very last Novanian when all had thought that race dead. The swamp monster felt a new and overwhelming responsibility to ensure that Ashton returned home safely. Not that that wasn't the goal before, but that now it was ever so much more important.

Then dear Morris began to doubt his wisdom in telling Ashton to be more himself, and wondered if the boy hadn't been right all along in wanting to remain hidden and unknown, there were so many dangers out there in the world. And Morris reminded himself that although Ashton was bold and courageous, intelligent and possessed of a remarkable foresight and wisdom, he was not yet that old, perhaps the amazing things he heard of Novanians before were things only achieved by those much older, and perhaps it was not time yet for the rest of the Aethermarinus to know that here in this boy was the beginnings of hope, no, Ashton was right, it was too dangerous yet for the world to know. But again he resolved, that when this was over he would urge Ashton to go back to the hidden realms, to visit Ile de Novo, his home.

The swamp monster felt so strangely alone when it had been so long with just he and Dew on board and barely the sight of the swifts so far out. It was terribly quiet too, without the men on board anymore. Morris begun humming a hesitant tune as he watched the skies ahead and held firm the wheel.

Santee, on the other hand was shouting out with delight, at the speed and the turns and the fun of the flight, as she lay there upon the swift's back, holding onto the feathers, and holding oh so tight.

But then in the distance, far up ahead, some flares could be seen, orange through the cloud, and then the fire of cannon shot could be heard, so at once the swift changed course and headed towards it. It was still so far and invisible yet, but the sound continued, then a silence so ominous.

Through a convergence of cloud Ashton flew, then all at once out into the startling brightness of the clear blue, but below, not far now, a sight to be dreaded, the thing Ashton feared, Calegra's Descalabro was there in the distance, sailing away in a manner triumphant, but here right before them, was the faithful old caravel, the Eventide, with part of its deck ablaze, yes, and part of its hull, dreadfully burning!

The swift swooped to it and flew quickly through, gathering there were men still on board trying to douse the flames as they could, but a hopeless task it really appeared, with the smoke billowing around, blinding and choking them as they worked, and by the looks of things they would not have enough water, but the fire would grow and take hold and then the Eventide would break up and fall. But what worried Ashton, even more, was that there was no sign of his brothers Simon and Lucas, and no sign of the Silvertip Sedge that they carried, could this mean that Calegra had them and had it?

At once he sped back to the Avaeste, faster than any swifts had ever flown it was certain, falling to his knees on the top deck, puffing, gasping, out of breath, putting his hand on Morris's shoulder as the faithful first mate came up. 'Descada's hit the Eventide, she burns, make way 15 degrees starboard, full ahead.'

Morris ran and made the adjustments, and Dew got the message down in the engine room and fired it up ever faster, not that he didn't already have it turning over with much pace and power.

On they went, Ashton stood impatient to get to the wreck, but afraid they'd be too late, or that Calegra would see them and come back.

'Don't get too close,' Ashton commanded, 'We can't let our own sails catch fire, go in away and slightly higher, I'll jump across with ropes and send up the survivors.'

He ran around, with Dew helping now, soaking ropes in water then securing several strong ones to the side ready to throw over, and he climbed up the rigging securing more ropes, the ones on which he would swing out and over to the Eventide to help.

They sailed up and the exhausted crew from Aeloran hailed them, leaving the flames as they burned uncontrollable, as the old ship began to break, there was no hope for it now, and down into the smoke and in between the flames as they grew ever higher young Ashton took his courage and jumped.

The men caught him and helped him in, taking the ropes as he motioned for them to take them and swing away and out of the burning, and they did, these survivors, one by one they escaped, and lastly Ashton on the final rope, just in time, as the old ship broke up beneath them and fell away, burning to no more than cinders as it plummeted down through the ether.

Morris turned the Avacste sharply aside so as not to be catching any stray embers that might be floating through the sky, and then he and Dew got to work helping pull in the crew from the Eventide.

Naturally the men were surprised and alarmed when the hands that took theirs to pull them in were warty and bubbled with a green tinge, and the faces that smiled and asked them if they were alright were the toothy smiles of a swamp monster and a goblin. But soon they found Morris and Dew quite attending and just the friends needed at a time such as this. Ashton too, when he made it back up, made sure all their wounds were dressed and bandaged, and that their thirsts were quenched.

'What of Simon and Lucas?' Ashton asked one man, who sat with his back against the railing as the young captain bandaged his hand. The man was covered in soot and his skin red from being too near the flames, and his breath came out very roughly as he spake.

'Captured,' he said, then breathed in again with difficult intake, 'captured, Prince Ashton, by the tyrant.'

'No!'

'It is so, I'm afraid. The man was truly maddened with an unfounded rage.'

'Oh, he left us to die further back, but later he would have discovered that he was fooled and we had long escaped. Perhaps that would explain his madness.'

'Aye, that would do it.'

'Do you know of what my brothers were carrying for me to the king, is it safe?'

The sailor shook his head, then explained, astonished, 'Somehow Descada knew we had it.'

Ashton sighed, a hint of guilt in his eye, 'Yes, he had a spy on this ship around the same time my brothers were here, unfortunately.'

'Oh, well at least that explains it. Yes he took the plant, but Prince Lucas asked why he wanted it, it being a curative and Descada not ill, and though he answered I did not hear, but whatever he said enraged Lucas so, and you know that is a hard thing to do for Lucas is the most placid person I've met in the world, and I've met quite a few. But so, Lucas, he near lost his mind and as they scuffled the plant was knocked from the hand of Descada into the fire. It was destroyed in the flames even though the tyrant near burnt his hands trying to salvage the thing. I'm sorry Prince Ashton, it was gone in seconds.'

'No! The Argentius! My brothers! What should I do?'

'Head straight to Aeloran.'

'But my brothers? I cannot leave them at the mercy of the tyrant.'

'Neither can you fight him and his men, only go now as fast and direct as you can. When they hear what you have to tell they will send out more ships.'

'But it may be too late! Aeloran is still days away.'

'So what's your plan?'

'Well,' Ashton said, thinking it through, 'Yes, I will head for Aeloran as you say, for if I'm not mistaken I won't have to look for Calegra at all, he'll be looking for the Avaeste with a furious revenge, he won't stop.'

'And he had his whole fleet near about when he came to us.'

'Yes, we saw it when he boarded us too. He must somehow

disguise it, for it quite suddenly turns up.'

'Aye, that it does.'

Although, Ashton thought to himself, the fleet could be an illusion, for he did not see it around Calegra's ship as he had sailed away from the burning wreck, when he had been scouting about as swifts. An interesting concept, perhaps Haim Clogh was right and the tyrant was defeated and just roaming the ether like a writhing dead serpent, with a power that was all empty and no more than deception. Still, deception and writhing can do a lot of damage, for instance the recent battle on Meridian, and Ashton decided he would not take the risk of becoming complacent.

'I must think,' he said to the sailor, 'I must get prepared. Just sing out if you need anything.'

'Thankyou, young prince, but where is the rest of your troop?'

'Home, they are from another port.'

'So it's just these monsters and you?'

'Just about.'

'Well. I thankyou for stopping for us, it was a brave thing to do, especially seeing how sparse your current crew,' he grinned, 'you have risked much, and done more than enough. You just tell us if there's anything we can do for you. Until we're back in Aeloran we'd be happy to serve under you.'

Ashton was touched by the sailor's words, and thanked him for them, but said, 'For now, you rest up, for who knows what will come tonight, or tomorrow.'

'Aye Cap'n, we will.'

So Ashton wearily checked the course. They were still going in the general direction, so he only had to alter the wheel ever so slightly, and slightly more, to account for the draft that had begun to sweep down from the north, then he tied the wheel where it was and went below to his cabin.

'More men,' sighed Santee.

'Aye.'

'At least they're good ones, I suppose.'

'Yes.'

Ashton washed his face, then sat down at the desk. Picked up the tools to draw the path they had come, and calculate the expected time to reach Aeloran, but put them down before a mark was drawn. His hand shaking, he couldn't steady the lead. He put his head to his hands, so tired and with such a weight on his slight shoulders and upon his weary mind.

Santee flew down and tip toed on the islands, between Ashton's arms and looked right up to him, into his eyes as the tears condensed, at his lips as they quivered trying to keep the pain in. She put up an umbrella in case of showers, but asked sympathetically, 'Boy, what's the matter?'

'Calegra Descada has my brothers, Simon of Cierrecay, and Lucas of Gaardevaran. The other sedge plant has been destroyed, so the one you have hidden is the last one there is, maybe the last one in the world. And we are still three days out at least from the safe harbours of the king's city, and without doubt the tyrant is near, seeking the Avaeste, if not on our trail already.'

'Oh dear.'

'Exactly.'

Morris knocked, 'May I come in?'

'Of course Morris, come in,'

'I have an idea,' he said, looking quite serious, and almost grim. He too understood the situation and the precarious predicament they found themselves in.

'Calegra will still assume you're dead, so take the aeroplane and the Argentius and go now. Then when he comes we will claim no knowledge of it and he will have to search the whole ship, without finding it.'

'No, I can't leave you and Dew and these sailors to near certain death. I know him Morris, next time he comes he won't leave any alive, besides, Gualtiero explained that the tank in the aeroplane only holds enough fuel for a day, and that at a stretch, he said, better to stick to twenty hours.'

'Is there nowhere you can refuel along the way?'

'No, not really,'

'Or maybe Dew can fix it up so that there are extra tanks, to give you another two days.'

'It might work.'

'There is always the other way.'

'What other way?'

'*You* could fly.'

'For three days and nights? No, not even I could do that, I'd fall from the ether into the sky.'

'Well, do you have any other suggestions?'

'Dew could alter and take the aeroplane himself. I must stay here, they are my brothers, and this is my ship, and you are my friends, I can't let you face Calegra alone.'

'But there is your father, the king, the reason why you have done all of this. And besides which, I have never been to Aeloran, will the people there take the word of a goblin? For I've never met any who'd dare without first knowing him.'

'I don't know. It is a city where it is rare to see unusual creatures certainly, but they are good people, the best,' Ashton said.

'But I hear an element of uncertainty in your voice,' Morris pressed.

'Yes, they are still just ordinary folk, and Dew does seem rather devious until you get to know him.' Ashton thought, and sighed, 'Perhaps I should go as you said.'

'Aye, go, and send out the king's fleet for us. Who knows, we might even evade him and arrive ahead of you.'

'Ahead of me?! Never,' Ashton laughed. 'Alright, ask Dew to see if the tank can be extended, and then if he thinks it can, ask him to do it.'

Morris nodded. 'Oh and Morris,' Ashton called after him, Morris looked back, 'thankyou, for everything.'

'No need, it's my duty and pleasure, Captain, and I should say also, that I believe I was mistaken, you are quite right in your decision to remain hidden. Don't let me convince you otherwise.'

'Thankyou, I'll still practise though, and I do value your advice.'

Morris nodded, then left.

The night went without incident, but that the crew barely slept, for the banging of hammer on tin below deck. Dew worked all night to finish the project, to add the extra tanks to the aeroplane, and he commented to Ashton, as Ashton went to see how he progressed, that the fuel should last even longer for gold was heavier than glue and canvas, and so less energy would be needed to keep the plane moving forwards.

And though the young captain could only grasp the basics of those particular mathematical dynamics, he understood what the goblin was saying and gave him a pat on the back.

'Well done Dew,' he said, 'anything else I should know?'

'Hm, let's see now. This stick here you push forwards to go faster, back to go slower, tilt the wheel to go up or down as you will, tilt it left to bank left and right to bank right, hold it steady to land, and land it slow at an angle almost parallel to the ocean, understand?'

Ashton nodded.

'Now, go and get yourself a good breakfast.'

'Thankyou Dew, you've been a great friend.'

'Don't talk like you'll never see me again,' the kind goblin laughed, though his eyebrows grew together in a worried frown. 'We goblins are made of tough stuff you know.'

'Yes, I know.'

'And so are you. And besides, nothing might happen.'

'I hope nothing will.'

'Either way, I am certain this aeroplane is the quickest way to get the silvertip sedge to the king.'

'I hope you're right.'

'When am I wrong? Now go, get some food into you.'

'Alright, I'm going.'

'And put some clothes on!' scolded Dew, laughing, for Ashton had not changed out of what he'd fell asleep in. 'You can't fly into Aeloran in your nightgown!'

'No,' Ashton laughed, 'that really wouldn't do.'

So Ashton sat and ate a rather large breakfast, for him in any case. He began with a glass of freshly squeezed pineapple, followed by toast with grilled cheese, relishing the crispy bits that chewed with a crunch and a crackle, then he had a bowl of oat porridge, smothered in honey and milk from a coconut, the last that was left from the stores they had gathered while in Sucitabek. He was about to protest but Morris put more plates in front of him, walnut and banana cake, and a handful of nuts and preserved apricots.

'Is there any food at all left on the ship!?' Ashton laughed and couldn't see how he could finish it.

'Plenty,' said Morris, 'I'll go and pack you more for the journey.'

'Not too much now. And don't forget water, I'll need that more than anything.'

Ashton finished breakfast, and then headed to his cabin, putting a few things he might need in a satchel then getting out of his nightgown. He pulled on his trousers, his shirt and his jacket, buttoning it neatly from his waist to his neck.

'Well, I guess this is goodbye Santee,' he said, smiling up to the lantern.

She poked her head out, 'What? I'm not coming with you?'

'Were you thinking you would?' he said, surprised.

'Of course I was, how could you think otherwise?'

'Oh, but who will look after the Avaeste and the crew if you come?'

'And who will look after you if I don't?'

She had a point. Ashton didn't know what to say, he didn't want her to get hurt but who could tell which was the best way.

'You know,' Santee said with a giggle as she looked Ashton over in his suit and with his hair still that faded ginger from her blonde potion that had worn out. She pulled on his fringe as she stood on his shoulder. 'I really must practise.'

'Is it that bad?'

'I'm afraid it is,' they laughed, 'but you know, you carry it well as anyone could, you might even get away with it.'

'Well, I'll just have to. It doesn't really matter anyway does it? I just want to get home.'

'Will you let me come with you?'

'Santee, you're my friend, not my crew, do as you want.'

'Then I'm coming.'

'Alright,' Ashton smiled, 'let's go.'

Santee took some small items from her room in the lantern then flew after him, down to the room below where sat the aeroplane.

Dew put a scarf around Ashton's neck, then pulled onto his head an old, scruffy leather hat that smelt like it had once been the home of a wandering cat.

'Where'd you get that thing!' the young captain spluttered.

'Found it down here, but it'll keep your ears warm and no doubt about it, it'll be cold out there, particularly if you catch the winds of a storm. And I can't forget these,' Dew pulled out some goggles. 'My spares for doing dirty work in the engine, but they'll do just fine keeping the wind from your eyes.'

'Thankyou, you appear to have thought of everything.'

'But Captain,' Morris spoke up, 'aren't you forgetting something?'

'No, I think I've got everything, haven't I?'

'But the Carex Argentius?'

'Oh, how could I forget that! Santee, where is it?'

'I put it upstairs, in the lamp by the window.'

'I'll get it.'

Ashton ran back, found the precious little thing, just with the blooms budding and flowering, and he put it safely in a short little canister then tucked it away into the folds of a spare jacket in the satchel he was carrying.

But as he ran out, followed by Morris, Dew and the Eventide's crew, as he turned to wave goodbye, he saw behind them what he feared again to see, the mast of that terrible and all too familiar ship. Fast approaching with his fleet, real or deception, was Celagra Camba Descada, that terrible tyrant.

'Go Ashton, go!' yelled Morris at once, pushing the boy down the stairs despite his protests. 'You have to, take it, take it to your father, save him. Get in, get in,' they helped him up. 'Turn the engine, go on, don't give me your buts, there's no time for hesitance! Get out of here!'

Ashton gave them all one last look, haunted and afeared of all that was happening. But he did turn the engine, yes he did start it up, and strap himself in and pull the goggles down. He made certain Santee was ready to fly, then ordered the ramp be let down and at once he started to move. He waved to them one last time, then pushed the lever full forward. Then out into the blue morning

Ashton suddenly flew, this aeroplane was magnificent! If he met him again he would tell Gualtiero so.

Young Ashton could not help but turn now and again as the Avaeste grew further and further away, till he could see it no more, and no more know how things went as his dear friends met with the Descalabro.

Chapter 24:
NOW BRACE, NOW HOLD FOR THE CHASE!

Now the Avaeste was nimble and quick, and as Ashton had told Lucas and Simon, if they had warning they should easily be able to out-run the pretentious frigate. So all the crew worked hard to get the sails catching every bit of sympathetic wind to aid in their progress, but the gusts from the north were met with squalls from the east and the sails grew harder and harder to manage. Still they made forward and kept the distance between them and the enemy the same and never reducing, but the fact remained that he knew where they were and would keep on following.

They worked hard through the day as the clouds grew around them, as the rain began to come, not heavy, but cutting, and as the dim of the evening set in, that's when they really began to worry. The night would be long and they already exhausted, they were only a small crew, and Calegra's men many. And then, when the darkness took over the sky and the bluster turned into a raging storm, the lighting showed the great frigate behind, closer, ever closer, with every spear of light.

They thought they'd beat him, they thought they'd got away, when the light of the dawn grew with the hope of the day, but then they saw it, that terrible frigate, rise up from out of the cloud ahead, sitting between them and the way to Aeloran, with the fleet. There was nothing the crew of the Avaeste could do, they were overwhelmed as Calegra's heavy boots thudded down, and he ordered his men search the ship top to bottom and leave nothing unturned. But they found nothing that looked anything like the Carex, and so the tyrant's ire grew.

'Alright!' he shouted 'Who's the captain now?'

'I am first mate,' said Morris, stepping forward.

'Oh you are? What a circus! I don't believe you, where's the real captain and the rest of the crew?'

'You should know, it was your bullet hit him, and your ropes left them to die where they were tied.'

'Aye, but you must have got loose pretty fast for this ship was long gone when we returned to the area. Surely you've made a replacement, you've had ample time for a ballot. Is there no one with ambition?'

'Well, yes we did, but we haven't, and there isn't.'

'Alright, so you then, first mate, tell me where is it?'

'Where is what?'

'The plant, the Carex Argentius or the Silvertip Sedge?'

'I can't say I can help you,' said Morris, scratching his head.

'I say that you can,' Calegra stepped forward, grasping Morris around the neck, picking him up and strangling him. 'You will tell me where that plant is Walump or you'll meet your death!'

'I'll never tell you,' Morris croaked, 'do what you will.'

'Oh I think you might,' Calegra smiled, 'men,' he motioned and all at once Dew and the remaining crew of the Eventide faced imminent death at these cruel sailors' hands.

'Now, let's try again,' Calegra said, 'where is the plant?'

Morris hesitated, what should he do? How should he proceed? What would Ashton say were he in this situation?

'Well?' cursed the tyrant, making the stranglehold tighter.

'Who's to say if I tell you you won't kill us anyway?' Morris asked him.

'I can give no guarantee but that if you don't, their death will be a certainty. One, two, three-'

'Wait!' Morris yelled, 'I'll tell you what I know.'

'You will?'

'Yes, just let them go, and take your hand from my throat.'

Descada ordered the weapons lowered and released Morris from his firm hand. Morris rubbed his neck and recovered as he considered that Ashton would be far enough now to evade a pursuit whatever he told this man, and very close now to the safe shores of Aeloran. But what would happen when he did tell Calegra where the plant was?

'Don't keep me waiting Walump, I am not a patient man.'

Morris considered fighting them all, but they were ready and armed, that was not such a good plan, besides which, Calegra could stop him with a mere sweep of his hand.

'Well?' Descada threatened, looming large and fierce over the monster, scaring him more than if he had been in the marshes and met a troll eater. 'Where is the plant!?'

'Alright,' Morris said, such a frown in his brow, 'one of the crew took it when we realised we were closely followed.'

'Took it where?'

'They're on their way to Aeloran, probably almost there.'

'I saw no other ship, you're lying!'

'No, why would I lie when in your hands you hold our lives. There are other ways to get across the ether than by caravel or frigate.'

'How did they do it?'

'They left in an aeroplane.'

'An aeroplane?'

'Aye, an aeroplane,'

'What sort of beast is that?'

'A machine it is, a contraption of a madman's invention.'

'Explain it.'

'It's almost like a bird, it has wings but they're stiff, and it's big enough to carry a man or two in it.'

'How moves it, if it is not a living thing and is not a ship? Is it possessed of enchantment?'

'No, like these ships, it has an engine.'

'I must see this machine, and I must have the plant, before either one reaches Aeloran,' Calegra said, and it could be seen that there were plans forming in his head, but also an uncertainty, a fear his plans may not come about. He would know the aeroplane was far ahead and would also know that he would face opposition from Aeloran if they knew he was near.

'We will take my frigate,' he said at last, 'but it's not fast enough, take the engine from this ship,' he ordered, for he did not know the Avaeste's value, he did not know it was a little ship with a heart. 'Strip this little runt of its engine and put it in the Descalabro alongside the other ones, install the one we took from the Eventide too, then get as much power as you can from all of them. We must catch up.'

'She's not yours to dismantle,' Morris defended, he knew what would happen without the engine, and without a crew to manoeuvre the sails to catch the favourable winds, the Avaeste would fall through the mist, and down to the Teramarinus! But Calegra just glared at Morris and commanded, 'Men, take this lot to the Descalabro and lock them up in the hold, I'd kill them, but I may need them yet. And don't take your eyes off this one,' he sneered at Morris, 'I don't like the look of him, he's a bit too cunning.'

So the men of the Eventide, along with Morris and Dew, the only remaining of the Avaeste's crew, were taken to the Descalabro and thrown into a barred and locked cell. Other men were here too, but most importantly, here were the brothers, the princes, Simon and Lucas.

'Oh, it's so good to see you're alive!' Simon said to the men of the Eventide, 'but what happened, tell me, how did you survive? For the last we saw the ship was on fire.'

The men were about to explain when Lucas saw the two monsters and drew Simon's attention to them.

'Swamp Morris, isn't it?' said Lucas holding out his chained hand in greeting, 'from the Avaeste?'

'Yes,' said Morris.

'And Dew,' Lucas shook his claw too. 'Where's my little brother?' he asked, quite worried, 'what happened? Descada would have us believe Ashton's no longer alive.'

Morris looked around and said under his breath, 'He evaded death. Last I knew he was alive and getting closer to Aeloran with the second plant.'

'May he succeed in getting there. But how it is that you have come to be here with our men?'

'The Avaeste came to our aid, when we were almost spent,' said one of the Eventide's men, 'that young Prince Ashton has some skill in his hands, and in his head.'

'So I'm beginning to see,' said Simon, grinning, then sighed, 'but what a predicament we're in! And we can do nothing about it!'

'Watch and be ready,' Morris said, 'if he gets to Aeloran the fleet will come and we must be ready to act.'

'But that must be why we're alive, they won't attack with us on board, they might even give him what he wants.'

So Calegra Descada had the two engines taken from the Eventide and the Avaeste, he did not care, so maddened was he, that the little ship fell away, alone and un-crewed into the lower mists and then to the unseen Teramarine. No all he cared was that he sped and captured the Carex Argentius. He had those engines set up in the hot and steaming engine room, alongside all the others, while the Descalabro was readied and began to speed ahead, pushed beyond the limits of its normal capabilities, with the engines turning over much faster than was wise, and with the added power of the others.

The speed they flew was phenomenal, but dangerously fast, for they whipped through the clouds and sky at such a rate, yes even this great frigate was not set up to travel at such speed, and the ropes and sails, though they were strapped down, threatened to come loose and pull away from the frame, along with the rigging. But Calegra did not heed it, just looked to the ether ahead, he knew the way to Aeloran and had always avoided it, but now he went with rage and seething, saying to himself, it did not matter how close he got, how far the fleet of Aeloran came out, as long as he got the plant, all would be well, and he'd get it, yes he would.

'Is that it?' asked Santee, 'is that Aeloran?'

'Yes,' Ashton answered, a smile and pride on his face.

'It's beautiful,' she said, looking at the sight of the distant island.

It was still so far away, but she could see the mountains, the high peaks all white and green right down to the near sea, all glimmering. In between the beach and the mountains the king's city lay, and beyond it the lowlands spread, then the hills and forests of all different colours. It all seemed so majestic. And below, if one turned upside down, mountains grew into the ether beneath, all white and silvery. 'People live there too, or elves I should say,' said Ashton, and Santee was amazed.

'Can you do something for me Santee,' Ashton asked, 'Don't be afraid, but there is a ship coming in the distance, ever by ever gaining upon us.'

She looked, but she couldn't see it.

'I don't know by what means it comes so fast, but I believe it is the Descalabro and it may be that before we reach Aeloran it will reach us.'

'No! Oh, but I see it now, there in the very distance, a ship coming, just a pin prick on the far horizon?'

'That's it. I have to go and slow them down, so you can reach Aeloran.'

'No, what are you saying? Don't go, Ashton, no-'

'I must. You know I must, you have to get to my home.'

'No, you go there, I'll go back and slow them.'

'No, I won't let you, it's too dangerous. I want you to become person sized again, like you did to talk with Carter, I know you can do it.'

'Why?'

'So you can fly.'

'I can fly as I am, thankyou very much.'

'Please, so you can fly this aeroplane and land it and warn them on Aeloran, tell them to send out their ships, and take the plant to the king. Who knows, they may see us already and be preparing.'

'Me? Alone? As a person? Around people? Ashton no, I can't do it, and, and you shouldn't go back! Who knows what could happen – what if Calegra sees you, what if he finds out who you are?! What will happen?'

'Who knows, but we are close now, please Santee, take the controls.'

Ashton took the other seat as Santee gave in, as she became a life-sized girl in a pop of glittering, and said, 'Alright, what do I do?'

Ashton explained things as he gave her Dew's goggles and the scarf and the hat to protect her ears from the very chill draft, 'and when you land, take it slow, down to the water, little by little.'

'I think I've got it.'

'I'm sure you have. Alright then,' he breathed and was about to go.

'Boy wait!' Santee yelled, and she looked at him so, with a fear and a worry and a tear, just beginning. 'Come here.' She turned and hugged him so very tight. 'There, now go,' she pushed him away and he jumped, just as she shouted, 'take care of you, best boy I know.'

Santee watched Ashton, heading in the direction of the Descalabro, a sweep of black swallows. The great frigate was certainly gaining. Santee looked back to Aeloran, and sped on, afraid and alone, but very determined.

Ashton flew over the Descalabro to see how things lay, a couple of swallows even flew inside and down through the galley, the sailors quarters, and even lower still, to the cells and then on to the engines. Ashton saw all, his brothers, Dew and Morris and here, down here in the black and the hot he saw the Avaeste's trusty little engine. He flew out again, but it cut him so deep, the thought of his faithful ship floating companionless down through the ether, and it was just as he feared, Calegra had the Princes in heavy locks and chains, and his friends behind bars and far below deck. Could it be any harder?

Morris saw a swallow go past and wondered if Ashton was on board, but it was only one, so he couldn't be sure. But he grew alert, so when another returned with the keys in its claws he wasn't surprised in the slightest. The swallow dropped the keys at Morris's feet, Morris quickly hid them, and motioned for the other prisoners to stay silent. Then more and more of the little birds could be seen here and there.

'Plague o' birds,' said one guard, looking around.

'Aye,' said another, 'we must be getting nearer the island.'

'Yes, we must be getting close to Aeloran,' Simon whispered.

'I don't know,' said Lucas, 'I didn't think there were any black swallows on Aeloran, home maybe, in the Gaardevaran there were some, they liked to nest in the rocky outcrops there, on their way between Cierracay and Novania. They're so tiny, I wonder what they're doing here anyway.'

'What does it matter what the swallows are doing, we're supposed to be thinking of a way to escape,' Simon said, frustrated.

But Morris just grinned as he saw the birds all heading, in a vague and unreadable way, down to the room of the engines.

Now Calegra had not noticed the small birds that had flown in, why should he, they were so insignificant what threat could they be to a great and powerful man such as him? If he had even seen one it had not registered at all, no he just watched the aeroplane ahead, yes, he could see it now, flown by one single man, how easy would it be to stop it!

They were still gaining ground and the tyrant could see that the ships of Aeloran were still only just leaving the beach. He could have the plant and use it far before they reached him, and then, once he used it, none of this would matter, would it.

Santee looked back time and again, seeing the gap between her and the frigate close up further and further, and she flew and manoeuvred, and wondered after Ashton, hoping he would not be captured or anything worse. And it did her heart good, yes it jumped with relief when she saw the grand ships of Aeloran rise up from the beach.

They all sailed with the flag of Mathis the king, and fast they did rise and come so swift, 'Oh but still so far to go yet!' Santee said to herself, 'Come on, hurry up you ships! Go and rescue my Ashton!'

The Descalabro grew terribly close, when Santee turned back all she could see was the great big prow. She turned and she dived, she ducked and she weaved, but still the giant frigate kept coming.

The ships of Aeloran grew closer too, the Aeolian was there, the Concordor too, but just when Santee thought her time was up and she would lose this fight and be overtaken before the good ships caught up, the Descalabro shook and stopped gaining so fast, still coming but for some reason slowing.

Ashton looked around the engine room and found a great hammer, indeed it was an oversized mallet, and before anyone could stop him he grabbed it with a great heave and yell, and ran to the bank of large engines and began a furious pounding. Parts went flying, steam shot out, spills of oil leaked everywhere and there where terrible noises, spitting and groaning and whirring sounds as the engines failed, sputtering out.

The two engineers working nearby came running and were stunned at the damage done by a mere boy, with a hammer meant for a giant. They pointed their pistols and told him to stand, but they didn't need to worry, Ashton was spent. He'd done all he could, he knew the damage would halt the Descalabro's fast progress enough for Santee to get home, there was no way they could fix it in time to catch her now.

The engineers caught him and bound him up, then marched him

on along to the ship's prison, no idea who he was, but soon again to meet with Descada, for the tyrant even now was running down, fuming at the interruption, wanting to know the reason for their slowing and the person responsible. The engineers dreaded the moment, but at least they had the culprit, and could put the ire of their master onto the boy with the mallet.

Now Santee flew through the fleet coming up, they did not give her a worry, but could easily see that she was a friend to Aeloran. She lowered slowly, just as she'd been told, lower and lower to the sea, slowly now, slowly now, she flew smooth, but then noticed she had gone further than expected and managed to land very close, coming straight for the beach! She pulled back as far as she could and tried to turn aside, but still the aeroplane went on and only came to a stop halfway up a sand-dune. Santee jumped down, throwing off the goggles and head gear, running up with the canister, many crowded around the strange craft, and asked all sorts of questions, but she puffed, 'I must get to the king, please! Which way do I go?'

'He will be at his residence,'

'He still lives?'

'Yes, but only just.'

'How do I get there?'

'See the way through the forest on the hill up there, beyond the rooftops,' she did, 'his residence is at the end of it.'

'Thankyou,' she said, 'may I borrow this?' she asked of the man's horse, but before he answered, she was off.

Chapter 25

IT'S THE TYRANT VERSUS THE CAPTAIN

Meanwhile, Calegra arrived, down in the dim below deck, and got to the boy before the others had time to say anything to Ashton more than a surprised greeting.

'I thought I killed you,' Calegra said through the bars to his prisoner.

'It seems you haven't yet,' said Ashton.

Calegra sniggered, he liked this lad, he knew exactly what was in for him. But on the other hand, he had seen the blood upon his chest, he'd seen the deathly shaking, and could not help but ask, 'How did you do it?'

'Perhaps I was not as badly hit as it seemed.'

'You must not have been. And how'd you get on board and to my engines?'

It was a question his brothers were also asking. Ashton didn't answer but said instead, 'Your time is up Descada, the ships of Aeloran close in, turn around and leave.'

The tyrant laughed so horribly, sharp and dark and rattling, 'I will not leave. No, there are still more games to play here. I have on board the second, third and eighth sons of St Amalric, what do you think they're going to do to me?' he asked, sneering deviously, 'Nothing. That's what. It's like having a monopoly. I tell them to jump and they'll jump if it means your safety.'

'But it won't get to that, will it,' Ashton said, 'go and look, go and see, my aeroplane will have reached the king. He'll have the Carex Argentius in his possession by now, already his physicians could have prepared it and he could be taking it. So you'll never get it, no matter what you do to us!'

Calegra Descada just glared at the boy, then turned and hastened up to his telescope to see where the plane lay. It was true, there it was on the beach, empty. And the ships of Aeloran were almost upon him. But then his ears caught a sound back down below, a fight? Swords, gunshots and terrible great row. It grew closer, up the stairs, and broke out onto the very deck of the Descalabro, the prisoners, all of them, had escaped, they would not sit idly and wait to be used as the tyrants ransom! No they would not!

As soon as Calegra had walked out and the guards turned their back, the crew began singing rowdy tunes, and Morris turned and undid the locks that bound Simon and Lucas's hands. Then when the guard had turned to deal with a distraction in a second cell down the hall, Ashton opened the lock on this one. The crew had snuck quiet and knocked out the guards before they knew anything of it. Then the other cells were opened and all were let out, but that's when they were discovered, see, more soldiers were about and soon the fight started, but the prisoners kept pushing forwards.

So now the foray spilt onto the main deck, into the sun and the air. It was clear the soldiers of the tyrant were more, and had more weapons, but the prisoners were far more determined. Calegra looked down from the top deck and watched with his best men from there, he didn't expect this little venture to last long, so was quite happy just watching.

But when it seemed that the prisoners might have a chance, he began to look greatly concerned. So he sent in his finest rogues and he himself pulled out his pistol, picking off targets from where he stood, and laughing with perverse enjoyment as he did.

Ashton could see they were not going to win this, not with the rest of the soldiers all joining in. So fierce were they and so skilled and ruthless, it was frightening just to look at them. 'Get to the long boats,' he shouted, 'make off, and the fleet from Aeloran will pick us up before we fall.'

His call was repeated, and for the long boats they went, many jumping in and casting off as they filled them. Lucas was off, Simon pushed him to go ahead for he was not the strongest, many of the crew of the Eventide too. But faithful Morris, he still battled, he and Dew as well, with Simon and Ashton as the rest retreated.

The ships from Aeloran were close, just behind, picking the longboats up even as Ashton said they would. Even closer was Edward's schooner, Ashton could almost hear his brother's voice.

It was clear to Calegra that he could not win this battle against the nearing fleet of Aeloran, his own fleet was so far off still behind him. And even if he could fight off these prisoners, they were no good to him now. So he readied to run, and no one was better at running than him. But before he said the words to speed away, he gave an order, and lifted up his gun and grinning grimly he aimed.

Ashton heard the order Calegra had given to his finest men, and he heard the shots ring out, five shots meant for Simon, Morris, Dew, Lucas – on the boat away, and lastly, one for him.

'No!' Ashton yelled, not his brothers! Not his friends! If it hadn't been for him none of this would ever have happened in the first place!

Simon, Lucas, Dew and Morris all turned at Ashton's call and saw the guns raised at them and the spark in the barrel, and they knew this was the last moment they would ever draw breath.

But as the smoke rose from his gun, Calegra's mouth hung open, each bullet that was shot did not hit its target, but a stray white dove. Bloodied feathers were across the boards, but now Ashton sat upon the deck, white-blue hair, long face, thin limbs, quite elfin, holding his wounds, blood pouring down, as the rest of them gasped, 'Novanian!' Ashton had not thought about his life or death, or his secret being discovered, it had all happened too suddenly to think of the consequences.

'QUICK!' Morris shouted, snapping Simon out of it, 'get him to the long-boat, back to the ship.' And the last of the men from the Eventide along with those just mentioned, carried Ashton, running, to the last longboat, pushing out and away with him before Calegra or his crew could do anything, especially as Morris covered their retreat in a manner we know can be quite menacing. Lastly the loyal Swamp Monster ran and jumped, and they pulled him in.

Calegra knew himself defeated once more, besides, there was much to think on, so he put his hand to his ship and muttered, 'Terga Vertere!' and at once he and his ship, and all of his men, were gone.

The Concordor was closest and picked the last long-boat up, Edward had just hauled in the boat with Lucas and could not believe what Lucas said he saw. Edward had heard the shots, yes, but surely it could not be so. Either way, he and Lucas paced impatiently to get to the last boat.

At last they pulled them in, Simon's face was as white as if it was he that had been shot, 'Do you have a surgeon on board?' he shouted, 'Edward, it's Ashton!'

'Standing by,' Edward replied.

They all crowded as Ashton was brought out, and lain upon the deck. So, Lucas had seen what he thought he had.

Ashton was unconscious now, as the surgeon looked him over, as the crews from Aeloran, and the two from the Avaeste stood by, watching and praying.

'No wonder he couldn't tell us where he came from,' Simon said, saying again, 'Novanian!'

All the crew were saying this name to each other in amazed and worried whisperings. 'Ile de Novo, Novania,' and, 'Weren't they all destroyed? But here one is!'

'I can't believe it,' said Edward, 'little Ashton.'

Lucas wiped the tears away that were gathering at the bottom of his glasses, put down his staff and knelt down by his brother. Lucas too was from the hidden realms, and now he wished he'd been more open with Ashton from the beginning. 'Hold on Ashton, we'll get you home. You've got to live, hear me,' he put his hand gently to Ashton's head.

These were no small wounds the surgeon worked on. He ordered bandages be tied tight around them all, except the first on which he worked now. He removed a shot from Ashton's arm, then stitched the wound, and had it bandaged up. But he looked at the men surrounding, and said, 'I dare not touch most of them,' he shook his head, 'they are in places far too delicate to do while aboard the ship. That one in the thigh is close to the main line through which blood flows, one is close to so many vital organs, and this one in the shoulder it has shattered bone. Best left to the king's own man when we get back.'

'And the one meant for me, it must be,' Lucas said, going to Ashton's right hand, where he saw the bullet hole as the surgeon unbandaged it.

'Yes, at least I can try to sew this one up.'

'No bullet?'

'No, it went straight through.'

'But I'm not hit,' said Lucas, 'and I'm sure their aim was true.'

'His interference probably diverted it still,' explained Edward.

'Come on Ashton, we're almost home,' said Simon, 'Is he still alive then? He looks awful.'

'Yes, he still breaths, and his heart still beats.'

'Oh good,'

'But I wouldn't hold out hope, any of you,' said the surgeon, 'five shots to the body is a grim thing, I can't say I recall any that have lived after such an experience.'

Chapter 26:
THE ARGENTIUS AND THE WISE KING

Edward broke with etiquette and sailed the Concordor right over the beaches and the shores of Aeloran, over city and the forest, right up to the house of his father, berthing it right at the doorstep.

Surprisingly the first there to meet them was a barefoot girl none had ever seen, but for Dew and Morris of course, followed by the other sons and the attendants of the king.

'We need the king's surgeon,' Edward shouted as the longboat was readied to let Ashton down, 'get a table ready, there was a fight, it's Ashton, badly hurt.'

Many attendant gasped and sighed in grief at the news, then they ran around to get ready to receive the hurt son of St Amalric, and fetch the surgeon and a nurse, and heat water and cool water and prepare the instruments, and of course, though it would be hard, tell his father. The other brothers were there on the ground, Sebastian, Marcus, Ambrose and Phillip, and they helped steady the boat as the boat was let down and could not believe what they saw when it reached them.

Simon and Edward slid down on the ropes, followed hesitantly by Lucas.

'Novanian?' asked Marcus, as they prepared to move Ashton.

'Yes,' said Simon, 'you won't believe how this happened when I tell you.'

'Is he going to live?'

'Touch and go. Edward's surgeon says probably no, that there's not much hope.'

They lifted him up on a stretcher and carried him in, Santee following, holding Ashton's hand, teary, saying as his brothers had, in a whisper, 'Boy, hold on.'

For a moment he seemed to wake, his eyes opened slightly and seemed to blink, and his head tilted to one side, 'Santee,'

'Yes,' she pressed his fingers and he pressed back.

'Do- does-' was all he managed, but she knew what he meant.

'Yes, I saw your father, he has it.'

'Thankyou, I'm sorry,' Ashton said, but she didn't know what he meant, there was no reason to apologise, no reason, but then his hand grew limp.

'No!' She screamed, then cried, 'boy, come back!'

The brothers quickly placed him on the surgeon's table, but the king's man looked at them grimly.

'He's stopped breathing,' that man said.

'No!' Santee screamed again, and Lucas had to hold her back, even though he didn't know who she was yet, he gathered she was welcome here and a good friend of Ashton's.

'If everyone could leave us,' the surgeon's assistant recommended, 'give him space and let us work.' And so everyone was removed. They sat outside the room, or paced up and down. Santee sat on the floor with Morris and Dew, biting her nails and swaying back and forward.

'Who is she?' Lucas asked Ambrose.

'She came flying the aeroplane, and brought father the cure Ashton found.'

'Oh,'

'She is nice, but a bit strange.'

'Yes, she does look a bit wild, with her free hair and bare feet,'

'She's like a child. Sometimes she stands for minutes staring at the lanterns in the hallway, but mostly she's just been up in the tower watching the sky for your return like the rest of us.'

The surgeon spoke to the assistant quietly, 'Go to the king, get this cure from him. If I understand what has been said, it will cure anything, even this. I will keep trying to revive Ashton but I don't think I can. I know the king will not use it, so we may as well use it for his son. Go via the other door, his brothers may take too long if they have to make the decision between their father and him.'

So the assistant went and soon returned with the Carex, nearly breathless. 'It was as you said,' she told the man, 'he sends it with his wishes to do all you can for his son. The poor man, he terribly wants to see him.'

'Now steep the leaves in the hot water there,'

'How many leaves?'

'All of it,' he said, and the assistant looked at him surprised, so he explained, 'I'm not quite sure how it works, but this is no herb, no common potion, it's a relic of the enchanted pieces that fell to the Ether long before they closed the gates to the Ciel Marine. The more we use, the more potent it will be. And for Ashton's sake it needs to be potent indeed.'

So she took the little plant and dropped it in, stirring it there in the water gently with the end of a wooden spoon, watching as the leaves lost their silver shine, then turned from green to grey, and started to break up, as the flowers curled, became transparent, then completely dissolved. Even the leaves seemed to almost disappear as they watched them. Then the doctor took a beaker and filled it, and lifted Ashton's head.

'What if it kills him?' asked the assistant.

'Just hurry, help me, he's already dead.'

So she opened his mouth and the surgeon poured the concoction in, massaging Ashton's throat to try and get it down.

When that was done, they took cloth and soaked it in the water too, then placed it over Ashton's many wounds.

'Is it working?' the assistant asked.

'I don't know, wait, it must be, look,' there was a small rise and fall in the boy's chest, 'He breathes again! Quick, hand me the long pliers, I better see if I can get these bullets removed and stitched up while he's still out.'

As Ashton lay there on the surgeon's table the Carex Argentius started its working, it pulsed though his body with every beat of his heart, then found its way into his mind and the connections of his memory. Suddenly Ashton found himself back on Calegra's Descalabro, standing on deck between the bullets and his friends, but then everything was slowed, every second a minute it seemed.

Then a figure much like Aolani appeared on the deck, tall, elegant, intriguing, with a silver-white cloak from his head to his toes and inner garments of green.

'What am I doing back here?' Ashton asked, 'what's happening?'

'You are here to make the choice again,' said the figure, motioning to the scene that was happening around them. 'Would you choose to do the same?'

Ashton looked around, not realising that the Carex Argentius was in him, he thought nothing but of this situation, totally absorbed in what was happening in it, and of course not realising that this is why Calegra had wanted the plant so desperately, what was written on the second page about the remarkable curative. Yes, that page from the *Encyclopaedeae de Floradae cum Medicus in Orbis Terra Antiquituus* maintained that the Silvertip Sedge did not cure the ills one had by giving the body strength to fight them, or magically healing them, no, it cured the thing by giving the chance to change how it happened, and maybe stop it from happening, yes, to erase everything, and go back and live from that moment. Calegra had wanted to go back to the time before his banishment, and replay things from there, but now the last of the plant was in Ashton's body there was no hope for Calegra anymore to do that, if it had worked for him at all.

But Ashton stood and looked around, at the bullets coming slowly through the air, looked at the faces of his friends.

'Well?' said the figure.

'No, I would do the same thing.'

'But you may die, indeed it is likely, and if you don't you may be scarred and not able to be these birds you love, nor any other thing. What makes you Novanian may be taken.'

'So be it,' Ashton said, 'I wouldn't change what I did.'

At once time sped up again, and Ashton jolted on the surgeon's table as in his mind he was hit again by the five shots, and sat on the deck, watching his blood run out. The surgeon looked at the assistant worried, but on they worked removing the bullets.

But then the Argentius, so potent because of the doctor's methods, went further back in memory, it skipped over times of hurt and times of emotional distress and found the other time in Ashton's mind when he had nearly ceased to exist.

Ashton found himself below the battle on his home, Ile de Novo, moments before he first was struck, as he crept out of the shelter where his father had hidden him. It had been so long without knowing, too long and there were too many unknown noises, beside which the hollow where he was filled with smoke and ash, and he was near choking. He escaped and he looked up at the raging war, frightened and bewildered, he had seen the beginning of it, but nothing like this. Around him the fire and chaos grew, bodies lay broken and dead around him, their homes blasted to pieces, shattered, as Novania was mercilessly ruined.

Nothing was green anymore, nothing was beautiful, nothing flew in the air but the ships of destruction. Blasts shook around him, throwing debris through the air, explosion after explosion. Fragments tore at him as he ran, trying to get away, to somewhere safe, but there was nowhere. More and more he fell, but then the picture was stilled and Ashton watched himself.

The same cloaked figure appeared, and asked, 'Would you change this?'

'Could I?' he asked, hopeful, and amazed.

'Yes, we could go back as far as you wanted.'

'I could stop this?' he asked again.

'You might be able to alter something, but the outcome may or may not be eventually the same, depending on what it is you changed.'

'I could stop Calegra? I could warn them?'

'You could try.'

But then Ashton remembered, Aolani's brother had given them warning but it had been ignored, so why would anyone believe him, he was so young here in this picture.

'Or could I go to Aeloran and tell them what was going to happen? Or could I go further back?'

'Yes, perhaps. But take time and think before you make up your mind.'

Ashton thought of all the ways he might stop this from happening, from approaching the king back then, even to going to the Ciel Marine before Descada's banishment.

The tall figure seemed to know what he was thinking.

'Think Ashton, even if he is not banished to the ether, there may be some other one that rises here in the Aethermarinus, choices would be made again and who can say if the outcome would be different. This day was terrible I can see, but think not of all that was lost, but also of what was gained, of what has happened since, what might have happened if you changed things, if this moment was erased and all the moments since, and then make up your mind.'

Ashton looked around, the city that had risen here was nothing, completely flattened, and the people who had sung here, silent. The ships of Aeloran and Meridian were there in the distance. He had dealt with this, it had happened, it was over, he was healing, Novania was lost, those here had suffered, but now they suffered no longer, and that was it. But if he could go back and change the way things happened he would not want anything like it to happen again, it would be too much to go through a second time, and he could not escape the fact that the fault did not lie with Calegra entirely, but also with his own people, who chose to hear him and ignore the warning. They would make the same mistake again and he would not be able to stop them, in fact, as he had thought before, he may have done the same.

So then he thought, as the figure had said, of all that had happened since, of the hand of the king lifting him, up out of the burning fields, of the things that he had learnt along the way, of his brothers, who he may never know if he chose to make a change. And then he thought of Morris, dear Morris might have died, if Ashton had not been there, if he'd been living some other life. Santee too, might have fallen into a state most wretched if she had not found some similar feelings in this boy and gone along with him. And Dew would be whittling his claws and feeding on insects that landed upon him, without the motivation to move and repair the old, worn engine. Oh, and the Avaeste, it would have stayed sitting unused and unknown in the swampy, dark corner of a certain port. Many others too along the way Ashton thought of. And then most of all, Ashton realised, he would not know the truth, for the Novanians for the most part had shunned the real world and lived in a fantastical half-life, alone and ignoring the rest of the world, but there was so much more to experience, to know and love and care about, yes, nor would he have realised how astounding love could be, that there as he died, as the poisons and the thorns grew upon him, that even then the king should stoop to rescue him, and that his new brothers did not question but accepted him from the beginning. Yes, Ashton thought, things would be so different if he went back and changed anything.

To go back would be to undo so much, to unlive and unlearn so much, to take away so many who had been born and all that they lived for, to undo many wars that had been fought and won, and who knows if it would change anything in the end.

What of King Mathis in his current illness? Well, Ashton did not know that the figure in his mind was there because the surgeon chose to try and save his life with the very rare plant he thought his father had, no, he did not realise that the Carex Argentius was in fact at work within him, so the matter of his father the king and his illness did not come into all his deliberating, apart from thinking that he did not need to come back here to stop the king from saving him, for surely the king now had the plant and would soon be well again.

He tossed about between yes and no, between going back to that time or before and carrying on from there, or staying here where he was. This was his home, this was Novania! Even to see it green and living one more time would be so wonderful, to see his first father, his mother, and his friends. But would it be a wise decision? Much would be lost and gained either way.

'Have you decided?' asked the figure, kneeling down, taking Ashton's chin into his hand and peering into him.

'Yes,' he swallowed.

'And what is your decision?'

'I, -' Ashton paused, looking around once again.

'You hesitate?'

'It is a difficult decision.'

'I understand.'

'But I won't change it. I will leave things as they happened.'

'You will leave things remain as they are?'

'Yes.'

'You're certain?'

'Yes.'

'You realise with that answer I have to send you back, back to pain and possible death, five bullets in your body and not much life?'

'Yes, I do, it's alright if I die.'

'I can see you have thought deeply and I accept your answer. You have chosen not to take the paths that I offer, but perhaps I can give you a little help anyway,' said the figure, and touched Ashton upon his forehead, saying, 'Now, go back and live!'

The surgeon leapt back, shocked, as Ashton sat up, gasping and wondering where he was, but quickly the man and his assistant went to the boy and bade him lie back still or else undo the stitching. Not that Ashton needed any urging, he fell back at once, so pained, and so weary.

The assistant took his hand, 'You're home, on Aeloran,' she comforted, as she studied his eyes, so questioning, so sparkling blue like the sea in the sun, like none in the world but a real Novanian's. 'Try and rest,' she said.

'My father?' he asked.

'Fine for now,' she answered. 'Just rest Ashton.'

Chapter 27

THERE'S A HEART IN HER HULL,
AS WE ALL KNOW

Unbeknownst to anyone in the Aethermarinus, there was quite a stir far, far below them, for the Avaeste had flown with the drafts in the sky and landed safely in the Terra Marine, yes, she glided upon the ocean. And once she had landed that little ship went to that certain port she knew of, that little harbour with rascally crew, indeed our friends' harbour, Althorn.

The rain had stayed off so Tom Needle played with his friends in the street, kicking a ball around, it would only be two hours now since Ashton had left, hadn't it? Could it even be that long? No, it hadn't been very long at all. When Tom stopped and the ball hit him because of his distraction, and his friends asked him what was the matter.

'It's the Avaeste, for sure it is, I'd know her make from the horizon I would. Be back soon lads, just give me a minute.'

So young Tom ran down the wharf, and up to the fine little ship. She was in a bad way, he could see that she was, and he yelled, but there was no one aboard.

'What happened here?' Tom wondered and climbed up himself, ran all about but nothing was found, only everything inside messed about. And then Tom thought maybe Dew was still here, hiding below for fear of being seen, so he ran below, but all was empty and desolate, and, no! there was nothing in Dew's little room, not even the engine!

Quickly Tom ran and found others of the men who had been on the mad adventure, and sent them hurrying back to the ship to see if they could make anything out of it.

Soon all had turned up and were mulling around, investigating and muttering, even old Gragan had come back again, wondering how this had happened.

'Maybe Calegra caught up with him,' said Banks.

'Maybe he met violent weather,' said Jennings.

'Maybe he went too near Diamantine and they were still unhappy,' said Phillips.

'Maybe, oh I don't know what to maybe,' said Carter, 'I just want to get back up there!'

'Here, here!' said Tom, and the crew called it out again after him. 'There's only one problem, sails we can replace,' Tom reminded them, 'but the Avaeste has no engine.'

'How do we get one?' said Berens, 'surely it was of an Etherean construction.'

'I saw it,' said Tom, 'it wasn't that complicated, it was almost like that generator thing the barman connects to the contraption he uses to keep the ice from melting.

'Ah yes, I know the thing,' said Carter.

'Do you think we could borrow it?' Tom suggested.

'We could, but I don't doubt we've enough money now to buy it.'

And so Carter and Tom set off to that fine establishment to find the little engine, and you can see the eyebrows rising on the bartender with doubt, but the sly smile of his wife as Carter handed out the gold coinage. But the bartender just shook his head, there were strange happenings occurring today, and he couldn't make head nor tail out of it, but he knew, oh yes he knew, that it had started with the appearance of a certain boy and Marsh Walump.

Phillips organised the men into groups, some he set mending the sails, others checking the ropes. Still others yet he had go up and down, over the ship's fine timbers, making sure she was quite sound and patching her up where she wasn't. Then when the engine came Tom crawled into the space to install it, saying what he needed they'd hand it into him, be it extra sheet, extra tubing or anything.

'There, I think that's it,' he said peering out, his face full of grease. 'Shall I give it a try men?'

'Aye, set it going.'

Tom turned, but then frowned, nothing happened.

'You made sure there's fuel? You have to have fuel.'

'Yes, I checked that first up.'

'And you know which connections go where and everything I suppose?'

'Well, no, but I have a rough idea. Come on Tom think!' he said to himself, 'You where there, Morris was there and Dew was here, and then that plug there, that lever like that, oh, here,' Tom laughed, 'how simple, I just got two turned about the wrong way, it'll be all good in a minute.'

Tom changed the wires to the appropriate places and then tried the engine again, and you should have seen the smile on his face and heard the cheers of the men as they heard it.

'Woooohooo!' Tom yelled, bouncing out of the box, and dancing around with old Gragan. Now it was only a matter of time before they would be up and flying.

So in a short time the men all boarded and sailed out of the harbour, slowly testing the Avaeste to see if she would be alright. But she seemed the same, the same dear ship, and Phillips lifted the lever to rise, and soon they were up from the sea beneath and flying up into the skies.

Chapter 28:
OUR HERO IS RECOVERING

Ashton lay still, sleeping mostly, as many visitors came and went. The surgeon's assistant wouldn't let many right in, only those who were very close, for too many came just to see if it was true, that the eighth prince was born Novanian.

His brothers were there by his side on and off, but she, whom they didn't really know, she never left him. Dear Santee sat in the chair constantly, and would not let anyone convince her to leave him. And though she longed to just be herself, the little sprite who could hide away, and though she was so tired from being disguised as a person for so long, she would not let herself change, for if she were small she couldn't hold Ashton's hand anymore, like she had been.

Morris and Dew were there as well, hiding in draws in the cupboard, for they had grown tired of the stares and the chokes and the having to be explained when they walked in the streets or even in the hallways.

Days he lay there, between sleep and waking, between life and death, but slowly he began to heal, and began to really open his eyes, but only for such short moments, usually they were missed.

Then one evening when Santee laughed at the antics of the monster and goblin as they played chess, sitting in the draws with the board between them, complaining at each others cleverness, Ashton took Santee's hand and pressed it, then looked up at her, smiling.

She let out a yelp of delight, took his head in her hands, then hugged him. He winced as she squeezed, but didn't say anything, just enjoyed her exuberance.

'It should have been you in the plane not me!' she said, 'I should have gone back.'

'No, don't be silly.'

'I'm so glad you're alive! Boy, can I stop being big yet?'

He chuckled, 'Whenever you want.'

She grinned, and held his hand again, 'Maybe tomorrow.'

For a moment he lay back his head, overcome with the throbbing, but then it passed and he was able to talk a little with Dew and Morris.

'Well, what are you two going to do? I don't have a ship anymore, and it looks like I won't be going anywhere for a while either, besides, I've done what I sailed out for.'

'Oh, we'll stick around a little longer,' said Dew. 'I was thinking I might visit Kebaticus to relate all these tales, but that is not urgent or important, so it can wait, and even if I go, I'll come back at some stage, but for the moment I'm going to stay here and play chess.'

'And you Morris?'

'I'm with you Ashton, wherever you stay or go.'

'The same goes for me,' said Santee.

Lucas stood outside and heard the captain and his crew, and it made him smile to hear such loyalty to his little brother, it made him smile just to hear his voice as well. Soon he knocked and entered, leaning on his stick and taking a seat by the bed, opposite where Santee sat, saying a greeting to all present, then turning to the patient.

'How are you little brother?'

'Getting there, slowly.'

'You just hang in, you'll get through.'

Ashton smiled in reply, it was all he had energy to do, then he fell asleep again, and his friends made the room dark and silent.

More days passed, more days with little waking. Once Ashton woke to find Simon sitting there with Ambrose and Marcus, holding a honeydew melon.

'Your favourite,' Simon explained.

'We rode all the way around to Halreagh to get it!' Ambrose explained.

'What would I do without brothers like you?' Ashton said, and thanked them as they helped him to eat it, the juice running down his chin, the taste and coolness of it so satisfying. Santee enjoyed some too, and Dew and Morris particularly liked the skin, saying 'No, don't throw that away, we'll eat it.'

When the surgeon checked up on him and pronounced his wounds were healing well, in fact quicker than he had expected, the news soon spread through the house, through the streets, and even out to the villages that it looked at last like Ashton was out of the woods and going to survive.

Then one day when Ashton had been awake for longer than just a few minutes or hours, and he had even got up taken a few steps just to the chair beside, he began to wonder why he had not seen his father.

'Have you seen king Mathis?' he asked Santee, she shook her head, no she hadn't.

'So he has not been in at all when I've been sleeping?'

'No, from what I gather he still lies in his room upon his bed,' she answered.

'Maybe it takes a while to work,' he said, stepping back to the bed, straining to do it without hurting, just as Edward walked in to see how his little brother was doing.

Edward held Ashton's shoulder to help steady him, 'What's taking a while?' he asked, thinking Ashton was talking about something to do with his own mending.

'Father,' Ashton said, 'isn't the cure working? I must have been in here for days, but I have seen nothing of him.'

Edward sighed and looked away, how could he say it? He rubbed his fingers through his hair and took a deep breath, 'Ashton,'

'What? What is it?' Ashton could see the worry on his eldest brother's brow, the knotted lines above the eyes, and bleakness in his countenance. 'Is he dead? Did he die before he could get it?' Ashton asked, afeared.

'No, Ashton, no he lives yet, but he gave you the Carex Argentius, all of it.'

'What?'

'Well, after what you did you were practically dead.'

'But, no, I've got to see him, he can't have done that,' Ashton stepped forward, evading Edward's grasp, ignoring the weakness in his legs and the pain of his wounds, it was nothing compared to the agony roused in his kind heart. He ran as he could, limping along, followed by his loyal crew, and the other brothers that saw what was happening, but Ashton made it to the king's chambers, and shut them all out.

Here lay the man, his father the king, not so old, indeed far too young to die, lying here sleeping, one arm on his chest and one by his side. Ashton collapsed, grasping sheets from the bed as he did, clutching them, crying, finding his father's hand and putting it to his forehead.

The fingers moved, then found Ashton's cheek, and held it. Ashton looked up, grasping that hand, finding his father's eyes, open just a fraction, looking back at him.

'My son,' said Mathis the wise, in a voice so low and weak Ashton could barely hear it.

'Father – why?' Ashton cried.

'I have waited many months for you to come back. There are things that must be said before I die.'

'Here I am, but father, why?' Ashton asked again, 'Why did you not take it? Why did you give it to me? You must live!'

'Ah,' the king grinned weakly, 'the silver sedge weed. The Carex Argentius yes, a pretty little plant. But it would not have worked for me. I would not change anything. Would I save you only to let you die at another time?'

'What?' Ashton remembered the figure now, and the choices, 'That dream, that was because of the Argentius?'

'Yes, it's a cure for all ills because it allows you to go back in time to change the event that made you unwell.'

'Oh, but, but I didn't change anything, if I'd known, I would have –'

The king hushed him, 'There is no way I would not come to your rescue. Do you know what would have happened if I took it and went back to that day on Ile de Novo?'

'You would be cured, you could have left me, why didn't you take it! You could have taken it and gone back yourself!' Ashton said, tears streaming down his face, 'I will go back all the way, I will find another plant –'

The king shook his head, 'No, it has all been destroyed. And besides, I would not touch it, for I would be well, but you would die. That is the price of this cure. I would make the same decision again, you know I'd make the same choice Ashton.'

'No, I don't matter! But you do –'

'Ashton, not only you, but many others across the Aethermarinus would cease to live, and all I have done and am doing would be undone. You had the opportunity to choose a different alternative yourself, but even you chose not to change anything, but leave things as they were, so, don't you understand my decision?'

'But you are wiser than I, you would know how to make it better, to save yourself and save Novania and to stop everything that happened, to go back and erase everything right from the beginning before all this started and start again.'

'No.'

'Why not? You needn't die! Novania needn't be destroyed!'

The king took some time, then answered, 'What happened on Novania and in other places was beyond terrible, and should not have happened, but it did happen, if I went back I could make my recommendations again, but I could not force their hands, else I would be the tyrant. And if I changed one thing, Ashton, you wouldn't be who you are,' Mathis said, and you could see in his eyes that that point was important, 'No, I would not change anything I did on that day, or before.'

They sat there together for a moment in silence, Ashton bowed over his father's hand, King Mathis watching his son and catching his breath.

'Did you know?' Ashton asked, 'Did you know when you saved me you would become unwell?'

'More than that, I knew I would die. But if that is the price I must pay for you to have life, I will willingly give it, and if I lived again, I would give it twice.'

'But how can I live – if I gave you this, this, what leads to your death?!'

A hint of a smile grew in the corner of the mouth of King Mathis the wise, but he said to Ashton seriously, 'You didn't give it to me Ashton, I took it, and took it willingly.'

'But you can't leave, not yet,' Ashton cried.

'Let me do this. Let me go,' Mathis touched Ashton's shoulder, 'I will not go very far.'

Ashton wept as he held his father's hand, it was such a long and terrible illness he had endured, and now he lay breathing his last breaths.

'Now, why I wanted to see you, the words that need to be said,' Mathis breathed with difficulty, 'do as I ask you Ashton, in a little while, when you feel ready, take a ship out to the hidden realms, go and visit your island.'

'Novania? But, no father, I can't go back there, I can't face -' but Ashton stopped, realising this was really the end, as his father's breathing further weakened, his eyes were nearly shut, he no longer grasped Ashton's hand with any kind of strength. 'Father no! No, stay with me!'

Then the last words he whispered out were, 'Trust me, and do as I ask. Do not be afraid Ashton.'

There the brothers found him, light from the window upon his head, leaning over the hand of his father, a hand now heavy and lifeless. It took a few of them to get him up, then Edward took him in his arms, back down the halls to his own room, back to his bed. Edward noticed the blood beginning to run again from Ashton's wounds, spreading across his gown and bandages, and he sent Sebastian off for the surgeon once again.

Edward tried to talk to Ashton, but the boy's head hung back, so weak, and near delirious, it had taken all his strength to sit and speak, and the conversation so heavy and the outcome of such consequence that all his adrenaline too was gone, all he had lived for all this time, to save his father, to save the king, to find the cure, and now all his father had said, taking time to sink in, feeling at once so overwhelmed, and so utterly empty.

Lucas stood and looked at their father, a tear running down as he pushed up his glasses then put the king's hair more neatly in place and smoothed the sheets. 'I will return to the Gaardevaran as you asked,' he said. And after him, one by one the brothers came to say their own farewell to their beloved father, Mathis St Amalric, the king.

Chapter 29:
WHILE MANY ARRIVE TO AELORAN'S FAIR SHORES

News spread quickly throughout the land, and across the Aethermarinus, taken by ship, aeroplane and bird, drigan, sprite and gryphon, out to the far corners, it was written and posted, etched, typed and scriven. Couriers rode, messengers ran, and fliers flew out to the farthest places, to remote and lonely outposts and all the scattered realms, with the news none of them wanted to hear, Mathis St Amalric, the wise king, had passed.

Within days of the news going out ships began to arrive from all over, filling the harbour of the king's city and all surrounding harbours. They continued to arrive for weeks, while Ashton watched and recovered, sitting up in a tower with his telescope watching until he was tired. Santee was herself again too, and sitting often upon his shoulder when they were alone, or with Dew and Morris, or hiding in his hair or his pocket when they weren't. And when anyone asked where the girl Santee was, Ashton would just say, 'Oh, she's somewhere around.'

The surgeon and his assistant came and went as well, observing how Ashton was healing, helping him to have confidence to move and walk around. His head was still so heavy and his balance quite unsteady, even apart from everything else, it seemed to take such a long time to Ashton to make every little bit of progress.

His brothers would come too, and help him to do the gentle exercises the surgeon had recommended, and every day the assistant would come and dress the healing wounds, and apply a bitter smelling ointment she insisted would minimise the scarring.

But at the moment, they were alone up in the secondary tower, the one hardly ever used, nearer Ashton's room, just Ashton and Santee, not even Dew or Morris who remained downstairs still playing chess. And Santee stood tall on Ashton's shoulder, watching the far harbour through the telescope as Ashton told her the countries from where came all these new arrivals.

From every nation that had ever heard the name of the king people came. A governor and his soldiers came from West Fall, from Hylethar a chieftain and bowmen. Craftsmen came from Oundin with gifts to honour St Amalric, and merchants came from the Atoll, they were rough yes, but their grief was heartfelt.

From so far out they sailed here, representatives came from Cierrecay, and from Gaardevaran the great Arceo himself, bearing with him others from his and near lands. Ambassadors came with kind messages from the people of Corrio and Lalapahue, and from Diamantine came the king, as well as Sir Rubra de Silva and his daughter Yvette. From all across they came, to honour and mourn the fallen king, and from Sho'Orakai came the queen.

'Look,' said Santee, 'I know this one, isn't that the flag of Meridian, of Annabella Bien,' she said excitedly. Ashton looked through the scope too.

'I see it, yes it is.'

'And who is that?' asked the sprite, looking far out beyond the other ships, far out into the setting sun, all golden across the sea.

Ashton took the scope and focussed, and saw the grandest ship he had ever seen, coasting in now on the waters, effortless, oh so smoothly. The young captain shook his head, 'I cannot but guess that that ship is not of this place, its design is not one belonging to the Aethermarinus.'

And there amidst all other craft, the magnificent ship sailed in, all the way from the Ciel Marine. It bore in it ones from across that realm, from Arazin, Uthain, Rhohavalan, and many from Aeranimh, they were so tall and proud and strong, but had a manner most thoughtful and kindly. They spoke with Edward when they came and it was agreed that his father's body would be taken home with them, for he was from the Cielomarinus and that is where he belonged.

Edward asked that they wait until tomorrow so that everyone who might could come and pay their respects before they took him so far away. Would they wait? Edward asked, until the planned ceremony?

Yes, they said, they would wait, though they could not really understand why everyone was so sad. They said to Edward, 'You need not mourn too long, for he is not lost, he just returns to us, but he will also remain here, in you, his sons.'

Edward thanked them for their kind words, but could not really understand.

That evening as Ashton sat there half asleep in the tower with the breeze upon his hair, with Santee sitting in the window sill and the telescope leaning untended, poking up at the stars, faint footsteps were heard below, coming up the stairs.

Ashton blinked and found Queen Annabella there. She sat, 'How are you Ashton, dear one?'

'I have been better,'

'So I hear,' she took his hand, and looked into him as she did, 'Dear one, how copes your heart?'

'Poorly,' he answered her honestly.

'I worried so for you when I heard the news of the king, but since I have arrived I have heard so many other things. Dear boy, you were so brave, I did not think that even you had such courage.'

'But I could not save him,' Ashton looked away, almost ashamed.

'Ashton,' said Annabella, 'you know him better than many, but may I suggest that perhaps it was meant to be this way, for was he not the wisest king that ever lived?'

'Yes, but-'

'And if he had wanted to be saved, don't you think he would have found a way?'

Ashton could not understand why she said these things, but then as he thought, he began to comprehend. The king had spoken like he knew all about the cure and what it did, he could have sent for it at the first sign of being sick, but he didn't, even Calegra had said he didn't think the king would use it, and Aolani had said he would not need it.

'I still don't understand,' Ashton said, and the queen saw the tears beginning and his face so desolate.

'Come Ashton,' Annabella said, and took him into her motherly embrace, 'maybe now it seems the Aethermarinus is bleak and things so uncertain and beyond us, and though you will miss his voice and his face, you will go out as you have done, as a son of St Amalric, and you will continue to be as I know you to be, brave, clever and kind hearted, and as you go on, some of these questions will be answered, and some of these uncertainties taken away. Life will again burst through the darkness.'

'I fear tomorrow,' Ashton told her what he'd not told anyone, 'they will hold the ceremony to farewell him. Songs will be sung, trumpets played, words read out by dignitaries, and there I will have to stand, but I don't want to say farewell, and I don't want to stand there as I am in front of everyone. If I had my Avaeste I'd sail far from here, I'd go on the sunrise, and I'd return when all this had passed.'

'It pains you to hear their words of mourning?'

'Yes, I know they are said with honour and respect but they give me no comfort. I would remember him by silent words, known only to myself and him, and by doing what he asked of me.'

'While you would be missed at the service, it is not wrong to do just as you say. Following your heart is more important than meeting these ceremonial expectations.'

Ashton hung his head.

'Another sadness?' she asked him.

'It's what he said. I want to do as he asks but I am afraid. He told me to go and visit Novania.'

'Ah. Yes, I too would find that difficult. You need not go alone, I'm sure there are many, your brothers particularly, who would accompany you if you waited until these proceedings were concluded.'

'No. I cannot ask it of them, and I don't want them to come. I will go alone as soon as I can find a way.'

'But you've another sadness yet? Ashton, what is it?'

'I cannot change. I cannot be the Ashton you saw before or anything but what you see, at the moment these wounds are still too severe.'

'But this is you Ashton, the real you, the Novanian, you need not be ashamed of your story.'

'But everyone stares. Who else has blue hair and pointy ears who isn't an elf?'

'It isn't that,'

'It isn't?'

'No, dear one, you represent what was lost, to look at you is to see hope. And hope is what we all need as we continue to rebuild.'

'I don't know if I will ever heal enough to really be myself.'

'I'm sure you will, but sleep now Ashton, you never know what might come with the dawn.'

'I should ask you before you go in case I miss you in the crowd tomorrow, how is Kielan?'

'He is very well,'

'And Highbury? And old Bartle?'

'Still going strong, and wondering how you went on your quest. One day you must come again and tell us everything.'

'One day perhaps I will. Thankyou for coming,' he added sincerely.

'Yes it took a while to find you out, hiding up here in your tower.'

Ashton grinned. Then Annabella said goodbye again and left.

In the not so distant Ether a foreign crew sailed closer and closer to the fair shores of Aeloran, the men spread out across the deck, and the lieutenants were arguing in the captain's cabin. Surely they should have found it by now if they'd have taken the right course and calculated the right distance? But no, there was nothing in sight in any direction.

'What should we do now?' asked Carter.

'Should we turn back?' suggested Phillips.

'Maybe just a little further,' said Jennings and Banks, studying the six pointed compass again, along with the many maps.

Then from up in the crow's nest the shout came down, there was a bright light up ahead that looked like it was maybe a city or something that big. 'It's got to be Aeloran,' said Tom, skitching down the rigging, 'I know it's dark and all, but take a look lieutenants.'

So one by one the men looked out to the point Tom pointed to, yes, there it was, a rising city in the darkness shining just like Althorn did when the ship was still distant and coming in through the night hours.

'I think you might be right,' Phillips smiled, 'what a sight for worried hearts.'

And so the crew sailed in on the very first faint light of morning.

The little Avaeste touched the silver waters and sailed in, holding itself up with pride, that is, satisfaction and delight. The men had her shining, and by some unknown trick their uniforms appeared again too and so they looked quite dashing as a crew as they stood smartly on the deck. These humble men found themselves in awe at the number of ships in the harbour, at the sheer size and make of some of these craft, and at those early risers that looked down intrigued at this tiny barque going past.

The men of Althorn were thankful for the Avaeste's small size as they took her further in and further in still, through all these larger craft, towards the wharf, and then they slowed and made anchor.

As the crew prepared a small boat to row in to shore and enquire after their former captain, they noticed a strange air hanging over this place, a feeling not quite tangible, until old Gragan lifted up his finger and said, smelling the air, 'Aye, it's a sombre wind, that it is.'

At once of course they feared all the more that something really terrible had happened to their young captain, and they hurried to row in and get news.

But Santee had woken early too, sitting upon the window sill and looking back out at the sea to watch as it glimmered with the rising sun, and watch the playful gulls and hear the rhythm of the waves. And then she saw what she never did expect, but she couldn't be certain without looking through the telescope, which as it was she couldn't move it. So she whispered in Ashton's ear, 'Boy, are you awake?'

'Maybe,' he said, still half asleep. 'Why?'

'There's something I think you should see.'

So he lifted his weary head and picked up the scope, looking down to where she pointed, at once falling backwards in shock, then bouncing up.

'It's the Avaeste!' he said, 'but she was lost!'

'Who's sailing her?'

Ashton refocused the lens and then laughed, 'You won't believe it! I see Harrick in the crow's nest! It has to be, haha, who else has a beard like that?! It's the men of Althorn! Oh Santee, what am I going to do? I can't get down there soon enough!'

Ashton quickly made his way down from the tower to his room, tapped the drawers, waking Dew and Morris and telling them the news, then he pulled on his trousers and his boots, pulled on a shirt, carefully though, minding his wounds, then found a hat and raced out, though a few called after him – 'Ashton, where are you going? What's got into you?'

He did not heed anyone, but picked a quiet horse, attached it to a cart upon which the three of them hopped, with Santee in his pocket, and then they rattled off.

Down through the tree lined path, all the way down the hill, out onto the main road from the village into town, then down with all speed through the streets of the king's city. But here he stopped for a moment, yes, in his mad dash he pulled up, here down the main avenue, and here in the middle park, and here at the harbour square, was where his father would be farewelled. He found a flower growing out of the cobbles there, picked it tenderly and placed it upon the memorial stone.

'Thankyou for bringing me here,' he said, then asked, 'but father, give me courage to make the way home.'

Then even as the men from Althorn set foot on the shore in trepidation at having to make their way in this strange and foreign land, without the confidence of Ashton's captaincy and feeling so small and out of place here between the grand ships and the grand city. But even as they searched the beach for a kindly face to ask the way, a little horse and cart stopped, just ahead, on the street beyond the sand. And who should come stumbling across, yes, no other than their captain, Dew, and Swamp Morris!

At least they had thought it was Ashton, but then as he neared they began having doubts, for Ashton didn't look quite like this boy here, nor did he have blue hair or pointy ears. But then the boy smiled, so wide and overjoyed to see his old sailors, and he said as he came, holding out his arms, 'Oh, it's so good to see all of you, you can have no idea how much you've been missed!'

And they could see that it was Ashton indeed, and they greeted him with the same exuberant greeting.

'Come on, let's go,' said Ashton, eager to be gone before everyone woke, stepping into the boat as the men followed and then began to row back out.

'But how came you to be here?' Ashton asked, 'Tell me everything Banks.'

'Well, the Avaeste she turns up at port in Althorn not so many hours after you left, all a mess and no engine.'

'That's right, Descada took it. But how'd you manage to get her back up?'

'Well we found another one, not quite the same but still runs pretty well.'

'Tell me, do you have enough fuel for another few weeks journey and returning?'

'Aye, we purchased all the red current juice that the bartender could find, equals the amount you took in black currant last time, and the engine seems to like it just fine.'

'Oh good, that's great.'

'I tell you what though, it took us a while to put your cabin back in order, everything was tossed around, and we couldn't go far without your compass, and for a while there we couldn't find it, but then Needle he says, 'You just give me an hour and I'll set it in your hands,' so he looks all through every cranny and nook and at last finds it up in a corner of the rafters. I'll say, the poor Avaeste, she really took a tumbling on the way down.'

'There's no doubt she really does have a heart.'

'Aye, I'll say she must. But what happened to you captain? Everyone has a hypothesis but we're all eager to know the truth.' Banks looked at the bandages all of them had noticed, 'You were in a battle of some sort?'

'Wait till we're on board,' Ashton saw the next question that was upon his lieutenant's lips, and said with a grin, 'I know I have to do much explaining.'

Very soon the rowboat got back to the Avaeste and the men

climbed back on board, and Morris and Dew received a cheer as they stepped onto the deck, but when Ashton was finally pulled up there was a cheer, but then there was silence.

'Blimey!' said Tom, always honest and open about what he was thinking, and expressing for the men what was their first question, about Ashton's slightly different appearance. 'You're not an elf are you?' asked Tom, direct and upfront as usual.

'No,' Ashton answered, a faint smile on his lips, 'I'm Novanian.'

'But how come you weren't like this before?'

'This is who I am when I'm not in any disguise, it's just easier not to be like this, there's less questions.'

'And what happened?' Berens put in, 'Did Calegra find you?'

'Yes, many things happened, there was fighting, but now he's fled once more.'

'And did you get the cure to your father?' asked Carter.

'Santee flew the plane and got it there in time, but he did not use it.' Ashton hung his head, 'My friends, he has died.'

They all were sad for they all knew the heart of their captain, and they had gone where he had gone through so much to get it. To hear that now the king had passed cut their hearts as much as if this was the king of their own country, more still than that, for he was the father of their dear friend, Prince Ashton.

'We are saddened to hear it Ashton, is there anything we can do?'

'I wish to sail out,' he said, 'I wish to sail up into the hidden realms, and go home. But it is far, and I would not expect you to come. You could always stay here till I return.'

'No Ashton,' said Phillips, 'here we stand, willing and ready to be your crew. Besides, look at yourself, you can hardly bear up! We'd not let you sail without our help.'

'Well,' Ashton smiled, sitting down on a barrel, 'there's an aeroplane on the shore you might want to stow, then let's up anchor, let out these sails, and let's go.'

Chapter 30:
IT'S HOW THE ODYSSEY ENDS,
AND BEGINS ONCE MORE

So as the sun really lifted its head and began to shine down on the king's city and all the ships in the sea, the little Avaeste was lifting up and sailing out into the open Ether Marine. Ashton sat there with Morris beside, with the wind in their faces, the wonderful freshness of the open sky so uplifting. Morris closed his eyes and felt the air in his whiskers, and flowing fast, pushing back his big ears, and Ashton sighed as he tried to still his heart, he had not been home for so many years.

Dew was as happy as he could be getting to know the new engine, it was a little different but worked much the same, and it smelt sweeter because of the red currants.

Now, to tell you everything that happened between Aeloran and Novania would be another story, but let me tell you the most important details that happened along the way.

Now the weeks went by and with every day the way seemed to grow a little dimmer, the nights were darker but the stars were brighter, somehow they seemed to be closer. Yes, with every day Ashton healed a little more, and grew stronger, though he grew more afraid.

Morris and Dew had told the crew all the details of what had happened, of the sail through the air, of finding the Eventide, and of being found out by Descada. Of the capture and of the fight, of Santee's flight, and of Ashton's brave actions.

'What!' said Tom, as Dew told of how the young Novanian had been a sweeping of swallows to bring them the keys and then doves to save him, Morris, and his brothers, from the terrible shots Descada and his men had fired upon them.

'What, Cap'n, can you really be pigeons?' Tom asked what they all were thinking, what they could not quite believe, 'Or is he having us on, this tale telling goblin?'

Ashton looked down a moment, then grinned, 'I prefer the term 'dove' over 'pigeon."

They all were astounded, naturally, but it was clear to Ashton that for many a demonstration would be needed for them to truly believe. But he just checked the course and let them wonder, besides which, he did not know if he could still do it, for he had not tried since he had been shot, and still wondered if it would be too dangerous.

When Ashton had withdrawn to his cabin, to his couch, to sleep one night, Morris sat on the deck with the men, under the closer stars and he told them the story to a more full extent, and explained to the men that Ashton could do what he could do because he was Novanian, and Santee said to the listeners quietly, 'He can even be a sprite, that's how he saved my life that time.' And Morris warned them to be prepared for a terrible sight when they reached Ile de Novo, and explained that even the captain was afraid to go back, but was going in any case to see the way things lay, and Morris told them of the battle, the original assault, when everything had been destroyed and how of all that had lived there, Ashton was the only survivor.

The simple men of Althorn were astounded by the story, and even they grew sombre when they realised what might lie ahead, and they thanked Morris for the warning, it would help them to understand just what was churning now in their young captain's heart and head.

Then one day they passed through darkening clouds, through unexplainable shadows, through light that smelt like rain and fog that felt like tiny bursts of ice upon the skin. Then there was a long time they sailed through silence so encompassing, where the beats of their hearts seemed echoed around and repeated back to them, through a place where nothing, not even clouds, could be seen in any direction, and where nothing moved, not even a hint of a breeze, and they were mightily thankful for the engine then, and thankful too when they finally passed through it and out into the ordinary sun.

Then they saw islands in the distance, but Ashton bypassed them, one all greens and browns, with golden-orange cliffs and a sea as full and blue as any they had ever seen.

'That would be Cierrecay,' Ashton said, 'and far beyond it where we cannot see would be Oundin.'

He did not need to look anymore at his maps, and the crew noticed.

'So, we're getting close?' asked Jennings.

'Yes, we're in the hidden realms.'

The men stood all on deck, gazing around in wonder at the place. There was a feeling in the air even, something they couldn't quite place, so different, something like a child's wonder, it was all new and unknown, the colours, the birds that flew around, the songs they heard across the air carried so far on these unseen currents. On they went and Cierrecay grew out of sight behind, when suddenly around them sped one then two then numerous flying beasts they'd never thought to see, small and large, bright and dark, cute, and frightening.

'Dragons!' they gasped.

'No,' said Ashton, 'Drigans they are: Rhovan, Reigcaq and Branagh.'

'Call them what you will, I'll still call them dragons,' gasped old Gragan, 'aye, I never thought I'd see the likes of them but in the pages of a fairy tale. Blessed my eyes,' he gasped again, 'that I have seen them in real life! Then turned to Tom, 'Pinch me lad, I'm not dead am I?'

Tom laughed hysterically, 'You'll be right Gragey, you just wait, your rheumatism will play up soon enough and then you'll be complaining.'

And then they saw the land from which these dragons came, the high peaks of rugged rock, the dim and distant plains, and the sea which crescented the land, so deep and dark and grim. Ashton thought of Lucas, this was his home. Somewhere beyond those mountains there were villages hidden, where the people lived with these fearsome beasts as friends.

One of the larger Rhovan screamed in welcome, seeing Ashton, and then a face appeared, it had a rider on its back, and the rider saw what the Rhovan had seen, her face lit up, surprised and overcome, and she stood up, spreading her arms to show her delight, and yelling down, 'Hail, son of Novania!' then at once she turned and flew back to Gaardeveran to spread the message.

Many came out and flew with them as they went on, an escort while this one of which they had heard whispers sailed back to his land. But as they left the far extents of what was considered Gaardeveran, one by one the riders left, saluting Ashton, then flying home.

Night drew in, then night withdrew, and another day passed by. 'Just how far is this place?' many of the crew began to ask. Then Ashton began to go higher, just a little by little more, and more clouds grew here, but just little puffs here and there around them, not above, and that night the stars seemed even closer, so close one might think you could reach up and get their golden dust on your fingers.

The new morning brought still no sight, but Ashton was not worried, he knew Ile de Novo was so far up and out it would take many days to get there. Then one afternoon as they sailed with the sun behind them, as they broke through another bank of clouds and came out into the open, there ahead lay a little isle, quiet, still, and with its mountains blackened.

Ashton swallowed the lump in his throat, he didn't know if he was ready, but Santee leaned upon his neck and Morris stood by him as always.

'Alright,' he said, 'let's do this, let's go in.'

And so the men prepared, getting to their posts to carry out the landing.

They came in close, and they could not see where they were supposed to sail, for all around the island, beyond the narrow beach, was a ring of mountains, impassable. But Ashton guided the Avaeste around until he found the gap in the rocks, a wider arc of sea where the mountains abruptly tapered down, letting the sea further in with an opening big enough for ships to navigate.

Down they came smoothly upon the silent sea, perhaps the only ripples that had been felt here for all these years. It was strange to come back here for Ashton, and stranger still for those that had never been. Here even the sea looked black, but it was so clear and still, you could see to the very floor, to the silt which now lined the sand, to the burned fragments of ships and memories of the battle that had been.

The young captain set his face and looked ahead, up to the pass before them, between the black mountains where had once grown flowers and ferns so full and flourishing, and where had played the happy swallows, darting down and around the boats as they sailed in. But no birds to greet them, no green welcome.

Ashton asked that they anchor out here, he didn't want them all to see what he feared lay within. He asked that they lower a boat, and that they let him go on alone. But after much back and forward argument, Ashton relented, he would take Morris with him.

So the two good friends rowed the little boat slowly in, through the break in the mountains, it was almost as dark as an underground cave for a moment there in the middlemost part. Then as they rowed further and towards the light, Morris noticed an interesting thing, that as Ashton looked around, up at the steep cliffs through which they were passing, Ashton's hand met with the water and unbeknownst to him something was happening. Where his hand met the water life had grown in an instant, a little glimmering in the bleak flow, a little clearing of the blackness, little fishes went from that spot and where they went darting, through the black rocks and the silt, life grew also.

For the moment Morris didn't say anything, perhaps it was just a coincidence, an irregular happening, but he couldn't help wondering at why and how it happened and as they continued to row and go forward many thoughts went through Swamp Morris's head. The one which seemed to make the most sense to him as he thought it through, was that maybe Novania itself had ceased to want to live for it too had lost hope. But here at last its son returned, how overjoyed this land must be, if it could only speak.

But then they came out of the passage into the openness, both Morris and Ashton held still their oars, yes they had to stop rowing. What met their eyes was not smoke, not burning or silt or brokenness, no, but a land of green hills and forests, growing again and blooming out of the ashen slopes, so vast indeed and so full of life that Morris could hardly believe all this could fit inside the small island they'd seen from the outer.

Waterfalls in the distance fell, the rivers ran again, and as Ashton set foot upon the land birds appeared everywhere, of all kinds from out the forests and from the cliffs, from out the bulrushes in the river, and they darted through the sky and swooped across the fields. Life grew everywhere, all animals that had ever lived here, as Ashton stood wide eyed and overcome with so full and broad a happiness he feared his chest would burst.

Then he saw a trodden path leading up into the mountains, a path he did not recognise and he ran, following it because his heart urged him. He ran so far and fast that Morris was soon lost behind, and on he went higher and higher amazed at all this newness, then he came upon a bridge, low over a the rushing river, the highest in the land that became the waterfall they'd seen from lower down. He crossed it, wondering who made it here, for certainly it had been constructed and had not grown here on its own. Finally he reached the other side and hurried up a rocky path, narrow and overgrown with lichened boughs and dense heath. The boy did not think he'd been this way in his lifetime, and wondered why his heart urged him on, and what would be at the end of it.

Then there upon a fallen log sat a figure ahead, a figure tall and sitting straight, but with his head down in thought, and with a loyal hound by his boot. The dog pricked up its ears as Ashton neared, and the figure looked up.

'Father!' Ashton cried, seeing the face, not believing it could be, but stumbling forward all the same.

Mathis stood, and smiled wide, and lifted Ashton up in his big arms, a fatherly embrace, then put him down, put his hands on Ashton's shoulders. 'I was hoping you would come.'

'Is it really you?' Ashton asked.

'In person,' Mathis laughed.

'You're alive?'

'So are you,' the king smiled.

'But how? I don't understand,'

'Ah, well, don't you see the gates back to the Ciel Marine?'

Ashton looked where the king pointed, and there in the rock was a door, wooden and unassuming, opening into shallow sea with a great sky beyond, where a ship lay waiting, the ship he had seen in the golden sunset that day on Aeloran. And here at the doors a little boat sat, only temporarily pulled in.

'You're not staying?' Ashton asked, comprehending that the ship out there belonged to his father.

'No,'

'But you could come back to Aeloran, and remain king,'

'What, after they farewelled me in a manner so moving? No, though I will always love the Aether, my place is in the Cielomarinus. Kings come and go Ashton, I could not stay forever, but I did what I came to do, and now I return home.'

'What did you come to do?'

'Many things, but most of all, I saved you. And Ashton, I have spoken with my father, and these gates will always be open from now on, indeed they have been closed for far too long.'

'Oh, I should ask – what of the wolves, the men from the rebellion?'

'Those whose remorse is true may return whenever they will.'

'But what about Calegra? He's still out there, and men like Von Marax.'

'Just keep alert and ready and they won't get the best of you, my son.'

'But what if he tries to find this gate and get back?'

'He cannot, unless his heart changes. You may not see them but I have posted guards around the island. They will protect Novania, and the doors to the Ciel Marine.'

'Guards? Like Aolani?'

'Yes. This is your safe haven whenever you want it, and when you grow weary of being here in the Ether Marine, you can come through and visit me. The islands of Aeranimh are the closest to you here, I'm certain you'll find them astounding, but I think you might also find that you are most welcome, and you'd fit right in.'

'But how is all this? How is Novania once again living? Did you bring dust here from the Ciel Marine to make it happen?'

'Ah, no, perhaps a little, but I believe it started when you were looking at maps with Highbury, when you cried for Novania. When your tear fell on the map your tear fell here and life began again.'

While Ashton talked Morris stood down in the grass, finding insects and wondering if he could eat them, while at the same time wondering what Ashton was doing, he had long given up trying to go after him. And out on the Avaeste the crew began to be worried, for the others had been gone so long, yes the sky would soon be darkening.

So they made the decision to sail into the island after their boy captain and Morris and there try to find out what was taking so long. So the Avaeste sailed between the dark rocks and the same sight met them as met the others when they came into the light, a scene so grand and so unimagined that many were quite overcome, staring around with wide open mouths and hands holding onto their hats as they looked up.

The crew disembarked and explored the shore, all the creatures so strange and so wondrous, and soon they found Morris and that good monster explained that Ashton had run up the path into the mountains and had been gone for some time now.

Ashton was in thought, 'Out in the ether there is so much happiness, but so much sorrow father, half my heart wants to go with you now,' he said, knowing his father was leaving presently.

'And the other half?' Mathis grinned, knowing Ashton's heart already.

'It just wants to be me again, it just wants to explore and discover everything there is in the Aethermarinus, I want to live.'

'So live,' smiled the king.

'Do you think I can? I think maybe I am too scarred?'

'There's one way to find out, what is it your father used to say? You don't know if you can fly-'

'Until you're thrust into the sky,' Ashton finished it.

Mathis gave Ashton a parting embrace then took his seat in the little boat, his dog jumping in after him. He took up the oars and began to row back out to the ship. Ashton stood at the doors and waved goodbye. When he finally stepped away the doors closed, looking like nothing more would be behind them than a deserted shack of a hermit, let alone the entire world of the Cielomarinus!

Then a spark lit in Ashton's eye, a spark had Morris seen it he would have known that the young captain was about to do something irrational and possibly dangerous, as Ashton ran back down to the river and began to wade out, not across the safe bridge no, but out into the rushing waters. The waterfall could be heard up ahead and Ashton neared it with every step, finding rocks and jumping from one to another, ever closer to the edge.

Then he stood there atop the falls, surveying his home again, looking down to the far stream below and hoping that it wasn't madness within him, as he stood there and longed to jump, and test if he could still fly.

'Look!' shouted Tom, 'is that him? There's someone up there on the waterfall!'

'Oh no,' said Morris, 'is that what he's doing? The madcap, he'll kill himself, surely he's still not well enough to try anything. Santee quick, go and stop him.'

But as they all watched, before they could do anything, they saw the boy jump out. He fell a little way, but then he disappeared, and they all wondered what had happened, but then they saw the blue swallows dart past, and over them, then they heard a splash in the water behind them.

'Come on,' laughed Ashton, as the boy captain they all knew, 'what are you waiting for? the water's lovely!'

Tom didn't wait, and splashed in as well, soon followed by many others, and they laughed and played until the stars came out, like nothing had ever worried them.

In a distant place, with a bleak outlook and a festering, mouldering anger, Calegra Descada gasped again the word, 'Novanian!' and said to himself in a voice so seething, 'I thought I'd dealt with them from the youngest to the last!' Then yelled out and stamped his boots very hard, and growled to his men some oath and muttered command. The captain of the Avaeste was to be found, everything was to be searched and turned upside down. 'I'll get my hands on his scrawny bones, I will,' growled the tyrant, 'and I'll tear him apart, if it's the last thing I do!'

Oh, but that is another story, for now let us be at peace, as the crew of the Avaeste, as they lay there on the hill, full on the fruits that Ashton had showed them how to eat, and looking up at the constellations.

Ashton told Santee, Morris and Dew about his meeting with his father and of the door to the Cielomarinus. They were astounded of course, and Morris asked, 'So what are you going to do now? Are you going to follow Mathis and go through yourself?'

'No, not yet, we are still young and there's so much living to do here in the Ether Marine. I thought maybe we could take Dew to visit Kebaticus.'

Morris gulped, as Dew laughed.

'A whole island of goblins!' moaned Morris. 'I'll be murdered before I set foot off the ship!'

'Not when I tell them not to,' said Dew. 'But it might be a bit hairy captain, perhaps I should make that journey by myself.'

'Nonsense, I think we'll be alright Dew, we've been to the end of the Ether and back, through unknown ways and stranger days, and lived to tell the tale.'

'What about the men from Althorn,' asked Santee, 'will they be coming too?'

'I don't know, what say you men? Do you wish to return home or continue on with us?'

'It will be awful quiet without them,' said Santee.

'I will miss listening to their fiddles,' said Dew.

'I think I will even miss the times they get themselves into trouble,' said Morris.

'Aye, don't take us back yet,' said old Gragan, 'there's plenty time before we need to go back.'

'But I thought you had a fear of falling?'

'Well, maybe I'm over it.'

And all of them agreed with Gragan, to continue on with Ashton as their captain, besides which, three years up here, and they might still make it back for tea tomorrow.

And so it was that the eighth son of St Amalric was seldom seen at home on Aeloran, although he did return to see his brother, King Edward, crowned. But Ashton had found that sailing was in his bones, and in the little Avaeste he travelled the Aethermarinus, to the very outer realms, yes, ever discovering, ever exploring, and always living, and knowing that out here in the hidden realms was a place he could always return at any time, it was not what it used to be, there were no people there, no villages, but it was a haven nonetheless, with a certain doorway, the thought of which gave him peace wherever he might be.

~

'It's another day Morris.'
'Indeed Captain, it is.'